KEEPER'S TEMPEST

CODE OF THE KEEPER, BOOK 3

MARIE ANDREAS

OTHER BOOKS BY MARIE ANDREAS

The Lost Ancients
Book One: The Glass Gargoyle
Book Two: The Obsidian Chimera
Book Three: The Emerald Dragon
Book Four: The Sapphire Manticore
Book Five: The Golden Basilisk
Book Six: The Diamond Sphinx

The Lost Ancients: Dragon's Blood
Book One: The Seeker's Chest
Book Two: The Finder's Crown
Book Three: The Hunter's Chalice
Book Four: Diviner's Scroll

The Asarlaí Wars Trilogy
Book One: Warrior Wench
Book Two: Victorious Dead
Book Three: Defiant Ruin

The Code of the Keeper
Book One: Traitor's Folly
Book Two: Destroyer's Curse
Book Three: Keeper's Tempest

The Adventures of Smith and Jones
A Curious Invasion
The Mayhem of Mermaids
An Intrigue of Pharaohs

Broken Veil
Book One: The Girl with the Iron Wing
Book Two: An Uncommon Truth of Dying
Book Three: Through a Veil Darkly

Books of the Cuari
Book One: Essence of Chaos
Book Two: Division of Chaos
Book Three: Destruction of Chaos

Magic and Sorcery Chronicles Trilogy
A Touch of Magic
A Slice of Sorcery
A Dash of Devilry

CHAPTER ONE

VAS FROZE AS TEREL AND Pela raced off the bridge with an unconscious Deven on their gurney. The voice Vas heard was a disturbing combination of the Deven she knew and one of the three Devens he became when he returned from dying and was in three bodies a year ago.

It was the worst of the three—the asshole pirate.

She forced that issue aside for the moment. She wasn't certain what she'd heard—aside from the voice of a dead Pirate of Boagada saying that even though Deven had been the Clionea nuns' Pirate of Boagada before, he was tagged to be it again.

Something supposedly impossible.

He'd also said that Deven would save or doom everyone. Then Deven channeled the jerk pirate persona.

Mac jumped the *Destroyer's Curse* through a dozen gates escaping the Nhali mining world as it blew up. Vas finally told him to stop, but this system looked too busy. She didn't enjoy the idea of hiding and licking their wounds, especially after a fight they mostly won. But that was what they needed now. Too many things had gone on lately.

The issue with Deven could be catastrophic.

"Mac, find us a less busy system. We have no idea if the Nhali can connect us to that planet, but if they can, they *will* blame us for it blowing up." Never mind that the Nhali had been digging up a converted planet left behind by the Asarlaí thousands of years ago. An extremely unstable and dangerous planet.

Mac nodded and blasted them back through the gate. He slowly went through another two systems, before Vas agreed to a location. No signs of advanced technology. And the only planets were far from the gate.

"Good work. Gosta, Hrrru, find us a place to hide. I'll be in the med bay." Vas fought the urge to race after Deven immediately. But they were now in a safer spot and she trusted Gosta and Hrrru to find a place to settle and hide.

She needed to know who was in Deven's head. If it was that jerk pirate, she'd lock him up immediately. She wasn't happy about him being the new Pirate of Boagada, but she'd take that over the asshole pirate any day.

"He'll be okay." Aithnea's voice coming out of her comm as she jogged down the corridors wasn't as soothing as it might have been if she wasn't dead.

"That pirate. I heard that pirate's voice."

Aithnea wasn't around when Deven reappeared after being blown apart. But she'd read the files. "He was seriously injured on that mining planet, that could be behind it," Aithnea sounded too soothing. She was the mother superior of a group of dead Clionea nuns, but they were warrior nuns. Soothing wasn't high on her list of descriptives. Even when she was alive.

Vas slowed as she went down the corridor to the med bay. If Aithnea knew something, Vas needed to know before she went to see Deven.

"What do you know? You heard that he's our new Pirate of Boagada, is this something because of that?"

The Pirate of Boagada wasn't a member of the Clionea nuns—at least not a regular one. The nuns were a female order, but the Pirate could be any gender. They served for a year or two, doing things in concert with the nuns. Oftentimes they worked around the nuns' stricter agendas.

Then they had their memories wiped out—something they agreed to before accepting the position.

"Yes. And while that did sound like Tilthias, the last Pirate of Boagada, it might not have been. No one has held the position twice." Her voice dropped and seemed to be talking to herself. "At least any that survived."

Vas was almost to the outer med bay doors when Aithnea muttered that. She stopped and glared down at her comm. "What did you say? Rather, what did you mean by what you said?" As far as Vas had been told there had *never* been someone to hold the position twice. But the nuns weren't against lying if they felt it necessary.

"You shouldn't have heard that. It's our fault, you're coming into some Keeper skills that I didn't think would be there yet."

She went silent and Vas was ready to find a way to drag Aithnea out of the comm by force by the time she spoke again.

"There were two times that circumstances required duplication of holding that position. They both died. I can give you the boring details now, or you can check on Deven." There was a level of sameness to her words. A balanced and non-emotional way of speaking that Vas remembered from when she was taken in by the Clionea nuns when she first escaped her home world as a kid.

It never boded well.

"After this, you, me, Jasiel, and Nitya are talking." Vas ignored any further responses and pushed open the med bay doors. Deven, Terel, and Pela were nowhere to be seen. Divee was monitoring the new bio bed and the unconscious Kantari prisoner inside. He jumped to his feet as Vas raced in.

"Captain!" He was startled but both snub blasters remained in his hands.

"Where is Deven?"

"Terel and Pela are with him in the clean room. She

didn't tell me why, but she has a full contagion warning lockdown on them."

Vas ran the way he pointed. The *Destroyer's Curse* was a new ship to her—well, new enough and she'd been so busy she hadn't fully explored the massive thing. The back of the med bay was huge and contained more rooms than hopefully they'd ever need.

She rounded a corner and found one room with enough warnings splashed across it that no one would be crazy enough to enter.

Aside from Vas.

She used her palm to override the warning code and entered a clean room decon area. The system checked her, and then she knocked on the inner doors.

Terel and her assistant Pela were in decon suits and Terel pointed to more of them hanging inside the decon area. It wasn't clear whether she was afraid that Deven might be contagious—or if he was the one in danger.

Vas scrambled into the suit and was sealing the helmet when the doors whooshed open.

"Terel, what the hell is wrong?" She'd barely stepped past the doors as they shut.

"I don't know. We almost lost him coming down here. *Three times.* I didn't have a chance to call you. We've been resuscitating him."

Vas looked down at Deven. He was even paler than he'd been on the bridge, but she couldn't see any external injuries. "Did something get inside him on that planet?"

"It might have?" Pela glared at the screens she was monitoring. "Whatever is going on, it's seriously messing with our ability to scan him."

Vas watched as the two furiously fought to save him—from whatever was killing him.

"Damn it, Aithnea said that people who'd been the Pirate of Boagada twice died—could that be it? He was declared to be the next one on the command deck."

"We need those damn nuns in here, now." Terel looked ready to snap something at the mention of the nuns.

"I'm here," Aithnea's voice came from one of the speakers. "And Jasiel is on her way down. Nitya is having some issues with the ship; we didn't escape unscathed. But I don't believe this has to do with that. Bluntly, the two Pirates of Boagada died *after* they'd completed their tasks. And yes, in both cases, they were aware it might happen. I'm not getting much from Deven's mind, it's too unstable right now. However, I don't think Tilthias' announcement caused this."

"Keep trying to reach him." Terel settled down, but she didn't seem convinced that the nuns weren't at least partially responsible.

A ringing came from outside the decon clean room behind them. Pela hit a button and Jasiel ran inside and quickly put on a suit.

Even though she was over eight hundred years old, Jasiel appeared to be an extremely fit woman in her sixties. Unlike Aithnea and most of the Clionea nuns, who almost all kept their hair cropped, she kept her gray hair long and coiled atop her head.

She was the founder of the most recent incarnation of the Clionea nuns and the only nun still alive. For now.

"What's happened?" Jasiel winced and shook her head as she came into the room. "And what is that horrific sound? How can you stand it?" She started to approach Deven, but stopped and took a step back.

"What sound?" Vas always had good hearing, and since her Keeper training it had improved. But aside from the low-level sounds of the machines fighting to keep Deven alive, there wasn't anything that would cause that reaction.

"A high-pitched...oh." Jasiel grabbed her helmet and collapsed.

"Pick her up, get her on a table," Aithnea said. "I'll try

and find what she was talking about. For the record, I'm not sensing anything. But being disembodied does have its limits."

Vas and Pela lifted Jasiel onto a bed and Pela scanned her.

"She reads fine. Simply unconscious. Without a reason." Pela narrowed her eyes and looked between Jasiel and Deven. "She's not in danger of dying like he is, but could these two be connected?"

Terel glanced up from Deven. "That would probably be a question for Aithnea. Well? Did the nuns have disorders we need to know about?"

"No. We were possibly the healthiest people in the Commonwealth. But there's something between the two of them. I still can't hear anything that would have caused Jasiel to collapse, but there's a strange vibration between her and Deven. Vas, can you roll Jasiel's cot to the far end of the room?"

Vas looked at Terel, but at her shrug went ahead and rolled Jasiel against the far wall.

"She's twitching." Vas stepped within Jasiel's eyesight and gently shook her arm. "Jasiel? Are you awake?"

"Yes. But wishing I wasn't." Her eyes didn't open but her face was lined in pain visible even through the faceplate of the decon helmet. "What crushed my skull?"

"You reacted to a sound and collapsed," Aithnea's voice came out of a closer speaker. "Not terribly gracefully, however."

"A sound?" Jasiel cracked open her eyes. "Oh, gods, my head."

Pela came over and gave her a shot, then ran back to Deven.

"Better. Thank you." Her face still showed pain, but she opened her eyes. "Let me guess, no one else heard it?"

"No. Do you know what it was?" Vas returned to Deven's side.

"I might. Tilthias could have passed something on to Deven. And Vas. Until this is sorted, I'll keep my mental shields up." She didn't move to get up from the cot.

Vas wanted to touch Deven but unless she took off her suit she couldn't. He was still pale and appeared to be twitching. She had no idea if that was good or not. "Tilthias shared thoughts with me in the cave where his body was buried. Or rather, his spirit did. I felt them but haven't been able to go through them. Maybe that's it?"

Jasiel slowly got off the cot. Whatever shields she put up, they must have worked as she moved next to Deven and peered closely at his face. "It shouldn't have caused a problem, but then all of those memories should have gone directly to Deven as the next Pirate. Not to the Keeper. I'd say Tilthias' spirit had no choice. Aithnea and I need to sort this out. After we stabilize Deven."

"Which is what we've been trying to do." Terel waved at the monitors. "Any idea how to do that? Something is trying to kill him and I can't find it, let alone stop it."

Jasiel turned to Vas. "I wasn't on deck, but you said you heard an odd voice come from him right before he collapsed?"

Vas gave her a brief rundown of Deven dying and then coming back as three people more than a year ago.

Jasiel gave a low whistle. "No wonder he was chosen again. There's a lot of mojo in him that I've never even heard of before. He's Kilesh, right? They are known for being strong espers, and have hearty recovery systems—but that's beyond anything from any species."

Vas shrugged. "Marli said that something in him had changed. She had scans of him from years ago that didn't match the ones she read last year." She frowned. "And that was before the 'dead and back as three' situation."

"The Asarlaí woman who helped in your prior battle? It's sad she was lost. For many reasons." Jasiel nodded as she continued to study Deven's face.

"I doubt we'd be alive now if she hadn't done what she did. But I agree. We do have access to her secret home though." Vas shook her head. "Except it's in the Commonwealth. Damn, for a moment I forgot that we still can't get through there."

Deven began twitching more and Terel increased the sedatives.

"Wait." Jasiel held her hand up and looked closer at Deven's face. "He's trying to come back. I believe those twitches aren't random."

"Let me try something," Aithnea said then went silent.

The twitching turned to spasms.

"Oh no you don't. Knock this off now!" Aithnea's voice echoed through the room. And inside Vas' head.

"This is mine." Deven's words were good to hear, but the voice wasn't. His green eyes were almost black.

"It's that damn pirate." Vas looked around. "Not the Pirate of Boagada. The other one."

Terel nodded. "I agree that's him. Have we lost our Deven?"

"Not if I have anything to say about it." Jasiel rubbed her hands together—which wasn't as effective since the suit had gloves—she put both hands on Deven and pressed down.

"You can't do this!" The voice coming out of Deven shifted. "This body is mine!"

"It was never yours, go back to whatever spawned you!"

In her Keeper training, Vas had learned that the higher-level nuns had almost magic-like powers. Or at least ones that couldn't be explained in an easy-to-understand manner. That was what she felt at that moment. A powerful fight was going on between Jasiel, Aithnea, Deven, and that pirate.

Just not one she could see.

CHAPTER TWO

———◆———

DEVEN'S BODY AND HIS FISTS pounded the bed. Then he crashed and the monitors went blank.

Vas grabbed him and he seemed to be breathing.

Then the monitors came back.

"What happened?" Deven's normal voice, rough as if he'd been yelling, was the best sound Vas ever heard. His green eyes peering at her were good to see as well.

"That we don't know, lad. How do you feel?" Jasiel stayed near his other side with Terel ready to move in.

Vas knew it was only because this might be beyond Terel's level of expertise that she hadn't forced Jasiel out of the way.

"Like someone has been punching me from the inside. Why are you all in decon suits?"

"Because you kept trying to die and I wasn't sure why." Terel moved closer now. "Your scans appear normal at this point. Any strange thoughts or voices in your head?"

"No more than usual." His grin was good to see. "But seriously, no. I remember the fight on that mining world. Then waking up here."

"You don't recall being on the command deck?" Vas wanted to touch him with her bare hand, just to confirm he was okay—and really him. But if Terel hadn't removed her suit, there was still something concerning the good doctor.

"No. Was I awake?"

"You sounded like that asshole pirate you were a while ago. We can talk more when you've been cleared by Terel. I'm glad that you're back." Vas held his hand tightly.

His eyes narrowed and he looked ready to demand a full explanation now.

Terel took off her suit but waved to Vas and Jasiel. "I'm sure you all have much to share and discuss, but right now, I need to make sure he's okay. Even though I'm not certain what was wrong with him."

Jasiel started to say something, but Vas took her arm and spun them toward the door. "Better to give in on this one right now. You probably want to come with us, Aithnea."

Unlike Vas and Jasiel, Aithnea couldn't physically get in Terel's way. But she tended to ask a lot of questions. Right now, Terel didn't look to be up for interruptions.

"Aye, I'll follow you two," Aithnea said, as Vas and Jasiel entered the decon room and removed their suits.

"Terel would have made a fine nun." Jasiel meant it as a compliment but Vas wasn't certain Terel would have taken it that way.

"She loves doing what she does." Vas hung up the suit to be cleaned. "I know you need to rebuild the Clionea nun order, but I wouldn't recommend starting with my crew."

"I wouldn't think of it." But her innocent smile gave away that she might have already been searching for them.

"Am I the only one upset about what happened?" Aithnea asked from the speaker in the hallway. "Can we go to a room and sort this out? I doubt that most of your crew cares what we talk about, but some things might need to be kept secret."

"Deven is going to be okay now, right?" Vas paused. The nuns had their agenda and it might or might not go with what Vas or Deven would want.

"As far as we know," Jasiel responded before Aithnea. Judging by the frown on her face, Vas figured there was a reason for answering so quickly. "Once your doctor has cleared him, we do need to look at him more closely.

Not to mention that as a Pirate of Boagada, one who did not come up through normal channels, we will need to work with him. So will you."

"I want this to be—"Vas' words were swallowed as the ship's klaxon blasted through the speakers.

"Damn it! What now?" Vas shouted as she ran toward the lift and onto the command deck. The alarm was too loud to use her comm to find out what happened.

Gosta and Hrrru were each working two stations at a frantic speed.

Something had gone extremely wrong.

"What's wrong?" Vas yelled as she and Jasiel ran on the deck. "And someone turn that damn thing off!" Every damn ship was playing a one-up game of who could have the worst alarm.

"I'm trying!" Mac had taken over an empty station and was hitting the counter with a wrench. "It won't die!" The last two words were shouted much louder than intended when the klaxon finally cut off. He turned bright red and put down the wrench.

"Thank you whoever did that, now what caused it?" Vas reclaimed her captain's chair and Bathie went to one of the science stations. The *Destroyer's Curse* was a former Hive ship that had been seriously retrofitted. It also had twice as many stations on the command deck as necessary.

"We're still trying to find out, captain," Gosta answered but didn't slow down what he was doing. "I believe that we might not have gotten away from that explosion as cleanly as we thought. Something latched on to us."

"Captain, what was that horrific alarm? Queen Shien is in a meeting, but asked me to find out." Khirson didn't run onto the deck but he moved quickly. His blue skin didn't disclose much, but he appeared winded. He probably ran from the Pilthian quarters but slowed once closer to the command deck to maintain decorum.

Khirson spent fifty years in a missing Pilthian sleeper ship that ended up being boarded by Vas and her crew. The Pilthians were a race no longer common in the Commonwealth, and he joined Vas' crew when his people betrayed him.

A short time ago another group of Pilthians sought shelter at the space station Vas and her people were stuck on—that group was ruled by Queen Shien. Khirson fell hard for the Queen and now was officially courting her and stayed in the Pilthian section of the ship. Mostly.

"We're looking into it. You're welcome to stay up here until we find something." Vas smiled. Khirson had proven himself to be an excellent crew member while he was with them.

He started to shake her off, then took another open science station. "Anything specific I should be looking for, captain?" His grin indicated that while he was in love with Shien and enjoyed being around more Pilthians, he missed the activity of a command deck.

Shien's people had been attacked months ago and their world destroyed. Vas planned to give them the Zqui space station once her crew could leave, but that was canceled when the megalomaniac Ome forced everyone out. Since then, the Pilthians had remained with Vas' crew.

"Khirson, could you search the data records I'm sending to your station?" Gosta didn't mind that his question had been directed at Vas—he and Hrrru were still racing through data and information. "Look for anything from that angle that might have hit the ship." He scowled at another screen. "We're also losing power. Not badly yet, and we are staying in one place for now, but if we can't stop it, we'll be in trouble."

Vas watched as images taken from multiple angles on the ship showed the massive explosion of the mining planet. "Is it me, or was that larger than Mayhira? Was someone *trying* to blow it up?"

Mayhira was their first exposure to one of the Asarlaí failed attempts at creating power and the ability to push between dimensions through planetary manipulation. From what Marli told them, Mayhira wasn't the only world the Asarlaí had tried it on.

Looking at the vids of the explosion, this felt far worse. She thought they'd gotten away mostly unscathed; the vids told a different story.

Hrrru flipped up a new series of images. "It was larger by fifty-five-point two percent, captain. There are signs of other shuttles trying to leave the planet but they were all swallowed by the explosion."

The Nhali were at war with the Lethian Assembly, a massive conglomeration of worlds —or at least they'd been showing signs of preparing for war. If the Lethian Assembly knew what the Nhali were attempting, they might have instigated the explosion.

Vas shook her head as the images played through. "The Nhali lost everything and everyone they had on that planet. But this seems like a difficult way to strike back at them. They couldn't have had more than a few hundred people there."

"Which means we weren't the only ones who knew what the Nhali were mining. The Lethian Assembly might have wanted to stop them. Or there are other players involved." Jasiel stood with her arms locked behind her back while she watched the screens.

"No one should know about that." Vas added, 'unless they have access to an Asarlaí' in her head. That wasn't something she was willing to say out loud.

Jasiel didn't look away from the screens but nodded. "How did Empress Wilthuny know about Mayhira? I've read the reports, an abandoned Asarlaí experiment and she took advantage of it."

"She was working with the clones…we think." Vas scowled. "That's not an issue we can deal with right now.

Has anyone seen anything that could have hit us when we fled?" The ship's power level showing in the corner of the main screen continued to drop.

"Nothing…wait. A flash?" Khirson replayed what he'd been watching and sent it to the main screen. "Right… there. A flash. That wasn't accidental debris, something shot at us."

"From what? The planet was exploding, no other ships were there…oh." Gosta froze the image right before the flash and magnified it.

A familiar silver ship appeared, fired at them, and then vanished. It was too much to hope the explosion had swallowed the ship after it shot them.

"Is that Ome's Ralith ship?" Vas grabbed the armrests on her chair.

Ome felt he owed Vas and her crew for some mysterious way they'd helped him. He was still a homicidal jerk, but one who was marginally on their side.

It appeared their grace period was at an end.

"I believe so." Hrrru couldn't stop watching the image.

Vas shook off the fear that Ome might be after them now. "What did he hit us with?"

A normal ship wouldn't have been able to survive being that close to the planet as it exploded. But the Ralith ship was beyond anything ever heard of during the Asarlaí control of this region a thousand years ago. It was more myth than reality.

But Vas and her people had seen it slice through ships, asteroids, and planets without pausing.

"Make a note to search for any signs of that damn ship in the nearby systems. Look at local feeds for planets. Someone had to have seen it. But right now, I need to know what the hell they hit us with."

"It's hard to say, captain." Gosta sounded hesitant, a rare enough occurrence that it freaked Vas out when it happened.

It also meant he could have an idea but for one reason or another, he didn't *want* to say it.

"What do you think it might be?" She watched the replays in slow motion.

"I'm not sure yet." He was extremely distressed. Knowledge was his thing—this admission was hard. "But it appears to be a small device that is embedded near our aft. It's giving out low emissions of sending out data—so probably a tracker—as well as pulling in power."

Vas' gut went cold. "Like a leach mine?" They'd run into them once before—nasty things that drained a ship's power and then used it to blow up the ship. "But why would Ome use something like that when he could have simply run us through? And why add a tracker to it? To see where we blow up?" Ome wasn't the most balanced of beings, but he was scary smart. A leach mine wouldn't be the best way to get rid of them.

"I don't think so," Hrrru added without looking up. "It is draining our power, and it is storing it...but it's creating its own backup storage module on the skin of our ship."

"And that's different from a leach mine, how?"

Bathie beat the other two. "There's no explosive component. Unless someone is seeing something I've missed—nothing is there to blow up. It's creating a strange storage of power."

Vas rubbed her forehead. "Can the power drain be stopped?"

"Hypothetically? Yes," Gosta said. "Right now, no."

"And the alarm we had was because of whatever Ome shot at us?"

"Yes, captain." Hrrru looked over at her and seemed calmer than before. "At least we haven't found anything else that could have triggered it. The alarms didn't react until it started pulling our power."

"Mac, any signs that anyone in this system has noticed

us?" There was only one populated planet but it was at the furthest distance from the gate. They were hiding behind the remains of a destroyed planet.

"Not that I've seen. I've checked the gate and it hadn't been used in months until we came along."

"Let's hope it stays that way." Vas hit the open comm for the ship. "Folks, we're hiding right now. In case you missed it, we were near a Nhali owned planet that exploded, we don't want to be attached to that event. We'll be here for at least a few days. Consider it R&R." She tapped the comm off.

Xsit had been listening to something during the checking of Ome's gift, but she now took off her earpiece. Xsit was a Xithinal, a bird-like species. Her yellow feathers didn't go pale, but her eyes were wide as she turned toward Vas. "Captain? I think we're being hailed. By the Commonwealth."

They'd been unable to reach anyone inside the Commonwealth once the Lethian Assembly feinted an invasion a few months ago. Vas didn't blame the government for shutting down its borders—not after they'd gotten their asses handed to them by the Asarlaí clones. But the Assembly backed off after a week, never firing on any former Commonwealth planets fallen outside of the border.

Vas waited over a month for the border to drop, or at least for communications to be reopened. The bulk of her crew and her base planet, Home, were inside the Commonwealth.

Vas ran to Xsit's station and took a headset.

The sounds were faint, but it wasn't just any chatter, it was the *Warrior Wench*. Vas left Ragkor and his crew in charge of her when Vas needed to run this operation outside of the Commonwealth. Her flagship was sending a repeating hail from the border of the Commonwealth.

CHAPTER THREE

———

"DAMN IT, CAN WE RESPOND?" Vas could barely hear the call, and it was clear it was a recording, but it was the first sign of getting ahold of the rest of her people in far too long.

"Not yet, captain." Xsit trilled and glared at the console. "But I'm working on it. It might be better if we were closer to the border. Much closer."

Vas handed her the headset back. "Keep tracking it. And anything else from the Commonwealth you can find. The Lethian Assembly backed off on their attack, why is the Commonwealth still locking down their borders?"

Had this happened when they were closer to the Commonwealth, she would have sent them immediately over. They were too far to consider it at this point.

"That's a good question." Jasiel ended her standing watch and took a seat at an open console. "They must have a reason. I still haven't found information as to why the Lethian Assembly was going to invade the Commonwealth anyway."

Khirson pursed his lips as he turned to them. "Maybe they weren't. Think about it, the data my people have indicates that the Assembly has been slowly expanding for years. But it was nowhere near close enough to take on the Commonwealth. And the information I recovered from your end showed that the Commonwealth was making a quick recovery when we came here. If they were going to attack, right after the Asarlaí defeat would have been a better time."

"They did it to make the Commonwealth shut its borders? But to what benefit?" Now Gosta was pulled into the debate. "It's not as if the Commonwealth can't open them again. Even though they haven't." His brows lowered. "Or maybe they can't."

"You think that somehow the border the Commonwealth put up is now locked against them? By the Lethian Assembly?" It felt unlikely, but there was a tiny part of Vas' mind that said it was true. Whether it was a Keeper thing or intuition, she had no idea.

The Commonwealth wasn't big about helping worlds outside of its borders. But they did if they had a large commerce with them. To deliberately cut off that financial supply would never happen.

"Damn it. They're too greedy to do that, they're trapped." Vas nodded to Gosta. "New topic of study, how could those border mines on that barricade be turned against the Commonwealth?"

"Are we going back there? I thought we had to stay out here and gather nuns. Or save the Universe. Or both." Mac sounded confused, yet hopeful.

"Not yet. We need to get that thing Ome gave us off our hull, figure out what happened on that Nhali mining planet, and a few other Keeper-type things. We do need to save the Universe, or at least try, but I think our best bet is to get more allies. Including our people from inside the Commonwealth. Besides, if the Assembly wants the Commonwealth trapped, then we want it open."

"Well put." Jasiel got to her feet. "Might we talk in your ready room?" Her face was calm—almost as scary as a non-emotional speech pattern with the nuns.

Vas nodded to Jasiel then turned to the crew. "Keep doing what you're working on. Deven's still with Terel, so don't bother him. Bathie, take the chair, call my ready room if you need me." Her crew might be mercs, but they'd gotten exceedingly good at digging into data and information over the past two years. If anyone could find out what was going on, they could.

"We have some great minds over on the Pilthian side. Would you like me to speak to them about the Commonwealth border situation? It's a good sign that some communication is now coming through, however." Khirson remained seated—he was still working on what he'd been asked to look for.

"Yes, please do, and tell Queen Shien thank you in advance. We need to find out all we can before we go back there." Vas nodded as she and Jasiel left the deck.

Jasiel waited until Vas shut the door and took her seat behind her desk before taking one of her own. The captain's ready room on this ship was large like everything else on it was. After puttering around in the tiny *Traitor's Folly,* this thing felt like a palace.

"We should call in Aithnea and Nitya if she's settled things down. I'd like Flarik as well."

Vas wasn't surprised at the first two, she'd figured this was another Keeper training situation. Flarik, her pregnant Wavian lawyer, however, wasn't related to that at all.

"Do I want to know why you want her? You do realize she's been staying in her room because she doesn't want to be around others until the egg comes, right?" Flarik wasn't initially happy about staying on the ship at all when she found out she was pregnant. She finally agreed to stay but kept mostly to herself.

"I do. But I feel she might be involved in our situation. Because of her child." Her frown said a lot more than her words did. Whatever the reason, Flarik wasn't going to be happy.

Unhappy Wavians were a dangerous thing.

Vas contacted Flarik before the two dead nuns. "Flarik? Could you come to my ready room? Jasiel wants to speak to us." She shrugged when Jasiel raised her eyebrow. It was fair, Vas had no idea why Jasiel wanted Flarik to be included and wasn't going to pretend that she did.

"Now?" The sound of sharp teeth clacking wasn't good. Flarik only did that when annoyed. Extremely annoyed.

Jasiel heard her and nodded.

"Yup. She says now."

"I can be there in ten minutes. Flarik out."

Vas looked at the comm as Flarik clicked off. The fact that she didn't argue and that she would need ten minutes were both unheard of. This pregnancy was seriously impacting her.

Jasiel reached out to Aithnea and Nitya. Both verbally appeared via the speakers. Nitya was a long-dead nun who'd been stranded outside of the Commonwealth five hundred years ago while trying to save the order of nuns inside the Commonwealth from her homicidal sister, Kalth.

Kalth had somehow survived and managed to claim the position of Keeper—the person who, along with the Pirate of Boagada, would restart the order of the Clionea nuns. Kalth's worldview wasn't good for anyone except her—the new order of nuns would have been used to control the Commonwealth, then the entire Universe.

Kalth was killed in the explosion of the mining planet. Nitya had shown nothing but relief at that.

"What are we discussing? Shouldn't we wait for Deven to recover?" Nitya sounded distracted but she was running the ship. The Hive had been forced to surrender this ship to Vas' people—but they'd done some internal damage that would probably take a few weeks in space dock at Home to resolve. Time and equipment they didn't have.

Nitya embedded herself inside the ship to save the crew. It was believed there was no way to get her out. After five hundred years in limbo, she was ready to leave this world. But she would stay with the ship until the end.

"This doesn't directly involve Deven, yet. He can catch up once he's recovered. We're not sure what the complications will be of him being the Pirate of Boagada for a second time." Jasiel sent Vas a sympathetic look but Vas shook her head.

"I already know about the prior two duplicate Pirates dying. That's not going to happen this time. We won't let it." She could only glare at Jasiel, but she meant it for Aithnea as well. They had enough nun power between all of them to keep him safe. Agenda or not, she was going to make certain they did.

The door opened and Flarik stalked in and narrowed her eyes at Jasiel. "I'm here. Now the question is why?" Even though she'd been sequestered in her room for a few days, she looked as immaculate as ever. Wavians could change their feather color and their gender—up to a point. Flarik had elected to keep her pure white feathers and her female gender. Wavians were descended from ancient birds of prey and now she looked at Vas and Jasiel as if they were prey.

Jasiel gave a beautiful smile and nodded. "Aithnea and Nitya are here as well, Flarik. I wanted us all to get together to talk about your child."

Flarik pulled her head back and put a protective hand over her belly. "My child is no one else's business. Not even the Clionea nuns. If there is nothing more, captain?" She hadn't sat yet but took a step toward the door. Watching Jasiel the entire time.

"It's not that we *want* to pull you into this," Aithnea's voice came out of the nearest speaker. "It's that there's something in your child that is somehow connected to the nuns. Or perhaps the Keeper and Pirate." She paused. "Jasiel, we didn't think of that. Vas and Deven are your selected co-parents, correct, Flarik?"

Jasiel's eyes went wide but she didn't say anything.

"Yes. Again, I don't see what business that is of anyone."

Flarik didn't move closer to the chairs but she also didn't leave.

"They are the current Keeper and Pirate of Boagada. There is a spiritual connection for co-parents, is there not?" Aithnea's voice was dropping into levels of soothing that Vas never heard before.

It was almost scarier than the way Flarik's eyes went wide as she stared at Vas. Vas was no longer potential prey; she was now something far worse.

"That was said long ago, that yes, it was true. Their job is to protect the child if the parent cannot—against *any* type of threat. But those were ancient myths. Nothing more." She didn't seem to notice as she took two steps forward and dropped into a chair.

"That might have been what your people believed." Jasiel leaned forward in her chair. "But I think that at one time it was true. Your people have changed a lot in the past few hundred years. I recall Wavians far differently." Her look was gentle, but at over eight hundred years old, she did have memories few others could claim.

"Is this a threat to my child? We can leave immediately if needed. There are colonies of my people out here." Flarik looked more like her no-nonsense self, but also more rattled than Vas had ever seen.

Had it been anyone other than Flarik, Vas would have reached over to comfort them. Flarik's face was a combination of shock, terror, and anger. But it didn't seem to be directed at Vas or Jasiel.

"I believe your child is to be one of destiny. And they are already reaching out to Vas and Deven on levels beyond normal comprehension. Because of who they are, your child has now become part of the Keeper and Pirate paradigm. They will have a part in the renewal of the Clionea order as well as the battles that we will face." She gave a genuine smile. "Like their mother, they are already a force to be reckoned with."

Flarik looked down at her clenched hands, then nodded slowly. "What do I need to do now and once they are born?" Since Wavians could change gender, no gender was assigned until the child was old enough to determine what they wanted to start with.

"At this point, I'd like you to study both the Keeper and the Pirate duties, if you wouldn't mind," Jasiel said. "To be honest, I've never heard of this happening. I called you in to see if you knew why your child was connected to the situation. I didn't know about the co-parents."

"I wasn't sharing that information." Flarik looked between Vas and Jasiel. "Please send me the information. Once Deven has recovered, he, Vas, and myself should confer." She smoothed her feathers and got to her feet. "Is there anything else?"

Vas grinned. Flarik was back in charge.

"Not at this time. Thank you." Jasiel gave a small hand gesture and then bowed.

Flarik narrowed her eyes but gave a small smile and put her hand on her belly. "Thank you. My people follow a different path now, but all good wishes to my child are welcome." She gave a small hand movement as well, but it was too fast for Vas to see.

Jasiel smiled as Flarik left the room.

"Was that all you needed me for? We do have a lot going on." Vas knew being the Keeper would be more than simply finding the Pirate—but mentally she'd been focusing on that task.

Jasiel watched her thoughtfully. "I was going to work on a different sort of training, one that you can do without Deven. But I believe Aithnea and I have much to rethink."

"And I have to go over parts of the engines," Nitya said. "Our escape from that planet wasn't smooth and I fear we might have issues when it's time to leave if I can't take care of things first."

"Go take care of the ship. Sorry, nuns, but that's her primary focus at this point unless you want to try swimming in space." Vas didn't get to her feet but waved toward the door. "We can discuss Deven's situation in a bit. I need some downtime." Vas didn't feel the exhaustion from her fight on the mining planet, and everything that followed, until this moment—but she was crashing now.

The quarters she shared with Deven would just remind her of the problems they had. Deven had no recollection of channeling that evil pirate persona, but that didn't mean that it hadn't been there.

Jasiel and Aithnea left Vas' ready room, already planning.

Vas almost went for a glass of something strong, but instead hit a button that brought out an uncommonly comfortable sleeper sofa from the wall. Her crew added it during the retrofit out of kindness—they didn't want her passing out on her desk anymore.

She meant to stretch out, the adrenaline was fleeing her body now that the immediate threats were over. If Gosta or Terel needed her, they would find her. Right now, she needed to close her eyes.

She was drifting off when a soft knocking came at her door. Ignoring it seemed to be the best idea at this point—if it was something serious, there would be more than a knock. She hadn't turned off her comm but nothing came through that. Which wouldn't have been the case if things were bad.

The knocking came again and Vas rolled off her sleeper.

She tapped open the door, ready to chew out whoever was there, but stopped. It was Deven. He was wearing medical scrubs and appeared confused.

"Did Terel release you? How did you get here?" He was back to being pale and his green eyes narrowed with worry.

"I don't know." He held up his hands. Both had cuts

and blood on them. "I woke up in the lift. I don't recall what happened."

Vas' comm chirped. "Captain! Terel and Pela have been attacked! And Deven is missing." Divee's voice was on the edge of hysteria.

CHAPTER FOUR

VAS PULLED OUT HER SNUB blaster and aimed it at Deven before she responded to Divee. "Deven is here in my ready room. How badly injured are Terel and Pela?" She mentally kicked herself. She loved and trusted Deven—but if that bastard pirate persona was floating around in his head, he'd have to be locked up.

Deven didn't move or speak but looked concerned about Divee's answer.

"They're both unconscious but seem to be okay. They fought back before they were knocked out." Divee paused. "Is Deven okay?" Those words were weighted. Okay as in not injured, but also okay as in he hadn't attacked Terel and Pela.

"I don't know right now. Take care of Terel and Pela, contact me when they're awake." There was a slim chance Deven's injuries and confusion weren't tied to what happened in the med bay. But she couldn't afford to assume that.

"Aye, captain." Divee cut his comm.

Vas used her comm to call Gosta. One problem with such a large command deck, her ready room was away from everything. "Gosta, I need you to come to my ready room with whoever big and fierce is near the deck." She kept watching Deven and didn't lower her snub blaster, but he didn't move.

"Aye, captain." Gosta didn't ask questions, but moments later he, Roha, and Gon came in.

Roha was the tallest and she could probably pick up

Deven. Gon was one of the nicest people Vas knew, but he was also huge and strong.

Gosta tilted his head as he realized that Deven stood in her doorway.

"There was an attack in the infirmary. Deven should still be there, but has no memory of what happened or of coming here." She didn't lower her blaster but did take a step forward. "Deven, you need to go with them. We have to lock you up until we know what happened."

He sighed and flexed his bloody hands. "Did *that person* do this?"

At least he remembered what she'd said about the pirate persona. "We don't know. Once Terel and Pela are conscious, we can ask who attacked them." She turned to Gosta and the other two. "Get his wounds looked at, and have them documented. But only after you reach the brig."

Gosta opened his mouth then quickly shut it and nodded.

Deven didn't put up a fight as Roha and Gon each took an arm and Gosta led them to the lift.

Mac came running over the moment the lift doors shut. "What happened to Deven? Where are they taking him?"

"Don't know what happened." Vas sighed and hit the button to retract the sleeper into the wall, then pushed Mac out and shut the door behind her. She'd prefer to keep Deven's lock up quiet until they figured more of it out. But the odds of that were slim. If Mac was asking about it there was no way that the rest of the crew wouldn't know that something happened within ten minutes. "Something is going on with him and until we sort it out, he's being confined."

Mac had a gift of gossip. Telling him not to say anything would only make things worse.

"What did he do? It's that pirate guy, isn't it? I heard

him before." Mac's blue eyes were round and he was too close to her.

Vas had also hoped no one else had been close enough to hear Deven's voice when he collapsed on the deck before. She should have known if anyone did, it would be Mac. "We don't know. My answers on this are going to be the same. When we know something, I'll share it with the crew."

Mac bit his lip to silence the rest of his questions. "Aye, captain. I'll go back to researching things."

Vas went to Hrrru after motioning for Bathie to stay in the command chair. "I'm going to check on a few things. But, as Mac already knows, Deven's having some issues. I'm not ready to discuss it at this point as we're not sure what we're dealing with. But from this point, until I say otherwise, do not obey any commands from Deven. As some of you know he is now the Pirate of Boagada, but he might also be channeling that jackass pirate persona he came back as a year ago." Deven had come directly to her, but as her second in command, he could have done a lot of damage if he hadn't. And if he was under the influence of that jerk pirate.

Most of the deck crew nodded. A few, like Xsit, looked extremely concerned but refrained from saying anything.

Even though he'd been the first to hear this, Mac looked ready to launch questions again.

Vas cut him off before he started. "Mac, I need you to form a crew to go on a ship walk and get whatever Ome tagged us with off the hull."

Hrrru's eyes went wide.

"*After* Hrrru and Gosta have cleared it to be removed." The task needed to be done, and since there was no flying at the moment, she wanted to keep an easily bored Mac busy. "Until they do, make plans on who and what."

Mac wasn't usually in charge of big projects, but the grin on his face pointed out she made the right call. Not to mention, she could add someone a little more experienced to his group if needed.

"I'll be making a full crew announcement concerning Deven, then will be going to the med bay and brig. Bathie, you still have the deck. The rest of you, keep looking for your answers." At nods all around, Vas opened the ship-wide comm. "Attention, Deven has been compromised from an attack on that mining planet we just left. He will remain under guard until I feel it is safe for him and the ship. From this point on, until I say otherwise, do not obey any orders issued by him. That's all."

"Thank you, captain. We will keep an eye out," Shien's was the only response.

Vas responded to her. "You're welcome. We've borrowed Khirson for a project on the deck. I hope you don't mind?"

Shien laughed. "He was your crewman first. If something comes up that we can't handle, I know where to find him." She ended the comm call.

Vas turned to the deck crew. "Stay out of trouble. And Mac, notify me before your group goes out." She knew that Hrrru and Gosta would tell her once they resolved the issue of that parting gift from Ome. But better to remind Mac.

The toss-up between med bay and the brig was a hard one, but right now there were more possible answers in med bay.

Divee and Larrisa, another doctor, were carefully helping Terel and Pela into sitting positions on their cots—which was good. The pain and confusion on both patients' faces wasn't.

Vas went to Terel's bed first. "How's the patient?" She kept her voice low but both Terel and Pela winced.

"The patient has a super nova-sized headache, thank you very much. Divee won't tell me what happened, is Deven okay?" Terel squinted at her.

Vas looked at Divee but he shrugged. Obviously, Terel didn't recall what happened.

"What do you remember?"

Terel closed her eyes and slumped back into her pillows. "We were working on him, checking to make sure there was nothing odd going on…with those nanites?" She sounded like she wasn't sure. "Then something came up and attacked us. Next thing I knew Divee and Larrisa were hovering over us like mother hedgepigs."

"You didn't see anyone? And why were you concerned about the nanites? They said they would remain dormant in him until we can return them to their part of space." Vas was trying to keep her voice neutral, but she was now freaked out that they could have an unknown attacker on board. Not to mention what those nanites could do if they'd betrayed them.

There had been a group of them on the Zqui space station, trapped by the former operator, Gerl. They'd held Deven hostage until they were sure they would be released back home.

Unfortunately, that home was near the domain of the mysterious and deadly Clongari—who appeared to be aiming to take over all known space.

"I didn't. Just a dark shape. Tall, like Roha's height. We fought back but it moved too fast for us. I looked into the nanites because we don't know enough about what they can or can't do. Just being thorough." Terel opened her eyes and glared. "Why aren't you telling me where Deven is and why he's not here with us?"

"I'll get to that." Vas patted her arm. "Pela? Do you have anything more to add?"

"Not really. Big, fast-moving shape." She winced and rubbed the side of her head.

"Did either of you see it attack Deven? Or see him get up to fight it?" He had injuries to his hands, but until they were cleaned up and examined, there was no way to know if they'd been defensive or offensive.

Terel scowled. "No. He didn't move. I don't think."

Pela shook her head. "It happened so fast. But I don't recall him fighting it."

Vas rubbed her temples. Either Deven was the attacker, or some weird thing got on board when they fled the mining planet. Both options were bad. Deven was a powerful enough telepath that if he had been possessed and was the attacker, he could have masked it from Terel and Pela.

"Deven showed up at my ready room. His hands were bloodied and he was confused as to why he was there and what happened. I have him locked up in the brig."

Terel started to get up, but Vas pushed her down. "Mathias is with him. He's documenting everything, but until we solve this, I can't have Deven, or more importantly anyone who might be inside him, roaming the ship. I told everyone else, but until I say otherwise, do not obey any orders from him."

"Damn. This isn't good."

"Understatement. Oh, and while you two were down here with him, Xsit picked up a recording from the *Warrior Wench*. The Commonwealth border is still up, but Ragkor is trying to punch through communications."

"What? That's great." Terel squinted up at Vas. "Or it would be if we could reach them. From the unhappy look on your face, I'm thinking we can't."

"Not yet, but our best and brightest are working on it." Vas looked to Larrisa. "What's the verdict about our patients?"

Larrisa was a synergian, a full-blooded version of Gosta. They'd recruited her to step back into the medical doctor role she'd moved away from twenty years ago when they were stuck on the space station and needed more medical support. She was tall, thin, and normally unflappable.

This was the first time Vas had ever seen her distressed—even during major battles.

"I still want to run more tests." She held up her hand to stop the protest from Terel and Pela. "Until I say you two are ready for duty, you aren't going anywhere. Isn't that right, captain?" Larrisa didn't turn toward Vas, but she didn't need to.

Vas grinned. "Sorry, she's right. And you know you'd do the same damn thing if you weren't the patient. Don't you think it's odd that neither of you remembers anything about your attacker? You fought them. I see the gel patches on your fists. Yet neither of you saw them?" She shook her head. "I'm sending over Gosta once he finishes securing Deven and updating me. He can work with Larrisa on figuring out what happened." She started to leave but turned to Divee. "I presume the cameras weren't on?"

He shook his head. "They were on, but are shorted out. We'll need to have them repaired."

"Get someone on it." Vas nodded to everyone and marched out. Divee had started on the command deck, but over the last two years had shown he didn't like being in charge—at least not of an entire crew. He seemed to be fitting in well in the med bay.

With no resolution of the Deven attack issue from Terel and Pela, Vas picked up speed and jogged toward the lift and down to the brig.

That no one from there had contacted her was hopefully a good thing. But Vas never wanted to become complacent.

Roha and Gon stood at the entrance of the largest cell. Gosta must have returned to the deck as only the medic Mathias was with Deven. But Deven appeared unconscious.

Vas nodded to Roha and Gon then went to the locked cell. "What happened?"

Mathias looked up with a shake of his shaggy head. He was a Welischian half-breed and while taller than most of his people, still had their fur. And the claws. "I don't know, captain. He was fine, making light of the entire situation, then as you came into the brig, he passed out."

Vas let herself inside the cell and locked it behind her. "No one in or out unless I say." She aimed her comment at Gon and Roha and they both nodded.

She walked to the side of the cot and crouched next to it. "Deven? Can you hear me?" He appeared to be sleeping, but she kept one hand on her snub blaster, just in case.

He twitched and Vas almost pulled out her weapon. But he only slowly opened his eyes. "What happened?"

"You passed out." Mathias stood back but his claws were ready to defend his captain if needed. "You were complaining about your head hurting more than your hands, then collapsed."

"My head does hurt. And now I remember our conversation." He turned to Vas. "And why you locked me up. Did I attack Terel and Pela?" He was calm but there was fear in his voice. He honestly had no idea what happened.

"We don't know. They're both conscious. Larrisa and Divee are taking care of them. But neither recall anything beyond a dark shape attacking them. They also can't remember if you were attacked or what happened to you."

"Could someone have gotten on board when the shuttles fled the mining planet?" Mathias was tapping his claws on his arms.

The same thought crossed Vas' mind.

"I don't think so, but it was hectic at the end. We can't

ignore that might have been what happened." She turned back to Deven. "You still don't remember anything?"

Deven shook his head. "No. I remember talking to you and Jasiel, then mostly nothing after the two of you left." He paused. "They saw a tall dark shape just appear and attack them? How could anything have gotten inside that room without being picked up by the cameras?"

The Hive had a lot of cameras in the original version of the ship. Vas had her crew remove the ones in private quarters, but leave the rest. With the amount of times her ships and space station had been attacked out here, it was a good idea.

"The cameras were dead." Vas dropped her head and massaged her forehead. "But I don't know that anyone checked the ones in the decon room or the corridor. He's okay? As much as he can be right now?" She stood up and turned to Mathias.

"I'd say yes. But his recent blackout is concerning. And I'll want to set up monitoring equipment."

"I *am* right here." Deven sounded the closest to his normal self since he had appeared in her ready room.

"Patients don't get to have a say. Especially ones I've had to lock up." Vas leaned over to give him a quick kiss then marched to the gate. "Get everything set up, Mathias. Then head back to the med bay. We'll keep guards and alarms on him. I need to go track down video evidence."

With instructions to Gon and Roha to keep two people on guard at all times, one inside the brig and one right outside the door, Vas jogged back to the command deck. She could pull up the vids at any station. Even though she hadn't gotten a nap, she wanted to get away in her ready room to search.

She was working hard to keep the fear of what was happening to Deven out of her mind.

CHAPTER FIVE

GOSTA WAS ON HIS WAY down from the deck as Vas was heading up. "Captain, I was looking for you."

"Change of plans. You and I are going to see what we can find on the vids from the corridors and lifts. Terel and Pela said it was a tall dark shape—let's see what was really there." She took his arm and swung him back toward the lift.

"How was Deven going to the brig?" Vas knew Gosta would have noticed any oddities.

"Normal, yet subdued. Honestly, he felt as if he wasn't himself."

"The pirate?" Vas felt a chill. So far that voice had only appeared once and she wanted it to stay that way.

"No. Not at all. Just extremely subdued. I wish I knew what happened to him."

"Don't worry, Gosta. No one has an idea of what's happened." They arrived on the command deck. The night crew would be coming on soon, but Mac was already looking bored, again.

"Since we're not yet ready for your ship walk, I have a new task for you. Bathie too, when the night crew comes on. I need people to examine the two shuttles we took to the mining planet. Scan the interior, exterior, and all cameras."

"I'm game." Bathie got up and stretched as her replacement entered the deck. "What are we looking for?"

Vas paused. "Anything out of the norm." Sometimes telling people what they should be looking for biased their judgment. If they didn't know what they were looking for, they'd question everything. "And both of you double-check the other. Thank you."

She turned and led Gosta to her ready room. Exhaustion was hitting hard, but she needed to do something. There was no way she was losing Deven.

Gosta waited until the door shut before he spoke. "You need to eat." He went to the basic food machine in her ready room. "What would you like? Sandwich? Soup? Solie, obviously."

Vas shook her head and laughed. "When did you get so pushy?"

"When I realized it was part of my job, particularly when your other protectors are injured. Neither Deven nor Terel would let you continue without rest or food. I know that you'll fight me on the rest, but food and solie are required. What would you like? Or perhaps a synergian delicacy?" His grin was evil—synergians had radically different versions of good food than humans. Even as a half-breed, Gosta's tastes leaned more toward them than his human half.

"No. Thank you. I have a soup and sandwich dish programmed in there." She yawned. "And you're right about the solie. A large one. Thank you." Vas moved things aside so they would have room to watch the vids while they ate.

Once he brought over their food, he'd duplicated her order for his food, they began pulling up the vids. Vas drank about half of her massive cup of solie immediately. The caffeinated hot drink was an odd combination of sweet and bitter but always woke her up.

Food wasn't a bad idea either.

Gosta started with the vids of the hall and Vas took the decon room. "I'm starting when Jasiel and I took the suits off and going frame by frame. There might not be anything, but I would think if someone was working through Deven they would have used something more solid than a vague dark shape."

"Excellent point." The two settled in to eat and search. After almost an hour the food and solie were gone and Vas swore she was seeing things in the vids that hadn't been there before. No mysterious black shapes though.

"Haven't found a single thing. I see Jasiel and me leaving. Then nothing until Deven stumbles out of the room. He looked worse than when he got to my ready room, but he was walking like a man asleep. I see Divee go in, but then nothing. Damn, we need to see what went on in that decon room." She ran her fingers through her hair. At some point, she'd removed her braid and her hair was roaming free. And was a wild mess.

"Nothing in the halls either. I followed Deven the entire way, but until he came out of the lift on the command deck, he was stumbling along. Once he gets to the deck, he still looks confused, but more aware of what he's doing." Gosta rocked back in his chair.

"We still have no idea what attacked Terel and Pela, or what in the hell is going on with Deven." Even the massive amount of solie she'd drunk wasn't enough to fight a huge yawn.

"I'm afraid not, captain." Gosta's sigh turned into a yawn. His eyes went wide in embarrassment.

Vas laughed. "Don't worry, it's been an incredibly long day for all of us. I'm ordering all the day shifts to bed, tasks or not. And yes, that means me as well."

"But captain, I can run another filter over the vids."

"You can get some sleep and battle on tomorrow. That is an order."

He got to his feet and put their dishes into the slot near the food dispenser. "Aye, captain." With a characteristic head bob, he left.

Vas was tempted to pull out the sleeper bed, but she needed real sleep. The aches and pains of her fight with

Kalth and her fake Pirate of Boagada were making them-selves known.

She wasn't surprised to see that Bathie and Mac were not on the command deck. Scanning both shuttles would take a while. She called them. "Make notes of where you stopped and secure both shuttles. You need to get sleep."

"But captain—"

"Have you found anything?" Vas cut Mac off.

"No, we haven't," Bathie responded. "We'll secure everything, captain. Have a pleasant rest."

Vas closed her comm with a smile. Bathie was going to make an excellent captain one day. With nods to the night deck crew, Vas went down to the quarters she shared with Deven. The ship lights were dimmed to give the feeling of night. Vas and most of her crew spent more time on ships than planet-side but it was still comforting to have the day-night cycles.

She normally kept minimum lights on in their quarters but turned all of them off once she came in. The entire day was now slamming into her.

The problems had kept her mind away from what occurred on the planet—and all the information Tilthias' spirit had dumped in her head. Something she would have told him if he wasn't so compromised.

She made it through a quick sonic shower and fell into bed before she let herself cry.

Vas wasn't a crying person. She had nothing against people who were, it was simply that after growing up the way she had, she'd learned not to.

But right now, she needed it. If Deven were physi-cally injured she'd know how to deal with it. But this vague weird shit wasn't something she could get her head around.

"You need to sleep."

Vas initially thought Aithnea had found a way to get

back in her head, then realized she was speaking through the comm station next to her bed.

"That's what I'm working on. What do you need, Aithnea?"

"You're crying. That's so unlike you that I'm concerned. And while you've gotten ready for sleep, you're not even under the covers." Aithnea had limited input in the visual area, but she could see some things. "You have much to sort out and need to be rested and ready."

"How do we fix Deven? I'm not even thinking about what I need to do next as Keeper—we need to get him back. *I* need to get him back." She wiped away her tears. She felt better being pissed.

"Jasiel, Nitya, and I are looking into it. We don't need sleep, well two of us don't, and Jasiel has gone weeks with almost no sleep. Deven is our primary focus."

Vas felt better about them being focused on him—even if she knew it was mostly for the benefit of the future Clionea nuns.

"Fine. I'll sleep. Just keep an eye on him while you're working, okay?"

"I promise," Aithnea's voice was soft. "Now, sleep, child."

Vas smiled. Although she never admitted it to the rest of the nuns, Aithnea had peeked into Vas' novitiate room every night to say the same thing. The fierce mother superior warrior nun comforting a lost child who wouldn't admit she was falling apart.

Kind of like now.

"Thank you." Vas crawled under the covers and was out as soon as her head hit the pillow.

It seemed she'd just fallen asleep when images came racing at her. They first seemed to be dreams, dark ones that sometimes haunted her sleep.

Then she realized they were images from what Tilthias, the prior Pirate of Boagada, had sent to her when she'd found his spirit on the Nhali moon. Once she fought to contain the rampaging thoughts, she saw they were connected images and maps covering the space they were in, the Commonwealth, and the vast edges of space where the nanites and the vicious-looking Clongari lived.

Everything was tied together as darkness covered them on the massive map in her mind. The Clongari were everywhere.

And no one else survived.

Vas woke up swearing and commanded dim lights on. It was almost time to get up, even though it felt like she'd just fallen asleep. She grabbed a pad next to her bed and began scribbling everything she could recall.

It felt far more terrifying in her head. The Clongari would destroy everything and everyone that wasn't them. Right now, no one would survive.

CHAPTER SIX

—◆—

VAS WAS ONE OF THE best merc captains in the Commonwealth in part because of her ability to see the true threats in any battle situation and prepare for them. Even as her heartbeat returned to normal, she realized she didn't have a clue as to how to approach this. They knew the Clongari were deadly and would have to be faced, but the absoluteness of the images was horrifying.

She quickly changed, braided her hair, and ran to the command deck. If Deven was himself, he might have some insight into what the hell they were facing. But there was no way she could take that chance right now.

The thought that this was nothing but a nightmare didn't cross her mind. There was a horrifying realness to it. Increased by the terror that Tilthias, the last Pirate of Boagada, was fighting against this situation becoming reality when he was killed two years ago.

Kalth murdered him to take over the new Clionea nuns. Vas was pissed about that when she first found out.

Now she was terrified. They were two years behind in solving this issue.

Gosta got up from his station. "Captain! I was going to call you. Mac and Bathie returned to the shuttles a short while ago and said they think they've found something."

"And I might have found a way to communicate with the *Warrior Wench*." Xsit bobbed her head excitedly, then frowned. "But we need to go closer to the Common-wealth border. A lot closer."

Vas held up her hands. "Excellent work, folks. I'm going

to the landing bay." She started to the lift, then spun back. "Unless we've heard anything new about Deven?"

Gosta shook his head. "No, captain. The vid feed shows him resting quietly on his bunk."

Vas nodded and ran into the lift. And hit her comm on the way. "Jasiel? Can you and Aithnea meet me in the landing bay? They found something."

"Aye, captain," Aithnea's voice came through the lift speaker.

"On my way," Jasiel responded, sounding far too perky for possibly having been awake all night. Maybe when you got to her age sleep was optional.

Vas picked up speed as she neared the landing bay. It was clear which shuttle they'd found something in, as only one had its doors open.

Bathie stuck her head out and waved. "We have an intruder. Or two." She stepped back as Vas came inside.

Mac split his attention between some odd gizmo in his hand and a panel of vid screens. The shuttles only had three internal cameras. His panel showed vids from seven. "Ha! Good to see you, captain. We're closing in on catching what it was."

"Is it still in here?" Vas had her snub blaster but she wasn't certain how effective it would be if the thing wasn't visible.

"No, captain. What he's chasing are the images it left behind. We've added cameras and connected them to this thing to expand the width of the residual images." Bathie scowled. "Not sure where it came from, because Mac won't tell me. But, according to it and what we've captured so far, there was at least one extra being in this shuttle when it returned from the planet."

Vas took a step outside to see which shuttle it was. "Damn it. This is the one Deven was on."

"Aye, captain." Bathie shook her head. "Unfortunately, Mac's toys haven't given us anything to work on. Until we can see for sure who was here, it could simply be a glitch in the system."

"It's not a glitch! I just need to get this thing working." Mac swore and smacked the long metal box he was waving around. "This will work, it will…oh." His tirade cut off as the gizmo in his hands started flashing a bunch of colors, and then the screens with the vid images came alive too. "It's working!" Mac sounded as surprised as anyone.

Streams of color slowed down and faint images of people appeared. Two of them had an odd glow and were only on the return flight.

Deven lied about the severity of his injuries, as most of the crew, aside from the pilot, were clustered around him as the shuttle headed for the ship.

The shuttle was almost to the *Destroyer's Curse* before the two faintly golden glowing shadows solidified enough to see their features.

"Is that Pol and Relin? Ome's brothers?" Vas started swearing as the two, identical to their maniacal brother, became visible. They still had the weird glow and it appeared no one on the shuttle noticed them. One of them held a small square device over Deven's head. The triplets looked identical so there was no way to know which was which. One could even have been Ome, but she didn't think that it was. Now that he had that Ralith ship, he didn't sneak anywhere.

"They look like it. Weren't they supposed to be locked up somewhere?" Mac watched as the shadow images finished whatever they were doing, then followed the crew out of the shuttle.

"A lot could have happened in the past few months," Bathie said.

"If they came on board before Ome shot us, then that device was probably aimed either at them, or to help whatever they're up to. We need to figure out more of what it's supposed to do." Vas looked at the screen again. Yup, both golden-encased entities followed the rest of the crew out. "Mac, do you have a frequency read on whatever shield those two used?"

"Good call, captain." Bathie held out her hand to Mac. "You know I can isolate it faster than you."

Mac shrugged and handed the pad over. "Always let people play their strengths."

"Spoken like a Clionean, Mac." Jasiel smiled as she arrived. "Sorry for my delay. Aithnea is stuck in a system loop and can't get out yet." She leaned over Bathie's shoulder to peer at the pad, then looked up. "You already found something?"

"Yes. Two shielded people, Ome's fellow triplets, boarded with the crew on that Nhali mining planet, then left once the shuttle landed here. Completely unseen. Bathie is sorting out their frequencies. Gosta and I searched the decon room and corridors yesterday, but without that frequency, even if they were caught on vid, we'd never know."

Bathie swore a few times. "I'm almost getting it, then it's like it's alive and slipping away."

"May I?" Jasiel held out her hand.

"By all means. But I'd like to see what you do." Bathie grinned as she gave her the pad.

Jasiel's fingers moved so quickly that Vas was glad she wasn't the one trying to follow them.

Bathie gave a yell as Jasiel raised the pad over her head in triumph. "We've got them. Shifty little buggers. And, I've confirmed they are not in here."

Vas smiled. "Excellent work, everyone. Secure this shuttle and let's take this to Gosta. Once we get a scanning frequency set up, I'll need the two of you to search the vids, along with a few more people. We need to search everything from the last day." Vas left the shuttle and waited as it was locked up. "Jasiel, do you think that

Nitya could use that frequency to find them in real time? Knowing where they've been will be helpful, but better to know where they are." Normally she'd use the comms to tell Gosta what they found, but even in a tight comm, their invisible friends might hear it.

The landing bay was rarely on full lockdown, but once the others came out, and Jasiel verified that the two brothers weren't anywhere in the landing bay, Vas locked it tight.

Jasiel nodded. "She might. We can call her when we're on deck. Altered personalities aside, Deven was most likely not involved in the attacks. I am concerned about the device those invaders held over Deven's head."

"Agreed." The only thing to calm her fears was that the brother didn't look happy as he removed the device. Hopefully whatever it was supposed to do failed. Vas tapped her comm to the med bay. "How are Terel and Pela doing?"

"We're both fine, thank you for asking." Terel was in one of her moods, but Vas couldn't blame her. She knew that being attacked was secondary to Terel's annoyance at having no solid memory of what happened.

"We might have found something of interest. Could you join us on the command deck?"

Terel paused. "I'll be there before you."

Vas laughed as her friend cut the comm. Terel might be annoyed, but curiosity usually resolved that.

The day crew was settling into their stations when Vas and the others arrived. She tucked away the pad she'd written down the weird visions she had last night. It would need to be addressed, but not until they found the invaders.

Vas waved to Jasiel and dropped her voice. "When you contact Nitya, could you tell her to secure all high-risk areas? In a nuns' cant?"

Jasiel handed Mac's pad to Vas. "Aye, and good thinking. Once she gets the frequency in her system, she can verify they aren't there and shut access down area by area. Might I use your ready room?"

Vas nodded. The nuns' cant was a shorthand lingo used only by them. Hopefully, if Pol and Relin were around, they wouldn't have a clue as to what was being said. Too bad only three of the beings on this ship knew it.

Gosta got to Vas' command chair before Vas did, and Terel was right after him. At least they waited for her to sit before speaking.

"Sorry I'm late. Delimara started twitching. But she remained unconscious and it eventually stopped." Terel's frown indicated how disturbing it was, although she tried to downplay it.

Delimara was their Kantari prisoner—so to speak. She'd kill them all in a heartbeat, but was currently under control, and sedated, by a massive amount of nanites in her system. The same ones who were in Deven's body.

"Anything to worry about?"

"Nothing yet. It only lasted a few seconds. I have Cassil watching her since I sent Pela down to check on Deven. Now, what's happened?" Terel folded her arms and started tapping her foot. Patience wasn't always a strong point of hers.

Vas pulled Gosta and Terel closer to her and quickly went over what they'd found and showed them Mac's pad. "If we can get this into our system, we can find them. And see if they were in the med bay when you two were attacked."

Gosta's hands were twitching with excitement as he reached for the pad. "Might I, captain?" It was such an afterthought that Vas almost laughed.

"Here you go. Terel, do you want to go with him? See what you can find?"

"Aye, captain." Terel also watched the pad.

"Good, then I—" Vas' words were cut off as the ship

rocked hard to the left. "Belay prior orders, what the hell hit us? No one should know where we are." The voice in her head that said, aside from Ome through the toy he stuck on them, was ignored and shoved aside.

He could destroy them at any point. He knew it and she knew it.

Gosta ran to his station, gently setting down the pad as he worked on both of his consoles. Terel stayed nearby. Hrrru remained at his spot, so he was quicker in getting the images up. "A Nhali gunship, captain. Only one." Never mind that even one Nhali gunship would be a challenge for them in their current condition.

"Damn. Raise all shields. Xsit, contact them." Vas knew that if the Nhali had reached out to Xsit, she would have told her immediately.

"My hail is bouncing back, captain. Nothing but static." The feathers on the back of Xsit's head were starting to rise as she continued calling out to the approaching ship.

"Walvento, how are we on weapons?" Vas had nothing personal against the Nhali, but she didn't believe they felt the same. Not to mention she had fled their secret mining planet as it exploded.

"We're fine, captain. I'm tracking that ship." It wasn't surprising that Walvento sounded happy about that.

"Hold your fire until my command."

"Aye, captain." The sigh in his voice was also expected.

"Xsit, switch communications to me."

"Aye."

As soon as the console on the arm of her chair lit up, Vas opened communications. She had Gosta add a narrower, but stronger, punch to her communications than the ship in general. "Nhali vessel. We have done nothing to cause this attack. Stand down now."

Gosta got to his feet making a slash across his throat.

Vas cut the call. "What, Gosta?"

"Captain, with all the furor when we escaped, Deven

collapsing, and everything, I forgot to tell you that I left some new drones hidden in the debris around this planet we're hiding behind. According to my readings, that ship is seriously damaged. Even if our regular scans aren't showing it yet."

"Good work, Gosta. They still have weapons though?"

"Not many. They hit us with enough to say hello, but not cause any real problems. If we'd been at full shields, we probably wouldn't have felt anything. They might not be responding because they can't. The drones are picking up wild power fluctuations."

"Ideas on how else to reach them? And do we have enough control over our power to move out of their way if they can't stop?" Knowing that the ship was in distress, their continuing movement forward—putting them easily within range of the weapons of the *Destroyer's Curse*—

was far less aggressive.

They had more than enough enemies out here. If they could help that Nhali ship, they might get someone on their side.

"I might be able to help with that," Flarik called in from her room. She wasn't on the command deck much at this point, but she paid attention to what was happening. "That's the ship that warned us off before. The one with a Wavian captain and many Wavian crew members. Let me try a lower frequency attempt."

"Go ahead."

Vas heard the clicks that were part of the Wavian secret language. She believed the lack of communication from the Nhali ship was due to their damage—but Flarik felt differently.

The Nhali ship began to list to one side. The movement was odd, but it changed their trajectory enough that they wouldn't hit the *Destroyer's Curse*.

"Are they going to hit the planet?" Vas asked as the Nhali ship slowed, but continued forward.

"They have been attacked by a power drain—they believe it was put on them by a Ralith ship. They're having trouble shutting down their engines and stopping forward movement," Flarik said.

"Damn it, what the hell is Ome doing?" Vas watched as the ship continued to slow. "Gosta? Hrrru? Ideas?"

"Captain, if they kill all power except life support, they should stop. Or I can break into their system and do it for them. It'll be faster if they drop their shields."

Flarik was talking to them, but also listening to the command deck. "They are dropping their shields, but move fast."

Gosta's hands flew over both consoles for almost a full minute, before the Nhali ship halted, dead in space.

"Flarik? Are they okay?" The sensors showed life signs and limited power. Nothing else.

"Yes. The Captain says thank you. And she'd like to speak to you."

Vas nodded and opened the ship-to-ship comm. "Thank you for not hitting us. Is everyone over there okay?"

"We have many injured, but I believe we've gotten our system to purge the contaminant. That silver ship hit us with something as we came into this sector."

Vas shared a look of concern with Gosta and Hrrru. The Ralith ship hadn't come to this sector. And they'd completed a bunch of jumps before hiding here.

Flarik came stomping on deck looking pissed and made a sharp motion to cut communications.

CHAPTER SEVEN

VAS DID SO WITHOUT SAYING anything to the other ship "What is it?"

"That isn't the person I spoke to before. It could be another Wavian or someone who knows our speech and can replicate it. But something is wrong with the speaker and with the ship. Far more than what that person is telling us." Flarik clicked her claws together rapidly. It was a good thing for the crew over there that she wasn't on the other ship.

Vas scowled. "I gathered something was wrong when she said the Ralith ship tagged her as she came into this system."

Mac folded his arms and scowled at the screen. "Captain, no one has come through that gate since we arrived yesterday. *No one.*"

Bathie nodded in agreement from her station.

"Then where did these people come from, why are they acting like a ship we ran across, and what is their real agenda?" Vas glared at the screen as if it could give her the answers.

"There's something on this ship they want. Nitya is looking into it, but according to her, that is not the ship Flarik spoke to before. It appears to be the Nhali ship, but something's extremely wrong." Jasiel came out of Vas' ready room and caught most of the conversation.

"And they were lurking here on the chance that we'd come to this sector to hide? That seems a bit much." Vas believed Mac and Bathie about no other ships following them through their jumps. But how in the hell could someone know where they were going to stop?

"When did the shuttle carrying Deven unload in comparison to our jumps?" Jasiel approached Mac's station and walked with her hands behind her back. Always a sign there was something she needed others to learn.

"Damn." Vas shook her head as she caught what Jasiel was aiming at.

"Almost thirty minutes. We had to get Vas' shuttle up here, then get the hell away from that exploding planet…" Mac swore. "They remotely took over my station. Or did something to it." He looked ready to tear the entire thing apart.

"Then we assume that our visitors are working with Ome. All of our visitors." Jasiel continued her pacing.

Vas shook her head. "That makes no sense, if there was something he wanted, he would simply take it."

"The Nhali ship is contacting us," Xsit said.

"I would like to speak to them again." Flarik looked ready to break heads. Or bodies.

"By all means." Vas turned to Gosta. "Those drones of yours, are you sure of their information? That ship looks to be in bad shape and they did allow you to shut them down."

Gosta's eyes went wide and he furiously started punching up information and swearing. "Not this time!" He hit something extremely fast and then glared at the screen of the Nhali ship. "They were trying to use my hack to get into *our* systems!"

"But you blocked them, right?"

"I did, but it was close. I saw more of who they were before I shut them down. It is the skin of the destroyed Nhali ship, but it's manned by members of the Lethian Assembly. The substructure of the vessel is theirs as well. This was a trap, but I'm not certain they are working with Ome." His long fingers were no longer dancing across the consoles but kept clenching like they wanted to reach out and strangle someone.

"They mimicked *my* people?" The feathers on the back of Flarik's head shot up. When that happened with Xsit, it meant she was terrified. With Flarik it meant she was hunting. "I will speak to them. *Now.*" Her eyes became hooded and Vas forced herself not to dive out of her chair. She did step aside and activate the communications array on it.

"Gosta, can those modified drones do anything in terms of attack?" Vas figured he wouldn't have simply sent them out to watch if there was a way to weaponize them.

"Yes, captain."

Vas nodded. "Have them ready for Flarik's command. Then attack that ship." Walvento would be disappointed, but at this point, Vas wanted to keep their heavy weapons for a bigger fight.

Flarik smiled and opened up the communications. "Listen—whatever you are. I am an extremely annoyed pregnant Wavian. If you do have any of my people low enough to work with you, they will explain to me what in the hells you are up to."

"We explained our situation—"

"And we know you aren't Nhali but part of the Lethian Assembly. You also tried to access our ship's systems. *Explain yourselves.*" Flarik shot off a round of nasty-sounding clicks. If there were Wavians on board, they got an earful.

"Their systems are powering up and weapons are coming online." Hrrru kept his voice steady but his hands were shaking. "They aren't as damaged as they look."

Vas swore. She had a feeling they needed to know what this damn ship was up to, and how they hacked Mac's system to find them. But they were out of options. "Gosta, hold back on your drones. Walvento, ready a full barrage of weapons on my mark."

"Aye, captain!" He sounded happy. But most of the faces that turned toward her were surprised.

Flarik nodded. "Excellent choice. Soon, before they figure it out. There is something evil in that ship." Her feathers were still up.

"Walvento, now." Vas couldn't say what Flarik felt, but a wave of malevolence now flowed from the ship.

Walvento wasn't kidding around and the amount of weapons fired was impressive. They might not have done as much damage as hoped if the other ship hadn't been launching their attack a few moments behind them.

Unfortunately for the Lethian Assembly vessel, their weapons were still in the process of firing when the array from the *Destroyer's Curse* hit them.

"They got some shots out. Our shields are dropping, captain," Bathie called out from her station. "Seventy-six percent, but there's more debris coming in."

"Nitya? Are they going to hold?"

Static came through first, and then Nitya's voice sounded like it came from a distance. "Yes, captain. I'm not letting them fall."

"Sixty-seven percent."

"Fifty-four percent."

"I believe we're staying at fifty-two percent, captain."

The Lethian ship was in pieces and drifting dead from the combined explosions. "Xsit, keep scanning all channels for survivors. Nitya, how long to get our full shields back?"

"Aye, captain." Xsit's feathers were up but they appeared to be in keeping with Flarik's. The scowl on Xsit's face as she listened didn't seem frightened but pissed.

"Unknown," Nitya said. "Hopefully within the hour. That drain on the hull is affecting everything."

Vas leaned back in her chair. She needed Deven to get back to being himself. But she didn't want him out of the brig until they captured Ome's brothers. "Damn it, what are the odds that two groups snuck on either via the system or the shuttle at the same time?"

"Good catch." Jasiel took over a station but turned to nod to Vas. "I couldn't gather much before they were blown up, which I agree with by the way, but they might not have been part of the Lethian Assembly after all. There were layers of subterfuge. I will examine the data we pulled in before they were blown up." She glared at the screen. "And I normally would agree on saving survivors, but in this case, I say leave them."

The Clionea nuns were known for giving little quarter, but the tone in her voice indicated there was more than that.

"Captain, there is a pod hailing us." Xsit broke in.

"Patch them through." Vas hit the comm on her chair when the light flashed. "What?" She was a merc, not a murderer. But in this case, not knowing who might not deserve to be blown to dust was making her pause.

"You cannot—" A high-pitched whine cut the voice off.

"Cut the comm!" Flarik jumped. "Cut it!"

Vas ended the call but the screaming whine echoed.

"Destroy that pod, immediately!" Jasiel's eyes were wide.

"Walvento, blow that thing up. And any other pods from that ship." Vas watched Flarik and Jasiel and they both nodded.

The whine cut off as the escape pod blew apart.

"What the hell was that? That thing *really* wasn't a Lethian Assembly ship, was it?"

"It's a Clongari, or was." Deven's voice coming through the comm was great to hear, even if there was a lot of pain in it.

"How do you know?" Vas didn't doubt him, but they still weren't sure someone else wasn't in his head.

"I felt them. And they were trying to kill me. Bastards."

"With that sound?"

"Yes. Deadly for unshielded Kilesh telepaths for any length of time. Debilitating for all other telepaths. Terel might want to have her team check all the espers on the ship."

"Are you safe now? We don't know if they had other survivors." Vas knew that normally Deven didn't keep his mental shields up while on their ship. But she'd never heard of an attack like this.

"I am. I'll keep my shields up and stay here in the brig. Just safer for everyone."

"Damn. I have to see you. I'll be down in a moment." Vas swore. She needed to tell Deven about Ome's brothers. And scan the brig for any invisible intruders.

"I'll be waiting." He ended the call.

"Gosta, I know you're doing a lot but I need the frequency on Mac's pad to be duplicated."

"I'll have it ready post haste." He nodded to Hrrru, then worked on another station with a blank pad.

"Bathie, you have the deck. I need to see Deven." Aside from the fact the brothers weren't showing on the deck, they had no idea where they were. She needed to tell Deven about the attack on him.

"Everyone keep looking for more escape pods from that ship. Bathie, if you see one, tell Walvento to destroy it."

"Aye, captain," echoed around the deck. Vas hoped there were no more pods.

Gosta waved a pad at her. She grabbed it and ran for the lift.

Terel easily caught up to her. "Sorry, the doctor needs to check on this new development. I've never heard of a sonic telepath attack." Her annoyance was clear. She would check Deven, but also give him a sound chastising. They'd had problems with him not sharing information for years—ever since he'd been declared dead during a fight, was buried, then hunted the ship down when he recovered a few weeks later.

Marwin and his sister Glazlie were now on watch, with him outside the brig doors.

"Nothing to report, captain. Aside from Deven screaming out in pain once. Pela said he was fine though." Marwin was short and powerful like his sister and brother—and, also like them, a deadly fighter.

Terel almost ripped through Marwin and the door at his words.

"Easy doc." Vas nodded to Marwin and he stepped aside.

Glazlie raised her weapon as the door opened, but lowered it when Terel and Vas came in. Not that it mattered, Terel raced past her to Deven's cell.

Pela and Deven looked up from chatting as Terel ran in.

"I would have called you if there was a problem." Pela shook her head as Terel let herself into the cell.

"I know." Terel held out her hand for Pela's diagnostic pad.

Vas followed Terel, then nodded for Glazlie to lock the cell again. "Hold on a second, everyone." Gosta showed her the scan would work with a push of a button—for smaller spaces anyway. Luckily, it did and Vas held her other hand up as she slowly aimed the scan around the entire room.

"We're clear, for now. Glazlie, don't let anyone open that outer door until I say."

At Glazlie's bolting of the outer door, Vas turned back to Deven and Pela. "A lot has happened." She filled them in on Ome's brothers and the attack by a fake Nhali cruiser.

Pela and Deven were both swearing when she finished.

"You're certain they scanned me with something when I was on the shuttle?" Deven got to his feet.

"Yup. I can show you the vid, but I don't think it's

on this pad. A small, rectangular item. Whichever brother was trying to use it, he looked pissed when he removed it."

"About this big, curved slightly, and green lights along the edges?" Deven held out his hands to mimic the thing she'd seen in the vid.

Terel beat Vas. "Yes. It's a miontain thought scanner, isn't it? They were on the planet and saw a chance to pull something from your mind."

"But why are Ome and his brothers nosing around Deven? Why were they on that damn mining planet to start with?" Vas accepted that Ome was extremely powerful and more than a little insane—but this was odd even for him.

Pela was also annoyed. "And why did he tag this ship? Sorry, still playing catch up."

"I would say someone wants the Keeper and the Pirate—or information on them," Aithnea's voice came from the nearest speaker.

"Glad you're back." Vas hadn't been concerned about whatever tied up Aithnea because Jasiel hadn't been upset. Also, there were a lot of other things to worry about.

"Eh, I was investigating. Fine, I was stuck. Gosta's work installing the scanning frequency for your friends to the entire ship jogged me loose."

Vas wanted to know how a dead nun who was living inside the computer of a ship got trapped and freed so easily. But that could wait.

"Why would Ome be interested in the Keeper or the Pirate?" Vas aimed her question at Aithnea's speaker. "How are they connected?"

Deven nodded at Vas' question. He might not recall what happened yesterday, but his mind was still one of the best on a ship of extremely bright people. "They could have found something that would help them on whatever megalomaniac thing Ome is working on. But the brothers were trying to get the Pirate information from me." He started swearing. "And probably triggered that damn persona in my memories by accident instead, since I didn't have anything to steal."

"We have to find those two and get them off my ship. Immediately." They'd been watching what they said after they found out about Pol and Relin. But they hadn't before that. With them wandering around invisible there was no idea what they could have heard.

Vas was surprised they hadn't come after her yet.

CHAPTER EIGHT

"AGREED ABOUT GETTING THOSE TWO off this ship. And whatever Ome hit this ship with. Once our ship is sound, we should leave as soon as possible." Deven nodded. "Now that I know what triggered it, I will be able to suppress that pirate persona. Permission to rejoin the crew?"

Terel responded first. "I'd rather you stayed here with that door bolted until we catch those two. But you do appear to be yourself."

Vas shrugged. "Yes, you can resume duties—once you get something other than med clothes on. But we wait here until Gosta has the scan fully working on the entire ship. I'm not leaving until we have those two and that tracking gift from Ome off this ship."

Deven shrugged and pulled at the loose top. "They are comfortable, but not imposing."

"Gosta? How are we doing ship-wide?" They cleared the brig of hidden people, but that didn't mean the brothers weren't listening in to the comms.

"Bit of a setback on that, captain. Mac's coming down to show you the problem."

"Understood." Vas ended the call. "They must have something that's working, or he wouldn't need to send Mac down. You can let us out now, Glazlie."

She unlocked the cell and then started for the larger doors. "Wait for Mac out front?"

Vas had been following her but stopped. "No, bring him inside. It's doubtful that he scanned on the way down. When Marwin knocks, I'll stay behind the door.

Get Mac in quickly and I'll scan around him to make sure he didn't bring a friend or two."

"But the brothers are only invisible, right? They're still physically there." Pela stood near the door as well.

"That's a good question. By the way you described the scene in the shuttle, they would have been stepping on people." Deven reached over to borrow Vas' second snub blaster as he shook his head and swore under his breath. "They moved themselves out of sync. A dangerous and deadly thing to pull off." His smile was evil. "And they wouldn't have been able to maintain it for more than an hour at the most. They might still be invisible, but they now have a body presence. Much easier to catch."

Mac made good time, as a knock came from outside a moment later.

"Glocvb et din?" Glazlie shouted through the door.

"Din et yawin!" Marwin shouted back.

"Maybe you and your brothers should share that native language of yours with our troops for codes."Vas laughed. The triplets were from a remote and distant world in the far reaches of the Commonwealth.Vas had never run across anyone else from there.

Glazlie grinned and opened the door.

Pela kept her foot on the back of the door so that Mac barely squished through.

Vas scanned around him, but he was alone. She nodded and Pela and Glazlie slammed the door shut again.

Mac stood back with an armful of odd gizmos watching Deven warily "He's okay now, right?"

"I'm fine, Mac, trust me. What are those?" Deven was using his 'soothing an animal' voice, but Mac still took another step back. Deven sighed. "I wasn't the one who attacked Terel and Pela, and that pirate isn't coming back."

"I believe you." But Mac's grin was weak as he turned to Vas. "Gosta can't get the scan ship-wide. That thing from Ome is throwing off enough sensors that it won't work. But we've been converting any free pads into these." He pulled the top one off the pile and handed it to Vas.

It looked like a toy blaster had been attached to the top left of a pad. "And what's the fake blaster about?"

"It's a repair gun for some of the ship systems. Really old though, no one in the Commonwealth uses them anymore. Nitya found a bunch in storage and Gosta connected them to the pad scanner. Aim at the far wall and pull the trigger."

Vas did. A light-colored beam came from the gun, then covered the entire wall once it hit it.

"The repair gun focuses and intensifies the scan, but disburses when it hits a solid object. Had one of our friends been there it would have blown their cover and even stunned them a little." Mac sounded as proud as if he'd invented it.

"Not as good as ship-wide, but I'll take it." Terel grabbed one from Mac. "Those bastards beat up Pela and me, we get the second shot at them after Deven."

Deven grinned and also took one, with Pela right behind him.

"How many more do they have?" There were two left. Mac would keep one obviously, but she'd like to give the other to Glazlie or Marwin.

"When I left, they were at thirty. Khirson took a bunch down to the Pilthians."

"Glazlie, do you want this? Or to go up on deck?"

Glazlie took the pad with a smile. "Always take the new toy."

They left, locking the brig behind them, and sent Marwin up to the command deck.

He would tell Gosta where Vas and her team were going to cover. This level from here to the med bay.

They spread out but overlapped each other with their scans so nothing would be missed. The targeting with the repair guns made scanning much easier and they quickly arrived at the med bay.

Cassil looked up from his desk in the front. "Good to see you up and about, Deven." He gave an odd look as they all came into the med bay, scanned, and moved further in. "Everything okay?"

Vas felt the hair on the back of her neck rise even though the scans in this room revealed nothing. "Glazlie, you and Mac stay here with your backs against the doors. Keep them locked and only open on my or Deven's command. Cassil, keep a weapon handy. Everyone else, let's keep going."

Terel snarled but kept her voice low. "They're *here*?"

"Not sure. But something feels wrong. My Keeper senses are tingling." That she found the thought comforting disturbed Vas more than the fact she had them.

Terel stalked past Vas, scanning the walls and ceiling of the corridor that led further into the medical area.

"Are you sure they aren't able to physically hide at this point?" Vas asked Deven as they followed.

"Yes. Maintaining a shift like that is dangerous. My people did studies, anything longer than an hour or so and the person died."

Vas turned to Pela. "Move up alongside Deven and me, but stay near the wall." Vas moved over to be a couple of inches away from the other wall. There were only a few inches between them.

The weird feeling continued the further they went. Terel didn't get too far ahead and would wait at each doorway. They all scanned the room, then shut and locked the door.

Finally, only a small lab remained at the end of the corridor.

Deven looked to Vas. "Still feel odd?"

"It's even worse now. Damn, is this what telepaths feel?"

"Some. At least until they are fully trained. But I feel it too. Something is near."

Vas swore at his choice of term. If something was down here, it better be those damn brothers.

Terel waited for the three of them to catch up, then opened the final door. She raised her blaster instead of her scanner but stepped aside for Vas, Deven, and Pela to flood the room with the scan.

It took longer than Vas expected, but two shapes appeared in the far corner. It was the brothers, but they looked bad. They collapsed as Terel stunned them both in rapid succession.

"Couldn't wait?" Vas ran to the closest one—he was out cold but breathing.

Deven checked the second one, then patted them both down. He held up the small machine they'd tried to use on him, four smaller blasters, and pulled off a disk that was embedded in each of their biceps. "This was how they pulled their invisibility trick." He dropped the disks to the ground and crushed them with his boot heel. "Sorry, any information that we could have obtained from those would have been offset by the risk. We should be able to get something from this though." He held up the scanner. "I suggest we keep them in separate cells in the brig—where they can't see or hear each other."

"Agreed. As for shooting first, they're lucky I kept my setting low since I wanted answers." Terel darted out of the room and came back with two pairs of cuffs. "The blaster shot should keep them out for at least an hour, but I don't trust anything about these two." She had them both cuffed and on their backs in moments. Glazlie and Mac came down the hall after Vas called them and nodded to Terel.

"You got them." Glazlie grinned.

"Yes, and we need to get them in the brig. Separate, sealed cells."

Deven grabbed one of the brothers and flung him over his shoulder. Glazlie took the second one and did likewise, even though the man was a foot taller than her.

Vas left the room. "Terel? Are you staying down here? We might need your medical assistance when they wake up."

"Yes, Pela and I need to get back to our normal day. But don't fear, I want to speak to those two." Terel narrowed her eyes and Pela nodded in agreement.

Vas led Deven and Glazlie out.

"What do you want me to do?" Mac drifted behind.

"Have you sorted what that thing is on our hull and how to get it off? And who's going with you? Once we learn what we can from these two, and find a good place to dump them, we need to get the hell out of here." The weird feeling she'd had before they found the brothers had faded, but there was still something wrong.

Not to mention that hiding in a compromised location was not a good plan.

"Aye, captain." Mac gave a sloppy salute as he jogged past them outside of med bay. "I'm on it."

Vas shook her head as he vanished and then hit her comm. "Gosta? We found them and are locking them up. New priority is to get the hell out of here. I want everyone working on it."

"Aye captain. Good to know."

"Is there anything I should know about?" Gosta often sounded distracted due to usually working on ten projects at a time. But this was different.

"I don't think so, captain. Just checking a hunch. Nothing to report. Yet."

Part of Vas wanted to run up and make him tell her his hunch, but she needed to see these brothers secured first. "Send Marwin back down to the brig, these two need guards." She'd get Gosta's new theory out of him eventually.

She switched her call. "Nitya? Can you get heavier security on the brig?"

"Aye, captain, all defenses will be increased around them. I think one of those two, or that scanner they had, was working with the object on the hull. I still don't have full control or power, but it's better." There was no static in her voice coming through the speaker this time.

Marwin beat them to the brig and held the door open for Deven and Glazlie. "Good catch. I already set up the two furthest cells and put up the screens."

The two cells were apart from each other and the sound and visual screens would block them from seeing or communicating with each other.

Deven checked the brothers as he and Glazlie dumped them in their cells and removed their cuffs.

"Keep watch on them and report anything odd," Vas told Glazlie and Marwin, then she and Deven headed for the command deck.

"Eh, I'll meet you there after I change." Deven kissed her quickly and left.

Vas was in the lift to the command deck when Aithnea's voice popped up. "He really is okay."

"I didn't say he wasn't. He's fine."

"Um hmm. I know you better than you do. Or maybe you're aware that you're lying to yourself. You have concerns."

Vas halted the lift. "Hells yes I do. First off, all second Pirates of Boagada die? Then that scanner brought back the other pirate? That person was a dangerous asshole. My concerns are justified."

"Your concerns could cause problems. If we have to fight our way out of here and you don't fully trust Deven—you could kill everyone. Not to mention, if that doesn't happen—you're supposed to be the Keeper to his Pirate. Trust is essential."

"I trust him and I trust me. I don't trust all of this

mystical stuff we've been shoved into. I thought once we found the Pirate of Boagada my job would be done. Or at least I hoped so." She muttered the last bit but didn't release the lift.

"You're tired," Aithnea's voice was gentle. "The last few years haven't been your normal life and it's catching up. Go do what needs to be done. We won't start training for you and Deven until we're in a more secure spot."

"Thanks. But shouldn't I get the Pirate stuff out of my head and into his?" The thoughts, memories, and information sent to her from Tilthias weren't intrusive. But still, she had enough extra stuff in her head.

"Everything has a time. Never fear, child, there are reasons for everything. Oh, Nitya is calling." Her voice popped out and the lift started again.

Vas shook her head. She realized saving the Commonwealth was important. And whatever part she and her crew had to play in saving everything around, including the Commonwealth, was even more so. But she wished she could go back to being a simple merc. It wasn't her fault the Universe changed the regs on her.

Knowing who to fight, when to fight, and how far to take the fighting made life so much simpler.

And if she was honest with herself, mind-numbing. She hadn't gotten into a good bar fight in a long time. She hadn't needed to.

The lift doors opened as she gave a massive sigh at how things had turned on their heads.

"Captain! What's wrong?" Xsit had sharp enough ears that she heard Vas sigh even though the deck was buzzing with activity.

"Just thinking." Vas forced a smile and walked to her chair. Bathie must have known she was on her way up as she was already at her science station. "Any new information? It doesn't look like there were more escape pods?"

"No, captain. There was one but it had seriously damaged controls and crashed into the remains of their ship." Hrrru hummed to himself as he pulled something up on one of the large screens. "However, I was able to single out this image from the debris. It has no life signs but appears intact."

The picture at first looked like a piece of shattered metal filled with sharp edges. Then Hrrru tightened the focus again.

"That's a body? That's one of the mysterious Clongari?" It didn't look that scary from this distance. And all of those jagged spikes were most likely an encounter suit. But Vas still felt a sense of foreboding seeing it. And fear.

"That's what it appears to be. Since they are myths in the Commonwealth, and even out here—no one has an image of them." Jasiel was in the station nearest to the screen but she sounded interested, not afraid. "We should bring it on board."

"What? Why? What's wrong with you?" Vas got it out first but the rest of the command crew appeared to be thinking the same.

"Hear me out. We can keep it in a specially secured room. Nitya, Aithnea, and I can make sure nothing from that suit can get out. There's a good chance we won't be able to get the Clionea nuns up in time to stop this invasion, our best bet would be to slow it down. Right now, the Clongari are doing simple feints—they're trying to find out who everyone is out here. Disguising themselves as a Nhali ship hiding as the Lethian Assembly tells me they might have been helping build the fight between those two. But no one knows for certain what the Clongari are." She turned her seat to face Vas and the crew. "We need to understand the enemy before we can defeat them."

CHAPTER NINE

THE BRIEF MOMENT OF HER crew listening to Jasiel with deference due to her age and station was gone and everyone spoke at once.

Most in increasingly loud tones.

The lift opened and a freshly showered and changed Deven came on deck and whistled loud enough to rattle the wreckage hanging in space in front of them.

Vas shrugged. She was too stunned by Jasiel's suggestion to engage in the conversation and planned to let the crew yell themselves out. But this worked too.

"What's going on with you people?" Deven asked as he walked through the new silence to his station.

"They're upset about what's on the main screen. Hrrru found it, so he—" Vas stopped. Hrrru looked ready to find a way to dig under his console. "Jasiel made a radical suggestion based on the find floating on the main screen."

Deven's swearing pointed out when he figured out what was out there. "What was your suggestion, Jasiel? Blow it to dust? I agree with that."

"I thought you might agree that we need to know more about them." Jasiel shook her head in disappointment.

Deven returned a full glare. "Those things haven't been seen in almost a thousand years. But even my people feared them. *More* than the Asarlaí."

"Your people, like everyone who even knows what they are, fear what is unknown. I repeat, we can't hope to fight an enemy we don't understand." Jasiel tapped her comm. "Nitya, do you believe once we remove the object on the hull, you, myself, and Aithnea could create a safe way to store the body drifting in space in front of us?"

"I'd have to investigate further, but there is an empty storage area on the lowest level that we could secure. There's no one on that level or the three above it."

Vas let out a deep sigh. She hated when deadly, dangerous ideas had merit. "Can we create a way to jettison that holding area if needed? I can send you the details from other ships with that ability, but that is a must before I agree to anything."

Deven continued to glare at Jasiel but softened it. "You're right. But I want to be involved. It's not that I don't trust everyone here, it's the fact that not everyone seems to have the proper level of fear."

"Agreed. And I want Hrrru to work with you all as well." Vas had only seen a few things disturb Deven on this level. But she nodded and sent the specs from *Warrior Wench* and the Pilthian ship the *Fairthien* to Nitya. The *Warrior Wench* had detachable decon rooms; the *Fairthien* could detach entire sections of the ship. This probably wasn't the time or place for something that advanced, but the data should help them set up a smaller version.

She reluctantly agreed that they needed to know what they were facing, but caution was paramount.

Vas shoved that issue aside for now. "Mac? How are we doing on that tag that Ome left on us? And Gosta, please find a planet with air and food nearby where we can dump the brothers once we're finished interrogating them." Vas turned to Xsit. "Anything on communications with the *Warrior Wench* or anyone else in the Commonwealth?"

"Still working on it, captain," Mac shouted as he hunched over his station in order to appear busy.

"I'll find one, captain." Gosta was calmer but he also was already working on two stations.

Xsit frowned. "Nothing yet. I'm trying different frequencies, but no results. Permission to go into the dark web?"

"Go ahead. Just take the usual precautions." Vas didn't like using the dark web, it could leave a ship open to a system attack, regardless of how well-defended it was. But as long as Xsit was her usual paranoid self, they should be fine.

They needed to find a way to reach their people in the Commonwealth. And get that damn barricade down.

"I found it!" Mac yelled as if he'd won a race. His look of disappointment when no one besides Vas appeared to care was clear. "Ah, captain, I think I've found how we can remove that object."

"Very good, Mac. Take who and what you need for your ship walk. Have Walvento get you a shielded box to put it in. I don't want to destroy it, but let's leave it with Ome's brothers when we drop them off." Vas wasn't completely certain the brothers were working with Ome, but she'd let them sort it out.

"Will do." Mac looked around, then pointed at Bathie and Gon to join him. "Maybe Walvento could help on the removal too?"

Vas nodded but watched him carefully. Bathie was a brilliant engineer, so having her along made sense. But Gon was more for muscle and so was Walvento. Mac, Gon, and Bathie ran off the deck as he explained the details of his plan to them.

"You didn't even ask what his plan was." Deven grinned.

"I'm trying to be more trusting. Not to mention, I trust Bathie and Walvento to keep Mac out of trouble."

Jasiel looked up from her oddly one-sided appearing conversation with Nitya about the body storage. "Aithnea could help get that Pirate information over to Deven while we're working on this." The seemingly innocent smile from Jasiel indicated that she had most likely been speaking to Aithnea as well. Or she'd picked up on Vas' concerns about Deven on her own.

No time to deal with things like the present. Although she would have liked more time to sort out her issues on her own. Time might not be a luxury they had right now. "Good idea. Gosta, you have the deck. If you need us, we'll be in my ready room."

"I'll be there in a shake, working on something," Aithnea's voice came through the nearest speaker.

Deven was already on his feet but motioned for her to lead.

Great. He picked up on the weirdness too. Vas forced a smile and marched to her ready room.

Deven came inside and shut the door before she gave him a kiss that expressed all the concerns she had.

"Thank you?" He grinned when they finally broke apart.

"Damn it, weird stuff can't keep happening to you. I need you." She sighed. "In more ways than one."

"And part of you is worried that I might not be completely me."

"I was concerned about that, but that kiss was all you." Vas went to her desk and sat. "But how can we be sure the other persona is being repressed? I thought it was gone completely when Marli and Terel put you back together."

Deven also sat and ran his hand through his hair. "Marli told me there was a slim chance of residual. But she also said that she'd blocked the personas completely. I need to take apart that scanner the brothers used and find why it triggered that reaction."

"And we need to get what Tilthias put in my head, into yours." Vas sat back and the pad she'd tucked into her pocket jabbed her. "Oh, and there's something else going on. Almost a dream, but I think it's more than that." She brought out the small pad and told Deven about whatever happened during the night. Vas was glad she'd made notes, the entire episode already seemed vague and distant.

His frown deepened as she finished the story. "That was something more than a dream. But whether it was from your Keeper training, Tilthias' memories bouncing in your head, or something completely different, it's hard to say. It's not good he knew about this two years ago."

Vas leaned over her desk. "You want to look in my mind." It wasn't a question. Deven knew how she felt about espers—even him. But she also knew this was most likely how they were going to get Tilthias' info into Deven's head once Aithnea got here. "How would I have been able to give you what Tilthias gave me if you hadn't been an esper?"

"He must have known who it was going to be before he told us. Are you sure you're okay with this?"

Vas' concerns about him faded even further at the honesty on his face. "Yes. Not happy okay, but okay as in we need to do this. Since Aithnea isn't ready yet, let's see if you can find anything odd that triggered my non-dream. When our resident dead nun is here, we can get this stuff into your head and determine if last night's images came from Tilthias." She felt they had—there was a sorrow attached that he'd been killed before he could find out more.

Deven got up and secured the door. "I don't want anyone interrupting this. No idea what all is in your head."

Vas nodded and hit her comm. "Gosta, don't let anyone interrupt us. Unless the ship is under attack. Seriously under attack."

"Aye, captain. I'll block access to your comm and deal with any issues myself."

Aithnea was going to help with Tilthias' information,

but she had a lot of projects going on for a dead woman. If they could do it without her, all the better. If not, at least Deven might have a better idea of what was going on in her head and what she'd seen last night. "Do I need to sit closer to you? Stand? What?" Deven had been in her mind before, but this was different.

"I'll come to you." Deven pulled his chair to the side of her desk. "Just turn to face me and relax."

Vas took a deep breath and shook out her shoulders. "I'm ready."

He leaned forward and gave her a light kiss. "It'll be fine, I promise."

A moment later the world collapsed around her.

CHAPTER TEN

VAS TRIED TO SCREAM, BUT nothing came out. There was darkness and cold but nothing else.

"It's okay. I promise." Deven's voice was all around her but still so far away that she could barely hear him. "Calm down."

"Calm down? I'm drifting in a mass of nothingness!" Vas shouted. Her throat felt it. Yet the sound vanished immediately. "Deven!" She put as much force as she could into it, but it didn't do much better.

"I'm here. It's okay."

"Don't say that when I'm drifting here. Fix it." Vas would have liked to have slammed her foot down, but there was nothing for her to push against.

A vague hug enveloped her. Nothing physical beyond the hugging feeling, but it was comforting. "This isn't right. What the hell is happening?" Her worry was turning to annoyance—a better setting for her. She'd had telepathic encounters before. Some weren't voluntary when she was young, thanks to her late brother.

But nothing like this.

"I'm not sure." Deven's voice was stronger now. "Something in your head is causing this. My view is fine. You're standing in the middle of an empty room in your mind. But your heart rate is elevated and you can't see me."

"I feel like I'm floating in a dark space. I can hear you better now, but I am having to focus."

"Let me try something."

Vas felt her mind lighten. She hadn't realized how

heavy it was until the pressure vanished. Faint light and shapes began to appear around her.

"That's better. Keep doing that."

"It's the Pirate—the good one. His information sort of hopped to me. The things he shared with you were far more than his thoughts alone. It's everything from every Pirate—ever. There's too much to go through now. But your visions last night were from them."

"What do we need to do?"

"I think I need to deal with this alone. It's all in here right now. So many voices…so many spirits." Deven took in a sharp breath. "Savan?"

The world shook again and Vas found herself on the floor of her ready room with a groggy-looking Deven a foot away.

Also, on the floor.

"Did you call out for Savan? As in Marli's boyfriend telepath who died with her when she shot them both into the sun to destroy the Asarlaí clones?" Savan was probably as strong of an esper as Deven if not more so. But she doubted that even he was able to reach out from beyond death.

"I felt him. It was fast, but it was him." Deven blinked rapidly as if he'd been rudely awakened and was trying to focus. "He's included in the memories of the Pirate of Boagada."

"As in he was the Pirate once?" That was disturbing to think of but since the Pirates normally forgot everything after—he could have been and not known it.

"He might have been." Deven shook his head. "Or Marli was."

Vas was slowly getting to her feet at his last words and almost fell over her desk. "What? How in the hell could an Asarlaí have been the Pirate?" She hit her comm. "Jasiel—in here, now!"

"What happened? Sorry I'm late," Aithnea said from the desk speaker.

Vas had no idea how someone dead and existing inside a ship's systems could sound out of breath, but Aithnea did right now.

"Hold on, we need Jasiel in here too."

Deven unlocked the door as Jasiel raised her fist to knock.

Jasiel ran in and took a seat. "You found something?"

"Sort of," Deven said. "I was checking Vas' mind for some odd dreams she had when the information from the Pirate came over to me. There are presences of all past Pirates in my head now. Was Marli or her partner, Savan, ever a Pirate of Boagada? I'm not going to drill through all the information in my head right now. But I sensed Savan—or someone close to him."

Jasiel responded first. "Marli was that Asarlaí woman, right? I think we would have noticed if one of them had been selected."

"Not if she hid it well enough and the prior Pirate selected her," Aithnea sounded far more worried than Jasiel. But she had more than a few run-ins with Marli. The two didn't get along.

"There's no way that could have happened…is there?" Jasiel rarely sounded at a loss; eight hundred years of questionable living could do that to a person. But she did now.

"I would have said no. Not at all. But Deven felt something. We have to trust what was passed to him." Aithnea calmed down but still sounded pissed.

Vas didn't like any of this. "Maybe it was only Savan? He was a powerful telepath, maybe he left a big mental footprint?"

"It could be him. Deven, what made you suggest Marli was involved?"

Vas almost laughed as an image of Aithnea in the convent popped into her mind. None of the novices were happy when she used that tone.

"I felt her." He frowned. "It might not be her, but her influence on Savan. Damn it. She might have been fully aware of him being the Pirate. She probably orchestrated it for something she needed." He rubbed the side of his head. "Until I can wade through all of this stuff in my head, we can't discount it might have been her. One of them was the Pirate. We need to find out why and when."

"I agree. If the last Asarlaí was either the Pirate or set up another to become one for her purposes, we need to find out when and what happened during that Pirate's reign." Jasiel also regained her calm.

"What if I can't find those answers in my head?" Deven asked.

"Then we'll have to find the archives." Aithnea was too flip for that to be as easy as it sounded.

"You have other archives? Beyond the one you had me find after you killed yourselves?" Vas had a small amount of the stuff from the nuns with her. Enough books to fill a good-sized smuggler's bin. And she'd only gone through four so far. There were ten times as many books, scrolls, and tablets hidden on Home.

"Yes, a few. They were created before I left the Commonwealth." Jasiel paced. "And they're still hidden in the Commonwealth. They could have far more information than we need. Aithnea, why didn't I remember these until now?"

Aithnea laughed. "Because you dropped a mind wipe on yourself, and me, for that matter, when you took off twenty years ago. I only recalled them a few minutes ago. Your block either wore off or our current situation triggered its release. This is good news—there were copies of many records I couldn't get out of our nunnery before we had to destroy it."

"Aside from the issue that the Commonwealth is still barricaded," Vas said.

"We can get past that." Jasiel's grin was edging toward dangerous. "Now that I recall them, I think there will be a lot of things we can use. Not only the information collected by the Pirates but resources for our war against the Clongari."

"I remember now why we both decided that hiding and blocking the information was a good idea twenty years ago. But we could have used some of that information in the past year." Aithnea paused. "Nitya has found something. I'll be back."

"Hopefully something good. Things have been a bit intense." Vas didn't mind intensity, but she preferred it to be something she could physically fight.

"And as a merc captain, you're so used to relaxing." Jasiel laughed as she headed for the door.

"No, but it was a far more organized chaos. What do we do now?"

"Keep working on getting us the hell out of here." Jasiel paused at the door. "Do you want me to help deal with those two scoundrels in your brig?"

"Not yet. We need to review the vids with the overlay on them. I want to see what they were up to before we caught them. Depending on what they found out, we might not be letting them go." Vas knew in her gut that Deven didn't attack Terel and Pela—but she needed to see what else the brothers did during their time lurking on the ship.

"Good thinking." Jasiel nodded to both of them and left.

Vas turned to Deven. "Are you okay with delaying looking into what you have in your head for a while? I'd like a second pair of eyes on this."

"I am. I have a feeling there is going to be a lot of

things to process inside here." Deven tapped the side of his head.

Vas hit her comm. "Gosta, can you send the footage from the vids and the scanning file to my room?"

"On their way, captain."

Vas pulled up the files and Deven created a second workstation on her extra computer. She could have assigned this to others, but with the programs they had, it shouldn't be hard to sort out once they found the brothers on the scanned vids. They might have separated at points, but being as they didn't when they were on the verge of being caught indicated that they probably didn't.

Ome was the brains of the three.

The scan overlay of the vids created an oddly colorless image. It was clear enough to see where the vid was coming from, just devoid of any deep colors.

Deven swore. "Found them leaving the landing bay. They're hard to see because they were still able to run their out-of-sync program then."

Vas searched and found the corridor they were in. After ten minutes, she paused the screen. "They're meandering. I don't get it." She wasn't sure what she expected, but these two looked like they were on a tour. Seeing them pass through others was disturbing.

"I know. I would have thought…damn. There I am." Deven swore.

Vas watched as Terel and Pela came running down the corridor with an unconscious Deven on the gurney. "The brothers are following you three."

"They are. And they have that scanner out again."

The two invisible men followed Terel and the others into the med bay. She saw Terel resuscitate Deven three times and each time, the brothers held back. There was a jump in the vid as it switched to the med bay system. Terel took them to the decon room.

Terel and Pela were working hard as they ran and Vas cringed when she saw them trying to revive Deven again. Terel ran scans and Vas could almost hear the swearing even though the vid was silent.

"Did one of them stick his hand in that machine?" Vas shook her head. It happened quickly, but one of the brothers ran to the machine Terel was fighting with and put his hand through it. Everything changed on the monitor and the Deven on the screen relaxed. "Did he save you?"

Deven replayed that section ten times. "No…damn it. Yes. I think he did. Watch the screen here." He tightened the focus on the monitor and reran the clip.

Vas wasn't a medical professional of any sort, but even she knew that Deven's numbers said he was dying.

Until the brother fussed with the machine. The numbers changed and Deven began to breathe normally.

"He saved you?" Vas was trying to find the connection but it wasn't clear.

"Whatever he did, it ran through the cables to the equipment Terel was using to try and save me. We need to talk to those two." Deven started to get to his feet but Vas pushed him back down.

"We do, but I want to know what else they did and why they attacked Terel and Pela." Before they went after the brothers they needed to find out what they'd done in the time they were roaming the ship.

CHAPTER ELEVEN

DEVEN CLEARLY WANTED TO TALK to the broth-ers now. It was rare that he was more impatient about something than she was, but she couldn't blame him for this.

After saving Deven's life, the two brothers remained in the room but didn't do anything but watch.

Then Vas in her decon suit appeared on the vid.

The brothers didn't respond.

Jasiel came in as well. Again, no reactions from the two brothers.

"How long had they been on the ship at this point, with the additional time it took them to get up here in the shuttle?" Vas asked as Deven slowed everything down and ran through the segment again.

"At this point, they had to have been closing in on an hour. They were going to be solid soon—even if they'd still be invisible. They had to have known that, maybe that's why they stayed in the med bay. Limited the chances of running into anyone once they became solid."

Deven let the vid go forward slowly. Vas and Jasiel left. Then the two brothers walked toward Terel and Pela. The way they avoided walking through anything indicated they were now solid.

Deven was relaxed and cracking some joke with Pela when a dark shadow appeared and flung Terel across the room. She slumped to the ground. Pela freed Deven's hand from the restraint but then she too went flying. The cloud vanished and revealed one of the brothers.

Deven freed his other hand and his legs, but one of

the brothers was pushing him down. Even though he couldn't see them, Deven got a few well-placed hits in and the brother staggered back.

Vas knew how good of a fighter Deven was. Yes, he had almost died a few times not long before this fight, but she was still shocked at how quickly he lost. Hell, she was surprised he lost at all.

As soon as the Deven on the screen slid to the floor unconscious, both brothers ran to the machine that had been tracking Deven and pulled something off the back of it.

"Terel is going to kill them. What did they take, and why didn't she notice?"

"They were taking something off that they put on before," Deven swore as he closed in on the image. "That damn scanner. Good thing I didn't have the Pirate of Boagada's memories at that point."

They went through the rest of the vids; invisible or not, the brothers were easy to follow now. But they didn't go near anything important.

"Aside from saving you, attacking Terel and Pela, and whatever they downloaded off that machine—they didn't do much." Vas stepped back after the third time watching them loop through corridors aimlessly.

"They were waiting," Deven said. "I guess they figured out we would be trying to find them and needed to find a place to hide until they were retrieved. I'd say that item on our hull from Ome is tracking us because of them."

"Then where's Ome? He could come through here and take them at any time. They don't have the Pirate's secrets if that's what he was hoping for. But he wouldn't know that."

"No idea. There's a lot of weird things going on." Deven got to his feet. "Shall we go speak to our friends in the brig and ask them?"

"By all means. Might want to bring Terel too."

They came out to find a mostly calm command deck. Gosta and Hrrru were conferring quietly and Vas waved for Gosta to remain in the captain's chair.

"We're going down to speak to our friends in the brig."

Gosta's eyes went wide. "But captain, you told me to have them escorted to the landing bay ten minutes ago." His neck bobs went up and down rapidly. Something that only happened under extreme stress.

"I did not." She hit her comm. "Roha, Marwin, Glazlie—go to the landing bay now."

"We're coming back from there, captain. You told us to take Pol and Relin there for pick up. A shuttle came to get them a few minutes ago. They said thank you and left."

Deven and Vas both ran for stations. "Gosta, pull up anything moving out there. I didn't order that. Roha, you, Marwin, and Glazlie need to report to med bay." At their affirmation, she called down to Terel and told her those three needed to be checked for any tampering.

Terel agreed once she heard what happened.

"Captain, it was you. I know it was you." Gosta continued scanning the area around them, but his hands were shaking. "You told the guards in the brig to escort the brothers to the landing bay ten minutes ago."

Vas found new swear words. "We've been played. Not sure what they were up to, but some massively strong telepath broke those two out."

"And they were focused enough that I didn't feel it at all," Deven said. "Ome or someone else? That's the question. Neither of the brothers are espers, I would have felt it."

"Agreed." Vas hit her comm again. "Nitya, is that scanner we took off the brothers secure?"

"Yes, captain. But I think the people on ship walk aren't." The front screen switched to four people on the surface of the ship. The smallish item that had been planted on the hull was growing at a pace fast enough to make it hard for Mac and the rest to get away from it quickly because of their grav boots.

And it completely blocked access to the hatch.

"Damn it. Mac? Why didn't you call in?"

"This just happened, captain. That shuttle left and this thing started growing. We need help."

Deven was already running for the lift.

"Hang on and link yourselves together. Are you all tethered?" Vas waved for Deven's lift to leave.

"Yes, captain," the tone of Mac's voice indicated he was insulted that she'd ask him that. Never mind that he'd gone out untethered before.

Mac wasn't stupid, he just got easily distracted.

"We're on our way." Vas went to Gosta. "Gosta, this wasn't your fault. I need you to focus on getting our people back."

He paused and gave a nod. "Aye, captain."

"Keep an eye on our people." Then she ran for the lift.

Vas got off on the landing bay level and contacted Terel. "I know they just got there, but do you think those three I sent down are okay? We've got people in danger on the ship walk."

"I only started my scans, but yes, aside from some quickly dissipating brain fog, of which I've pulled enough data to sort out, they're fine."

"Send them to the landing bay." Vas ran and grabbed her space suit from the locker.

Deven already had his on. "Everything is ready to go. We're going to have to grab them and haul them in."

Vas secured her suit and nodded to Marwin, Roha, and Glazlie to get on theirs when they ran in.

Deven took the pilot seat and Vas slid in next to him and then tapped her comm. "We're coming out in the shuttle, Mac, hang on."

"A-cap," his words were chopped up but who knew what that thing on her ship was doing to communications.

Or anything else for that matter.

Vas looked back and noticed that Marwin, Glazlie, and Roha were all armed with heavy blasters. "I'm not sure that shooting that thing is a valid idea." They were going to have to do something about it, but not until they got their people back.

"Better to be safe than sorry, captain." Roha beamed and patted her heavy blaster fondly.

"Good mindset, just don't forget our primary goal is getting our people back. And not blow up our ship."

"And take close-up scans of that damn thing before we get rid of it." Deven left the landing bay, then circled the shuttle back to the ship to fly over their people. "Nitya said it's starting to work its way through the outer ship's hull."

"Damn it. Ome waited until he rescued his brothers, and then set it to attack us. Still makes no sense considering what his ship can do." Vas swore as Deven held the shuttle over their people.

They were clumped together but had run out of room to escape. The growing tech monster was closing in on them and pushing them up against a sensor array that was too large to safely climb over.

"What in the hell did that bastard put on my ship?"

"*Our* ship." Deven flashed her a grin, then frowned. "But now that I can see it better and get clearer scans, I'd say that's a Kilesh ground clearer. They're old but they were used as a passive way of claiming land. Before he modified it anyway. They would never be this aggressive on their own."

"The brothers are Kilesh?" Glazlie asked from her seat near the door.

"They could be." Deven shrugged. "I didn't think so,

but they got a hold of some interesting Kilesh tech at the least."

Vas joined Glazlie at the door and waved to Marwin. "Marwin will be with Glazlie and me. Roha, stay inside the door in case we have visitors. Deven, remain as you are."

Vas clicked the tether of her suit to the bar next to the door, then stepped out. Her grav boots kept her from wandering into space and let her slowly drift down to the ship. Marwin and Glazlie followed behind her. "Just a simple grab and bring back folks." Their tethers were designed to pull them back to the shuttle but they still needed to go slowly.

One of the forms below slumped forward, and the other three caught them.

"Captain, Mac is unconscious," Bathie was usually calm and collected but she sounded neither right now. "Something is wrong with his suit."

Deven cut in. "Did he or any of you touch the growing part of that thing?"

"Yes. There was no way not to when it first expanded. But why would that…oh crap. I don't feel so good." The second form to slump must have been Bathie.

Vas got down to a foot above the surface of the ship and locked her boots to stay there for now. Whatever that techno-mechanical thing was, it was only a few feet from her crew. She reached Mac and pulled him to her.

"Do you want us to disconnect the tethers?" Even Walvento's voice was odd.

"No!" Vas reached down to pull Bathie up as well. The tethers would keep them together, but better to bring them up slowly. Marwin and Glazlie hovered as best they could but it was taking longer than it should to drop down enough to pull up the others.

Vas should be able to bring all four up on her own, but something was pulling them back down. "Damn it, that thing is interfering. Deven? Did your people have something that could adapt like that?"

"Not when I was there—but it's been a long time. Most likely it's something Ome added."

"Captain? Gosta here. I'm picking up odd readings from that thing—almost like it's alive."

"We didn't have anything that could do that," Deven said. "And given the way my people view artificial intelligence; they couldn't have changed that much to have created it."

"Damn. Why didn't we pick up on anything like that before it expanded?" Vas held on to Mac and Bathie, both unconscious. Judging by the names on the suits, Marwin had Gon who was slowly moving. Glazlie grabbed Walvento. He seemed the most aware.

"Captain, this stuff will destroy the ship. Permission to shoot it?" Walvento still held a blaster the size of his leg.

"No shooting. Not yet. It will get into my system." Nitya had the distracted tone of someone doing a dozen things at once, but she was fierce about this.

"What the lady ship said. Shit, is that thing rising to us?" Vas pulled the others up but getting back into the shuttle was going slower than it should. And it looked like the mechanical mess below them was growing taller.

"It is. I'm going to pull up, the shuttle's winch is making odd sounds." As Deven spoke, the tug on her tether jerked, pulling Vas and the rest up a foot more, and then stopped.

"Is that thing supposed to grow spikes?" Glazlie was the closest to the bottom of the mob. "Cause it's got spikes now."

"Let me shoot it." Now Walvento sounded groggy but he was still the only one of the original four who was conscious.

"No!" Vas, Deven, and Nitya all yelled through the comms.

"Those spikes look like the suit that Clongari wore, is it related?" Vas held on to her people tighter as the tether jerked again then started going back up.

"I don't kno—" Deven's words were cut off as the shuttle took a hit. Roha swung out of the shuttle door but grabbed a hold of the door.

"Hang on!" Deven yelled as he fought to control the shuttle.

"Gosta? Who the hell fired at us?" Vas couldn't see much beyond the shuttle, but there hadn't been anyone alive out here before—at least nothing that showed on the scans.

"I don't know," Gosta never liked to admit that, and right now he sounded terrified. "We're not seeing anything. Oh." His pause wasn't good. "Captain? That thing on the hull fired at the shuttle. I'm not sure how though."

"That's *not* something from my people. Get up here!" Deven regained control of the shuttle and Roha grabbed the tether and helped pull everyone in. The winch was working after a fashion but the noise was getting worse and it was slow. Dragging four unconscious people up with a semi-functioning winch felt like forever.

They pulled up Walvento when the shuttle took another hit.

"Close the door and hang on to something!" Deven yelled as he took off.

Roha and Vas got the tethers disconnected and the door secured. They managed to get everyone buckled into seats before the shuttle rattled again.

"Hold on, that thing is getting ready to fire again!" Deven wove through the destroyed fake Nhali ship and a huge section of it exploded behind them.

CHAPTER TWELVE

—◆—

"THAT DIDN'T COME FROM OUR ship, or rather, the thing on the hull." Vas ran to the seat next to Deven and pulled up the shuttle's weapon system. She didn't see where the shot came from but it wasn't from behind them.

"No, it didn't," Deven swore and did a few more swerves around the wreckage. Dangerous, but if anyone could navigate that, she knew he could. "I'm not picking up on anything ahead of us."

Vas also swore as a familiar silver ship suddenly appeared ahead of them. "He's come back to finish us." Why he had drawn this out was a damn good question. And one she'd probably never know the answer to.

"Captain Vas, you're welcome for me saving you. There was an attack pod of some kind hiding in that wreckage. It was taking aim." There might be a communication problem with her ship, but Ome's voice came through clear and annoying.

"You put that thing on *my* ship. Snuck your brothers onto *my* ship. And now you're *saving* us?" Vas was too annoyed to be cautious. This guy could destroy them with a snap of his fingers.

"I did attach a simplistic tracking device to your ship. I needed to do so to make sure I could find my brothers once they completed their tasks. Which they failed to do, but thank you for not killing them. Something from that wreckage around you mutated my tracker and has been using the power stored in it to attack your ship. I'm not sure who the pod was, I had to destroy them too quickly for any analysis."

Vas shared a look with Deven. She almost admired a villain who was so honest about his actions.

Deven looked like he wanted to snap Ome's neck.

"Then you didn't mean to disable my ship with that tracker or have your brothers attack my second-in-command?"

His laugh was rich and only slightly unhinged. "Caught me. The power drain was to keep you down for a while. And they were simply retrieving information for my ongoing projects, nothing more. I had nothing to do with the disguised Clongari who attacked you, although you defended yourselves admirably."

"Captain? I can't see the shuttle on any screen. Something's emitting from that wreckage and it's getting stronger." Gosta's voice was clear now.

"This is not good. The Clongari did not go peacefully, and they planned on their vessel being destroyed," Ome sounded angry now. "They rigged their ship to release a toxin when it broke apart. That is what changed my tracker, and what is killing your ship. You need to go back to your ship and leave this sector. Immediately."

"We would love to, but your toy, mutated or not, is making that impossible."

"I agree. Buckle in and tell your ship to do the same. Even my vessel can't hold off the effects of that gas for long." For the first time since she'd met him, Ome sounded almost scared.

Vas called to Gosta. "There's a gas being released by the dead Clongari ship. Ome might be able to help us but we're bugging out. Now. Have everyone secure themselves." Ome wasn't patient even when manically happy—he sure as hell wasn't going to be so at this point.

Gosta had enough time to say, "Yes, captain," before

the shuttle and the *Destroyer's Curse* were grabbed by the most powerful tractor beam Vas ever felt. It was like the one the Net and Club Hive ships times ten.

"Hang on! Whatever he's pulling us with is shaking this shuttle apart!" Deven yelled as he tried to maintain control. The sounds coming from the hull weren't good, but they were moving away from the wreckage at a pace faster than the shuttle could have gone on its own.

"Captain! I don't know if I can keep the ship together!" Nitya's panic wasn't a good sign.

"Tell your ship to release the outer hull panels that have that monstrosity on them immediately!" Ome was shouting, something else she'd not heard much of.

"Nitya, can you do it?"

"It won't be pretty. We'll need to do some serious repairs, but yes." Panels under the mutated tech monster flew off the *Destroyer's Curse* and slipped out of the tractor beam. "I hope this works."

Deven's swearing grew admiring and Vas shared the sentiment. She had no idea how this beam was doing what it was doing, let alone being able to separate the hull pieces.

The speed increased, far beyond what the *Destroyer's Curse* could have reached on its own.

"Captain, we can't keep like this for much longer, not with the damage to our hull," Nitya yelled through the comm.

"I'm trying to help, but yeah, what she said," Aithnea responded.

"And…go!" Ome shouted through their comms as the shuttle and the *Destroyer's Curse* were suddenly flung out of the tractor beam. "You can thank me later."

The Ralith ship vanished a moment before the wreckage far behind them exploded.

"Is everyone okay?" Vas looked around the shuttle as she called to the ship. Luckily everyone remained secure

in their seats. The unconscious four were still unconscious, but they didn't appear to be worse for the trip.

"We have calls coming in of injuries on some levels,
but no one is reporting anything serious," Terel said. "Are
we going to slow down?"

"We are slowing, captain," Gosta added. "Slowly, but
we are decreasing speed. We'll be extremely close to the
only inhabited planet in the system, but we won't crash.
Hopefully."

"I can't land this shuttle until we both reduce enough
speed." Deven turned to Vas. "But miraculously, we're still
intact. I think we'll have to scrap this shuttle afterward,
but it lasted better than I would have guessed."

"Good." Vas got up and went to check on the unconscious crew. "Any idea about what happened to them?"
She looked inside Mac's helmet but he appeared to be
asleep. "You said something about them touching that
mutated tracker?"

"That was when I thought it was something related to
my people," Deven said. "No idea now. But you might as
well take their helmets off. If it was something that could
go through their suits to get them, then we're all already
contaminated."

"I heard that," Terel's voice popped in. "Sorry, I was
going to report on current injuries, we have a few more
serious ones coming in. But what contamination?"

Vas explained what happened to the four people on ship
walk as she removed Mac's helmet. Deven was right—if
it was something contagious that went through the suits,
then everyone in the shuttle was already exposed.

"Damn it. Can you scan one of them and send me
the data? We can't risk bringing anything contagious on
board."

"Full-level scan, I assume?" Vas fussed with the medical
scanner that she kept on all of her shuttles. It wouldn't be

the same as if Terel and her equipment could see them, but it was something. The ship was slowing, but still approaching the far end of this sector quickly.

"Yes. Hold on." Terel's voice went distant as she yelled commands to her medical crew.

Vas scanned Mac. It showed nothing. She tried again. Finally, on the fourth try, the scanner began flashing. "Terel? We've got green, orange, and blue contagions here. I know the basic ones, but what in the hell is this?" Different types of contagions initially showed a color category before the scanner could completely isolate the issue.

Green was bio, orange meant artificial, and blue referred to technological. All of them appearing on the same scan was disturbing.

"What? Are you sure? That's impossible." Terel's focus was now all on Vas.

"I got nothing the first three times, so the med scanner could be broken. But I have four unconscious crew, and five more of us who might have been exposed to whatever in the hell knocked the others out. I'm transmitting the scan now."

The others removed Bathie, Gon, and Walvento's helmets as well. Like Mac, they all looked like they were sleeping. Aside from the fact no one could wake them.

Vas scanned them all and sent the results to Terel as she continued to curse.

"Did the others not work at first also?" Terel's furious typing was almost as loud as her voice.

"No. Scanned on the first run. As you see, the same colors are showing on everyone."

"There's something familiar about this. Damn it, I can't pinpoint what it is. Give Mac a shot of 2 percent kinlo, but watch his reactions closely."

Vas looked to Deven but he shrugged. Kinlo wasn't a strong sedative, but it worked well. But Mac was already as sedated as he could get. Roha handed her the pre-loaded hypo.

Vas injected the hypo into the side of Mac's neck. "Okay, but I think it'll just—" she jumped back as Mac yelled and tried to scramble to his feet when the hypo did its job. Or rather, the opposite of what it should do.

"I'll kill you all! Who did this? Why can't I move?" Mac twisted and turned but couldn't seem to figure out he was belted into the shuttle chair.

Then again, the way he frantically looked around, and yet seemingly didn't recognize anyone, indicated he had no idea where he was or what happened.

"Terel. He's awake and freaked out. Please tell me this was what you expected?" Vas stepped back as Marwin came forward to distract Mac.

"Damn it. Yes. Not what I'd hoped, but what I feared. It's a nano bug."

Mac suddenly appeared aware. "I have nanites? No offense, Deven, I'm sure yours are fine. Why am I tied up? It's the nanites, isn't it? They did something bad." He was no longer angry, but confusion was still clear on his face.

"Not sure if you heard that, but Mac is back. Nano bug isn't the same as nanites, right?" Vas watched Mac as she spoke.

"That's a good sign. And no, it's not the same. Nor is it communicable. Those four got it from that damn mutated thing on the hull. Give the same dosage to the other three. Once you land that shuttle, we'll come get them."

"Can I get up?" Mac was calmer but watched Vas before trying to release the safety belt.

"I'd rather none of them moved much until we can do a full diagnostic. I don't think there should be any actual nanites involved. But better to remain still."

Vas was pretty sure Terel was trying to freak out Mac

enough for him to stay out of trouble—but judging by Mac's wide blue eyes as he froze in the reclined seat—he believed her.

Bathie recovered the quickest, with Gon being close behind. Walvento wouldn't listen, nor calm down, so Roha stunned him.

"He's not going to be happy." Vas agreed with her action. Walvento could cause a lot of problems before his system brought him back to knowing who they were. A damaged shuttle wasn't the place for it.

"Captain? We're under full control now. Nitya and Aithnea are both deep in the ship's systems but they strongly suggest we get the shuttle on board and get the hell out of here." Gosta coughed. "Aithnea's words."

Deven laughed. "We're coming in. Do you have an idea on where to go or are we sector jumping again?" He navigated the shuttle to approach the landing bay.

"Yes." Gosta's abrupt response was surprising.

"I'll come up on deck the moment we've landed." Vas wasn't going to hound him here.

"Aye, captain. Gosta out."

The landing bay of the *Destroyer's Curse* began as state of the art when it was a Hive ship and was even more impressive after their retrofit. But that wasn't noticeable from their horrible landing.

Deven fought to keep the shuttle from skidding into any others in the bay, but it was a close thing. Vas was glad all the Pilthian ships were in the larger secondary landing bay. She'd hate to have to explain to Shien that they'd destroyed their only transportation.

Terel, Divee, and two medics were waiting behind the bay shield with medical beds at the ready. They ran forward once the shield dropped after the landing bay doors slid shut.

Terel ran a scanner over Vas, Deven, Roha, Marwin, and Glazlie, but shrugged at the negative results. "You're all fine. Please go get us the hell out of this place." She grinned. "If you don't mind." Then she and her crew loaded the patients onto the medical beds and raced out of the landing bay.

The shuttle behind them groaned and the front landing struts snapped.

"On that note, might want to put a shield around this thing until we can salvage it. I'd rather not have it take out more of our shuttles." Vas jogged to the lift with Deven alongside her as the other three worked on a shield. This way if the damn thing exploded, nothing but it would be destroyed.

CHAPTER THIRTEEN

—◆—

"GOSTA, WE'RE ALL IN AND ready—what did you mean by your answer? You have a location or we're hopping some more?" Vas slid into the empty captain's chair. Gosta was now working on three stations and Hrrru had three as well.

"My 'yes,' was because we're still sorting things. I don't believe that we want to get too close to the Commonwealth until we're sure they've dropped the barricade or that we can get through. There are reports on the dark web that they have armed drones on the perimeter. Many Commonwealth planets were deemed too remote and were excluded when the barricade went up. Many outside Commonwealth worlds have reported automated attacks on any of their ships that went too close to the border. Even though they are registered as Commonwealth."

Vas leaned back. "And we're a converted Hive ship. Even showing the Wavian registry won't be enough since we don't have an official Commonwealth registry. Damn it. What's the plan?" Random jumping through gates wasn't something she was fond of. After having to do it for a few months, she hoped Gosta had a miracle solution that didn't involve unsystematic jumping.

"I've found a way in." Gosta's smile as he turned was scary. It being echoed by Hrrru and Xsit made it even more so.

"And what is it?"

Deven pulled up some of their screens and nodded at what he saw. Whatever the three planned, he agreed.

"Someone?" Vas didn't mind they wanted to be dramatic, but she wanted answers.

"First, I think we should get out of this sector immediately. A random jump or three would be a good idea." Deven continued to pull up information.

"Fine, keep your secrets for now. Khirson, do you feel comfortable enough to stay in the pilot seat?" If she had to, she could take over, or Deven could. But it would be better if they both remained free. And bringing in the third shift, unless it was an emergency, wasn't the best idea.

"I'm ready to jump." Khirson flashed a grin.

"Then let's do it, three jumps. Then I need someone to explain to me what this great plan is." Vas was glad to get out of this sector, after everything that happened. She hit her comm. "Nitya and Jasiel. Did you two get that Clongari body in the ship and secured? If not, sorry, it's too late." As much as she agreed with the reason for looking into the Clongari, she wouldn't be crushed if they hadn't brought the body on board.

"Aye, captain," Jasiel responded. "It's secure and is in a fully detachable room. It's an old trash lockup but that was the best we could fortify quickly."

Vas laughed. "Better than nothing. Keep cameras and monitors on that thing. The first sign of anything, and I do mean *anything*, questionable, you will eject that trash bin." It was good thinking actually. Trash bins were often fully detachable on larger ships in case a contagion got in.

There were no signs of other ships as they went to the gate. Most likely Ome was a million light years away at this point.

The first two jumps were fine, and it didn't appear that they'd been picked up by any traffic in the area.

"We have it!" Gosta yelled and Hrrru and Xsit followed suit. "If we can go to the coordinates I'm sending, we will be close enough to work on dealing with the barricade, far enough to be safe from drones, and hidden enough to make the needed repairs to the ship."

"And I should be close enough to reach our people." Xsit bounced in excitement.

"You heard the man, Khirson, take us to that system. Where are we going by the way? Coordinates were one thing, Vas preferred names.

"To the Solar system." Hrrru was now also bouncing. Something he never did and it was honestly a bit disturbing. "Well, that's the only planet in it and it's called Solar. Many of my people relocated there before the Asarlaí war. I'm looking forward to visiting."

"It's a small planet that the Commonwealth considered taking over a few months before the Asarlaí clones attacked, but it doesn't appear they went through with it." Gosta didn't bounce, but he was clearly pleased with himself.

"Any idea as to why the Welischians started relocating there?" The Welischians had decimated their oppressors on their home world not that long ago but mostly seemed to stay on their own world. She hadn't heard of any mass exodus.

"I've heard of Solar." Deven was still pulling up information, but he turned to her. "They have a high ratio of telepaths—which might have been why the Commonwealth was looking at it."

"Doesn't the Commonwealth distrust you guys in general? They seem to lock up enough of you."

"They do. But before the war, there was talk of building a telepath corps. And having the Welischians move there would fit as well. Being as they're immune to us." Deven flashed Hrrru a grin.

"That could be true. There were many opportunities for my people to relocate," Hrrru said.

"If everyone believes that's our best place, let's go. Given our situation and that we still have people looking for us,

I'm limiting visitation on the planet. Hrrru and Deven will need to go down, but I'm hoping not to have to stay here for long." Hrrru appeared ready to object until she said he could go down with Deven. He never showed it, but she knew he missed being around his people. There were a handful of Welischians on her planet of Home but they were all much older. Mathias and he talked sometimes, but Hrrru was much younger.

Khirson gated them to an extremely unimpressive system. But Vas was grateful they were out of Lethian Assembly and Nhali space for now. What they needed to do down the line wasn't forgotten, but they had to get more people with them first.

The lone planet of Solar was as far away from the gate as possible. Rather, the gate had been built far away from the planet.

An unhappy thought crept into her mind. Most gates were near worlds—or deceased worlds. There was an asteroid belt but it was even further from the gate than Solar was.

"Damn it. Gosta, scan Solar."

"Anything particular, captain?"

"Yes, the Asarlaí created crap that was inside Mayhira and that Nhali mining planet." If the planet Solar had been modified and moved here, it could explain why it was so far from the gate. It would also explain the Commonwealth wanting to annex it.

Empress Wilthuny might not have been the only one aware of these modified worlds and the power they could create. The Asarlaí had abandoned their plans for them, but others didn't.

Deven started swearing as he dove into the search as well. Hrrru looked crushed.

"Damn it, yes. I'm picking up on trace amounts." Deven turned to Gosta. "I'm thinking it's throughout the planet's core? But nowhere near the amount on Mayhira or the Nhali mining planet."

Deven was smart, but he also knew that Gosta was better at this—and faster.

"I'm only seeing trace results as well." Gosta frowned at the screen he was working on. "It's as if it was begun, but not finished. I do see evidence this planet did not begin in this system, however."

"Is it in danger of blowing up? Or being made to open a portal to another dimension?" Vas got to the point. Wilthuny had done a lot of serious manipulation to get Mayhira to transform and eventually explode. Without knowing everything the Nhali had done to that mining planet, there was no way to know how much they triggered and how much had been the planet. But Vas doubted the Nhali who died there would have stayed if they felt the explosion was imminent. "The Nhali planet didn't change the way Mayhira did, did it?" Mayhira became a new sun after it exploded.

"No, captain. It blew to bits. There was nothing left to scan." Hrrru was less cheerful now.

"Damn it, more things we need Marli to answer." Vas got to her feet and moved closer to the screens. "I want that planet being scanned and tracked the entire time we're here. And how safe are we going to be from the locals? They might not be fans of the Commonwealth, but they might not like us either." And there were no places to hide the ship for repairs that she could see. The belt here was small and they were tricky to hide in during repairs to the hull especially.

Deven nodded. "There's a pocket of space behind the belt. Not natural and it does allude to Asarlaí interference. But I think it will hide us."

"Can we still go to the surface?" Hrrru asked.

Vas watched the screens, then the printout of the condition of the hull. She knew Nitya had been able to protect the damaged areas, but it had to have put a strain on her. "Yes. But take Roha with you. Deven and Hrrru, check out your respective people. Roha will keep an eye on both of you. We won't be far, but I want the hull repairs finished immediately."

"Will do." Hrrru almost ran for the elevator, then caught himself and slowed down. Deven caught up to him and they left together.

Vas tapped her comm. "Roha, I want you to go down to the planet with Deven and Hrrru. Keep them safe."

"Aye, captain!" Roha laughed. "By the way, Mac is complaining about being trapped in the med bay while exciting things are happening."

"Tell him to wait, or Terel will run more tests. A lot more." Vas was glad to hear that Mac was bored though.

Roha laughed again and signed off.

Once the shuttle left, Khirson turned to Vas.

"Get us to that pocket, Khirson." Vas hit her comm. "Nitya, who do you need to help on this?"

"I'd like Bathie and Mac, once they've recovered. Divee and Cassil as well. Most of it will be myself, Aithnea, and Jasiel."

Vas nodded. She meant they were going to do some nun mojo. And Vas wasn't crushed at being excluded. She leaned back in her seat as Khirson moved them into position.

Space looked like space everywhere, but knowing how close they were to the Commonwealth, and the rest of her people, gave her hope. They were facing the Nhali, the Lethian Assembly, and who knew how many other groups they needed to get on their side. Then they had to stop the Clongari from destroying everything.

When she and her crew came back to the Commonwealth after the Asarlaí clones had kicked the Commonwealth's ass—she initially faced them with only her ships from Home. They gathered others, but it was easier to get survivors on their side. Convincing the Nhali and the Lethian Assembly of the seriousness of the Clongari threat was going to be a hell of a lot harder. Smaller systems might join, but only once the two large ones did.

The pocket of space they hid in was clearly not natural. But Gosta was happily muttering to himself as Khirson brought them into it.

"Do what you need to do, Nitya. Shout out if you need more help. Once Terel clears Mac and Bathie I'll send them where you want them."

"Thank you, captain. Oh, based on that chemical the Clongari released, I've increased the shielding around the body we retrieved. I suggest we don't try to examine it until it is even more secured and off this ship."

"Good idea. You haven't been to Home before but there are some extremely secure research areas there." It would be interesting to show both Nitya and Jasiel Home. Vas had no idea what Jasiel's plans were once they finished this fight, but if the *Destroyer's Curse* and Nitya survived, they'd have to remain together.

Before two years ago, Vas rarely went to Home, maybe once a year. But after being stuck out here for the past few months, she found she missed the place.

"Xsit, what did you say about finding a way to reach our people? Is that beacon from the *Warrior Wench* still sending?"

"I believe I can punch through the communications block. The *Warrior Wench* is still transmitting so I'm locking on to it. But I might only have a few chances once I try. The barricade system is extremely aggressive and not friendly."

"And it's not Commonwealth," Gosta said. "I believe the original blockade was theirs, but then the Lethian Assembly, or some other enterprising sort, created their own. The Commonwealth can't get out. And judging by the lack of ships near their side, I don't know that they're even aware."

"Damn it. That's something we need to deal with after we've fixed this ship. The last thing we need is to draw fire without being ready to fight back." Vas turned to Xsit. "Keep monitoring everything you can reach, but we'll wait until we know we can fight or flee before reaching out."

"Aye, captain." Xsit scowled at her monitor.

"Vas? Can you come down here?" Deven's comm came through.

"To the planet?"

"Yup. We might have some help, but they want to meet and talk to you." Deven sounded like he was fighting a grin.

"Okay?" Vas nodded to Gosta to take the command deck, then went down to the landing bay. "Anything I should be prepared for?" Back when they were mercs, she sometimes did have people who honestly wanted to meet the great Vaslisha Tor Dain based on her reputation.

She seriously doubted anyone in this odd backwater world even knew who she was. She knew that she'd never heard of this place until today.

"No, be ready to talk. Possibly a lot. By the way, there is a much higher than average number of both espers and Welischians than I expected. At least from what I've seen so far. And the people of Solar staged a coup not too long ago. The Commonwealth did attempt to take them over supposedly, but the people of Solar kicked them out."

Vas picked up her speed down to the landing bay. This world could prove helpful.

Taking the shuttle away from *Destroyer's Curse* was easy, but seeing the damage to the hull was painful. Seeing that new hull pieces were being applied and the ship was beginning to look better helped. Sort of.

"Shuttle on approach, welcome to the free world of

Solar. Please follow the directions to your landing coordinates." The voice was polite. Not hostile nor overly friendly. Nice change.

Vas secured the shuttle, then hit her comm as she walked across the landing field. "I'm here. How do I find you?"

"We'll find you. Look to your left."

Vas spotted Deven, Hrrru, Roha, and five others walking her way. Roha had her massive blaster at her side, but not in her arms, a sure indication she felt safe around those five.

"Captain Vaslisha Tor Dain, I'd like to introduce you to Yesenia, Lucan, Abiel, Qaan, and Tobias." Qaan was a tall Welischian half breed, the rest appeared to be of human stock.

The woman in the front, Yesenia, almost looked like Vas' younger sister. If she'd had one. She had a mass of flaming red hair that was barely under control and looked a lot like Vas'.

"I can't believe I'm meeting you." If Yesenia shook Vas' hand any harder, she was going to break it. But her grin was wide. She was in full idol-worshipping mode.

Vas smiled back but glanced to Deven for reassurance. He nodded and shrugged.

"Nice to meet you too. I'm surprised that you've heard of me."

Abiel, an older man with a long gray ponytail laughed. "After the battles to free the Commonwealth? Everyone knows you and your fleet. I'm not a fan of having been a Commonwealth world, but I and everyone on this planet are grateful for what you and your people did to save all of us."

Vas didn't recall specifically coming anywhere near this world, but things moved fast. She put on her best smile and nodded her head. "I'm glad we were able to help." She looked around the busy shuttle port. "Maybe there is a more private place we could speak?" She hoped Yesenia and Abiel were exaggerating, but she didn't want to take a chance of being spotted by too many people.

"Of course, come this way." Abiel turned and headed to the street outside of the landing area.

Hrrru paused. "Captain, might Qaan take me around to one of the Welischian villages? I won't be long."

"By all means, thank you for reaching out to them for our ship."Vas knew she'd said the right thing when Hrrru stood a little taller. Going to talk to them had been his idea, but she still wasn't giving up on her hope of one day getting more of his people to join her crew.

Hrrru and the Welischian woman turned and left.

Abiel led them down a narrow road, then into a neat little house. Even though they didn't appear worried about the Commonwealth trying to reclaim their world, Vas expected more hiding from them.

Abiel put his hand on an elaborate palm lock embedded next to the door, then motioned for everyone to enter.

CHAPTER FOURTEEN

VAS HAD NO IDEA WHAT she'd been expecting, but the elaborate high-tech interior of the house wasn't it. Even after she saw the tech of the palm lock. The building might appear to be a cute little country home, but it was a center for some sort of operations.

And looking down the hall that stretched out from the front room, it was a hell of a lot larger than it looked on the outside.

"Let's go to my office." Abiel led them down the hall. Yesenia and Lucan remained with them, but Tobias nodded and went in a different direction. The place was a warren that appeared to go underground.

"Your freedom has come at a cost." Deven nodded as they entered into a large room.

Abiel shut the door behind them and motioned to a group of luxurious chairs. "Getting it hasn't been easy and as you see we're still fighting for it. We do realize this latest attack on the Commonwealth in terms of that barricade has been in our favor."

Roha remained standing as the others sat.

"Please, you don't need to worry about being attacked." If Abiel was concerned about Roha's massive blaster or the fact that both Vas and Deven were also armed, he didn't show it.

Roha smiled. "Thank you, but I'm good here."

The tall slender man named Lucan appeared wary. Not hostile, but Vas noticed he glanced at their weapons a few times. He also watched Yesenia. Mostly when she wasn't looking his way.

Which, as she continued to watch Vas closely, was often.

"Have you ever met a dozer pilot named Janx?" Vas finally asked Yesenia as Abiel brought out a cart with bottles and packaged snacks.

Yesenia shook her head. "Not that I know of, why?"

"You remind me of her." Vas smiled. It wasn't in looks, Mac's cousin Janx was taller and blonde. But the idol worship was close enough. Vas was a merc captain, and knowing that people she'd never run into in person thought that highly of her was disturbing.

Judging by the smirk playing around Deven's mouth, he found it amusing.

"Now, as much as we appreciate a visit from the great Captain Tor Dain and her second-in-command, I have a feeling there is more to it than a visit of the local Welischians and telepaths."

Lucan nodded. "Not to mention that a Commonwealth merc and crew are on the wrong side of the barrier in a converted Hive ship." He wasn't smiling.

Abiel didn't look happy at the comments, but he didn't stop him.

Yesenia appeared annoyed. "You can't distrust everyone, Lucan. They were probably on a secret mission and got trapped out here. My sources say that both the *Warrior Wench* and the *Victorious Dead* were still in the Commonwealth when the barricade went up."

Vas lifted an eyebrow. "You're tracking my ships?"

"Only in my downtime." Yesenia shrugged. "I mostly track the Commonwealth enforcers—or did before the barricade went up. Solar is a free planet, but I don't think they agree, so we keep watch."

Roha leaned forward. "I do recall hearing about this world now. Your former government was selling it to the Commonwealth?"

"Aye," Abiel sighed. "We were in the process of trying to overthrow the prior government, then the Commonwealth came in and messed up those plans. So, we started again." He waved to the cart. "Please, take some refreshments. I have a feeling there are deeper reasons for this visit." He gave an odd hand gesture to Deven.

Deven returned it and gave the same to Yesenia.

Her light brown eyes went wide and she returned it awkwardly. "Sorry, still not completely sure about this telepath thing."

"Are telepaths treated badly here? I understood this was an open planet?" Vas watched the three closely. She knew that Deven would tell her what the secret signals meant, but better to find out now if the telepaths were in danger.

Solar was primarily chosen for its closeness to the Commonwealth, but between the telepaths and the weird Asarlaí stuff in its core, even if minimal, she figured there was going to be more than a simple repair stop involved.

"Our prior government mostly ignored us. The Commonwealth had other more nefarious plans." Yesena shook her head. "As I said, I'm new to this—long story—but there's still a feeling of mistrust for espers."

Deven nodded slowly. "It was probably tied into what the Asarlaí did to this world."

Vas took a sip out of a bottle and almost spit out the drink at his words. She figured they would inform someone of leadership stature here about their planet's issue, just not this soon.

This crew still seemed too secretive to be the primary government for the planet.

"The Asarlaí?" Abiel ignored Vas' choke. "If you mean the copies that attacked the Commonwealth, they never came here."

Deven shook his head. "The real Asarlaí. A long time ago." He gave a brief version of what happened to Solar.

Even Lucan was silent when he finished.

"Are we in danger?" Yesenia cut to the important part. Her idol worship was gone now.

"We're looking into that. As Deven said, it appears that the Asarlaí relocated Solar to this system, began their process, and then stopped. Have your people ever found evidence of Asarlaí in this world?"

Lucan paled. "We are still talking almost a thousand years ago, right? Those people were creepy."

"Yes, a thousand years ago. Don't worry, we'll share whatever we find out about the core of your planet. But you should be safe." Deven hadn't mentioned Mayhira.

"And maybe tell us why your ship is now hiding?" Abiel asked. "We picked the *Destroyer's Curse* up when you got close, but now it's gone." He waved a hand. "Don't worry, we know your ship is hiding in the pocket space. We've had to use it before too."

"We're working on repairs and thought it best to avoid being picked up by the Commonwealth until we're recovered and can reach the rest of our crews." Vas continued to watch all three. "Deven wanted to talk to some local telepaths, and Hrrru wanted to speak to his people. Then you fine folks wanted to meet me." Vas held out her arms and did a small bow.

"You can't break through. Some of our people had been on a recon trip and got trapped behind the barricade. No idea why they haven't dropped it yet." Lucan was less hostile, or at least appeared that way.

"We have some pretty good hackers—I think they'll make it." Vas wasn't going to tell them everything, regardless of Deven telling them about their planet.

"And we don't think the Commonwealth is in control of the barricade at this point," Deven added. "We'll know more when we can reach our other ships."

Abiel nodded and watched Deven closely. "We should—" His words were cut off by a high-pitched alarm. "Damn it." He hit a button on the side of his desk.

"Stations people, we have an intrusion in quadrant G-23. They're trying again."

Roha raised her blaster but looked at Vas.

Vas and Deven both stood with the three Solar locals. Abiel, Yesenia, and Lucan ran for the door.

Vas followed them as the alarms continued but greatly reduced in volume. "Who's trying to break in and where? And where is quadrant G-23?" Hopefully, wherever it was, it wasn't near here—or the landing field.

Lucan ran alongside them as Abiel shouted orders with Yesenia on his heels. "There are still Commonwealth guards on Solar. Many withdrew right before the barricade went up, they didn't like the Lethian Assembly any more than anyone does. But a few either remained behind on purpose or missed their ships." Lucan gave an actual smile. "Sorry for not trusting you, but we're still not in a stable position."

Vas grinned back. "Not a worry. And I hope you stay free of the Commonwealth." Even though Home was in the Commonwealth, as a registered merc, and former hero of the Commonwealth, Vas knew she and her people had far more freedom than some planets.

And if the Commonwealth wanted Solar for what was inside the planet, as well as the high percentage of telepaths, it was probably much better if they stayed clear of it.

Abiel shouted again and Lucan and Yesenia, along with six heavily armed people, ran out a side door.

Satisfied that his people were doing what they were supposed to, Abiel stopped and turned to Vas, Deven, and Roha. "To expand on Lucan's comments, G-23 is a section of town not far from here that some of the Commonwealth guards have been trying to get into. We've pushed the known Commonwealth elements into distant villages where they can't interfere much, but one group keeps trying to get into G-23."

"Why?" Vas luckily hadn't had much interaction with the Commonwealth military guards, but she knew they wouldn't have been accidentally left behind. No matter what Lucan or Abiel thought.

"That's an extremely good question. We have defenses around the high-risk areas, but didn't originally have one there until they started trying to get inside. It's mostly storage buildings for seeds and farm equipment." Abiel added two blasters to his person and held up a third one to them. "Although you do look well-armed."

Deven waved him off. "I think we're fine. You don't mind us joining you?"

"Not at all. Come on."

Vas watched Deven as they ran alongside Abiel and another group of heavily armed people. Not that he didn't like a good fight, especially for a decent cause, he did. But there was something in his face that indicated he had other reasons.

"You'll share later, I presume?" Vas kept her voice low.

"Of course, my captain." Deven flashed a smile that faded quickly. "There's more on Solar than we are seeing—probably more than Abiel or his people know. But to find out, we need to keep them safe."

They loaded into two heavy transports and drove away from the landing field. That at least was good. Vas would rather not lose another shuttle. She hit her comm to the ship. "Gosta, we might be out of contact for a while. There's a situation down here."

"Understood, do you need reinforcements?" His distracted tone was in play.

"Not yet, any ETA for the ship repairs?"

"Maybe a day." He coughed. "Three at the most. Gosta out."

Vas frowned at her comm. Gosta was developing a bad habit of cutting off when he didn't want to discuss something. A situation to address later when she wasn't bouncing around in a transport off to possibly fight Commonwealth guards.

She came here to get back into the Commonwealth, not pick a fight with it.

"What's in the sector that they are after?" Roha asked from her seat in the back. As always, none of the bouncing bothered her at all.

"We're not sure, to be honest. Like I said, only farm buildings." Abiel shook his head from his seat next to the driver. "They started focusing on it about two weeks ago. For the most part, the Commonwealth people left behind have stayed to themselves and tried not to be noticed."

"Did any Lethian Assembly ships stay after the rest left?" Deven watched the view outside the transport. But his hand remained on his blaster.

"Not that we tracked." Abiel turned back to them now. "You think they might be behind this?"

"Might be. We're not sure what the Lethian Assembly is doing. But it looks like they modified the Commonwealth's barricade to use it against them."

"Which means we need to get that thing down. I know the barricade being in place has helped you, but if the Lethians are trying to cut off the Commonwealth, they're after something big. There's a lot at risk right now." Vas wasn't going to tell him everything at this point, but Abiel needed to know there was far more at stake than Solar.

"Maybe Flarik could help this world gain legal freedom," Deven said.

"That sounds like a Wavian name," the driver said as he avoided a massive pothole. The trees and plant life started to hug the road now.

"Yup, and she's a top lawyer as well. If she can help you legally get free of the Commonwealth, she'll do it." Hopefully. Flarik was usually helpful in these cases—but it was hard to say with her pregnancy.

Their transport, and the one behind it, came to a halt near an electric wall. An extremely high electric wall.

Vas let out a whistle at the size. "Do you have these all over?"

"Just around the Commonwealth guards. Damn it, there's a hole there." Abiel left the transport and then dropped to the ground as blaster fire came from a gap in the fence.

CHAPTER FIFTEEN

———

THE DRIVER JUMPED OUT, KEEPING low as he went around to Abiel's side. Deven, Vas, and Roha followed, ignoring the calls from the other people in the transport.

Abiel slid under the transport but waved to them. "I'm fine. Get them."

He must have said the same to his people in the second transport as they all came out. Half ran toward a clump of squat windowless buildings on this side of the wall, and the rest ran through the gap.

"Roha, stay here." Vas looked where Abiel was crawling out from under the transport. "Hope you don't mind, but we don't like leaving our vehicles unguarded."

He blushed. "Excellent point. I'll wait here as well, then." He pulled out a snub blaster and nodded to Roha.

Vas and Deven took off through the gap.

Normally Vas might try to stay out of this, but although it was the proximity to the barricade that brought them here, there was something more going on. Something she wasn't going to be happy about if it followed recent patterns.

Part of this was the weird feeling she got around Yesenia. She hadn't noticed it until Yesenia and Lucan took off. But there had been a weird pressure in Vas' head that lifted then.

She wanted to ask Deven if he felt it too, but not while running through the jungle looking for Commonwealth guards.

Two blaster shots aimed at the transports came from

ahead and to the right. Deven darted over and Vas followed. The area was rough and uncivilized. The guards might have been breaking in to get supplies.

Doubtful.

Deven gave her a nod and he broke right again and she took left.

The hooded shooter was focusing on Abiel's people and didn't look up until Deven tackled him.

The two tussled as Vas stayed back inside the tree line to make sure there was no one else around.

Deven knocked the person's blaster out of their hand and kicked it away. Then he pinned them down and pulled back the hood.

"A Hivian? You're not part of the Commonwealth."

The Hivian gave a loud 'oof' sound as Deven sat on his chest. Hivians were rarely seen in the Commonwealth, and it wasn't likely that this one was a Commonwealth guard.

"I'm a Commonwealth guard. Have lived there for many years."

Vas took a step out from the trees. "Oh? Where?" She kept her blaster aimed at his head although she knew Deven would kill him first if the Hivian tried anything. "And don't call for help. My people have this area surrounded."

"From Fiolth. Just left there for this assignment."

"Really? The bastard fake Asarlaí clones pretty much decimated that *moon* almost a year ago. And it was mostly filled with scientists and researchers. Want to try again?" Vas continued to scan the area around them without looking away from their prisoner.

His tattered uniform under the dark hooded jacket was of the Commonwealth guards, but it was an old style. As in before the Asarlaí attack old. Years before. Hopefully, they could get some real answers out of this one, or grab another one.

"No." He shut his mouth as Deven pulled his blaster and held it an inch from his face as he continued to sit on him.

Hivians weren't large people and Deven had a lot of muscle on him. It was amazing the Hivian was still breathing.

"Don't say anything." Three more Hivians, also in outdated Commonwealth guard outfits, stepped forward.

"Look, we know you aren't Commonwealth guards." Vas pulled out her second blaster and covered them as they were covering her. "We're from the Commonwealth. That uniform hasn't been seen for probably a good fifteen years."

Deven kept his blaster against the forehead of the one he sat on. "Probably twenty. Didn't we use them for a job once?"

"Stop talking! We have you surrounded."

"Actually, we have you, and your friends further back, surrounded." Lucan stepped forward with Yesenia and the six others they left with. Each of them was fully armed and grinning far too much.

Vas waited for the weird pressure to return when Yesenia appeared, but she felt nothing. She did happen to see Deven's face develop a tick at her appearance that he quickly subdued.

There was something odd with that woman.

"These people aren't Commonwealth?" Yesenia had two blasters out, both aimed at the Hivian on the ground.

"No, they aren't. Which makes me question many things. All of you in Commonwealth uniforms, put down your weapons immediately or I start shooting. You might or might not have heard of my crew and me. I'm Vaslisha Tor Dain, an extremely successful Commonwealth merc captain. That man down there is my unbelievably deadly second-in-command. Our ships are overhead by now and have all of you tracked." She paused. "Weapons down now or we blast you off this planet." There were no ships overhead, but bluffing was part of the game.

The sound of thunks filled the area as the weapons around them were dropped. "Can some of your people gather their blasters, please?" Vas asked Lucan and Yesenia and kept her weapon on the fake guards.

Weapons were picked up, and the rest of Abiel's people with Lucan and Yesenia herded the fake Commonwealth guards into the clearing.

Six more Hivians, and five beings from other smaller Lethian Assembly worlds.

"None of you are Commonwealth? That's brilliant." Vas nodded to Yesenia and Lucan as the rest used ties to restrain the fake guards.

Deven got off his prisoner and used a pair of ties on his wrists. "Have any of you seen Commonwealth guards here without these uniforms? Something different?"

Lucan shrugged. "I don't think so. Mostly if I saw a uniform, I took off running."

Yesenia tilted her head, then shook it. "Sorry. I mostly ignored them until recently. But those look like what I've seen."

"This could be more interesting than we thought." Deven got the group of captured fake Commonwealth guards moving back toward the transports.

"These people aren't Commonwealth? What about the ones who fled?" Lucan stayed on the outside of the group with his blaster out. From the tone in his voice, he might be coming to the same conclusion Vas was.

"No idea. But I think something is going on. How long ago did the Commonwealth try to take over this planet?"

"A year ago? One day the government we had vanished and we were told the Commonwealth was taking over." As Yesenia spoke, she moved closer.

This time Vas was waiting for the weird pressure and felt it. If she focused on it, she was able to push it away. It was an odd feeling, as if someone was calling to her from far away.

"I wish we could see the ones who left. And their ships." Deven joined in herding the prisoners back toward the transports.

Roha and Abiel both raised their blasters at their arrival but quickly lowered them.

Vas went to Abiel. "Do you have secure places to hold these people? By the way, their uniforms are about twenty years out of date and neither Hivians nor other members of the Lethian Assembly would have been allowed to join the Commonwealth military. They're seen as unfriendly by the Commonwealth government."

"Yes, we have secure prisons." Abiel started swearing as he looked at the fake Commonwealth guards. "That's not good. Solar was always independent, and honestly, their uniforms looked close enough for us. Not to mention that they claimed that they bought Solar and the prior government vanished directly after."

"Most likely they were killed or are being held somewhere on a Lethian Assembly planet." Vas nudged the stragglers into the transport. They needed to speak more about this entire mess, but not in front of the fake guards.

They were also going to need to round up the rest hiding out here and make sure they didn't have a way off the planet. She might have to call for more people to come down from the *Destroyer's Curse* to help clean things up.

Lucan started to say something, but Abiel cut him off. "Not here. Take the people in your group and find whoever else you can easily bring in."

Lucan, Yesenia, and the six with them nodded and ran past the buildings.

It was even more curious as to what these fake Commonwealth guards had been going after inside the farm storage. But that was something to be left for interrogations. She hoped Flarik was up for it.

The ride back was mostly silent. Some of Abiel's people stayed behind to guard the farm buildings. None of the buildings showed signs of being broken into, but the attempts at doing so were clear.

The fake Commonwealth guards remained silent, aside from a few grunts as they tried to get comfortable with their hands tied behind them. Abiel frowned as he watched them but didn't say anything.

Vas didn't blame him. Since Solar was a small, non-Commonwealth planet, its people wouldn't have recognized the older Commonwealth uniforms.

Deven watched them carefully as well. Most likely it was to see which one he thought would break first.

They approached the house from the back this time. It didn't look like a cute country home, but more like an industrial complex. A large gate rolled back at their approach and armed guards stood on either side. The fact that they were wearing full armor and gas masks wasn't reassuring.

The prison was down underground and the prisoners were marched inside.

"We'd like to question them if you don't mind. But first, I think we should talk."

Abiel frowned as the prisoners were secured, but it was at them rather than Vas or Deven. "You're right. This new information is disturbing."

Vas thought that was a massive understatement, but silently followed Deven and Abiel inside. Roha volunteered to help watch the prisoners and Abiel agreed.

Looking around, Vas wondered if he was also questioning some of his people.

This time it was only the three of them in Abiel's office and he locked the door once they entered.

"I am at a loss for how they did this. I think my people

and I were so focused on winning our freedom that we failed to pick up on clues." He took his seat but looked like he'd aged a few years.

"How many times have you been in the Commonwealth?" Deven leaned forward as he sat and Vas felt him trying to calm Abiel down.

"Never. But still, we should have noticed something." Self-blame and confusion were heavy on his face and in his words.

Vas wasn't as calming as Deven, but she did smile and change direction. "Can I get a list of the items that are in those barns they were after? I have some smart people on our ship who can sort out why those fake guards were so focused on them."

Abiel pulled himself out of his thoughts and nodded. "I can send them to your pad."

"Do you have images of the shuttles or ships they were using?" Deven asked.

Abiel's frown was back with a vengeance. "I do. Close up on one, in fact. We had an altercation a few months ago. It didn't go well for them and I can say that I hope you're right and the Commonwealth wasn't behind any of this."

Vas knew there was a story there. But at this point, they needed to figure out what was going on. Once she saw the data appear on her pad from Abiel, she got up and walked to the far end of the office.

"Let me speak to my people and send them this. They can get started on tracking down what was going on here." There was still a huge chance that the incomplete Asarlaí planetary core transformation was at the center of this entire ruse, but there could have been more going on.

Especially since Solar was a non-Commonwealth world, coming in as the Lethian Assembly would have made more sense. So why didn't they?

Abiel nodded and he and Deven continued their discussion.

Vas hit her comm. "Gosta? I need some data looked at. Things are weirder down here than expected."

"Aye, captain. Can you send it to Bathie? Things are weird up here too." Gosta's voice was rushed and Vas couldn't recall him ever saying 'weird' before. Nor handing off digging into data.

"I can. Is there anything we need to know about?" She doubted that he wouldn't have said if there was, but this was a day for Gosta firsts.

"No! I mean, no, captain, everything is just busy."

Vas took a deep breath and reminded herself that she trusted her people—and Gosta was the most trustworthy.

"Bathie?" she switched to her. "I'm glad you're fully recovered. Can I send you some data? We have people who were pretending to be Commonwealth guards but are Lethian Assembly and they were after something on this list."

"Aye, captain!" Unlike Gosta, Bathie sounded happy to work on something. "Got it. I'll dig in and Aithnea is bored so maybe she can look as well."

"I'm not bored." Aithnea's voice cut into the comm call. "Well, maybe a little. And I do love a good mystery."

Now Vas really wanted to know what was going on up there. Gosta was in full panic mode and Aithnea was bored. She sighed. If Aithnea was bored, clearly whatever was going on with Gosta wasn't a danger. Yet.

"Thanks. And can you have Xsit watch for any incoming ships and tell me or Deven immediately?"

"Of course!" Xsit's slightly insulted chirp indicated she'd been listening in.

"All of you, we're looking for anything that explains why the Lethian Assembly took over this planet, pretended to be Commonwealth, and left some of their people behind to go after seeds. Report back once any-one finds anything."

Vas rejoined Deven and Abiel in their discussion. "Any progress?"

"Aside from me missing many red flags, no." Abiel blew out a bunch of air and looked annoyed with himself. "I'm glad you folks needed to hide here."

"So am I. And at least now you don't have to fear the Commonwealth once we break down that barricade. Do we have enough information to start questioning the prisoners?" Vas would still like Flarik to be here, but that might be better after they'd gone a round or two. And she wasn't sure that she wanted more of her people here until they figured out more of why this was happening.

Deven got to his feet. "Yes, look at these images. They even used old mock-ups of Commonwealth shuttles and ships. This one was barely appearing as a Commonwealth cruiser." He handed over his pad. Still images of shuttles and a few distant shots of ships.

"I wish we knew what in the hell was going on." Vas knew at some point they needed to work together with the Lethian Assembly to stop the Clongari. But that was beginning to appear impossible.

"You and me both." Abiel handed a set of cell keys to Deven and then pulled up a bunch of images at his desk. "If you don't mind, I'm going to work on things from my end. Maybe between myself and your people, we can get a better idea of what in the hell happened."

Vas and Deven wished him luck and left. The door locked behind them.

"I don't know that he trusts all of his people." Vas kept her voice low even though there was no one in the cor-ridor.

"He doesn't. I didn't scan him, but he is worried about more than those fake Commonwealth guards." Deven handed her his two blasters as they left the house and went toward the prison. "I'm assuming that I'm doing the talking?"

Vas grinned and put away the extra weapons. That was how they dealt with interrogations back when they were simply a merc crew. He went in unarmed and politely questioned them, she stood outside with a glare and multiple blasters.

It usually helped because the people they were fighting were extremely aware of who Vas and her crew were. She figured it would still work even if the prisoner was clueless.

Roha was stationed outside the entrance and nodded. "There are a few of Abiel's guards inside, but nothing has happened so far. Any news?" She tilted her head up toward the sky.

"Not yet, but we have Bathie and Aithnea working on it. Stay here in case things go bad."

Roha grinned. "Always up for some action. Good luck." She dropped her smile and returned to watching.

It was hard to tell what had been here before. But Vas doubted that most cute country houses had a massive underground area with cells. The way wound through some serious food and supply storage areas. Far more than Vas usually had for most missions. Abiel was expecting a siege.

There were four guards down the main aisle and they nodded in acknowledgment, then returned their watching.

Deven passed the first few cells before he found the person he wanted. It was the Hivian they'd first captured.

His Commonwealth outfit had been removed and he somehow looked younger in a dark blue jumpsuit.

Deven used the key Abiel gave them to open the door, then handed it to Vas. She locked the cell after him, then stood near the bars with a pair of blasters in her hands and a blank face. She'd switch to looking angry later if needed, but better to start neutral.

"Hi, we want to ask some questions, nothing more." Deven took one of the stools in the cell and smiled at the Hivian. "I'm Deven, what's your name?"

"You're Kilesh." It wasn't a question, only a statement. The Hivian's voice sounded younger now too.

"I am. Well, I was. I left there long ago and have lived in the Commonwealth longer than you've been alive. Why did they leave you and your companions behind?"

The Hivian pulled back. He'd been expecting something else. "I'm just a grunt. They couldn't get all of us back to the Commonwealth."

Deven shook his head. "We know you're not Commonwealth. The locals might not, this world had never been in the Commonwealth, so they didn't know. But we know." He dropped his voice. "My captain is behind me and she doesn't have patience."

Vas leaned closer to the bars and snarled.

"I'm seriously a nobody. They wanted us to stay behind to find some entrance or something." He shrugged. "And then grab the seeds. They told us to get as many of these weird seeds as we could."

"What seeds?" Deven gently asked.

Vas was more interested in the secret entrance and where in the hell it went, but Deven was skirting it to keep their prisoner calm. No one could be freaked out about seeds.

"I can't remember. They had a weird name. Flame-throwing? Something like that."

"Falian thring?" Vas asked. Normally she wouldn't interrupt Deven's questioning until needed, but those words crawled their way out of her deep memories. Rather, out of the Keeper ones.

Deven briefly turned back to her and looked paler than he had a moment ago. "Was that the name?"

Falian thring were literally seeds of destruction. The original Asarlaí created them a thousand years ago. They could transform a lifeless planet into a growing one—for a while. They could also destroy a formerly healthy planet. The Asarlaí used them to destroy enemy planets who refused to surrender.

Supposedly they'd been lost when the Asarlaí empire imploded.

The Hivian looked between the two of them. "That sounds like it. Why do you both look upset? They're only seeds after—" his words were cut off and he was flung to the ground by an explosion.

Followed by the sound of blaster fire.

CHAPTER SIXTEEN

———◆———

VAS THREW DEVEN ONE OF his blasters as he dove to cover the Hivian. Vas turned her back to them as more blaster fire came from deeper down the underground area. And from the entrance.

Damn it. There must be another way to get underground and some of the remaining fake Commonwealth guards were staging a jailbreak.

"What the hell is that?" The Hivian didn't sound worried about being on the ground. Probably the smartest thing he'd done all day.

"It sounds like people are trying to rescue all of you." Vas stayed low. There was more weapons fire coming from the entrance, but there was still some below.

Then the screams started. A lot of them.

"There aren't that many guards down here to make that much sound." Vas glanced at Deven.

He closed his eyes and tilted his head for a moment. When he opened them again he was furious. "No, there aren't. The guards and a group of fake Commonwealth guards are slaughtering the ones we have locked up. We need to leave." He got to his feet and lifted the Hivian as Vas unlocked the door.

"What? No, they're with me, they wouldn't…oh my gods." The Hivian froze as two guards shot people who'd come in with him.

There was no time, they were going down the line killing everyone in the cells.

"Follow me, and don't let him go." Vas took off at a run,

shooting Abiel's guards in between them and the exit when they fired at them.

Roha got one as Vas got to her. "Glad you made it; I was coming to get you when I heard the blaster fire. None of the rest of Abiel's people have come out."

"Get to one of the ground transports and protect our friend. Bug out if we don't come back in five minutes." Vas yelled to Roha as Deven shoved the Hivian toward her. Then she hit her comm. "Hrrru? Where are you?"

"Captain? I can barely hear you." Hrrru's voice sounded like he was shouting down a long tube.

"Are you okay? Don't come back to the compound, we're under attack."

"We're on our way, captain!" Hrrru cut the comm.

Hrrru wasn't a serious fighter, but he sounded fierce as he disobeyed Vas' orders.

"Damn it." Vas covered the exit as Roha picked up the Hivian, ran to the nearest armored transport, and locked them both inside.

"Gosta, we're under attack down here. Might need backup."

"Aye, captain. We're almost able to move. I'll also have some shuttles readied."

Vas rolled her eyes and looked to Deven who shrugged and led the way back into the house. There was no blaster fire inside as they ran to Abiel's office and pounded on the door.

Abiel unlocked it. "What's wrong?"

"The prison is under attack and some of your people are helping to kill the prisoners we brought in." Vas pushed open his door.

"What? Damn it." He hit a comm-like tag on his shirt. "Lucan, everyone fall back. We're under attack from without and within." As he spoke, he ran to his desk and pulled out two smaller blasters. "Only bring the people you left with."

Vas couldn't hear the response, but it was short and Abiel ended the call with a nod.

"I trust Lucan and Yesenia and the six with them with my life. But we had some recruits after the Commonwealth put up their barricade. Did any of the prisoners survive?" He hit a button on his desk and a low-level alarm rang through the house. And the sound of bolts locking ran through as well.

"One that we know of, he's with Roha. But why are they killing them and not freeing them?" Vas asked as she and Deven followed him down the hall.

"Very good question." Abiel went to the front room as the people who'd been in the house joined them. He quickly filled them in on what happened.

Vas hoped that these were trustworthy people, but all they could do at this point was hope. She stepped away as her comm pinged.

"Captain, more armed people are coming this way." Roha was calm and most likely wanted to know if she needed to kill people more than bugging out.

"You're still out there?" It had been more than five minutes.

"Yup. This transport is tough, while I was waiting I checked it out." She paused. "Our friend is tied up again. He kept trying to open the door." A muffled sound came through the comm. "And he's gagged because he won't shut up."

"Good. If they want him and the others dead, we need him alive. Are the people coming in on foot?"

"Yup. This thing has some sweet firepower. Permission to shoot?"

Vas looked over to Abiel, but he was busy sorting his people. She and her people were involved in this whether they wanted to be or not. "As needed. If you can push them back, do so. Lucan, Yesenia, and their people are coming in their transport. I'll make sure Abiel lets them know you're friendly."

"Deal." Roha cut the call and heavy weapons fire came from outside. She wasn't as focused on it as Walvento was, but Roha did enjoy blowing things up.

Abiel had about twenty people arming themselves. Heavy metal shutters slammed down over all the windows, and the lights dimmed.

"They were expecting something like this," Vas said to Deven.

"We were, just not right now, and not against our people." Abiel adjusted the armor he wore. "Honestly, we'd been preparing for this since before we broke free of what we thought was the Commonwealth."

Vas told Abiel about Roha and their prisoner remaining in the transport. More heavy weapons fire from outside accented her words.

Abiel nodded to the walls. "This is a fortified building, but we have to meet the enemy. Too many people can overwhelm our defenses."

"And some of the enemies are your own people," Vas added.

Abiel gave a small smile. "I already changed any codes I had. Only the people here and Lucan's group can use them. I have other scouting groups out, but none of them have responded yet, so I blocked all of them."

Vas' comm buzzed.

"Captain? We have a Welischian contingent of sixty armed and ready to defend you." Hrrru sounded excited about fighting. Maybe being around more of his people was making him feisty.

Abiel answered his comm and nodded to Vas. Most likely Qaan reporting she was bringing reinforcements.

"How far away are you? Come in cautiously, we're not sure how many enemies are out there."

Abiel was talking too low to hear, but he was gesturing

broadly. Even though Qaan, or whoever was on the other end of the conversation, wouldn't be able to see them.

"They say we'll be there in about ten minutes. We're in these nice transports."

Hrrru was bouncing right now, Vas could hear it in his voice.

"We'll see you when you get here, Vas out." Her comm immediately pinged again.

"Captain," Bathie didn't sound nearly as excited as Hrrru. "The only things of interest in the list of things in those barns are some massive drills and way more Falian thring seeds than anyone aside from a megalomaniac Asarlaí would ever need."

Deven was close enough to hear and started swearing.

"Are those seeds as dangerous as I think?" She asked but the look on Deven's face gave her the answer.

"Yes," Aithnea cut in. "And they could activate the mutated core if they were sent down that far—even though it was never completed in the change. If the Lethian Assembly did deliberately leave behind their own people, it was a suicide trip for them. Provided they were able to get to the seeds."

"How can we stop that from happening?"

"Don't let anyone get those seeds."

"Damn it, they pulled back the people watching the barn."

Deven hit his comm as he heard her.

"Gosta?"

"Yes, most of the trouble has been resolved and we're moving over the planet. What do you need?"

"We need the ship overhead. We have to destroy a building." Deven kept his voice low as he gave the coordinates of the barn while he watched Abiel and his people. Even if they were sure of what they had, they might not want it blown up.

Vas hit her comm. "Aithnea, will exploding those seeds

activate them in any way?" Considering it looked as if whoever set this up was counting on that when the seeds got to the planet's core, it might not be a great idea. She doubted the Lethian Assembly was trying to open a dimension portal by exploding the planet, but they were planning on something.

"Ah, I heard Deven's comments. We'd need to neutralize them first with a counteracting chem drop. *Then* blow the hell out of them. But Nitya says the sensors are showing good-sized groups moving toward both your location as well as the building with the seeds."

CHAPTER SEVENTEEN

"DAMN IT. HOLD ON." VAS turned to Abiel. "Do you have sensors? My ship says a lot of people are coming our way." Granted, some were the Welischians, but there were only a few dozen of them.

"Yes, we do." Abiel nodded to one of his people who brought up an image of the area around the house and the barn. "The attackers are here and a few around the barn. But that thing is well secured." He pointed to two smallish clumps. One near the prison and one near the buildings with the drills and seeds. Neither group was more than a handful of people.

Aithnea started swearing through the comm as she overheard Abiel. "Tell him his entire system has been compromised. Over two hundred people are coming your way in transports. And at least fifty more are heading for that building."

"Damn it. Something is wrong with your system, Abiel. Two hundred people are heading our way, and a second group is going for the barn." Two hundred combatants with her entire crew fully armed and ready wouldn't be a problem. But Abiel's people were unknown, and some had already been shown to be traitors. And as good as she, Deven, and Roha were, Vas didn't think they could do it alone.

"What?" Abiel spun to two of his people. "Where's Loen? She set up that system. Find her immediately."

"She went outside right before these two came in." The man nodded to Vas and Deven.

"Maybe she went to the jail?" another said.

Abiel turned to Vas and Deven. "Did you see a tall, thin, pale Foorlian when you came left the jail?"

"Foorlians are pretty noticeable. And they don't like living off their home world. I haven't seen one here." Vas once had a Foorlian on her crew, Jakiin. He'd been Mac's best buddy and co-conspirator in all sorts of trouble. And he'd followed Deven to certain death to save their crew and a thousand refugees.

Deven made it back from death. Jakiin hadn't.

Abiel hit his comm. "Loen? Come in."

The responding static was loud enough for everyone to hear.

Abiel tried a few more times, but there was nothing but static.

"Maybe she got hit during the attack?"

"Or she was involved." Abiel turned to the people in the room. "We've been attacked from without by those fake guards and within by our own people. No time to debate or discuss, but right now I need Ila, and Mani to purge the systems of any codes input by Loen. All of them. She only took over as lead systems a few weeks ago, so you won't have to go back far." He tapped an older woman. "Grech, you're in command if I don't come back."

Grech nodded and turned to the other two. "You heard the man, get Loen's codes out now."

Vas figured Abiel was operating on the assumption that the people in here were safe. He could be right; he knew them all better than she did.

But if she were planning on a sneak attack like this, she would have left someone behind.

Vas wished she had someone to leave behind, but with only her and Deven, that wasn't an option.

Deven stayed next to Abiel in a quiet debate while Abiel's people either worked on purging systems or prepped to face their attackers.

Both men came to Vas. Abiel moved them down the hall, away from everyone else, for some privacy.

"Deven has convinced me to stay here and watch my people." Abiel's voice was flat.

"Did you trust Loen?" Vas asked.

"Yes." Abiel's face reddened. "But I didn't even know that those people we thought were Commonwealth guards were fake. Maybe I'm too old. It feels like I am."

Vas folded her arms. "How old are you?"

"Ninety-eight. I'm only middle-aged for my kind, but these are catastrophic mistakes."

"I have an eight-hundred-year-old human nun and an even older dead one in my ship. Literally. Age isn't the issue. You were focused on a goal and those bastards took advantage of it. That's done now, right?" She favored him with the glare Mac often earned.

Abiel pulled back, then smiled. "Aye, captain. Now I know why people are afraid of you." His eyes widened and he hit his forehead. "Aside from Yesenia, myself, and a few others, most of my people didn't know who you are. Loen did."

"And if she was working for the Lethians, then she had the timeline for their plans moved up." Deven looked around the people in the front room and dropped his voice. "Did any of these people join when she did?"

"No, but many of the ones guarding the jail did. I don't doubt they'll try to claim they weren't involved, but I'll handle them. But even if Qaan and her people get here soon enough, I'm not sure you can fight off that many." He handed both of them small comms. "These will come to me, Lucan, and Yesenia only. Call if you need us. What-ever you're doing."

"We have a plan." Vas flashed him a smile as she and Deven attached the smaller comms below their own while he led them to a side door and locked it behind them.

"I hope he's right about his people in there." Vas kept her voice low as they ran around the side of the compound to the jail and Roha's transport. There was no sound of blaster fire, but they still kept low as they ran.

Deven nodded. "If not, I don't think he'll have a problem killing them. Abiel is a good man, but he's got a lot of pride and it took some serious hits today. Anyone who crosses him again won't fare well."

Vas hit her comm as a call came in.

"Captain? We're here. Where are you?"

"Hrrru, keep your people back for now."

"Qaan is already leading us in." Hrrru's voice dropped. "She's swearing about a traitor named Loen. Qaan is extremely angry."

Good of Abiel to warn Qaan, but he should have had them stay back a bit longer.

"How close are you? Loen is a Foorlian so you'll know if you see her. Deven and I have a plan, but I need you to keep your people back."

"We're approaching the compound from the south, just passing the airfield. But I don't think Qaan will listen. She's not like most of my people." There was a lot of idol worship in his voice.

Vas turned to Deven. "How are we going to destroy those seeds with a stubborn Welischian?" Hrrru could be stubborn, but usually only with theories.

Deven tapped his comm. "Hrrru? Can you ask her to stop and let me speak to her?"

"Sure."

"Hello? This is Qaan." Her voice was low and sounded annoyed even through the distance of Deven's comm.

Deven quickly explained what they were going to have their ship do. And that a lot of the combatants might change their direction when that happened.

There was a pause, then a sigh. "More people are closing in on the compound. We will focus our attack there."

Deven thanked her and Hrrru then ended the call. "I'm assuming we want to get Gosta over there quickly?" He looked up into the sky. "There's a lot of wind higher up, and it's increasing."

"Damn it," Vas called Gosta and explained the change of plans. The ship would be more impressive, but it wasn't a good low-orbit flyer. And it would have to stay high enough because of the winds that the suppression foam could end up everywhere except that building.

"You want Mac and Bathie to go down in a shuttle with the foam?" Gosta started muttering. "Those two overheard me and are already running for the lift. I hope this works."

"Me too." Vas and Deven ran to Roha's transport as the engines kicked in.

Roha opened the driver's side and motioned to them. "Get in. Where are we going?"

Vas took the front seat and Deven climbed in the middle row. Their prisoner Hivian was in the furthest row. "Right now, getting clear of the compound and waiting in the woods near the barn. Why is he way back there?"

"He was beginning to bother me." Roha gunned the engine once the doors shut.

"He's fairly tied up. And still gagged." Deven turned to the man.

"I know, but he was breathing aggressively." Roha flashed Vas a smile as they pulled away from the compound.

"What happened to the guards?" Vas hadn't seen anyone on their way to the transport. That was good and bad. Bad in that it most likely meant all the prisoners were dead but good in that there were fewer combatants in the immediate vicinity.

"They never came out this direction." Roha drove quickly away.

"Wasn't the group with Lucan and Yesenia coming back here?" Deven turned from watching their prisoner.

Vas had completely forgotten about that transport. They should have been back by now.

"That's what I thought. What's the plan with the barn?" Roha must have missed being on a planet, she was having way too much fun taking various tight turns through the trees.

"Damn." Vas hit the comm Abiel gave her. "Lucan? Yesenia? This is Vas, where are you?"

Static came through and Deven got the same result.

"Did they get attacked? Could any of the people with them have been spies?" Vas switched to Abiel.

He answered immediately. Unfortunately, he hadn't heard from them either.

Vas briefly told Roha about Mac and Bathie. "We need to go to the barn and find Lucan and Yesenia and their people. That entire area is going to vanish." Vas hung on to the dash tighter, as Roha picked up speed. "Have you been hanging around Mac?"

Roha laughed. "He wishes. Just nice to be out driving on a lovely day. Saving people, destroying enemies. It's good to be back." She swerved sharply as the flash of a blaster came a few feet from the hood.

"Dodging people who want to kill us. How close are we?" They moved away from the blaster fire, but Vas had no idea how far they were from the barn. She was expecting an impatient fly-by from Mac and Bathie at any moment.

"Three minutes, tops." Deven secured his second blaster and had his hand on the door handle. "Permission to depart and take care of our shooter, captain?"

Vas rolled her eyes. "By all means, *second*. Go kick ass. Maybe Roha will even slow down for you."

"I can do better." Roha spun so the transport blocked

where the blaster fire came from, then almost completely stopped.

"Thanks." Deven opened the door and rolled out.

Roha returned to driving once Deven scrambled behind a boulder.

There was no one around the building on the side they approached from. But whoever had been there was most likely who shot at them.

"Shit. Is that the other transport?" Vas looked at the blown-out tires and shattered hood of a transport sticking out of a large gully.

"Let's find out." Roha stopped the transport behind a pile of stone and rubble then turned to the prisoner. "You probably want to stay still; those people want to kill you."

Their prisoner glowered but didn't move as they shut and locked the transport.

The sound of blaster fire was further away—most likely Deven—as they ran toward the gully and the downed transport.

Only one body was inside, and the massive hole in the back of the man's head said he'd been killed while inside.

"That could be one of the people with Lucan and Yesenia, hard to tell without a face. But was he killed because he betrayed them, or because someone betrayed him?" Vas took a quick look in the vehicle, ignoring the blown-out brain parts, while Roha kept watch but there was no other evidence that could tell her what happened.

Aside from the transport having been attacked.

"Shouldn't they have been heading back to the compound?" Roha continued to watch around them but she also motioned to the tracks. "They were attacked returning to the barns."

"Where the hell were they going and where are they now?" They'd both been speaking softly, but Vas froze as the sound of marching feet came from around the barn. She motioned for Roha to follow her around the back of the buildings.

Their transport was hidden but would be spotted if whoever was marching came this way. But there wasn't much they could do at this point.

Vas held up her hand for Roha to stay behind her and pulled out the tiny spyglass she carried in her pocket to look around the corner. "Shit, shit, shit. Those aren't lackeys they accidentally left behind." She rolled back against the wall and put away her glass. "Good news, aside from the noise, there are only ten. The bad news is they're all military Lethians"

CHAPTER EIGHTEEN

VAS LET HER BREATH OUT slowly as the marching went further away from the barn. "They had to have been hiding with the fake Commonwealth guards—Gosta would have noticed any other ships in orbit."

"Where now?" Roha was all merc professional now.

"We need to find Lucan, Yesenia, and the rest—if they're alive. Then get them and us the hell out of here. This thing needs to blow up." Vas was surprised that Mac hadn't either contacted her or buzzed over the building yet. They needed to get this place ready for the suppressant drop and the quick follow-up of a massive explosive barrage.

The blaster fire from the direction Deven was died down. That was good. Hopefully.

Vas led the way around the far side of the barn and started swearing. Getting inside wouldn't be a problem as a guard in a Lethian uniform was standing in front of the slightly open door. She seemed to be paying more attention to the opposite direction.

Roha wasn't a small woman, but she was deadly silent when sneaking up on someone. Vas kept her blaster aimed at the distracted guard's back and motioned for Roha to take care of her.

After securing her massive blaster to her back, Roha pulled out a wicked-looking knife and silently ran forward.

The guard didn't make a sound as she collapsed. Roha looked inside without moving the door, then motioned for Vas.

Vas joined her as they waited for anyone inside to notice the guard was gone. Nothing. Vas looked around the corner with her spyglass, but couldn't see much in the complete dark.

The people who had taken off might be hiding inside and they left the woman to guard.

Vas wished she'd brought night vision goggles, but as this started as a 'meet the locals' event, she hadn't thought to bring them.

Roha had though. She handed a pair to Vas. "Here ya go, captain."

"Thank you. I'm having you pack my standard away gear from now on." The night vision goggles showed what she'd expected—only more of it. Eight massive drills lined the walls and surrounded a mountain of crates so large even with the night vision goggles she couldn't see all of it.

"I don't see any heat signatures." Roha finished her scanning.

Vas and Roha dragged the dead guard into the barn and mostly shut the door with them inside.

"Captain, we're on approach. Ready to drop?" Mac always had great timing.

"No. Loop around and stay high. We're still too close and we're missing people." Vas was hoping if Abiel's people were still alive, but captured, they'd be held in here, but no life signs wasn't good.

"But I had the perfect approach—"

"We're good, captain," Bathie cut him off. "Pulling up. Mac's whiny because we're alternating passes. The next one will be mine."

Vas could hear the smirk in Bathie's voice.

Mac muttered in the background but didn't say anything else.

"By the way, how are you two standing on a bunch of people?" Bathie asked.

Vas adjusted her scanner to a tight search and started swearing. There were several faint heat signatures under the floor. They weren't supposed to be found. "Thank you. Now stay high until we call. There might be a hidden ship up there." She figured the Lethians were already down here, but that didn't mean they didn't have a ship stashed somewhere.

"Aye, we'll keep our eyes open."

Vas stomped on the floor and was rewarded by the sound of loose boards. "We need to get this up, and still watch the door."

"If you watch the door, Roha and I can pull the floorboards up. Those Lethians are still looking for me further out but they'll be back." Deven's voice coming softly from the darkness behind them almost made Vas jump.

"Damn it! How did you get past us?"

"I wasn't the first." Deven pointed to the far corner. "There was a hole back there. It looked old and well covered, but it still worked."

"Glad you're intact." Vas nodded to both of them. "I'll stay at the door, you two get whoever is in there out." Hopefully, it was Yesenia and her companions. And not more fake Commonwealth guards left behind by the Lethian Assembly.

It took a few minutes to find the trap door. Judging by the amount of stuff Deven and Roha had to move, whoever was down there had been left behind to die.

Which made Vas wonder why they hadn't simply been killed. The captors must have felt they could still use the prisoners for something.

Deven and Roha went down the stairs under the hidden door. Judging by the noise the two made, something exceedingly uncommon for either of them, those stairs were old.

Roha came back first with an unconscious Lucan over

her shoulder. He was tied and gagged, but still breathing. Roha dropped him behind Vas.

"It looks like the five remaining people from the six in that transport, plus a few other locals. Maybe four more. It's going to get crowded in our transport."

Vas leaned down to cut Lucan free and Roha went to get more people. Vas left his gag on, the last thing they needed was for him or one of the others to freak out when they woke up and start screaming.

Deven brought out Yesenia, also unconscious, and Vas cut her hands and legs free.

They had two people left down below when Vas held up her hand as Roha dropped her next person.

The sound of marching feet was coming their way.

Roha froze and Vas took a single step closer to the door. She'd kept it open an inch but knew if the Lethians came up looking for the guard it wouldn't help much.

There was a pause, then blaster fire, and the marching feet retreated.

"Damn, I don't know who's out there but they gave us some time."

Roha nodded and jogged back down the stairs.

Moments later she and Deven brought the last two out.

Vas stayed near the door as they cut the last ones free but there were no more sounds outside.

"We need to get them into the transport." The transport could fit ten people sitting. With all of them and their Hivian prisoner, they were thirteen. Cramped, but the bigger issue was getting them to the transport.

"I got this." Deven paused at the door, opened it, then raced out. Vas watched him until he rounded the corner then mostly closed the door again.

"Was there anything down there with them?" She asked Roha while they waited. Abiel's people looked roughed up. The others didn't but they had still been left behind.

"Explosives." Roha's face was grim. "A lot of them.

Which makes no sense. There were also signs of the remains of some sort of chemical shots, they were all knocked out with something."

Vas nodded. Hopefully, they'd stay out until she and the others could get them free from here.

The transport couldn't be quiet, they weren't designed to be that way. But Deven made up for that with speed. He raced up, flung open the doors, and they threw people in. They didn't have time to be gentle, saving their lives was more important.

"Whoever pulled the marching guards away from us is either dead or long gone, the guards are coming back." Deven had excellent hearing, Vas didn't hear anything.

But she trusted him.

Roha took the wheel again. Vas sat in front, with Deven crammed up next to her against the door.

A blaster shot flew out of the woods as Roha cranked the wheel around and raced away and off to the other side.

Their prisoner had two unconscious people piled on him and from his muffled exclamations wasn't happy with the turns Roha was making or the bodies.

Vas figured he should be glad he was alive.

Her comm crackled. "What?"

"Captain, we might have a friend up here. Gosta's tracking someone coming in from the gate." Bathie sounded tense for her.

"Keep me updated. How far out will we need to be to be safe when you drop the loads?" The suppressant would go right through the barn and probably all around the area. Not to mention the results when the explosives hit.

Mac cut in. "About twice as far as you are now. Providing you're that transport with a lot of life signs in it racing away from our target. And that the shield we're dropping with the suppressant holds."

Roha's response was to increase speed. She was going away from the compound as far as Vas could tell. Good idea if they were already under attack. Fighting with a bunch of unconscious bodies around them wasn't a great idea.

"That's us. Come in low, it'll take that ship a while to get here from the gate. Give us time to clear the area, suppress, shield, and blow that thing up." Vas hoped no more of Abiel's people were there, but they couldn't let the Lethians and whoever they were working with complete their plans. It would kill everyone on the planet as it transformed. Mayhira was designed to create a portal between dimensions, but Vas and her people changed that, and instead, it turned into a new sun.

The Nhali mining planet simply exploded.

There was a reason even the criminally greedy Asarlaí abandoned the planet conversion plan. There was no way to know what this partially modified core would do, but she didn't think any of them wanted to find out.

Mac and Bathie clicked off as Gosta called in.

Vas headed him off before he could speak. "Mac told us about the incoming ship. Lethians?"

"Yes, but it's a science vessel, not a warship. At least it's showing as such and has little in the way of weapons. And it's approaching cautiously."

Vas shared a look with Deven, but he shrugged. She didn't know that the expanding, violent, and greedy Lethian Assembly had science ships.

"Keep scanning them. Warn them off if they get too close." Vas paused. "Actually, have Flarik speak to them." Since the *Destroyer's Curse* was registered as a Wavian vessel, might as well have her take charge.

"Aye, captain. She's already on her way to the deck."

"Excellent," Vas swore when Roha zigged as more blaster fire came from behind them. "We're going to be incommunicado for a while."

At his affirmative, Vas cut the comm.

Whoever was behind them was also in a transport, but still hadn't come close enough for their weapons to be a real threat. But they did seem to be trying to nudge them back toward the compound.

"Roha—"

"Not a worry, captain. I'm not letting them push us around."

There were a few thuds, and a groan from the prisoner, as Roha made a series of twists and turns that Vas would have said was impossible for an overloaded transport.

Her comm buzzed again.

"Captain, you're almost clear," Bathie said.

The sound of a low-flying shuttle came from above them.

"That's you, I take it?"

"Aye. Mac wants to know if he can take out the transport chasing you. It won't interfere with our drops."

"Sure. Tell me when we're clear."

The explosion behind them was loud. That transport was closer than she thought.

"Clear!" Mac yelled.

"Go!" Vas turned to Roha. "Keep going in the direction we are. I trust Bathie, but things can always be off." The rear camera showed Mac taking care of the people following them and taking out a lot of forest.

Roha kept racing through the woods when a rumble rocked the transport. The second one lifted the back set of tires in the air and trees all around them were flattened.

CHAPTER NINETEEN

———

"EVERYONE OKAY DOWN THERE?" BATH-IE'S voice was distant and static-filled. "If so, you might want to keep going. There was an extra kick from the explosion. The shield expanded but can't be sure it will hold."

Vas imagined Bathie glaring at Mac. Most likely he did something he shouldn't have.

"We're okay, and yup, still running. Can you buzz the compound and see what's happening? I'm not sure what we're going to do with our prisoner and nine unconscious people."

"We're on it. Oh, Gosta can't get through to you due to interference kicked up by the explosion. But he says the Lethian science vessel has stopped halfway here. They did that as soon as Flarik told them to back off, but there's been no other response."

"Good." Vas grabbed the dash for the fifth time as Roha managed to get more speed out of the transport.

"Terel suggests we bring the people in your transport and all of you up to her." Bathie was still doing the talking but Mac continued to swear in the background. "And the compound has become a complete battleground."

Vas looked to Deven and Roha, but neither appeared ready to stand down from a fight. Not to mention that Hrrru was still with his people somewhere. "Might be a good idea for our prisoner and the others. They're still unconscious and were roughed up. But Hrrru's in the middle of things, and these people need help. Is there a clearing near here but away from the fighting?"

"Aye, captain. Just keep going in the same direction. Gon and Marwin tagged along on this trip and were hoping to get some fighting in," Bathie said.

"We can make a trade." Vas shook her head. Honestly, she was surprised more of her crew hadn't come along *just in case*.

Roha veered into a clearing where the shuttle was coming down at the far end. Once it landed, Roha drove up to it.

Mac, Bathie, Marwin, and Gon came running out and quickly transferred the nine still unconscious people into the shuttle. Vas wasn't sure how their prisoner felt until he fought to be taken as well. He finally figured out that if he wanted to live he needed to leave.

"Keep this one tied up until you have him in the brig. But the rest of them can have their gags taken off once you're on the ship."

Bathie nodded and kept a hold of their prisoner as the last to go in. But he looked like staying on this planet was the last thing he wanted to do.

Vas didn't blame him.

Deven took the second row of seats in the transport, with Gon and Marwin in the rear. Roha spun the transport and tore out of the clearing.

"These are sweet rides. Not at all like the junk the Commonwealth makes. Maybe they'll let us buy some? Not this one, it's damaged." Roha scraped the right side as she darted through trees. "Very damaged."

Marwin gave them what intel they had on the fighting going on around the compound. It wasn't much.

"We don't know where they came from? The ones we blew up were Lethian Assembly but some were trying to pretend to be Commonwealth," Deven asked.

"Not when we were still up there. Gosta was swearing as he tried to find out more. Even Nitya says the ground troops appeared out of nowhere," Marwin said.

"Cloaking? Damn, that's not good." Vas hit her comm for Gosta or anyone on the ship, but the interference from the explosion was still in place. "That Lethian science vessel might not be the only one up there if they have cloaking."

"There's no way they missed the explosion. Maybe they'll leave if their entire purpose here was to set off that core. The drills and seeds were incinerated." Roha was trying to sound optimistic but there wasn't much behind it.

They stopped back from the compound but fighting was evident. The enemy fighters would have seen the explosion as well, but it wasn't slowing them down on their attack.

"Hrrru? Where are you?" Vas wanted to help Abiel and his people, but she needed her man back first.

"Captain? I can barely hear you. That explosion knocked everything off. We're near the front of the compound. A Foorlian woman is leading the enemy."

"Thank you. We're coming in." Vas hit Abiel's comm. "We've got your people up in our ship, but there are five of us who can fight. Where are you?"

"We're trying to keep them out," Abiel's voice was masked by the sound of weapons fire. "They're coming in!" He cut off and Vas couldn't get him back.

"Shall we dump this thing and stop them?" Deven asked as they came around the corner. The Welischians were fighting a group of Lethian Assembly soldiers and a tall Foorlian woman was fighting the pissed-off tall Welischian. Qaan definitely had a grudge.

"Is that Hrrru?" Vas swore as he jumped at the Foorlian. "This is a good place to stop. Get Hrrru and go after anyone fighting the Welischians. Deven and I are going inside." She would have liked to bring everyone inside; the door was now blasted open. But Hrrru and his people were the priority.

Roha had barely stopped the transport when she, Gon, and Marwin raced out. Deven ran to the house with Vas right behind.

The attackers surrounding the house pulled back but t returned as they realized there were only two fighters. Oddly, they were using edged weapons.

"Is there a block?" Vas knew there were ways to disable blasters—they'd been used on that Nhali mining planet for one and Gosta had created his own a few years ago. She waited for Deven's head tilt and then a nod, and then they both switched blasters for knives.

Since blasters were still working on the edges of the compound, it was most likely a mechanism Abiel had in place if he had to defend his base.

The front room was full of fighters from both sides, but no sign of Abiel.

Vas ran toward his office and found him fighting at the entrance to the hallway, armed with a large sword that he seemed comfortable with. But he wasn't going to last long on his own.

More of the attackers were getting past his people and running toward him.

"You help him, I'm—"Vas spun and knifed a Hivian still wearing an old Commonwealth guard uniform as he charged forward. "I'll cover the front." She pulled out a second knife and grinned at the enemies clustered around the remains of the front door.

Three more attackers charged forward—all with non-functioning blasters when Roha joined her. "I can stay here. Hrrru is with Gon and Marwin. The Welischi-ans are winning." She glanced down at Vas' knives, swung her blaster into the holster on her back, and brought out her long dagger. "Thought I felt a tingle." One advantage of her merc crew, they were experienced in all types of weapons.

Vas grinned and ran through the room of fighters. Neither Deven nor Abiel were in sight, but they were a few feet around a corner in front of his office door. They were fighting in unison, something Vas was envious of. She and Deven could work together like that, but they'd been together for twenty years.

This was an example of two extremely powerful telepaths working as one.

The fighters were trying to get into Abiel's office but didn't seem like they were trying to kill either man. In fact, they were taking great pains not to, even though there were eight of them against Abiel and Deven. And all of them had knives, daggers, or short swords. Unlike the new wave outside, these fighters knew there was a blocker inside here.

Shit. The Lethians might be after telepaths as well as whatever they had been hoping to gain from activating the weird Asarlaí stuff in the planet's core. Maybe the barn explosion changed their plans but it didn't destroy them.

Vas yelled to get the attackers' attention from the other two, then started stabbing. And kicking. With knives in each hand, punching wasn't an option, but kicking felt good.

She'd been under a lot of stress lately and this was a great workout.

"Having fun?" Deven yelled over the fighters.

"I am!" Vas jumped back as one of the knives from the enemy got too close to her chest. They might want Deven and Abiel, but someone knew that while those two were telepaths, she wasn't. Her being killed wouldn't be a problem for them.

She could still see the front door and saw when Roha stood back and let a bunch of Welischians in. They yelled and ran toward the remaining attackers in the front room. For a mostly peace-loving people, they were channeling their fierce side well.

Vas kept fighting. Then she realized that both Deven and Abiel were slowing down. There were only three attackers left here, but they were going to overwhelm both at the slow rate they were now moving.

She stabbed and shoved the attackers out of the way to stand in front of Deven and Abiel. Deven scowled as he picked up on the problem, but whatever was causing it, neither man could shake it off.

Vas hunched lower with her knives ready as more attackers came around the corner. Everyone was moving at normal speed aside from Deven and Abiel. She'd bet that any other telepaths near or in the compound were in the same boat. Someone or something was targeting them.

"Gosta?" She didn't know how long the effects of the explosion were going to mess up communications, but she needed help. Two attackers were killed as they tried to charge past her. Luckily the hallway wasn't wide.

"Ca–ain? I can barely hear you."

"I hope I'm coming through better than you are." Vas swung with both blades and forced another attacker back.

Deven and Abiel were almost stationary now.

"Something is slowing down Deven and Abiel—he's another telepath. I can't see any others down here, but they're probably having the same issue."

"We're sending down mor- -roops. Han-tight." Then the comm shut down.

Damn it, she wasn't even sure he heard her. She wanted him to scan for anything impacting telepaths. More troops would be good, as long as none of the telepathically inclined were with them.

She used her comm to reach Roha. "I need help down the hall."

"Coming!" Roha yelled instead of using the comm. She was grinning as she entered the hallway and destroyed the attacker trying to run in and the last one attacking

Deven and Abiel. Not that more couldn't come, but at least these were out of the way.

She stood next to Vas and glanced back. "What's wrong with those two?"

"No idea. They just started slowing down. Abiel was fighting to keep people out of his office, so I don't want to abandon it."

"They're not moving."

Vas glanced back. Both men were now locked into position as they fought off people who weren't there anymore. "Nope." Vas hit her comm. "Marwin, Gosta is sending down more troops, when they get in place, I need you and Gon to come inside. Go down the hall."

"Aye, captain! Want us to bring Hrrru too? He's having fun it looks like."

"Not if he seems safe where he is. Is anyone out there slowing down?"

"Not unless they're injured."

"Then get in here as soon as you can." There might have been over two hundred attackers originally, but they were getting reinforcements. And while there might not be any telepaths in the outside fighting, the odds were slim—this planet had a high concentration. Most likely they'd been killed where they stood as they slowed down.

Which meant that whatever was hitting Deven and Abiel was aiming for all the telepaths. Vas took a step closer to them and motioned for Roha to do the same. No one was getting these two.

"Captain!" Marwin yelled from the front room.

Vas yelled, "Back here!" Another wave of fighters was coming down the hall, but Marwin and Gon made short work of them as they came behind them.

"What's wrong with Deven?" Gon had a sword almost as long as Vas' leg. Vas wasn't going to ask how he knew to bring it.

"Not sure, but the man next to him is a telepath also." The sounds of fighting in the front room seemed to be lessening. "How bad is it? And how many came down from the ship?" Judging by how quickly the shuttle came down after speaking to Gosta, Vas figured he had a group in the landing bay ready to go when they spoke.

"Gosta sent my brother and sister and five others. They're turning the fight in our favor, I think the enemy ran out of nearby fighters," Marwin stayed closest to the front room to keep watch.

An explosion almost knocked all of them off their feet.

Vas looked around but nothing appeared to be exploding inside. "That came from the jail and storage behind us. They killed all the prisoners, why blow it up?"

"Hiding evidence?" Roha turned and lowered the sword Abiel still held raised.

Probably a good idea and Vas did the same to Deven. There was some physical resistance, but not much. Deven's eyes didn't move and he continued staring ahead as she lowered his arm.

"We'll never know for sure. I'm not risking people going back there. And we need to get these two someplace safe." Normally Vas would be out there fighting until the end—but not with Deven compromised. Not to mention the attackers wanted both men, and that wasn't happening on her watch.

Another explosion, weaker this time, came from the same direction.

Vas swore. "Gon, go see if you can tell who is doing what out back. Do not engage unless attacked though." Gon wasn't as fight crazy as some of her people, but he looked too enthusiastic when she told him to go to the jail.

"Aye, captain." For such a large man, he could vanish quickly when he didn't want any more instructions.

The fighting was dying down when Deven, Abiel, and people from both inside and outside the house started screaming.

CHAPTER TWENTY

———◆———

"WHAT'S HAPPENING?" MARWIN YELLED AS he looked out into the front room, but didn't leave the hall.

"I have no idea. Roha, grab Abiel's weapon." It took a few moments, but Vas got Deven to release his. Neither man responded but tilted their heads up to scream louder.

Roha swore and punched Abiel in the jaw. Hard. He immediately stopped screaming, blinked once, and then slid down the door and collapsed.

Deven kept yelling, so Vas punched him as well. Same results, but when he blinked he briefly looked more aware. Before his eyes rolled back in his head and he crumpled to the ground.

"Marwin, go punch anyone standing and screaming but make note of who they are. Did any more of our telepaths come down in the shuttle?"

"Aye, captain. I don't think any did." Some of the minor telepaths kept it to themselves. And if Gosta hadn't heard her warning, they might have come down.

Marwin raced out into the front room. The screaming slowly stopped as the punching continued. There were going to be a lot of sore jaws when they woke up.

"What now?" Roha bent down to check on Abiel, but he wouldn't wake up.

Gon came running back but kept looking toward the front room. "The fighting is mostly over, why is Marwin punching the screaming people?"

"We're not sure, but something made the telepaths start yelling. Roha discovered how to stop whatever they were doing." She looked down at Deven. He didn't appear comfortable in his collapsed state, but his face was more relaxed now. "What were the explosions?"

"A group of Lethians wearing old Commonwealth clothing were launching grenades into the jail. I chased them off and they ran to a transport." He shrugged. "The jail is pretty much destroyed."

"Damn it, there's way more going on here than we can sort out right now," Vas said. There must have been something more important than dead prisoners inside.

Hrrru came racing around the corner. His fur was ruffled and dirty, but he was grinning. Until he saw Deven. He skidded to a halt. "I was coming to tell you we won, but what happened to Deven?"

"Something attacked all the telepaths. Can you find your friend Qaan and bring her here?" With Lucan and Yesenia up in her ship, Vas wasn't sure who else she could trust of Abiel's people.

"Aye, captain!" Hrrru was already running away when he yelled.

Her comm pinged. "Vas? What's going on down there?" Terel's voice was the clearest she'd heard from the ship since the explosion of the barn.

"Thank the gods." Vas quickly filled Terel in on Deven and the rest of the telepaths. "Not to mention, I'm sure there are plenty of other injured."

"I'm on it, we'll have a medical team down there immediately." Terel ended the call as Hrrru and Qaan came around the corner.

Qaan reached for her sword when she saw Abiel collapsed against the door.

Vas held up her hands. "We didn't do this. Well, we punched them both to stop the screaming, but something else attacked them." She stepped back to show Deven. "My man is down also. I have a medical team coming and they're ready to help your people too. The jail was destroyed by the surviving attackers as they fled. Lucan and Yesenia are being treated on my ship."

Qaan paused, looked to Hrrru who nodded, then did the same. "Thank you, Captain Tor Dain. Your man Hrrru has shown to be honorable, and I believe your words."

Vas wanted to take Deven and Abiel into Abiel's office until Terel got down there, but Abiel had been fighting to keep people out. Keeping it shut and locked was the best idea until he recovered.

"Qaan, could you and Hrrru check both groups for injured? I don't care what happens to the attackers."

She gave a tip of her head. "Of course, Captain Tor Dain." Then she and Hrrru left.

"Roha and Marwin, stay here and guard these two." Vas looked down at Deven. "I need to get a better idea of what happened." At Roha's nod, Vas jogged into the front room. A group of the Welischians were gathering the injured—and tying up the enemies.

Vas never liked having to take over another merc's group, but it had happened before when the leaders were killed during multi-troop campaigns. Granted, Abiel and his people weren't mercs, but they were close enough.

The front of the house was a minor war scene.

Glazlie nodded as she approached. "I saw another of our shuttles landing in the clearing. Medical?"

"Hopefully. How many of the seriously injured are ours?"

"Just two low-level telepaths. The other fighters didn't seem as prepared as they should have been. And to be honest, they were kind of shitty fighters. The two telepaths were Ziol and Roxien. They did the screaming bit until Marwin came out and punched them. I have them under those trees where they won't get stomped on."

Qaan and Hrrru came jogging from the back.

"The entire jail is nothing but rubble. Luckily there was a security shield on the supplies. Abiel would have been furious if we lost those." Qaan's face dropped. "He is going to be okay, right?" She previously appeared to be a consummate professional, but not right now.

"I have the best team of medics in the Commonwealth, the real one, coming in right now." Vas pointed to Terel, Larrisa, Pela, Divee, and two others as they ran across the clearing toward them. "They'll be okay. We should gather all of your injured together and give them a chance to work."

Terel set up a triage under the trees where the two unconscious crew were.

"I've got Marwin and Roha guarding Deven and Abiel. I can have them brought out once you're set up."

Terel looked around where mobile injured were making their way to them. "We'll be set up in a few, might as well go get them" Gurneys and triage beds quickly appeared. Terel motioned for Pela and Divee to grab two and follow Vas.

"Stay with Terel, just in case," Vas said to Glazlie. Then she, Pela, and Divee went to retrieve Deven and Abiel. There was no way to be certain that there weren't more enemies hiding.

The Welischians had moved the injured, dead, and captured people from the front of the house but Roha and Marwin were still standing guard over Deven and Abiel.

"How sturdy is that door?" Vas wasn't sure what Abiel had been protecting, but keeping his office safe was a good idea.

Roha knocked on it. "It seems solid. But one of those grenades could take it out."

"My thoughts as well." Vas stepped back as Deven and Abiel were loaded onto the cots. "I'm keeping you two here. There's no idea what the enemy is doing and until we know things are secure, we plan on everyone being out to get us. Or get what's in that office."

"Aye, captain!" Both said at the same time.

Pela and Divee took the injured men outside.

Vas followed but did a full walk-through of the entire building. The damage wasn't as bad as it would have been with blasters, but still impressive. Along with the front door, two side doors were blown open. The one in the back that Abiel originally sent Vas and Deven out of was still solid. A tap on it told her why—it was reinforced tilian. An exceedingly tough metal found and processed only on the Welischian home world.

Having so many Welischians living on Solar had many advantages.

She went to the front and found Qaan and Hrrru with a group of warrior Welischians. Vas didn't think there were such things, but they appeared ready to go back to fighting.

"Could you have some of your people guard the three destroyed doors? I don't think we can trust that the attackers are all dead or gone."

"We can do that, Captain Tor Dain. I hate to think what would have happened if this attack happened without your people here. We weren't ready." Qaan sighed and looked at the blasted front door. "I told Abiel we needed to fortify all the entrances."

After seeing the tilian door, Vas agreed with Qaan. "Why didn't he agree?"

"Abiel's a good man. But he's been operating in stealth mode since the old government was in charge. He still felt that was the best way, and that heavier defenses would give things away."

"I'd say that ship has flown."

Qaan looked around. "Very much so."

Vas' comm buzzed. "Excuse me." She nodded to Qaan and turned away to answer the comm.

"Captain, I've punched through!" Xsit was so excited

that her words were almost too high to hear. "I can reach Ragkor! And he thinks that together we can drop the barricade around the Commonwealth."

CHAPTER TWENTY-ONE

"CAN YOU SEND THE CALL to me?" Vas asked.
Xsit gave an unhappy chirp. "Sorry, no. I tried twice, I wanted to surprise you."

"You still did great. I'll come up with the injured. Keep Ragkor on the line as long as you can." Vas ended the call and ran to where Terel and Divee were loading Deven, Abiel, the other unconscious telepaths, and the seriously injured of Abiel's people into the shuttle. The rest of her people were treating the walking wounded.

"Are you heading up? Xsit has reached Ragkor."

"I have to. I can't figure out what's impacting the telepaths and need my labs." Terel grinned. "I could use a pilot, then I could leave Divee to help the others."

Vas gave an elaborate bow. "I would be honored to serve. Let me update the rest of the ground crew."

Vas hit her comm. "Roha? I'm heading for the ship. You, Marwin, and Gon are in charge. The Welischians should be guarding the busted doors now."

"Even better, they're already working on rebuilding the two on the sides. Qaan has some people getting special door material from their compound."

Vas could guess what that was, regardless of what Abiel wanted before. The time for secrecy for these people was long gone. "Keep me informed. I'll send the shuttle back once we're unloaded." She was surprised that Mac hadn't forced his way back down here as it was.

Roha confirmed and Vas went into the loaded shuttle. Deven and the other telepaths looked like they were sleeping—aside from the entire not waking up part.

Once Terel triple-checked that everyone was secured and the doors were locked, Vas lifted the shuttle into the air.

Terel slid into the seat next to her but continued to keep an eye on her patients. "How was the fighting?"

"Refreshing, but oddly not as bad as I would have expected. There were more of them than us, and even though the Welischians were fierce, I was surprised at how quickly we won. I'd guess that the Lethians, and anyone else behind the fake Commonwealth, weren't ready for a fight."

"None of them were Commonwealth?"

"They were using twenty-year-old uniforms. I seriously doubt that if the Commonwealth took Solar over they'd do that. Solar has been mostly isolated so no one on the planet had any idea."

"Why am I strapped down and why are my jaw and head fighting for pain dominance?" Deven wasn't putting much effort into getting out of his seat and his eyes were mostly closed in pain.

Terel went to check on him as Vas brought the shuttle into the landing bay. "I punched you. Something down there attacked all the telepaths and you all started screaming. It was annoying."

Abiel and the rest of the telepaths started moaning as they regained consciousness and faced the same discomfort as Deven.

"Damn, I remember something. I couldn't move and there was a force in my head trying to shut me down. It hit all the telepaths?"

"That we know of. There didn't appear to be any among the attackers—at least none that survived. But all of ours and Abiel's had the same reaction." Vas landed the shuttle as Cassiel and two more medical crew came out once the shields were in place.

"I'm fine now, I don't need to be prodded." Deven had

already removed the seat straps but laid back down at Terel's glare.

"No. What hit you all was a weapon, a damn scary one that we can't be certain is limited to Solar. I'm going to go talk to Ragkor—you can join me after Terel clears you." Vas flashed an evil grin and ran out of the landing bay.

Her smile dropped as she ran to the command deck. The Commonwealth mostly ignored or locked up telepaths, but they had never invented something that could take them out in mass like that. Whoever did this needed to be stopped.

The command deck was calmer than usual, mostly due to fewer of the normal troublemakers. Vas ran to Xsit. Gosta started to get out of the captain's chair once he saw her, but Vas waved him off.

"Stay there for now, not sure how long I'll be up here. Oh, anything from that Lethian ship?"

"Nothing. Aside from them annoying Flarik by remaining quiet. She's back in her room now."

Vas nodded and held her hand out to Xsit who handed over an extra set of earphones. They were far bulkier than normal ones but excellent at focusing sound.

"I had to bring out the big ones, but it's working. There's a short delay in the conversation but we think that's something to do with the barricade."

Vas nodded and adjusted the earphones. "Ragkor?"

His response came a few moments later. "Captain! It is so good to hear you." Even through the earphones, his voice was tinny and distant. But there was no doubt that it was her former second-in-command.

"Xsit says you have a way for us to take down the barricade?"

Another delay. "Aye. It'll involve shoving a ship through the barricade, charging it from both sides before the barricade can kick it out, and then exploding it. We tried it on this side, but the frequency is different for you. Someone on your side created that thing and latched on to the Commonwealth's barricade."

"Let me get Gosta." Vas waved Gosta over and Xsit handed him her pair of earphones.

Another delay. "Can we get Deven in on this too?"

"We've had some adventures out here close to the barricade and Deven has to be cleared by Terel first." Vas would like to ask Ragkor if he'd ever heard of a device to take out a bunch of telepaths, but the delay in communications was annoying. And it could wait until they took down the barricade.

Vas wasn't the science brain that a lot of her crew were, including Gosta and Ragkor. But she caught most of the plan. It wasn't as simplistic as Ragkor originally said, but it wasn't that far off.

"We need to wait until we've sorted out our telepaths and the people on the planet—and get everyone back home. I have a feeling there will be some backlash there when the barricade drops. And the news gets out that they weren't ever really part of the Commonwealth." Vas didn't visit Home that often, but just hearing Ragkor's voice made her want to go there sooner rather than later.

"Aye, captain. And we'll need to calculate the exact size of ship you'll need to find and what to hit it with on both sides."

Vas looked to Gosta. "You two can work this out, right? Hrrru will probably be one of the last of our people to come up."

Gosta grinned. He was in his element. "We can indeed."

Vas nodded to him, handed the earphones back to Xsit, and then ran for the lift—to find Bathie and Mac coming up.

"Bathie, take the deck, Gosta's working on getting that barricade down."

"Aye, captain!" She jogged over to the captain's chair.

"What do you need me to do, captain?" Mac asked.

Vas was going to send him to the pilot chair, but she wanted a shuttle on the planet as long as she had people down there. "Get a strike team and go down to wait for the cleanup then bring up the rest of our people."

Mac's eyes widened at 'strike team' but he didn't say anything.

"Yes, I want you to have backup. There's some serious stuff happening on that planet and I believe we caught the enemy off-guard—we can't underestimate them though. We can't get any more involved right now. Once their people are cleared by Terel, and sent back down, we're off to break that barricade. I don't need any more surprises."

Mac shrugged and followed her into the lift.

Vas got off the lift on the med bay floor, leaving Mac to continue to the landing bay.

The good news was that most of their patients were now awake enough to be annoyed at Terel and her people doing the final checks. Including Vas' crew.

The door slid open behind Vas and Jasiel came running in. "Oh good, you're back. There's something wrong with that planet down there."

"What's wrong with my planet?" Abiel's voice rang out from across the med bay. He might still be on a bed, but he sounded robust—and concerned.

"Aside from the fact that it was taken over by the Lethian Assembly and fake Commonwealth guards. And has a possibly extremely deadly mutation in its core, nothing." Vas answered before Jasiel could.

"Indeed, what the captain said." Jasiel gave a sweet old lady smile as she approached Abiel. "I'm Sister Jasiel, nice to meet you." She shook Abiel's hand and started asking simple questions about his planet and his life. Or seemingly simple ones.

Vas shrugged and stepped back. Jasiel worked on her

own agenda and it was often better to let her run with it. Within reason.

"I can't find what attacked the telepaths. There's no residue in any tests I've run, and they all seem fine now. But we do have another problem." Terel motioned for Vas to follow her to a back room as Jasiel continued interrogating Abiel.

Yesenia, Lucan, and the others who'd been rescued from the barn were in the decon chamber. And still unconscious.

"These are more concerning. They're fine according to the machines. *All* the machines. Aside from the fact that they can't, or won't, regain consciousness." Terel's glare at the people in the room was fierce. She often took patients' failure to behave rationally—whether it was their fault or not—as a personal affront.

"You think they don't *want* to wake up? What was done to them?" Vas watched as two medical personnel in full decon suits monitored the patients.

"I have no idea. I'm hoping that once Abiel and Deven are clear they can try and reach them telepathically. I don't believe it's the same thing that hit the telepaths during your fight, but it could be related. But I've no idea if any of them are telepaths."

Vas watched them. They simply looked to be asleep. "I'm pretty sure that Yesenia is a powerful telepath. And there was something odd about her. A weird pressure hit my head sometimes when I was near her."

"Really? That might explain things. I have a feeling that she was the focus of whatever attacked them. Then she affected the rest."

"The focus? Someone used her to take them out?" There were a lot of dangerous things with telepaths going on down there.

"Hard to explain, but…" Terel cut her comment off and her eyes widened while watching the patients.

Vas turned back to the decon room. Yesenia was sitting up. Eyes closed, but she seemed to be fighting to wake up. "What the? Ow!" Vas dropped to the floor as a stabbing pain went through her skull.

Terel grabbed her. "What's wrong? Vas, look into my eyes."

Vas tried but her eyes were watering in pain. "No idea. Something squished my brain. Yesenia?"

Terel looked back into the room but kept her hand on Vas' shoulder. "She still has her eyes closed. Four of the others are starting to twitch now, the rest are still. Are they telepaths?"

"No idea." Vas took a deep breath and pulled in some of her Keeper training to calm her mind. The pain slowly pushed aside. "Damn, that wasn't fun." She got to her feet.

"No, you stay seated until I sort this out."

"We can help with that." Deven and Abiel came down the corridor with Divee tagging behind and appearing annoyed.

"Sorry, Terel. They forced their way out of their beds." Divee scowled at both men.

"We're fine, trust me. But they might not be. Abiel told me how strong of a telepath Yesenia is. She's at least as strong as me—if not more so. Possibly a lot more." From the odd look on his face, there was something Deven wasn't saying.

Something he didn't want Abiel to know.

Vas nodded. "You two can go in there and check them, but in full suits." She raised her hand to stop everyone from complaining. "Terel, you're a great doctor, but you have said you're not a telepath expert. Deven and Abiel, I don't care if those suits can't stop a mental attack—there could be more things going on and they're the best things we have. Divee, thank you for trying to stop these two. But you can go back to work on the others."

Divee looked relieved as he turned and ran back to the main med bay.

Abiel and Deven were irritated, but Vas didn't care. The lingering pain from whatever hit her head gave her an annoyed disposition that wasn't even tolerating Deven's attempted refusal.

"Suits or remain outside." She folded her arms and noticed that Terel did the same.

Deven went for one of the suits. "It's easier to surrender."

Abiel shrugged and joined him.

"You going in too?" Vas asked Terel, as she seemed torn.

"Not yet. My people have this covered and those two will take care of any telepathic issues. And Yesenia is now fully awake."

Vas turned to the glass. Deven and Abiel—in their decon suits—were coming in when Yesenia jumped off the medical bed and ran toward both men, yelling. That it wasn't a language Vas had heard before was almost more disturbing.

Deven stepped in front of Abiel and held his arms out— he also brokenly spoke in the language Yesenia used.

"What are they saying?" Vas asked without looking away. They had translators everywhere on the ship. Yet whatever they were speaking wasn't being translated.

"No idea. But whatever Deven said, it worked."

Yesenia stopped with her hand raised to hit Deven. Then she started shaking and collapsed.

Abiel started swearing and carried Yesenia to her cot.

Vas hit her comm to Deven. "What in the hell was she saying and how did you know what language it was?"

Deven watched Yesenia for a few moments before answering. "She was speaking an archaic version of Asar-laí."

CHAPTER TWENTY-TWO

DEVEN PAUSED, THEN CONTINUED. "A dialect far older than Marli's, so I didn't catch all of it. But roughly, she said the Universe killers were coming and we needed to flee or be consumed."

"Are you sure?"

"Not completely sure about the exact translation, but the dialect was close enough to Marli's that I know it was a type of Asarlaí." His face and voice were neutral.

"How did she learn that?" Vas felt a chill. Could Yesenia be some new type of Asarlaí clone? One that missed being destroyed like the rest? Aside from the weird pressure in her head—which she didn't feel at all right now—Yesenia had seemed like a good kid. But they couldn't let any Asarlaí survive.

"She's not an Asarlaí." Abiel looked up fiercely. "I would have noticed."

"No one is saying she is, but the Asarlaí left behind some strange things." Deven kept his voice soothing, but Vas could tell he was upset about this.

So was she.

"I still have Asarlaí markers in my database and we can find out for sure." Terel slammed open the outer door and almost forced open the interior one when it was too slow.

"You didn't know that it wasn't the real Commonwealth who took over Solar," Vas said to Abiel as she came to the foot of Yesenia's bed. "How many Asarlaí have you met?"

Abiel's face flushed. "Good point, and I know you and

your crew fought the Asarlaí clones. But Yesenia is Yesenia—there's nothing else."

Lucan was the first of the others to get off his cot—not gracefully, but he stumbled over and leaned on the edge of Yesenia's bed. "What's wrong with Yesenia?"

Vas hid her smile. Even barely able to stand, that boy was smitten with Yesenia. Vas hoped for his sake that there was a simple, non-killer-Asarlaí reason behind what Yesenia was.

"They're not sure. Just some oddities." Abiel had been frowning but forced a smile as he turned to Lucan. "But I don't think you should be up just yet, right, Doctor?"

Terel had come back with a new machine and was pulling it over to Yesenia. "Ah, yes. He should be recovering in the front med room." She looked around. "Everyone from Solar who is awake should be. I'm sure you're all anxious to get back home. Aside from Abiel who will stay here with Yesenia until she wakes up." Her grin wasn't nearly as practiced as Abiel's but it worked.

"I should stay too." Lucan kept watching Yesenia's face so he missed the frown Abiel gave Terel. He wanted Lucan out of the room.

"Not right now." Deven took Lucan's arm. "Come on, everyone. They can help her faster without you all here."

With a final look at Yesenia, Lucan and the others followed Deven and one of the medics out.

"How's it going pulling up those Asarlaí files?" Honestly, Vas was surprised that Terel had brought copies with them on the *Defiant Ruin*, then the space station, and now here. But she was grateful for her friend's paranoia in this case.

"Not as fast as I'd like." Terel nodded to Abiel. "You can take the suit off if you'd like. Asarlaí blood or not, she's not contagious."

"What?" Abiel blinked his eyes and patted the suit as he

caught what she said. "Good idea. I was mentally trying to reach her, but it's like there's a block of some kind." He twisted around and took off the suit. "Is she really some sort of Asarlaí? If so, how? I knew her mother briefly. She didn't show any signs of being anything more than human."

"What about her father?" Vas kept an eye on Terel, but the level of annoyed muttering coming from her as she hunched over the machine she'd brought in indicated they couldn't do anything else yet.

Abiel shrugged. "Yesenia never met him and her mother wouldn't talk about him, beyond implying that she hoped he was dead and that keeping Yesenia away from him was essential. It was one of the reasons that she abandoned Yesenia when she was young." He frowned. "Not the best option, she had to hide her in the orphan system. But it kept her safe."

Terel jumped up. "I found it. I need to clean up these files. I grabbed copies of everything in *Warrior Wench's* medical data when we left the Commonwealth. *Everything.*"

"Well, you can sort it out when we go to Home." Vas looked up as Terel glared at her. "Oh, yeah. Xsit got through to Ragkor, and he and Gosta are working out how to take down that barricade." She shrugged at Terel's and Deven's looks of annoyed surprise. "Sorry, there's been a lot going on. I assume that Jasiel is working with the injured?"

"Yes, in her way." Deven went to Terel's computers. "She'd like to come see Yesenia, but wants to make sure the rest are okay first."

Abiel looked up from staring at Yesenia. "Nice lady, she didn't say what religious order she was with though."

"Jasiel is a Clionea nun. A very powerful one."

Abiel paled. "We'd heard they'd died."

"They had some troubles, but as you saw, they're here.

She's the eight-hundred-year-old nun I mentioned before."

He shook his head. "Wow. Well, good to know they're still around."

Vas shared a look with Deven. Right now, there was only one. But the more people who believed the nuns were in place and active, the better.

Terel spun through the files, stopped to draw fresh blood from Yesenia,

and then went back into data diving.

"Can you reach Yesenia?" Abiel looked at Deven as he held Yesenia's hand.

Deven scowled. "I tried when I spoke to her and just now. It's as if I can almost reach her, but there's a fog in the way."

Abiel nodded. "That's what I hit too. She will be okay, right?"

Terel nodded, looked back down, then up again. "Yes." She looked at Vas and Deven and tilted her head. There was more to say, but she was asking if it was okay to say it in front of Abiel.

Yesenia had no known living family, and it seemed that Abiel and his group had become that family. He needed to know. Vas and Deven nodded.

"Not sure how it got there, but there are faint traces of Asarlaí blood—not the clone Asarlaís, but the originals—in Yesenia."

"She's one of *them*?" Abiel appeared concerned but didn't release Yesenia's hand.

"Yes and no." Terel sent one of her files up to the screen on the wall. "These markers here, are Asarlaí. But as you can see, they're few and not strong. Someone way down her family tree was an Asarlaí—something always thought to be impossible, as they were genetically incapable of mixing with other species." She frowned at the screen. "Or so we thought."

Deven walked closer to Yesenia. "But that wouldn't explain her language acquisition." From the focus on his face, he was trying to telepathically reach out to her.

The decon doors opened and a clearly concerned Jasiel came in as Deven spoke. "She was speaking Asarlaí, was she? There's something odd afoot. Three of the others each said short sentences in what I assume was Asarlaí. They didn't act like they had any idea what they said, or even that they said it." Without asking, she came to Yesenia and put one hand on her forehead and one over her heart. Then closed her eyes.

Yesenia had been twitching, but not waking up. The movement stopped when Jasiel touched her and her breathing returned to normal.

Jasiel opened her eyes and took a step back.

"Abiel?" Yesenia's voice was rough and Terel handed her a cup of water. Which didn't do much for the confusion on Yesenia's face. "Where am I?"

Vas moved closer. "On my ship. What do you recall?"

Yesenia finished her water and then responded. "We were going to do recon on that barn. Tyil attacked Lucan, so Govlia had to shoot him, and we crashed. Armed guards grabbed us." Her eyes narrowed and she shook her head. "That's all until right now. Could I have some more water, please?"

Abiel watched Deven but didn't say anything. He did step back to let Deven come next to her.

"You don't remember anything else?" Deven asked gently as he put his hand on her forehead.

Jasiel watched both of them but didn't say anything.

"Some weird nightmares. Probably due to whatever they knocked us out with." Yesenia looked around. "The others made it, right?"

"They're fine, plus some more of your people they'd grabbed. We took them out of this room for final clearance. You were still unconscious and we were concerned."

Terel smiled. "I'm Terel, the chief medical officer on the *Destroyer's Curse*. It's nice to see you are awake."

Vas then introduced Jasiel. She had no idea how they were going to tell Yesenia that she had trace amounts of Asarlaí blood and had spoken an incredibly old dialect of their language.

Or even if they should tell her. Whatever had been used to knock her and the people with her out might have triggered the reaction. There also was a chance that even though Yesenia might have no idea about it, someone on Solar did.

Abiel, Jasiel, and Terel all looked toward Vas expectantly. Nice.

Vas let out a breath. "This is going to be rough, so I'll cut to the chase. Yesenia, we found trace, extremely trace, markers of the Asarlaí in your blood. Plus, the first time you woke up here, you spoke some version of their language."

Yesenia blinked a few times, then smiled. "This is a joke, right? I'm part Asarlaí?" She held up her hands. "I don't look like them, and I certainly don't feel like taking over the Universe. Although, their powers would be handy." Her words slowed down as she looked at the faces around her. "You're not kidding? Wouldn't that have been noticeable at some point?"

Jasiel patted her hand. "There are many mysteries in this universe. You only recently discovered your telepath skills, didn't you?"

Abiel looked up. "Do you think someone created this?"

"I doubt it." Deven remained standing back but continued to watch Yesenia closely. "From what I'm scanning, she was born with the markers and esper skills. But both had been repressed until recently."

Yesenia drank more water, continuing to look both annoyed and confused, while Vas and Deven went over how they found her and the others.

And what that barn's purpose was.

Yesenia stuck her hands through her hair and left them there. "I'm trying to process things, but this has been a hell of a day."

Jasiel's smile was full soothing grandmother now. "If Vas and Terel don't mind, what say we go and discuss things a bit more? Deven and I plus a friend you haven't met yet, Aithnea, might be able to figure out our next steps."

Yesenia gave a half-shrug half-nod, but Abiel scowled.

"I would like to be there as well." He didn't appear defensive, but he also looked like it wasn't an option. He viewed Yesenia as an adopted daughter.

Yesenia's smile was genuine. "I would like that. Could I get some food, too? Wherever we're going?"

Vas laughed. "By all means. The small conference room, Jasiel?" Along with the *Destroyer's Curse* being massively larger than the unlamented *Traitor's Folly*, it was exceedingly meeting focused. There were two floors dedicated to assorted meeting spaces. The smallest was the easiest to deal with in Vas' opinion.

"Of course. Come along, we'll have Aithnea order some food." Jasiel's smile faded when she turned away from Yesenia and met Vas' eyes.

Vas nodded—if they needed her they'd call. Jasiel was simply warning her that things might get weirder than they already were.

Jasiel led Yesenia and Abiel out.

Deven stayed behind until both sets of doors closed. "This is going to be interesting. I was trying to see if Yesenia was duplicitous, but she wasn't. She genuinely has no idea about any of this."

The three walked out but Deven turned toward the smaller lift that went to the meeting rooms. "I'll keep you both updated."

"I'm going to clear all the Solarians, but I won't release them down to the planet until you finish." Terel was sober.

Vas knew there was a chance that they couldn't let Yesenia go.

CHAPTER TWENTY-THREE

V AS RETURNED TO THE COMMAND deck. With luck, Gosta and Ragkor had made progress on bringing down the barricade.

"Any news?" Vas asked as she walked over. Gosta and Xsit were still wearing their earphones and from her animated stance, Xsit was actively contributing to whatever was being planned.

Bathie glanced up at Vas' arrival. "Those three are talking so fast that I had to tune them out. But, Gosta and Xsit became excited a few minutes ago, so I think they figured out something. Mac and Walvento made it down to the surface, but aside from the clean-up, and Hrrru not wanting to leave, things aren't exciting down there. Mac's words, not mine."

"As in Hrrru seriously wants to leave our crew, or not want to leave the planet at this point?" Vas had a policy that as long as it wasn't during a fight, or any other time that might cause difficulty to the rest of the crew, if any crew member chose to leave they were free to do so.

An unhappy merc was a dangerous merc. Not that she thought any of her people would deliberately cause problems—she wouldn't have brought them on board if that were the case. But if they were unhappy where they were, their focus was split. Fighting for the lives of yourself and the crew wasn't a good time to have a focus issue.

She honestly never thought Hrrru would leave.

Bathie glanced over to Gosta but he was intently debating something with Ragkor. "I don't know, to be honest. Finding a group of his people who have moved beyond their home world and are fighting to change things seems to be enticing for him. Personally, I hope he doesn't decide to leave."

"Same here. But it is his choice. I'm going to see what they've sorted out." Vas turned to the communications console but spun back. "Any changes on that Lethian science ship?"

"No movement and no comm response. I think we can assume they aren't what they want us to believe."

Vas glared at the screen that held the stationary ship before continuing to communications. "Agreed."

Xsit had her head tilted as she listened to Ragkor through the headset. Gosta was a few feet away and muttering under his breath, but also scribbling like mad on his pad.

Xsit looked up, removed her headset, and waved to Vas. "We found what we needed to blast through that barricade with a ship." She wasn't hopping, but her smile was huge. Then it dropped. "But the specifics of the ship needed might be a problem. The best one nearby appears to be that Lethian science ship. Of course, there aren't many ships in this area, so maybe something else further away could be found?"

"We need to get that barricade down soon. We don't have time to search for something else." Vas tapped on Gosta's shoulder.

His jump told her what she'd suspected. He was so caught up that he hadn't noticed her coming over. Or probably even that she was on the deck.

"Captain! Hold on, Ragkor, the captain's here." Gosta pushed over his earphones. "Is everyone up from the planet?"

"No. And we have people with us who should be down on the planet as well. Xsit says we can use that Lethian ship?" Not that she objected to blowing up one of their vessels, not with everything they'd done to create this barricade, among other things, but they might put up a fight. Science ship or not, they were most likely not going to agree to turn over their ship for destruction.

And theoretically, she and her crew were going to need the Lethian Assembly to fight alongside them when the time came to challenge the Clongari.

Stealing and destroying one of their ships wasn't going to win points.

"It does look like a perfect fit," Gosta said. "The only other ship anywhere near here that almost meets the requirements would be the *Solar*. But it's too short and narrow to carry the charge correctly. Neither Ragkor nor I believe it would conduct enough power to blow the barricade."

"Not to mention that I don't think the Solarians would be up for us destroying their ship," Vas said.

"Can I speak to Ragkor?" Vas held her hand out. If they didn't need these old headsets, she'd move them into her ready room.

Gosta handed her his set. "Here you go, I need to see what that ship is doing." He ran to his station.

"Hi Ragkor, so we can do this? For sure?"

"Hi, Captain Tor Dain…Vas." Ragkor caught himself. She might be the one running this show, but she had told him that as a captain himself, he should use her first name.

She'd been telling him that since she brought him on board as her second-in-command years ago. Maybe in a few more years that military training of his would fade.

Ragkor coughed. "Yes, we can do it. Gosta, Xsit, and I repeatedly ran through the simulations. The ship channeling the explosion will create a cascade collapse in the barricade and crash those beacons the entire way across the Commonwealth."

"Once we get a ship and rig it with explosives." Walvento wouldn't be happy about losing the explosives, but

Vas was still more concerned about getting the Lethian Assembly ship.

"There is that."

"Captain? That Lethian ship has engaged engines and weapons are now online. It's coming our way and continues to refuse to answer hails." Gosta didn't sound concerned compared to anyone else. But for him, he was heading toward full freak-out mode.

"Damn it. Sorry, Ragkor, but our best weapon for that barricade is being stupid. Stay on the line with Xsit in case things turn quickly."

There wasn't anything he or any of their people in the Commonwealth could do until they broke that barricade, but she didn't want to take the chance that terminating the call would mean they couldn't get Ragkor back.

Vas reclaimed the captain's chair from Bathie who ran to her science station. "Flarik? Did you get any further response from those Lethians?"

Flarik's voice was so annoyed that Vas was glad she wasn't on the command deck right now. "No. And my brief interaction didn't convince me they are Lethian Assembly scientists. The ship might be, but the beings on it are *questionable.*"

If it were anyone else, Vas would ask how she knew. But Flarik had already impressive instincts that were increasing in strength—most likely due to her psychic baby. "Thank you, Flarik. Similar to the fake Nhali cruiser we ran up against?" She had hoped the Clongari were staying at the other end of the universe. That they could be right here almost made her rethink destroying the barricade. Not that it would probably hold against those beings for long.

"I don't believe they are the same." Flarik paused and lowered her voice even though with a closed comm only Vas would hear her. "My child did not like them. *At all.*" Flarik wasn't into the entire bit about her unborn baby being an up-and-coming spiritual bigwig for her people. But she was sensitive to the changes inside her body.

"Thank you." Vas ended the call, then hit the comm to Deven.

"Vas?" he sounded distracted, most likely still sorting Yesenia out.

"We have a problem. Something's wrong with that Lethian Assembly science ship and it's coming our way. Sort of. Damn it, they adjusted their direction. Whatever's going on we need you up here." She cut the call as she watched the science ship slowly alter course.

"Gosta, is that vessel aiming for the planet?" It appeared to be entering orbit around Solar.

"It is. It will hit the outer atmosphere in five minutes."

"We have to stop them; we need that ship intact." And she didn't think whatever it was up to was going to be beneficial to the Solarians.

Vas' comm buzzed as Deven came on deck. Along with Abiel and Yesenia.

"Vas here." She nodded to the three. Not sure why he brought them up, but she wasn't going to worry about it right now.

"Captain?" Mac's voice was faint. Communications had cleared up with the planet, but whatever the Lethian ship was doing was messing with that again.

"What's going on?" Vas knew the odds of Mac contacting her in a case of less than a disaster were slim.

"We're getting shaken up—literally. Earthquakes all over. Qaan reached out to a group of Welischians on another continent, they're getting them too. Small right now, but seem to be growing."

"Get our people together and lift off if you have to." Vas turned to Gosta. "Earthquakes on the planet. Is it our friends?" The Lethian ship assumed orbit around the planet. At least it wasn't aiming to crash into the place, but being in orbit might not be that much better.

Gosta switched to his second terminal and started swearing. The specific words weren't loud enough to be understood, but the sentiment was. "It is. I can scan them completely now, those *are* Lethians. They might have been behind the incident with the core and are trying another tactic."

Yesenia and Abiel had been examining the massive bridge, but she walked closer to the screen that showed Solar.

"We need to get back and stop them." Then she muttered a few words in what sounded to Vas like the same language she used in the decon room and collapsed.

Abiel got to her first, but Deven was right behind him.

"What happened to her?" Abiel held her.

Deven checked her eyes and pulse. "She's asleep. Whatever is triggering this response is messing with her body. It's as if there are things it wants her to do, but she's not an Asarlaí."

Flarik came stomping off the lift. "That ship needs to be stopped. Blown apart if need be. They're secret ops of the Lethian Assembly." Her claws kept extending and retracting.

"And they must have known about the Clongari ruse we faced earlier. Options, people. We don't want that ship to continue whatever it is planning. And we do need it to blow up the barricade." She didn't feel bad about stealing their ship now.

Mac called her again. "The quakes on the planet are getting worse. I've got all of our people and as many Solarians in the shuttle as I can."

"Lift off, but stay away from that ship. Come up here. We'll send down more shuttles for as many of Abiel's people as we can get."

Abiel looked up. "Thank you."

Yesenia shook her head and looked around. "I heard

the weird stuff this time. But in my head it made sense. Can I have a pad and stylus?"

Bathie brought her both and Yesenia started scribbling furiously. "It's already fading. But here's what I recall." She handed it to Deven and got to her feet.

"This says that all who come this way will be killed. The people have claimed this world and no harm will come to it unless it is through them. Death to invaders." He paused. "The people refer to the Asarlaí. In their minds no other beings were people."

"Not as helpful as I'd hoped." Yesenia shrugged. "It made more sense in that other language."

"Solar is booby-trapped?" Xsit had been listening in.

"That's what it sounds like," Deven said. "But it sounds like a trap for any attackers, not the locals." Which might or might not be true. The Asarlaí *really* didn't like other races.

Yesenia rubbed her temples. "I know a lot is going on right now, but why did I hear them again?"

Deven shrugged. "I don't know. But something is working through you. Gosta, how are the earthquakes?"

Gosta looked up long enough to scowl. "Expanding. And that Lethian ship is definitely behind it." He called up a map. "Look at this. The earthquakes are following it."

"Then why are there quakes on the other side of the world as well?" Yesenia seemed glad to leave the Asarlaí issue aside for now and Vas didn't blame her.

Gosta's swearing increased and Deven ran to his station.

"Yup. From the readouts, it looks like there must be a smaller cloaked ship pacing the Lethian one on the other side of the planet. Whatever they are doing to cause this, they're working in sync. And they're picking up speed."

CHAPTER TWENTY-FOUR

"DAMN IT." VAS TURNED BEHIND her. "Abiel, can you get your ship to come help? We need the Lethian Assembly vessel intact, but we need to stop them both if we want to save your planet."

Abiel paled as he watched the destruction on the screen. Then shook himself and reached for his comm. "We leave a skeleton crew on board at all times." He pointed to an unattended station and went there when Vas nodded.

Deven turned from his station. "We can send fighters after them, but there's no guarantee that they don't have their own. Not to mention, if we want to keep that ship in one piece, we'll need a lot more fighters than what we have."

They'd picked up twenty-five Hivian fighters when they'd claimed the *Destroyer's Curse*. Nice, but Vas agreed, they weren't going to be enough.

Vas hit her comm. "Shien? Any of your pilots itching to see some action?"

"Vas, nice to hear from you. Yes, my people appear to be getting bored. What do you have in mind?"

Vas quickly told her about needing the Lethian ship intact, what it was doing, and what the Pilthian fighters would be up to if they chose to engage. She wasn't certain that Shien would go for it. This wasn't a life and death situation for the *Destroyer's Curse* and those fighters were the Pilthians' only way of travel if they had to leave Vas' ship.

But Shien quickly agreed to send half of her fighters out to help take down, but not destroy, the Lethian Assembly science ship.

Abiel rose from the station he'd been at. "We can help, but we don't have enough crew to man the fighters. Most of my pilots are still in the compound."

Vas called down to Mac. "Once you bring up who you have now from Solar, I need you to go back to the compound and find as many of Abiel's pilots as you can and take them to the ship *Solar.*"

"Got it. When I drop these Solarians up on our ship, can I swing by and swap with someone who's not flying a fighter to run the pilots to Solar? I'd like to take a fighter out."

Vas laughed. "I didn't mention us sending fighters."

"Nope, but it was implied. If they are, we are." Mac's voice grew choppy. "I'm heading for the landing bay."

"Thank you." Vas wasn't going to fight Mac—he was cocky, but he was also one of her best pilots.

Abiel watched the screen. "Thank you. My best fighter pilots are up here. Yesenia, Lucan, and Govlia have clocked more airtime than anyone else in my group. And I'd like to lead my ship in."

Shien and Khirson came on deck, Khirson was in one of the Pilthians' fighter suits.

"We can take you over to your ship. Or rather, my consort can." Shien gave a small bow.

Whoever Mac was switching with would get more of the pilots from the compound with the transport, but this would hopefully speed things along.

"Thank you!" Yesenia looked ready to start bowing. "I didn't know your people were still around." She flushed but it didn't dim her enthusiasm.

Shien grinned. "A few of us. Thanks to Vas." She nodded to Khirson and he motioned for Yesenia and Abiel to follow him as they went to the landing bay.

"The rest of the fighter pilots that I'm sending were going to the landing bay directly." Shien took over an empty station. "My people were getting bored but I don't know that this was what they had in mind. They're restless for a world we can call our own. Or at least a continent."

"I don't blame them. Maybe once we get the barricade down we can find something. I do have a planet called Home, but not sure how many open continents we have left. We were still taking in refugees when we left the Commonwealth."

"Thank you, and not to sound ungrateful, but my people don't have great historical memories of the Commonwealth. I think we can find something out here. Once things settle down."

The wings of fighters, both Vas' and Shien's, launched in waves from the bay. One larger fighter turned and went toward the ship *Solar*.

Vas turned away from the screens. "What do we need to prepare to blow up that barricade? Beyond getting that ship intact."

Xsit chirped. "Ragkor says the ship doesn't have to be functional. As long as the structure is there. We could tow it to the barricade if needed." She glared at the Lethian ship and the destruction on the planet that was visible on one of the large screens. Then snarled, "in case it gets damaged."

"Good to know." Vas turned away before she grinned. She'd thought about taking Xsit off her flagship a few months ago because she didn't have a fighter's instinct—unless drunk. But it seemed she was changing.

"They're using massively adapted sonic interrupters on the planet." Deven pulled up data from his station. "The two ships are working off each other. If we can shut down one of them, it'll stop the attack on the planet."

Flarik took the station next to him. "It is progressively getting worse. They are going to get that core triggered one way or another."

"Not if we can stop it." Vas hit her comm. "Fighters, engage the fake science ship. And we need to decloak that other one." Disabling the science vessel without destroying it was risky, but they had to stop what it was doing.

"On it, captain!" Mac was too enthusiastic when he called in. But as none of the fighters broke formation, at least he was sticking to the plan.

Shien was communicating with her fighters and they worked with Mac and the rest. So far the Lethian Assembly ship hadn't sent out fighters of their own.

"Captain Vas," Abiel's voice came from the comm he'd given her. "We're ready to send fighters and the *Solar* will be able to go after the second ship. Once you decloak it. We're calculating a general area for it, based on the location of the one we can see. But not enough to target."

"Keep your fighters with you when you go after it. I'll send some of ours to follow them." Vas kept looking at the screen of the planet, but the only ship lifting was one of her transports. "Doesn't your world have smaller ships? Transports? Garbage scows? Why aren't they leaving?" Hopefully, they could stop the quakes, but if not, no one down there would survive.

"They do. But with the fake Commonwealth government gone, there's no one to tell them how much danger they're in. Unfortunately, I'm seen as a crackpot and extremist." Abiel didn't try to deny it, but the frustration was clear in his voice.

"Give me the codes for your full planetary communications system." Vas waited until the codes came through then called down to the planet. "This is Captain Vaslisha Tor Dain of the Commonwealth. Your world is in extreme danger. We need everyone who can to board any available ships and lift off. And take as many people with you as possible. This is an order."

Calls started coming in but Vas cut them off with a snarl and broadcasted again. "Do not waste time, get on those damn ships. Your planet is under attack. Leave now!" She put a large dose of bitchiness in her voice and the comm calls from the planet vanished.

Deven grinned back at her. "Well done. I almost thought you were a Commonwealth official myself."

"You take that back." Vas shuddered. After she, Deven, Marli, and their crews rescued the Commonwealth from the Asarlaí clones, she and Deven were hounded by the restructuring administration to join the Commonwealth government. Getting away from them was part of the reason that she fled and took a job outside of the Commonwealth in the first place.

Granted, the biggest reason was Aithnea declaring that the entire Universe was in danger if they didn't get the Clionea nuns up and functioning. But avoiding the Commonwealth government was still enough to help with that motivation.

Deven winked, then turned back to his station.

While she was tracking things on the planet previously, Flarik switched to long-range images on her screen. "Captain, I'm picking up ships coming in from the gate. Two so far but they appear to be waiting for more." She let loose a steady stream of swearing in multiple languages. "They are Lethian Assembly warships."

"Damn it." Vas drummed her fingers on the arms of her chair. It wouldn't take them long to get here.

"Should I hail them, captain?" Xsit set aside her headset communications with Ragkor and looked poised to reach out to the other ships.

"Not yet. But keep watching them, Flarik. Xsit, report

if they reach out to us but don't respond." Vas had a feeling they wouldn't. At least until they got all their ships out of the gate.

"Transports are all back on the ship, captain. The extra Solarians have been taken to the holding bay for now. Should we send them down for more people?" Bathie asked.

Vas watched the gate information. The two ships hadn't moved and it appeared that whoever they were waiting for was having difficulty with the gate.

"It worked." Gosta looked up. "I hope you don't mind, captain, but I attached a virus to the gate as we came in. It was experimental and won't affect anyone leaving." He gave an awkward head bob. "I thought it might be handy in case someone was following us."

"Thank you. But why didn't it impact the Lethian Assembly ship circling the planet? Or those two?" Gosta was brilliant, but his inventions didn't always work on the first few tries. That he hadn't told her about this one before this didn't surprise her.

"There were bugs." He scowled at the screen. "But those two did come through slower than they would have. And from the readings from the gate, there are at least two more ships trapped on the other side."

"Then we have a little time, thank you, Gosta." She'd have Deven get the details and determine the long-term usability of the invention later.

"I've broken through the cloaking system on that second ship circling the planet." Bathie grinned. "I can send the coordinates to all the fighters and the *Solar*."

"Do it. Mac, take half the fighters to join the *Solar* and take that cloaked ship down." Cloaks were tricky beasts and difficult to keep secure. Which was why most people didn't use them.

"On it."

Xsit called out. "Captain, Jasiel has a way to get the

Lethian Assembly ship disinfested of its crew. Her words. She's on her way up."

"It wasn't just her you know." Aithnea's voice was good to hear through the nearest speakers.

"Yup, we both helped her come up with it." Nitya as well. Both sounded extremely smug.

Jasiel ran out of the lift. "I would have told them that you two were involved. We need Gosta to break through their shields and send a code that will trigger the ship to crash."

"We need that thing intact, Jasiel."

"Oh, it will be." Aithnea sounded excited as she responded before Jasiel could. "The ship won't really be crashing, but the fear of it will clear out the crew. I'll be tagging along with the code and Nitya will send support. It'll work."

Vas watched the gate. The two Lethian ships still weren't moving and nothing new had come through. She pulled up the visual of the ship currently shaking up Solar. "Gosta? How tight is their security?"

He grinned. "Not tight enough, captain. I can break into it but not sure how to send Aithnea through." His smile fell. "Nor how to get her back."

"We'll get her back when we claim the ship. I only wish I could go." That was the first time Vas heard Nitya regret, even if only a little, about her choice to meld with the *Destroyer's Curse.*

"This *will* work." Jasiel folded her arms and stood in front of the screen. She was full Clionea nun at this point and appeared ready to fight anyone who dared disagree with her.

Vas studied her for a moment, then shrugged. "We don't have time to look for other options. Do it."

Jasiel grinned and then told Gosta what to do. In minutes the Lethian Assembly ship stopped and its escape pods were flying toward the gate.

Vas gave the order to let them leave the system.

"Captain Tor Dain, we have taken down the smaller ship. Wasn't much of a fight. I think your fighters are disappointed," Abiel called in.

"Excellent. Once things have settled, we'll send down your people."

"Thank you. Do you need us for what you're planning?"

Vas looked around, but Deven, Gosta, and even Xsit all shook their heads. "We're fine. There are two Lethian Assembly ships stuck at the gate, so you probably want to keep in the air for now. Our fighters can stay with yours."

"Good to know, thank you. Abiel out."

"Vas, Aithnea has control of the Lethian ship," Nitya said through a speaker. "The good news is that we won't need to use many, if any, of our explosives to ram the barricade. The bad news is that the ones packed on that ship are going off in five minutes."

CHAPTER TWENTY-FIVE

"WHAT? DAMN IT, THEY WERE planning on crashing into the planet after they shook it apart. Can that ship move on its own?" Vas doubted the Lethians had enough time to booby-trap it, but they'd also been flying with a lot of explosives for a reason. Aithnea sent over the specs and it was more than what they calculated they needed to destroy the barricade.

"Barely. It's going to need a tow." Nitya sounded distracted as she was computing what would be needed. "And we have to get Aithnea out of it immediately."

"I'm fine. Seriously, I'll make sure this thing gets to the point of impact, then dart back. Just give us a boost."

"Captain, the forces that will be around that ship as it hits the barricade will make it impossible for anything to get out—even a disembodied nun." Gosta turned briefly but didn't stop whatever he was calculating. "I agree with Nitya on this. Before we move that ship into the barricade, Aithnea needs to leave."

"Aithnea, I might not be a mother superior anymore, but neither are you." Jasiel snarled. "Get your dead ass out of that ship. *Now.*"

Vas was impressed, there would have been no way she would have defied Jasiel had she been in charge when Vas was a kid.

"But—"

Vas cut Aithnea off. "Nope. You are part of my crew now and I'm still the captain. I agree with them. Gosta and Nitya, get her the hell out of there."

"Give me a second first." Aithnea didn't sound like she was giving up.

Gosta nodded. Ready or not, he and Nitya had a hold on Aithnea.

"Second is over."

"Fine, I'm going to be heavy though."

Vas turned to Jasiel but she shrugged.

"Damn it, something is fighting us." Gosta's hands moved faster than before and Nitya's swearing echoed softly through the comms.

"Got her!" Nitya yelled as Gosta slumped into his seat.

"Aithnea? Are you here?" Vas called out as a data dump filled the screens. "What did you do?"

"Yeehaw! I'm here and I brought over all the info on those buggers that I could grab. And it looks good. Oh, and I triggered the explosives on a two-minute delay, it was the longest I could do, so you might want to throw that ship into the barricade—fast."

"Damn it, Aithnea. Xsit, tell Ragkor to back up, we're sending the ship through. Gosta, give that thing a good nudge." Vas opened the ship-wide comm. "Everyone, secure stations!"

Even expecting it, the jolt as the *Destroyer's Curse* grabbed the Lethian ship with the former Hive grappling system and raced for the barricade was harsh.

Deven managed to move some of whatever data Aithnea brought over to a smaller screen so they could see the barricade flare as the Lethian ship was released and slammed into it.

"Ragkor says he can see the ship on their side—blow it!" Xsit's chirp went to the too high to hear for most species range.

Vas called to Walvento. "Give it some help if you would, but only a few." She didn't doubt about Aithnea setting it to go off. But better more explosives than fewer in a one-shot deal.

"Aye!" Walvento's response was in sync with a group of missiles hitting the Lethian ship. Then the ship exploded. They were still too close, so the *Destroyer's Curse's* shields took enough hits to cause a warning alarm around the deck. But the beacons lining the barricade exploded across the dark space as the collapse went to the far end of Commonwealth space.

Vas had a moment of concern when ten ships were facing them from the other side instead of only one. Then she saw the *Warrior Wench* and *Victorious Dead*. "Ragkor! You brought the entire team?"

"Most of them, captain. Don't worry, Grosslyn is on Home with two of our ships and has his massive guns ready for the hordes that will be rushing in once the barricade falls. His words, by the way."

Vas was so happy to see them, that she wasn't going to give him grief about calling her captain. "It's damn good to see you all. We still have fighters out around the planet, but we should be able to wrap things up—"

"Captain! My virus on the gate fell!" Gosta didn't yell or flail his hands often, but he was doing both this time. Things were bad.

"Hold on Ragkor, we might have a problem."

The *Warrior Wench* and *Victorious Dead* came out of the Commonwealth.

"You mean those Lethian Assembly ships? And a pair of Hive ships following them? I do like your converted Hive ship, by the way. Almost thought we were facing a crew of Wavians." Therlian called in from the *Victorious Dead*. A former novitiate of the Clionea nuns, Vas offered her the command of any ship after the battle against the Asarlaí clones. She chose to stay with Ragkor as his second on the *Victorious Dead*. Obviously, she'd taken temporary captainship when Ragkor had to take over the *Warrior Wench* after Vas and the rest took off on the *Traitor's Folly*.

"Thank you. The *Destroyer's Curse* has some perks. And that would be one of them." Vas looked to Gosta but he was moving almost too fast to see. "We're going to have a fight on our hands. It seems that the planet Solar has some of the Asarlaí compound that Mayhira had in its core. And the Lethian Assembly, or at least part of them, are trying to blow it up."

The rest of her ships crossed the former barricade.

Vas' comm buzzed. "Captain! Hrrru here. I'm on a Welischian vessel coming up from the planet. Well, one of them. There are five warships. Qaan asks what do you need us to do?"

Vas shared her confusion about everything Hrrru said in a look at Deven and Bathie. Gosta was still panicking so he didn't notice.

Welischians becoming serious fighters was one thing, but having dedicated warships? The specs she could see as the five left the planet indicated that while they weren't huge, they were heavily armed. And fast.

"We have incoming Lethians and Hive ships from the gate. We have to assume they are here to blow up the planet. Or they were trying to stop us from dropping their barricade. In which case they're just being pissy."

"We're on it, captain!" The joy in Hrrru's voice was impressive to hear. He might not have been one of her most bloodthirsty crew members before, but being with his people again was bringing it out.

The five Welischian ships took off for the Lethians and Hive ships.

"Captain?" Ragkor was chomping at the bit.

"Follow them. But leave three ships to guard Solar." There weren't any signs of more threats beyond the four seriously outmatched ships coming from the gate, but better to not be caught off guard.

"Deven, stick with our crew going to the gate."

The ships from the Lethians and Hive were slowing

down. Whatever they'd come for, they weren't expecting this kind of resistance.

Vas grinned. "Xsit? Please contact the lead ship." She was ready to talk to them now. If they were smart, they'd make an excuse for such a heavily armed arrival and leave. If not, she knew her entire crew would enjoy a fight.

"Aye, captain," Xsit repeated her hail four times before she gave up. The bright yellow feathers on the back of her head were standing up in agitation. "They are now blocking me."

Vas opened up a channel to all of her ships and Hrrru. "Our guests are refusing contact. Let's spread out and show them why that's not good manners." The affirmatives were good to hear. Vas had only had a fleet for less than a year and hadn't been sure how she felt about it.

Until now.

After being alone outside of the Commonwealth for the past few months—this was nice. And the spread of her ships as they pulled apart from each other and the five Welischians was damn impressive.

"Captain, Qaan, from the Welischian ships is calling."

"Patch her through."

"Hello, captain. Our fleet is small and new. Might we be allowed to take first strike? My people are still new to this. Aside from Hrrru, of course."

"By all means. I'll have my ships follow yours. Good luck, Captain Qaan."

Her laugh was rich. "I hadn't thought of that, but it's fitting. Captain Qaan, out."

Vas passed along the new orders and all of her ships held back in formation to look as imposing as possible. She wasn't sure what prompted the Welischians to venture into a more aggressive fighting mindset, but they did need to get their feet wet.

The Welischian ships looked small as they engaged the Lethian and Hive vessels. But the firepower they used was nothing to be laughed at. Plus, they had the ability to strike and move out of range far faster than the larger ships.

The *Destroyer's Curse, Warrior Wench,* and *Victorious Dead* waited until the Welischians got in two full runs before moving forward. Their remaining ships held back.

The Hive ships were both larger single vessels, there were no club and net pairs here. They were pure warships and their shields were still holding.

It looked like they and the Lethians were going to fight regardless of being outmatched in number. Four warships against eight Commonwealth ships and five Welischian ships wasn't a favorable set of odds.

"What are they doing?" Vas looked at the screen, but for a moment it looked like the aggressors were going to try to force their way through to Solar.

So much for them coming to stop the barricade from being dropped.

One of the Welischian ships took a bad enough hit that they turned back to the planet but said they didn't need help to land.

The Lethian and Hive ships launched a volley of weapons and then turned and ran for the gate.

"Nothing appears to have gotten through any of our shields. Should we follow?" Ragkor sounded like he wanted to.

"No. As long as they leave, we're good, we have too many things to deal with." Vas monitored the damaged Welischian vessel as it landed. From what she saw it wasn't a great landing, but anything that the crew could walk away from was a win in her book.

"Abiel? Are you seeing any signs of more enemies out there?"

"No, captain. And it appears that all the quakes have subsided. I'm taking everyone but the basic crew back down in shuttles. Thank you doesn't seem enough to say."

"I'm glad we could help," she paused. "I have an odd question. But do you happen to have a continent in need of inhabitants?" She wanted to talk to Shien about it, but Shien spun toward her when she heard her question and nodded.

"Actually, we do. It's smaller and at the bottom of Solar. Mostly only explorers go there, but it is capable of supporting a small colony. I couldn't offer anything until we establish a real government, but do you have people who want to relocate?"

"I might. We'll keep in touch." Vas ended the call. "Solar might be an option, Shien. If you want to take your people down there and wait until they reestablish a government, that would be understandable."

"I heard, and thank you. I was studying their world before we started fighting. But, I feel my people and I need to stay with you for what's coming. As long as you don't mind?" Shien got up from the station with a smile.

"Your people are welcome to stay with us anytime. And thank you. I have a feeling we're going to need all the help we can get."

Shien nodded and swept her way off the deck.

The Welischian ships were heading back to Solar and Vas sent Mac to the landing bay to coordinate the transport of the Solarians down to the surface.

One more thing struck her. She hit her comm for Hrrru. "We're returning the Solarians in a short while. Will you be coming back with them?"

"Thank you, captain. I would like request a temporary leave of absence and gather a few of my things, if I could. I feel there is much to learn and contribute here."

"I understand. You can come up with Mac, get the things you need, and explain it to Gosta. We'll be waiting when you want to return." Vas could face many things, but Hrrru and Gosta had become best friends—she'd rather not break the news to Gosta herself. They could work things out on their own. She felt better that Hrrru was only taking some of his things—he might still return.

"Aye, captain! Thank you." Hrrru ended the call.

Deven was studying some of the massive amounts of data that Aithnea brought back from the Lethian ship. "Gosta? How many drones do you have? Not connected to us."

Gosta looked offended. "My drones are all clean, Deven. But as it happens, I currently have twelve."

"We want to seed this system with them. The Solarians now know of the threat to their world, but until we can find a way to neutralize that core—the Lethians and others will keep coming." Deven pointed to the data on his screen. "Just from the part I've seen so far, they have some serious plans for it. Honestly, Solar might have been the primary reason that they feinted the attack against the Commonwealth and then corrupted the barricade to keep them inside."

"Damn, that's not good and completely plausible." Vas nodded to Gosta. "Coordinate the drones and send them out. Is there a way to send the results to both us and Abiel?" He might not officially be the leader of Solar, but he helped save the place.

"I believe so, captain." Gosta was making adjustments, but Vas noticed he glanced at Hrrru's station more than a few times. He hadn't said anything, but he clearly heard part of her conversation with Hrrru.

Vas called Ragkor. "We're setting some drones out in this system. I'm not sure the Lethian Assembly won't be back."

"Want someone to stay behind as well?"

She paused. She wanted to see all of her people after being gone so long, but leaving a ship behind was a good idea. "Yes, leave the *Aoenyth*. It's pretty impressive." The

Aoenyth was a massive warship, larger than the *Destroyer's Curse* and it simply being in orbit might help dissuade the Lethians from returning—at least for a while.

Hopefully, Gosta and the other brainiacs could figure out a way to neutralize the Asarlaí element in the core of Solar and make the planet less of a target. She knew it would be difficult, but if the core was only partially changed, there could be a chance it could be done.

Without blowing it up.

Not to mention, with three of these planets on record so far, they needed to have a way to deal with them—there were most likely more. She'd also ask Gosta to get a group together to find ways to scan for the element.

After they restored the Clionea nuns and saved the entire known universe from the Clongari.

Mac and the other transport pilots sorted out the Solarians and got them back home.

Hrrru returned on the first empty transport and he and Gosta had a quiet talk. Neither appeared happy when they separated, but Gosta hugged Hrrru tightly. Hrrru appeared to be crying as he nodded to the rest of the crew and jogged to the lift. Vas noticed that Mac volunteered to take Hrrru back to the planet once he'd gathered his things.

Gosta watched him leave and Vas thought she heard him mutter in Synergian but he focused on getting his drones out.

Deven came to her chair and leaned on the back "It's not going to be the same without him."

"No, it's not. But I think he's growing up. And hopefully, he'll come back." Vas had grown increasingly close to her command crew since they'd been out of the Commonwealth, and she felt the loss of Hrrru leaving.

The *Aoenyth* and *Solar* took up orbit around the planet along with one of the Welischian ships. Abiel assured Vas they were prepared for anyone coming for them. And he would contact her the moment any aggressive ships came to Solar.

"Does the Commonwealth even know the barricade is down?" Vas asked Ragkor. The *Destroyer's Curse* didn't have access to the Commonwealth frequencies. One of the many things they'd have to look into once they got back to Home.

"Not that we can tell. To be honest, captain, after initially stating concern at their barricade becoming locked on the other side, the official standing was one of uncaring. I think they liked being cut off."

"Maybe they know what's coming." Deven was close enough to hear Vas' open comm.

Flarik turned from her station and got to her feet. "I have filed the official documents transferring the *Destroyer's Curse* to Commonwealth registration. I will track the process but it should be swift. However, if I'm not needed up here, I will go back to my room." She didn't wait for a response and was halfway to the lift when Vas thanked her.

The last thing they needed were bureaucratic issues. Vas might or might not keep the *Destroyer's Curse* as her flagship, but she wanted to keep it in her fleet.

"Lead us to Home as soon as Mac lands that final transport in the bay, Bathie," Vas called out as the remaining ships went into the Commonwealth.

"Staying here or taking back the *Warrior Wench*?" Deven stayed next to her.

"That's a good question. I have grown to like this ship, but I think it might need another captain during our fight."

He narrowed his eyes. "And you have someone in mind?"

"I do. It'll come as a surprise to everyone if I follow through with it." Her smile dropped. "It's been an exciting day, still feeling like yourself?"

He laughed, gave her a kiss, and returned to his station. "Completely. I still want to know what they scanned me with that triggered the reaction, but I'm me."

CHAPTER TWENTY-SIX

———◆———

THE TRIP TO HOME WAS thankfully uneventful. Few ships were spotted and all were quite a distance away. Ragkor mentioned that once the barricade was locked, most travel lanes changed and more ships avoided the Rim.

Vas wouldn't admit it to anyone beyond maybe Deven in private, but she had to fight tears as Home came into scanning range.

"Approaching ship! Identify yourself!" Grosslyn's voice was great to hear barking through the comm.

That was one of the worst things about the past few months—not being able to even speak to her extended crew. Even on long sieges when they did mercenary work, she always kept connected.

"Who do you think would be leading this bunch of misfit ships in?" Vas laughed. It was doubtful that Grosslyn thought the armada was chasing the *Destroyer's Curse*. He would have put the cloak on the planet if he thought that. He liked being ornery though.

"Vas?! Captain!? Ragkor said he was going to find a way to get you—he did it! And you got the barricade down! What the hell is it that you're flying though? Ya lost that *Traitor's Folly* ship out there?"

"It was sliced in half by that escapee, Ome. But those tales will wait until we're back. Requesting clearance to dock at that lovely new station you have sitting there. I hope it didn't cost too much from our coffers." The docking station was the largest she'd ever seen outside of the Commonwealth's inner core planets. And even at this distance, it was clearly state-of-the-art. As the manager of Home, Grosslyn had some disposable income to keep things running.

Not this much though.

"Not at all, we had some income come in unexpectedly." He coughed. "I'll explain when you're back on the planet."

Vas shrugged. She had no idea where extra funds would have come from, but she doubted Ragkor would have turned to piracy. She told Grosslyn they'd need room for the Pilthians to comfortably stay together. They didn't have time for a long visit, but she figured everyone needed some downtime before heading out again.

While emergency repairs had been done at Solar, the *Destroyer's Curse* still needed some serious work.

Bathie guided the *Destroyer's Curse* into the largest bay of the station and the crew began connecting it.

Vas opened ship-wide to her crew and the Pilthians. "Attention everyone. We're going to be taking transports down to the planet. Only take what you need for a few days, we're not changing ships just yet. Queen Shien and her people will have accommodations on the planet. I don't recommend anyone remaining on board as we need to do repairs and modifications that will make things uncomfortable for a while. Head down to the landing bay once you're ready."

It was impressive to watch most of the rest of the ships dock at the station. Even the *Victorious Dead* did so and it could do a full planet landing. But Vas didn't like too many ships going to ground and had trained Ragkor that way. The *Warrior Wench* was landing on the planet, but it was the only one.

"Shall we pack an overnight bag?" Deven waited until the station clamps had hold of the *Destroyer's Curse*, then joined Vas.

"I think we should." Vas turned to Gosta, but he was

making no moves to get his things. "That does mean you too, Gosta. If you're not down in an hour, I'll send people to get you. You can work on your projects in your apartment." Prying Gosta off the ship was always an issue.

He sheepishly looked over. "Aye, captain."

"Aithnea? Are you staying up here?" Vas knew that Nitya could never leave the *Destroyer's Curse*, she was bound to it for the rest of her unnatural existence. But Aithnea was more flexible.

"I'm staying, I believe Jasiel is planning to as well. There are nun things the three of us need to work on. I'd say the Keeper and Pirate as well. But, while we will need you two eventually, a few days apart will be better." It wasn't completely dismissive, but the tone was clear. Vas and Deven would only be in the way.

"Have fun. Deven, let's pack." There was no way Vas was going to fight with Jasiel to get her off the ship. Besides, the more the three of them could get done without her and Deven, the better. She knew they were going to be doing some nun work along with saving the universe the old-fashioned way, by fighting. But the longer it wasn't needed, the better.

Vas and Deven got to their quarters before being buzzed by Walvento.

"Captain, request to stay on board. Also, there's that Hivian still in the brig."

Vas rubbed her forehead; she'd forgotten their fake Commonwealth prisoner. She needed these few days off, even if she wouldn't admit it to anyone. "Thank you, Walvento. If you can bring him to us in the landing bay, I'll let you come back after one night on the planet."

Deven raised an eyebrow as he quickly packed their bags.

"Aye, captain. I'll meet you there." Walvento didn't sound happy, but not upset either. One night wouldn't kill him.

"Who knew that even after all we've been through the past few months, we'd have to pry our crew out of the ship?" Vas shook her head as she ended the call.

Deven laughed as they left. "They're adaptable. And they adapted well to this."

Vas' comm hummed. "Yes, Flarik?"

"Hello, captain. I would normally not ask for an exception, but it would be difficult to move my entire nest down to the surface. I believe it would be better if I remained up here."

Vas shared a look with Deven. "Do you want us to stay?" She wasn't certain what co-parents needed to do before the child was born.

"No, I don't think so. The nuns are remaining, I believe?"

"They are."

"We will be fine."

"Call us if you need anything."

"I shall." Flarik ended the call.

Deven adjusted his pack as they went down the corridor. "I don't blame her. The nest she made is even larger than before."

Vas' comm chirped again before she could respond to him. "What's up, Terel?"

"Vas, I'm not sure what to do about Delimara. The nanites are keeping her and themselves unconscious, but I don't want to leave her unattended up here, and taking her down to the planet would be even worse."

"We can watch her as well as Flarik and her child," Aithnea's voice popped in from a speaker in the hall.

"Did you hear that? Aithnea, Nitya, and Jasiel will watch her. Get yourself and your people down to the transports."

"Understood." Terel closed the call with a sigh.

"She wanted to stay as well." Deven punched up the lift.

"This break came just in time."

The landing bay was chaos. The Pilthians' side was more organized and they were already using some of their larger transports to go down to the planet.

The first transports from Vas' side were full and finally heading down when Walvento showed up with a small duffle bag and their fake Commonwealth prisoner.

Vas nodded. "Thank you, Walvento. Do you mind guarding him on the way down?" The Hivian prisoner looked like even less of a threat than he had on the planet, but it would help Walvento get over leaving his weapons for a day.

The prisoner paused as he passed Vas and Deven. "I guess that you saved my life. Thank you. I don't know much, but I'll tell you whatever I know."

"We'll talk once things are settled. You'll still have to be locked up, but I promise it won't be bad."

His grin made him look younger. "I'm breathing and off that planet with all of my limbs. A jail cell is an improvement."

Walvento pulled him toward the shuttle that Vas and Deven would be taking. Mac waved from the pilot's seat.

Vas hit her comm. "Gosta? Are you already on a shuttle?"

"On my way, captain." From his faintly out-of-breath voice, he was running to his quarters now.

"I'm going to wait until he's down here," Vas said.

Deven took her bag. "I'll save some seats. I take it that we want Gosta to ride down with us?"

Vas grinned. "I don't trust him on leaving, so good guess."

The landing bay had mostly emptied, only a few folks waiting for a shuttle to come back up—and Mac waiting impatiently for Vas—when Gosta finally came down. He had four bags and all of them looked heavy.

"We're only going to be down there for a few days." Vas grabbed a bag and walked to the shuttle.

Gosta's bags were a tight fit, but Vas blocked him when he offered to wait for another shuttle.

"Nope, you're going with us, bucko."

Deven smiled and pointed to the two seats next to him as Vas secured the door.

"Ready, captain?" Mac sounded impatient, but that was fairly common.

"Aye, Mac. Take us down." Vas took her seat and patted Gosta's hands. "You can stand to be away for a few days. I promise. Besides, I need you to explain to everyone what we're facing out there." The detour to Solar had become far more than simply a repair stop and a chance to reach the rest of her crew. But they needed to get back to gathering enough intel and forces to take down the Clongari before they got a foothold.

Deven saved Vas the seat near the portal window and she took advantage of it. Seeing Home rising as they landed was beautiful.

"What are you thinking?" Deven leaned in. Most likely he sensed something but wasn't going to search her mind.

"Just that maybe after we save the universe and everyone in it, I might think about retiring. You were right. I don't spend enough time here."

Deven's laugh was low. "I said that almost a year ago."

"I know, it took me a while to think about it." The view below wasn't exotic. Just a large landing field with several hangars around it. The town itself was close enough to get to on foot but gave a feeling of being off on its own. It wasn't exotic either but looked damn good.

Vas had a feeling it was more than simply being trapped out of the Commonwealth these past few months.

CHAPTER TWENTY-SEVEN

GROSSLYN TOOK THE PILTHIANS TO a large, empty hotel not far from the landing strip. A brand new one. Vas narrowed her eyes when he told her he thought it might be handy to have for visitors.

A sixty-room hotel. On a planet that wasn't supposed to be visited by anyone. She and he were going to have a long talk when he got back from settling the Pilthians.

Which was most likely why he said he wanted to do it himself.

Deven took their things to his place while Vas went digging through the mountain of stuff piled on her desk. It wasn't that anyone had officially used it, it just ended up a dumping ground for anything even remotely interesting that Grosslyn or any of her ground crew thought she might want to know about when she got back. And that for some reason couldn't be stored electronically.

She would have to retire to have time to look through it all.

The smell of rolls, and not just any rolls, but the famously addicting ones only made at the nearby diner by Delilah, hit Vas before she saw the tiny woman carrying them come into the hangar offices.

"That basket is larger than you." Vas jumped to her feet and lifted the basket of amazing rolls, biscuits, and other baked goods. Delilah was a retired campaigner who'd been old when she joined Vas' crew back at the beginning. She was also a telepath and an incredible cook.

Vas finished one roll before she set the basket down on an empty desk. "It's damn good to see you." She hugged Deliliah hard enough that the tiny woman finally pounded Vas' back to be set down.

"Glad to see that you're still in shape. Even if you did almost give me a heart attack a few months ago." Delilah was about four foot nothing and mostly humanoid. She admitted to nothing.

"How did I give you a heart attack from outside of the Commonwealth?" She reached over and lifted two more rolls.

"You can eat as many as you want, as long as you save a few for Deven. I made them for the two of you specifically. You'll have to fill me in on all the tiny details after you've spoken to the troops." She pulled up a chair. "As for the heart attack," she shrugged. "I was nosy and kept sending out mental feelers. Worked until that damn barricade went up. Anyway—I felt your former ship explode. I barely sensed that you, Deven, and the crew were safe on a space station before those idiots in charge of the Commonwealth cut us off."

"You can reach that far?" Vas hadn't known Delilah was a telepath until two years ago—even Deven couldn't reliably sense things at that distance.

"Sometimes? I have a strong tie to you two. And it gave me a boost. Not to mention that dead nun of yours acts as a focus." She paused. "She's not still inside your head, is she?"

Aithnea and Delilah had met briefly when Vas was on the planet before they went after the Asarlaí clones that decimated the Commonwealth. It had been an interesting meeting of the wills.

"Aithnea has upgraded and now lives in ships." Grabbing another roll to rip apart, even though she was by no means hungry, Vas gave Delilah a summary of the past few months.

Deven came in a half hour later when she was finishing up. He grabbed Delilah in a hug as he scooped some rolls.

"It's good to see you, Delilah. And these are excellent as usual."

"It's good to see you two as well. No more having ships be sliced apart. Even if you're not in them." Delilah got to her feet. "Enjoy the rolls and biscuits, and I'd better see you both at my place for breakfast tomorrow. You can fill me in on the little bits over cups of solie and a mountain of food." She glanced into the hangar, then took off in the opposite direction of the crowd. Delilah preferred to run into old friends in her diner—not the hangar or airstrip.

"Grosslyn is back and currently out front gathering the troops for our update. Aside from the people who were with us, he's gathering everyone close by. Even some locals who might not be crew. He seems very excited." Deven finished off a few more rolls.

"It's almost like he's trying to make sure this goes on a long time and he can delay explaining to me the docking array and that new hotel. More importantly, the costs of those things."

Deven laughed. "I was thinking the same thing. What did Delilah mean about exploding ships?"

Vas frowned and told him. She trusted Delilah as she always had, but the amount of telepathic power she mentioned was scary.

"That is impressive. Maybe she'll be more forthcoming at breakfast tomorrow."

The noise level in the hangar was increasing. Always an indicator that Vas and Deven needed to get out there.

"Shall we? I figured Gosta and Terel would come in to get us when they got back. I'd like both to speak to the crowd about what we faced—and will be facing." Both Gosta and Terel had swung by their homes to drop things off, but neither lived far from the hangar.

Deven bowed and held open the door. "After you, my captain."

Neither Gosta nor Terel appeared. Which was concerning, but both of them could get caught up in things. They were probably puttering around the homes they hadn't seen for a few months.

Vas and Deven took turns discussing the original visit outside of the Commonwealth, skipping the Keeper and nun portions, all the way up to the short fight near Solar. Grosslyn played things well and brought up more questions every time there was a slowdown.

Vas called it at the two-hour mark. "Thank you all for welcoming us back." She raised her hands. "But we've had a long day and want to rest now. As we said before, there are a lot of things going on. Assignments will be coming shortly." Most of them were still awake, so that was a good sign.

"Where are Terel and Gosta?" Vas kept her voice low as many of the older crew members wanted to come to welcome them back individually.

"I was thinking the same thing. The crowd was so large at the start that I figured they were in there somewhere," Deven said as he and Vas moved back to the offices. "I searched, but they're not in the hangar."

They were almost to the offices when Mac and Bathie came running through the crowd. Both looked far more roughed up than could be explained by a few hours at a pub.

"They grabbed Gosta, Terel, and Walvento as we were coming back here." Mac got out before doubling over with his hands on his knees to catch his breath.

"What? Who did? *Walvento?*" Both Gosta and Terel were tough in their ways—but Walvento was a force of nature. Vas had a hard time imagining anyone short of an army taking him.

"They took him down first, then went after the rest of us. Gosta and Terel were also unconscious when we escaped. Mac and I were toward the back and drifted behind the rest when the attack came. They got us in the side alley of Nivers Road. They were blocking it from anyone on the street seeing the attack." Bathie was roughed up but looked better than Mac.

"Who did it? And how did you two get away?"

"No idea. Five fighters, all in dark red. No marks on their clothing or weapons, they wore face masks, and didn't speak."

"They almost had us, but Bathie turned into a wild woman and started screaming as she attacked them." Mac grinned. "That got their attention and they took the others and ran. I'm sorry we couldn't save them." His grin died.

"Damn it. I'm glad you didn't try. We wouldn't have a clue as to what happened to any of you. But who did it? No one but our people should be here." Vas went into the office locker and grabbed a pair of blasters. Deven did the same.

How had invaders landed on Home without anyone noticing?

The four went back into the hangar where Grosslyn was chatting with a few old campaigners who'd come in for the meeting. He jumped to his feet when he saw the look on Vas' face.

"I swear, I didn't touch the coffers—"

"That's not an issue right now. Gosta, Terel, and Walvento were grabbed in an alley by unknown forces." Vas motioned for Mac and Bathie to give descriptions. Now that they were both calmer, there was more detail. But not enough to know what the attackers looked like if they dumped their odd ensembles.

"I'll start scanning the vids." Grosslyn jumped to his feet.

The three retired fighters got to theirs as well. "What can we do, captain?" Sachi was older than Delilah, and probably still as tough as Walvento. The two men with her had more than a few years between them but kept in fighting shape.

"You three know our missing people, start searching the lower town. If they're keeping them here, that's a likely spot to hide them. They could have killed them, but they didn't. Which means we assume they want them alive. That gives us the advantage—I don't care if the people who took them are dead or not."

Sachi patted the blaster under her long jacket. "Full force as necessary." She frowned. "These two aren't packing though."

Grosslyn waved them over. "I've got weapons they can use. Captain? Should we call back the troops?"

Vas almost said yes, then shook her head. "Not yet. Even our people could muddle the search at this point. But needless to say, no one goes off planet. Notify the refugees there's a space storm and no one can lift off right now."

Space storms were rare and could be easily debunked if anyone looked close enough. But the only ones who might do that right now would be the people they wanted.

"And we'll need someone to see if the description of the attackers matches anything in any database," Deven added more weapons than he normally carried.

Vas almost said Gosta could do it, then shook her head. She was getting her people back. This was Home, damn it. A safe refuge from an uncaring universe.

"I'll get people on it, captain," Grosslyn yelled as he ran toward the office.

Vas and Deven followed Bathie and Mac to the place where the attack happened once they all armed themselves. Aside from a few extreme cases like Sachi, most people weren't armed on the planet.

The alley looked like an average alley. There was enough debris that it was clear how they'd been ambushed.

"Vas? What's wrong?" Aithnea's voice overriding her comm made Vas jump.

"We've got a problem." She wasn't going to ask how Aithnea knew—some nun tricks were better left unknown. "Three of our people were kidnapped."

"On Home? Sorry, of course on Home. What can we do to help?"

Vas dropped her voice. "We need to find where they took them. It was Gosta, Terel, and Walvento—can you do any nun magic and track them?"

Deven, Mac, and Bathie were slowly going over the alley. It was full night now, but their wristlamps were turned up.

"Not from up here. But you and your Pirate might be able to."

Vas would have glared at Aithnea if she were here. "I need to save my people, not do Keeper training."

The other three were studiously not paying attention to her one-sided conversation until she said that. Deven didn't stop his search but frowned.

"There's no reason you can't do both. You can work together and amplify each other's natural talents. It's part of what you do naturally, but now give it some oomph. Focus on Terel, she's unique."

Vas waved Deven over. "The nuns think that you and me, or rather, the Keeper and Pirate, can track Terel."

He shrugged. "She is biologically distinctive. Unless a sibling of hers is on the planet, I might be able to find her given enough time. But using what? My telepathy can help, but it needs focus. And we might not have enough time."

"Thank you, Deven," Aithnea said loud enough to be heard by him through Vas' comm. "And that's where the Keeper comes in. Deven will be the power, you'll focus it on Terel."

Vas watched as Bathie and Mac finished searching the

alley and both shook their heads. It had been a long shot that any evidence of the attackers would be here, but one she'd been hoping for.

"Our options are slim and the longer we wait the harder it will be. We don't know why they were taken or what the plan was." It could have been a kidnapping of opportunity, or they specifically wanted something from one or all the people they grabbed. "Hold on." Vas went to Bathie and Mac. "How hard did they try to get you two?"

"Not very, to be honest. They seemed surprised at us being along. They knocked out the others with hypos, but fought us and then took off when I screamed." Bathie shook her head. "I should have tried that earlier."

Vas nodded and spoke to Aithnea. "Most likely they did want those three specifically. But have Jasiel contact all of our crew to make sure they stay inside tonight—and that all of them can be reached. Warn Shien too." Even though the Pilthians weren't part of her crew, this wasn't the time to take chances.

CHAPTER TWENTY-EIGHT

———◆———

IT TOOK LONGER THAN VAS wanted, and both Jasiel and Nitya had to join in explaining the process, but eventually Vas and Deven were set to track Terel. It wasn't a difficult thing, once Vas understood it. She'd be using some of the same Keeper mojo she tapped into when working with Aithnea and Jasiel to zero in on Terel. Then connect that to Deven through the bond they shared.

"It would be easier if you had her blood, but you can't spend the time to come up here and get a sample." Aithnea was the only one still on the comm call at this point. It had been fifteen minutes, but Mac and Bathie were chomping at the bit. They'd decided that if Deven and Vas were the searchers, they were the enforcers.

Clearly, they were both still upset about not saving their friends. Even though from what it sounded like, they would have lost and either been killed or kidnapped had the attackers not taken off.

Vas felt the same and she hadn't been there.

The tracking was weird. She'd assumed that since Deven was the telepath, he'd find them with that ability. But it was the two of them together that did it. Interestingly, Deven's telepathic abilities wouldn't work on this—unless he was paired with the Keeper.

Aithnea put Vas into a trance and the alley around her dimmed. She felt Deven in her mind, but the other two were shadows. She didn't see Terel so much as see everything that wasn't Terel. And there was a hole in that non-Terelness that she had to focus on. Deven took her hand as they left the alley, reinforcing the connection between them. Mac and Bathie stayed on guard behind them.

It was an odd sensation as Vas led them through the town in the night, Deven lending energy to the search and her focusing it on the spark of Terel. Bathie moved in front of them since there weren't many people in this part of town, a few did want to stop and say hello. Bathie explained they were doing a training mission and needed to be left alone.

Luckily, they were soon outside of town and that distraction stopped. A chill ran through Vas as she realized where they were heading. The old solbilan mines.

Before she won this planet in a card game, it had been a powerful mining world. Solbilan was a dangerous mineral but one needed for starships a hundred or more years ago. The need for it died out, and so did the mines.

She only went near this mine once when she was first exploring her new planet. She'd left when it brought back too many memories of when her brother sold her to rogue telepaths as a kid. They'd kept her deep in a cave.

"Damn it."

Deven stopped. "What's wrong?"

"They're in the mines." Vas knew Mac and Bathie might not understand the importance of that, but Deven would.

"Terel is in there." His voice was calm and the connection between them flared.

"Do we call for backup?" Mac asked from behind her.

"No. We—"Vas cut herself off as pain tore through her gut. She was even more connected to Terel than Aithnea said she'd be. Now that they were closer, she knew that pain came from her friend. "We don't have time. They're being tortured."

A flood of support came through her hand from Deven. And fury at what she was feeling and why.

"Let us go first, you two call Grosslyn and tell him where we are. The remaining solbilan in those caves will mess up our comms," Deven said. "Then follow us in a few minutes." There was a chance that Mac and Bathie wouldn't be able to find them. This mine was supposed to be completely shut. But this way Grosslyn knew and could send more help. Hopefully, they wouldn't need it.

Vas was already pulling toward the entrance of the mine when Bathie grabbed her other hand.

"Take these. Drop them every few feet and we'll find you." She put a bag of what felt like pebbles in Vas' hand. "We were going to a club when the attack came; these glow bombs are popular there. Just don't squeeze them when you drop them."

Vas' vision was still odd, but she smiled at the Bathie shadow. "Thanks." Then she led Deven in.

His energy and power increased the moment they crossed inside the mine. He wasn't reaching out tele-pathically in a direct fashion but was going through her. Their abilities supported each other, making them each stronger.

Vas dropped one of the glow bombs at the first turn as she continued to be pulled forward by Terel's presence. And pain. They were still hurting her. Even through her enforced shadow world, the small green light she dropped flickered and glowed.

A sharper burst of pain hit her. "We need to go faster." She picked up speed, navigating through the tunnels as if it were bright daylight. She felt Deven pull out his blaster with his free hand. She'd forget the glow bombs and get her blaster out once they found Terel and the others. Right now, it might be more important that Mac, Bathie, and anyone else on their crew could find them. She'd lost count of how many turns they made. For a supposedly closed mine it was extremely open.

One advantage of sneaking up on people who thought

no one could find them—the attackers weren't bothering to be silent as they yelled at Terel.

Vas dropped the last glow bomb and then the bag as she pulled out her blaster. Deven released her hand as they raced into the cave.

Even though there were lights, the entire place was still dim because of the Keeper trance. Ten darker areas indicated the enemy. Terel, slumped in a chair, was the only bright light. Two still forms on the ground behind her made Vas yell and race forward.

She didn't trust her blaster with her vision still dimmed. Besides, the Keeper part of her wanted to physically fight. She holstered her blaster and jumped for the two cloaked people standing nearest to Terel and snapped their necks.

Deven was right behind her and took out three before any of them could yell out. He was one of the best fighters Vas had ever seen, but the Pirate mojo was kicking things up.

Three more of the kidnappers died before they could get their blasters out.

Terel raised her head. "Maybe keep some alive for questioning?" She was beaten but was already working on freeing herself from her binds.

"Good idea, I was focused on killing them." Vas shook her head as the trance that Aithnea helped create faded. She pulled her blaster back out, changed it to stun, and shot both of the surviving attackers.

Deven went to Gosta and Walvento. Both were unmoving. "They're alive, just unconscious."

Terel and Vas finished removing Terel's bonds as Bathie and Mac came running in with blasters raised. They skidded to a halt when they saw the bodies.

"Aw, man, captain. I wanted some payback." Mac nudged a few with his foot.

"Sorry, I was a little focused." Vas stopped as the world swam around her and she dropped to the floor.

Deven swore, and then he did the same. "What the hell just happened?" He looked fine, but like Vas, he also didn't look like he was getting to his feet anytime soon. "I have no energy."

Terel stretched and patted herself down, looking for any serious damage. Then went into full doctor mode. "I'd guess it's whatever you two took to move like you did. I could barely see either of you when you raced in."

"No drugs, only whatever Keeper and Pirate mojo Aithnea activated. Damn, this feels awful." Vas was grateful for the ability to find Terel and take down the kidnappers so readily, but right now she felt like her entire body was on fire. She'd never had this kind of kickback from a Keeper activity and hoped this wasn't a sign of the future.

"Grosslyn's sending a crew down here. Pela is coming with a medical crew, too." Bathie noticed the two stunned kidnappers and roughly tied them both up. "I do agree with Mac, though. You could have saved some for us."

"It was in the moment." Vas tried to adjust herself, but while she could remain sitting up, she couldn't do much else.

Terel checked on Walvento and Gosta, then nodded and stepped back. "They're still out from whatever those bastards used on us. Bathie and Mac, can you see if you can find their supplies anywhere? Whatever they hit us with was unlike anything I've heard of. Walvento has an uncommonly high tolerance for any sedatives, but they dropped him with one dose."

The sounds of running feet made Mac and Bathie turn and hide on either side of the entrance to the cave. Terel ducked to protect Walvento and Gosta, and Vas and Deven kept their blasters aimed at the entrance, but neither could get to their feet.

"It's okay! It's us!" Marwin held his blaster over his

head as he, Glazlie, Huglin, and Roha came skidding into the cave.

Mac and Bathie came out from the sides.

Vas lowered her blaster. "No one followed you? This seems like a small group for this type of operation. It was too well done to have been a spur-of-the-moment attack." Which meant far more people were probably involved. She didn't recognize any of the dead or unconscious kidnappers, but there could still be more lurking.

"Not that we saw. We left Gon and Kylia at the entrance as well. Pela and crew are right behind us with med beds." Roha came over to Vas. "Are you enjoying sitting there?"

Vas laughed. "Not really. But unless you're planning on carrying me all the way back to the hangar, I should wait until Pela gets here." She needed to talk to Aithnea about this thing. Great power burst, but the aftereffects could have been fatal for them all.

"Understood." Roha went to check on Terel, Gosta, and Walvento as Pela, Divee, and two more medics came running in.

Luckily they had a nice collection of collapsible floating med beds. Vas didn't doubt that her people would be willing to carry her back. But Deven wasn't light. Not to mention Walvento outweighed them both combined.

"Check Terel first, they were hurting her."

"I'm fine—"

"I felt what they did. You're not fine." Vas cut her off. "Terel first. You might as well load Gosta and Walvento onto some beds, they're going to need more help and time than we have here."

Deven pointed out the two unconscious prisoners as well and two beds went toward them.

"I found something." Bathie and Mac had resumed looking for anything that could help sort out what had been used to knock the others out. Bathie held up a large case. "It's got a lot of vials in it. Different colors and labels."

"Grab it and anything else you find. We need to figure out who in the hell these people are, who is behind them, and how they got here." Vas adjusted herself as feeling began to return to her legs. A good sign, but there was no way she could get up. The why of the attack would come once they figured out the who.

Mac and Bathie found a few more cases and bags, but that was it. Not enough for an evil lair, which meant this hadn't been their base of operations. Once Bathie and Mac secured their finds on a cart, they turned to Vas as Marwin was helping her on a med bed.

"We could go search some of the nearby caves."

Vas was about to shake them off as a chill went through her. Deven beat her before she could say anything.

"No. There's something wrong here. Very wrong. We need to leave." He rolled onto the bed after it took Huglin and Glazlie to lift him. "Now." He winced and grabbed the side of his head.

Vas didn't know if it was Pirate and Keeper related, or if she was still picking up on what was going on in Deven's head, but a wave of fear hit her. "We're all loaded, right?" There were six med beds with people and one with secured things. Terel allowed a brief examination but refused a bed.

"Yes, but—" Mac moved toward the entrance.

"No. We need to go *now*." Vas held her blaster across her body. Not knowing what was causing the feeling meant she didn't know what to expect. But something was seriously wrong.

Roha led them out, with Mac and Bathie running alongside her. The triplets stayed behind the cots. The cots moved on their own, but Pela and her medics remained with them.

"Keep running." Deven didn't shout, but he was still clutching his head in pain. Their speed picked up and the med cots followed.

"Are those explosions behind us?" Vas tried to turn around to look, but couldn't see anything. The next one was louder and shook the ground. "Shit!"

The direction they were running appeared stable, but this was an old mine.

Another explosion shook the tunnel hard enough that more than a little dust and dirt fell on them.

"Run!" Marwin called from behind, although he and his siblings were far closer to the cots now.

"Come on! You're almost out!" Gon yelled from the entrance.

They were nearly there when another explosion rocked the entire mine and the ceiling of the tunnel they were in collapsed.

Vas yelled as her med bed tipped over and everything in the tunnel went dark.

CHAPTER TWENTY-NINE

THE GOOD NEWS WAS VAS now felt like she could move. The bad news was she wasn't sure she should. It didn't seem as if as much of the ceiling collapsed as she feared, but there was still enough to make moving about dicey.

"Is everyone okay? Call out." Hearing from everyone in the tunnel with her was comforting. But they were still stuck with no light, no idea if their attackers had more people coming, nor what set off the explosions.

At least she no longer had the skin-crawling danger feeling.

One by one wristlamps flickered on. Vas' didn't work, and judging by the reduced numbers of them, hers wasn't the only broken one.

While the rockfall blocking the entrance wasn't surprising, it did tell her this was deliberate. The entrances to all the old mines were reinforced to specifically *not* do what this one did. Someone rigged it to collapse.

"Captain? Are you in there?" Grosslyn's voice coming through her comm indicated they were close enough for the comms to work and that he'd been worried enough to leave his beloved hangar. Grosslyn was one of the few people she had on her payroll who'd never been a fighter. She hired him as admin when she first started and he'd remained that way.

"We're here. Looks like we all survived the collapse, but not sure about the getting out bit. Please tell me you have excavation equipment?"

"Some? Sorry, captain, we were focusing on a rescue of a different kind. But we're working on digging you out."

"Thanks. We'll work on it from our end. I'm not sure if we have unknown hostiles in here or not." If there had been, and they set off the explosions, she would assume that they had another way out. But as she'd learned through twenty years of mercenary work—never underestimate the stupidity of people.

Deven eased off his med bed, then came to help her off hers. There was still a lot of tingling in her legs, but at least she was on her feet. "Thank you. First thing once we get back, we talk to Aithnea and Jasiel about what in the hell happened to us." Sudden superpowers were handy, but collapsing afterward made them more of a danger than a help.

Everyone conscious slowly got to their feet. Gosta and Walvento were still unconscious and remained secure on their beds. The two prisoners were the same, although one took some hits to the head. Terel nodded that Gosta, Walvento, and the one prisoner were okay, then shook her head at the other prisoner and pulled the sheet over his head.

The ones behind this might have been hoping to not only kill or trap Vas and her crew but also remove their own people from telling anything of their plans. After the stunt of that type on Solar, Vas wasn't going to be surprised if that was the case. She doubted the Lethian Assembly was behind this attack; whoever it was had to have come from the Commonwealth with that barricade being in place the past few months. But never underestimate your enemy.

"Keep a guard on that last man," Deven said before Vas did.

"Good idea. I need a crew at the entrance to slowly remove the cave-in," Vas said. "The rest of you, keep your blasters out and watch everything behind us." There were no splits in the tunnel this far up, but there were many not too far back. If the people behind this were stupid and stayed here, they could come from five different tunnels.

A crashing sound from outside was followed by a lot of swearing. It also let some light into the tunnel. Her crew might not have brought much in the way of excavating equipment, but they had powerful lights.

Vas turned to the tunnel behind them and kept her blaster ready. Another crash came from the front and then the way was clear.

They still had to do tricky maneuvers to get the three unconscious people, strapped in their beds, and the bed with the cases from the kidnappers over the uneven rocks. The med beds were semi-floaters but did rely on a mostly smooth surface to maintain their correct level. The rocks meant they were constantly shifting height. They took out the deceased kidnapper as well. There were sometimes clues found in death.

Once the beds were out, Vas and Deven sent the rest of their people to follow. The two of them walked out slowly and backward with blasters set on the dark tunnel behind them. Not easy, but while she didn't have the urgently panicked feeling of before, there was still a tendril of being watched.

Once they were outside, she turned to Grosslyn. "I need a security fence on this and guards until the fence is up and running. There might be another entrance. In the daylight have people do recon teams and search the surrounding areas. Do not let anyone go inside the mine."

"Aye, captain. I'm glad you're all okay and that you found them. Are Gosta and Walvento going to recover?" Grosslyn watched the med beds trundle past.

Terel walked over. "I believe so. I need to get them to a more secure place to do a full examination. Glancing at that case of chemicals the kidnappers had was interesting—and scary. If the labels are right, someone is dabbling in some messy stuff."

Grosslyn nodded, he didn't know about those things and liked it that way. He turned and started barking orders. He sent a team back to the hangar to get a mobile fence and stationed additional guards at the entrance to the mine. Facing both directions and armed with massive blasters. Grosslyn took the lead going back to the hangar for the med beds and everyone else.

Terel checked on her two unconscious patients and then came to Deven and Vas. "It's not a short walk back, are you sure you two are fine? You both look awful."

"We're fine." Vas tried to look less awful, but it was difficult when she felt that way. "Just some slap-back from whatever mojo Aithnea and Jasiel set us up for."

Deven nodded.

Terel narrowed her eyes as she looked between them. "Fine. But if either of you collapses, you're waiting until morning for a pickup." With a terse nod, she turned and marched ahead to where Gosta and Walvento were being wheeled. The heavily restrained, and still unconscious, prisoner was being guarded and rolled along behind them.

Mac came up alongside Vas. "Do you want us to stay as guards? Escort you all? Or?"

Vas laughed. She knew where that 'or' was going. Mac and Bathie were the most on-again-off-again couple she'd ever seen. But they'd been mostly on again recently.

And they'd been going out for a night on the town before all of this happened.

"We have enough people for both, I think. Go have a nice night. Just stay in if you don't mind. And return to the hangar in the morning." It didn't look like the kidnappers were interested in Bathie and Mac, but better to be safe. They had no idea why this entire thing happened or who was behind it. Granted, the kidnappers couldn't have known about Vas and Deven being the Keeper and Pirate—or what they could do.

Mac grinned and he and Bathie took off.

The rest made good time back to the hangar. Grosslyn nodded to the armed guards at the only open entrance as they went in.

They never had guards on the hangar. But in this case, it was a good idea. Vas had always felt safe on Home, one of the reasons she'd kept the planet after unexpectedly winning it. When you were a merc, a safe place to rest and recover—and keep your family safe—was worth more than any ship.

The fact that these bastards were able to land on Home and kidnap her people said that wasn't the case anymore.

The rear of the hangar held a full medical bay as well as communication stations. Although he didn't work on a ship, Grosslyn kept things similar to the ships for the crews.

Terel and Pela led Gosta and Walvento in, with Vas right behind them. The guards took the unconscious prisoner to the lockup, and the dead one to the morgue.

Terel turned to Vas. "While I want to do a full workup on you and Deven to see how you did what you did, I'll be working on these two first."

"Ha. I wanted to make sure you didn't need anything. And that you are going to have Pela confirm with more equipment that you're okay." Vas wanted to know the same things Terel did—but this wasn't the time. Not to mention she didn't think that standard medical equipment would provide any answers as to what Aithnea and Jasiel did.

"I was roughed up, but nothing bad. I promise. She can do a full scan and confirm it." Terel handed the case taken from the cave to Divee and he vanished into another room. "He's found his calling. He's good with patients but excels at analysis and medicine. I need to isolate what the kidnappers drugged us with to find the right solution—and what they used to bring me out of it. I'm going to compare my blood with Gosta's and Walvento's and see what we find. It might take a while, but they'll be hooked up to so many machines that if either sneezes an alarm will go off."

Vas nodded and watched as Gosta and Walvento were transferred to full medical beds and a lot of machines. "Keep me updated. Deven and I will be staying in one of the rooms here for the interim." Which did mean that she needed him to retrieve their stuff from his place. Along with the additional rooms for medical and communications, there were more than a dozen quarters in this part of the hangar for crew who didn't want to stay in town—or were working on projects.

She went out to the main hangar as Grosslyn sent off the crew with the fencing for the mine. She blinked as a yawn overtook her—it was two in the morning and she'd had a hell of a night.

"I grabbed a room for us, second on the left." Deven came over. "You need sleep. I'll get our things; you need to rest."

"Thanks. What I need to do is to talk to a pair of nuns. I'd say Nitya as well, but for the most part, she's stayed out of what's going on with us. I'll call Aithnea and Jasiel from the room."

Deven nodded and took off.

What Vas wanted to do was to contact all of her people and make sure they were okay. But two a.m. wasn't the best time for that.

The rooms in the hangar were basic. Bed or beds, table and chairs, and a serviceable bathroom with a sonic shower. Right now, that bed looked like a fancy suite. Vas shook off her fatigue and forced herself to sit on one of the hard chairs. It wouldn't help matters if she fell asleep right in the middle of chastising the two nuns. She hit her comm for Aithnea.

"You're awake late. Is everything okay? You did rescue them, right?" Aithnea was perky but she no longer had to worry about having a body to get exhausted. Sleep, or lack thereof, wasn't a thing.

"Yes, we rescued our people, but both Deven and I collapsed afterward. It was like the biggest adrenaline crash ever. Why didn't you warn us?"

"We weren't certain that would be the result. And even if we had warned you, would you have turned down those abilities?"

Vas glared at her comm. It had been a long few hours and she didn't need Aithnea to be so right. "No. Neither of us would have. But does that mean if we use them again the same will happen? And are they turned off now?" She hadn't thought of that until this moment.

"Yes, it is turned off. We only made a temporary adjustment. As for the collapsing happening again, we honestly don't know. This is new for us too. We need to work with both of you once your immediate crisis is over. We do have a universe to save after all."

"Aithnea, someone managed to get on Home undetected and grab three of *my* people. *On Home.* I need to fix this."

Aithnea was silent for a few moments. "I'm going to work with Jasiel and Nitya on ways to help you find out who is behind the breach. And I understand your concern. Now, get some rest." She cut the comm before Vas could respond.

That pause before Aithnea responded was troubling. It usually meant that Aithnea knew something, or thought of something, that she wasn't up to sharing yet. Vas finished her shower and came out in a towel when Deven came in.

He appeared concerned as he dropped their bag on the table.

"What happened?" Fatigue vanished as soon as she saw his face.

"I was briefly followed here. And one of the security alarms on my place was tampered with. I fixed it and verified that the others were in place, no one got in. The tail following me hung too far back for me to see them—and they were blocking me."

Vas grabbed fresh clothes out of the bag. Blocking a telepath of Deven's level was extremely difficult. And could only be done by someone stronger than him. "We have to go back out there."

"No, we need rest." Deven took the clothes out of her hand. "My fatigue contributed to their following me as well as why they could block me. They were probably outside my house and tailed me from there. It's too late and there's nothing more we can do until daylight. At least nothing outside." He took her towel, kissed her, and they tumbled into bed.

CHAPTER THIRTY

V AS FOUGHT HER WAY OUT of a collection of disturbing and terrifying dreams. It was as if her subconscious was purging a lot of random thoughts all at once.

The room was strange and dark, but the well-muscled arm thrown across her waist was familiar. It took a moment to realize where they were. Then the aches from her adventures in the mine kicked in and reminded her.

"Time," she asked quietly.

"Too early," Deven muttered but didn't move.

"I was asking the comm. Wherever it is." Vas would love to sleep for another couple of hours. However long they'd slept, it hadn't been enough.

But she knew they didn't have that option.

Deven rolled over and hit his comm. "Grosslyn, any news?"

"Grosslyn went to bed a few hours ago. I'm helping out," Sachi answered. "But, there's nothing new to report. Aside from Delilah saying that she's bringing breakfast for everyone."

Vas rolled out of bed. "She's good, I'll give her that. And I'm exceedingly hungry. Quick showers and let's eat." She needed sleep, but the sound of a good home-cooked meal was too much to ignore.

Deven ended the comm with Sashi and within ten minutes they were both showered, dressed, and following their noses.

Delilah was coming into the hangar—under the watchful eyes of the newest guards on rotation. She must have shut her diner down for the morning, as an army of her staff came behind her with enough food to feed the entire planet.

She waved Vas and Deven down. "Given what happened last night, I didn't think you'd be up for coming to the diner. And that you might be calling back more of your crew to the hangar. Can't face an attack on an empty stomach!" She scurried off to shout orders to her staff.

Vas watched as Delilah's people, with some help from the waiting crew, set up rows of tables and chairs. She'd like to know how Delilah heard about what happened early enough to have this much food ready, but it smelled too good to even think about delaying eating long enough to ask.

Besides, Delilah was like Grosslyn in that regard, if anything happened on Home, those two were the first ones to know.

"Feeling better are we?" Delilah came back as Vas and Deven were dealing with the mountain of food on their plates. "You two worried me again. I don't like that." The tone in her voice made both of them look away from their plates and toward her. "We need to find those assholes and kick them off our planet. I'm too old for this kind of stress." To accent her words, she added two huge scoops of breakfast potatoes to their already full plates. "Eat up and get back out there." With a sniff, Delilah turned and marched down the line of chairs with her vat of potatoes and a fast scooper. No plate was left untouched.

"We have been told," Deven said with a grin that dropped a second later. "She has a point though; we need to get this locked down fast."

"Agreed. Our people aren't going to take it well when they find out that someone broke onto our planet." Vas kept eating, even though she wanted to get out to the investigation. But she figured it was prudent to mentally drop into merc mode. Which meant eating as much as you could, when you could.

"Before you ask, no. I haven't woken Gosta or Walvento yet. I was up too late isolating the original poison, and didn't trust myself to be functioning enough to complete anything after that," Terel said as she wandered up with a full plate of food and dropped into a chair across the table from them. Most of the crew were still asleep, but a few were trickling in. "Good to see you two took my advice to get some rest, even if it obviously wasn't enough. I guess I should be happy that you two are looking better and eating. What did your nuns say?"

Vas gave her friend a long stare. "What, you got an hour or so of sleep yourself? Your eyes don't droop like that unless you're still exhausted." She'd force Terel to go back to sleep, but most likely Terel would do the same for her.

Leaving them at a stalemate.

"Fine. But we have to locate these people, find out what they want, and why some of the contents in that case were level ten pathogens." Terel shook her head but kept eating, even though level tens could wipe out an entire planet in weeks.

"What?" Vas knew Terel better than almost anyone—and she knew if there was a danger, Terel wouldn't be sitting here.

Terel laughed when Deven didn't do more than shrug and keep eating. Vas wasn't the only one in merc mode.

"It's no fun trying to shock you two. They had three vials of variant level ten pathogens—*neutralized* pathogens. They had killers but pulled their teeth. This raises an even larger question of why did they have them. The contents of that case have proven fairly useless in finding out anything about our kidnappers. Most of the rest of the items were simple supplies. I am closing in on finding any matches for my blood compared to Walvento and

Gosta. Once it runs through the process, I'm hoping to finalize the antidote that they used on me to wake me up but didn't have in their cases. And once I recreate it, I think we should keep some on hand."

"Agreed," Deven shoved aside his empty plate. "I'm going to go back to my place and see if I can pick up any trail of the person who followed and blocked me." He got to his feet, kissed Vas, nodded to Terel, and left.

Vas nodded to Gon who was standing near the door and he followed Deven out. Vas figured that Deven noticed as soon as Gon started toward him. But he wouldn't send him back.

Vas had no idea what was happening, but no one was going on their own outside. Deven's place having an attempted break-in and his being followed last night made that clear. She shoved aside the fact that Terel, Gosta, and Walvento had been grabbed in a group. The odds were still better with more than one.

"Where's Xsit? I need her to start contacting our people."

Terel pointed behind Vas. A small office with a familiar-looking yellow feathered head in the window sat against the wall. "She's been at it for over an hour. Roha was with her but went to join the guards at the mine. With a second guard."

Vas turned back to Terel. "There has to be a reason they went after you three. You're all officers, and it would seriously hurt my crews, not to mention me personally, to have you taken. But what are they planning? And why were they in old solbilan mines?"

"Damn good questions. They could have been after you and Deven as they might have known that you two would rescue us. Hopefully, Gosta can help us with it all when I wake him up." Terel got to her feet. "Check on Xsit, I promise to grab you once either of them wakes up, or I have some great epiphany."

Vas nodded and pushed her plate away and then went to the small office that Xsit was using. Xsit could be impressive when she wasn't being frightened. She was moving so fast on her calls that she was a yellow blur. Vas stayed off to the side to watch, then knocked on the door when Xsit slowed down.

"Just wanted to see how it was going. Any non-responses yet?" Vas came into the office and shut the door behind her as Xsit finished off her last two calls.

"Not yet, but I did have five that I had to call back. Of course, I'm only partially through the list. Most people are coming here. Shien's people are checking on everyone in their hotel and keeping the doors locked. But their comms were glitchy and they complained they weren't working well even inside."

"How much solie have you had?" Xithinals usually didn't drink the stimulant drink as it hit them extremely hard, but Xsit was so wired her feathers were vibrating.

"A cup. Maybe five? I don't know. But we need to make sure everyone is okay. This is bad."

Vas put her hands on Xsit's shoulders and looked down into her eyes. "Yes, we need to make sure everyone is okay. But Nitya and Aithnea could help from the ship too. I need you to be okay as well." To be honest, she hadn't thought of Nitya doing the checks until now. Having a dead nun controlling a ship was difficult to keep in mind and Vas was still exhausted.

"Oh. I should calm down." Xsit's speech was slowing down. She probably only had two cups.

"Yes, you should. Relax, let me contact Nitya." It took a few minutes but Nitya's voice came over her comm. Vas quickly explained what they needed.

"That won't be hard. I can do it while Aithnea runs the scenarios for what happened to you and Deven. I do apologize for that, by the way. There was no indication that would happen."

Vas laughed. "I'd hoped there hadn't been, but Aithnea and Jasiel can be extremely goal-focused sometimes."

Nitya's laugh was rich and not heard often. "That was true when we were all alive, it remains so to this day. Don't worry, Vas. You saved me, I'll keep an eye out for you. Figuratively."

Vas signed off and looked to where Xsit was gulping down glasses of water. "Are you going to be okay?"

"Yes. I might have gotten too worked up." Xsit downed the rest of the pitcher to offset some of the solie. "I can't believe they got Walvento."

Vas knew the thought wasn't coming from him being more important than the other two. Xsit and he didn't run in the same circles. She was concerned for the same reason Vas was. Drugs or not, Walvento was a seasoned fighter and had a unique makeup that made him difficult to drug.

"Agreed. Why don't you take a break and have some breakfast. Then come back and monitor for anything unusual in the lanes. We need to make sure our people are okay, but we need to find who's behind this. There's probably some chatter out there, somewhere."

"Aye, captain." Xsit was only slightly jumpier than usual as she made her way to the food. The tables were getting full and crews were dragging more tables and chairs out from storage.

Vas knew that Terel would find her, but she needed to check on her two crew members regardless. The med area was calm but busy as Terel and Divee worked on something with a huge machine.

When Terel gave a happy yelp and jumped up, Vas knew her timing was good.

"You found the issue?"

Terel and Divee turned to her and the level of the two smiles was almost frightening.

"We did. I can have a treatment for both of them in a

few minutes." Terel's smile dropped. "And make enough to keep on hand. The combination of chemicals they used to create this concoction is scary and detailed. Whoever is behind this has a talented and evil chemist working with them. Now that we broke it, I can see how it was done—but it's tricky."

Vas dutifully looked at the images of what was done, but that wasn't an area she was good at. Terel always wanted her to look anyway.

"It's done." Divee had been running another machine and took out two vials.

"Excellent. I'll take Gosta, you take Walvento."

Vas stepped back. "You might want to secure Walvento, he doesn't wake easily in any circumstances."

Terel shook her head. "It's been so long since he's been knocked out, I forgot. Secure him, and maybe I should take him instead."

Divee pulled himself up. He wasn't a good leader, nor as large as Walvento, but he could hold his own. "I'm fine. Or I will be once we get him secured."

Vas hid her smile and helped him run restraints on Walvento's arms and legs.

"Where am I?" Gosta's voice was weak and extremely confused, but a wonderful thing to hear.

"How are you feeling?" Vas went to his other side and took his hand. "You had us worried."

He tried looking around but even lifting his head seemed difficult. "Was it those people that jumped us? I tried to fight back; I did. But then Walvento fell, and Terel fell…and that's all I remember."

"Yes. They got all three of us. Luckily, they didn't want Mac and Bathie so they ran for help." Terel hooked up an IV to Gosta. "Just making a few more adjustments, then you should be your normal self."

"Whaaaa?!" Walvento's yell had his regular tone, but like Gosta, was far weaker than normal.

"Settle down, Walvento! You were attacked, we're try-ing to help." Divee was almost stretched out across him to keep him down, even with the restraints.

Vas ran over and grabbed Walvento's face to make him look at her. "You know me. You're going to be fine, but stop fighting."

He closed his eyes and dropped his head back on the pillow. "They took me out. I didn't even fight back."

Vas released his face. "You can have Terel and Divee break down exactly what they took you out with, but trust me, you didn't have a chance."

"Not at all." Terel forced him to open his eyes so she could flash a light in them. "And you're welcome for us being able to bring you back."

"Was I the only one?"

"Nope. They got Terel and Gosta as well. Mac and Bathie had a nice fight on their hands but it looks like they wanted you three. I need you back up and run-ning as soon as possible." Vas kept her face serious. Telling Walvento how worried she'd been wouldn't do a damn thing.

"They should both be fully recovered within the hour. Food will help though." Terel smiled.

"I'm on it." Vas let out a sigh of relief as she went to grab some trays. She still wasn't happy about her people being kidnapped or her planet being invaded. But having Gosta and Walvento back made her feel better about fac-ing whatever in the hell was going on.

Delilah caught her while she was making up plates and took over the job after shooing Vas away. "Grosslyn's in his office and said you might want to see something he's found. I think Xsit might have gone with him."

"Thanks. Don't forget one of those is for Walvento." Vas handed the food trays over.

Delilah nodded and added triple the amount of every-thing to one platter.

Vas looked toward the guards at the front while she jogged to the offices. She doubted Deven and Gon would be back yet, and they weren't.

Grosslyn and Xsit were hunched over a monitor in the back of the office and from their tones, a mild argument was going on.

"And what have we found?" Vas asked as she joined them.

"Captain! We were looking on the dark web." Xsit was calmer than when Vas last saw her but still a little too hyped. She also tried to hide a small cup of solie behind her.

"Anything worthwhile?" The dark web was hard to find and dangerous to navigate. Xsit had become proficient at it during their time trapped outside of the Commonwealth.

"Just that the Commonwealth doesn't seem to realize yet that the barricade is down," Grosslyn said. "Even though they set the original version up."

"And that's worthy of the dark web?"

"Mostly it's only chatter that this would be a great time to invade the Commonwealth. But they seem to be joking." Xsit shrugged.

Vas hadn't spent enough time there to know if people joked on the dark web, but she'd take Xsit's word for it.

"More importantly, and not on the dark web, is the fact that three Lethian Assembly warships are coming our way. They haven't crossed into Commonwealth space yet, but they'll be there in a few days."

"Damn it, there's no way that's good. Are they passing anywhere near Solar?" Vas was still hoping to get the Lethian Assembly on their side for the fight against the Clongari, but that was looking less and less likely.

"No. If I had to guess, I'd say they're heading for us or at least this end of the Commonwealth." Grosslyn shook his head. "But I don't like guessing."

"Neither do I, but I think with what just happened, we have the right to be paranoid. Gosta and Walvento are awake and recovering. Terel is creating more of the cure to keep on hand in case this is something common from our invaders. We need to know who in the hell is behind this."

CHAPTER THIRTY-ONE

———

VAS, GROSSLYN, AND XSIT MADE more inquiries on the dark web, but nothing helpful came up. Nor did any initial scans show indications of anyone other than their own ships coming anywhere near Home within the past few weeks. After an hour of not resolving anything, Vas got up to leave for her own office.

"Keep working, and Grosslyn do a comm check on all former crew members, better yet, get Sachi and Delilah to do it. Nitya is calling all the active crew, but you know some of our old-timers have gone deep. We need to find them and continue checking on everyone. We also need someone to do a deeper search for ships that might have snuck onto the planet a while ago. This was too well planned to be last minute." Ignoring the fact there would have been no way for these invaders to know Vas and crew would be coming back—or when.

But there was also no way to know how long these people had been here waiting.

"What would you like me to do, captain?" Gosta came into the office with Walvento behind him.

"Or me? Terel cleared us to return to duty." The way Walvento's hands kept curling into fists made it clear he was hoping for a chance to break some heads. In all the years he'd been on her crew, Walvento had only gotten sick or injured enough for bedrest twice.

He didn't take losing any fight well. He might have understood Vas when she pointed out there was nothing he could have done based on the drugs the kidnappers used. But that didn't mean he accepted it.

"Walvento, do a full analysis of the weaknesses in town and the surrounding areas. Including the newer buildings, which Grosslyn can help you with. Also see if you can find out why the comm relay at the Pilthians' hotel is glitchy." Walvento wasn't a data digging guy, but looking for strategic weaknesses—usually of the enemy—was something he was good at. The Pilthians' comms could simply be some bug of the new hotel, or the start of something more sinister. Communications were vital during a fight.

Walvento nodded and left to find a monitor.

"Gosta, come with me, we have more digging to do. We need to find how those bastards got here." She'd been planning on having Xsit work on a deeper search of the records of all traffic in the area, but Gosta would be better. And that way Xsit could maintain general communications when people tried to reach them. Vas knew that as word got around, anyone too far away to drop into the hangar would be calling to see what they could do.

Vas sighed as she and Gosta went into her office. Returning to Home had been wonderful for a brief while. Not so much now.

Her comm buzzed as she settled in to do her search for hidden ships. "Vas here."

"You need to come up here," Aithnea's voice had that extremely calm tone which meant things were bad—not what Vas needed to hear right now.

"Damn it. Things are bad down here."

"I know, and if you don't want things to get far worse, get up here. Deven too."

Vas got to her feet. "Deven is tracking who followed him last night. Do you absolutely need him?"

"Not if you have a second Pirate of Boagada handy. If not, I'll need you both in your official functions. Soon."

"I'll find him. Something is impacting comms in one of our buildings, might just be them, might not. I'm bringing a radio just in case. If you try to reach me again and it doesn't go through, use the radio frequency. Flarik knows it."

"Find him and get up here." Aithnea cut out.

Vas pulled out a pair of radios and set both to be on-call. Along with various weapons requirements and technological limits, there were a few worlds which feared comms. They'd only had to use the radios a few times in battles but they might come in handy now. Hopefully, the comm system wasn't under attack and they wouldn't need them.

Gosta also got to his feet.

Vas motioned him to sit. "Aithnea needs Deven and me for something, so I'm going to hunt him down then take a shuttle to the *Destroyer's Curse*." She held up the radios. "Don't stop what you're doing, but can you send out a request for everyone to see if they have these? I know some made it to storage, but many are probably in closets."

"On it, captain." Gosta looked odd only working with one computer but his speed made up for it.

Vas jogged back to Grosslyn's office and told him what was going on.

"Who will you be taking with you if he doesn't respond to your hail?" Grosslyn asked with an immobile face.

"Good point. How about Walvento? Have Xsit take over his project." Vas probably wouldn't have left without a guard, but she hadn't thought about it.

Walvento was halfway to the hangar door before he responded. "Aye, captain!" He was fine doing things at a desk, he just preferred doing about anything else.

Vas nodded to Grosslyn and Xsit, then followed Walvento as she hit her comm for Deven.

"Vas?" It was Deven all right, but the comm was scratchy. Damn it. Not a good sign.

"Where are you? Aithnea needs us." If the comms were

compromised there was a slim chance someone could hack in. Telling their enemy that they would be in a shuttle soon wasn't a good idea.

"I can barely hear you. We're near the wharf."

Vas swore. They were further away than she'd like. "Go into the pub we used to go to and watch your backs." She couldn't explain it, but a chill went down her spine. It wasn't the wharf area specifically; it was everything between here and there. Deven would know which pub she meant, the Conweigh. Also, something better to not say on the comm.

"We can come back—"

"No." Vas cut him off. She couldn't explain it, but she didn't want Deven roaming around without her. "Can't explain now, but stay at the pub. And if you can find some old timer to sell you a radio, buy it."

"That's a good idea, we'll be there. Deven out."

Walvento had taken the time she was speaking to Deven to put on full body armor, grab a set for Vas, enough weapons to launch a small war, and two extra radios. "Anything else?"

"I think we're good." Vas slipped into the armor. Not common on the streets of Home, but this *was* a merc planet.

Double checking that everything was secure, she and Walvento marched out of the hangar. Five guards were visible, but she knew at least two more were hidden.

The distance to the wharf wasn't far, but there were places that would work well for an ambush. They usually didn't have to worry about things like that as this was her world and only certain people should be able to land. The weird feeling of foreboding—mostly relating to Deven and Gon—hit her again.

It was an odd time of day so there weren't many people out, and no one to trigger the feeling of being watched.

The wharf looked completely deserted. Which, weird

time of day or not, never happened. The fishing boats had left the dock hours ago, but there were always old fishermen and fisherwomen hanging around chatting. And retirees who never fished but liked being down here.

Even if she didn't already know something was wrong, she would by this.

Walvento unbuckled his massive blaster from its place on his waist, and Vas took out her two more normal-sized blasters.

She still wasn't great at telling when Keeper things kicked in, but the creepy feeling down her spine grew worse and didn't feel like normal instinct.

"Do you see anything?" Vas dropped her voice and spoke on an outgoing breath. A trick she'd learned from Aithnea and taught to all of her crews. The pub appeared as she remembered, but looked deserted.

"Nothing." Walvento wasn't as quiet as her, but it was doubtful anyone else could have heard him. Even if there had been more people around.

"I want you to go to the left and circle behind the pub. I'll be bait." She put both blasters in their holders but kept the guards open.

Once Walvento nodded and vanished, Vas walked out into the open and headed for the pub.

The armor should have been a clue for anyone watching her. But it was all black and she knew that from a distance she just appeared to be bulkier than she was.

The Conweigh was silent as she approached. Unless he was unconscious, she knew Deven wouldn't let her walk into a trap.

She grinned as her comm gave a series of clicks. Then repeated the pattern and stopped. Deven. His code said his group was fine, or in this case, he and Gon, but the location was compromised. They didn't use the comms that way often, as in the middle of a fight, you wouldn't hear them. But she was glad he thought of it now.

She tapped out a simple 'yes' reply. Then sent a tapped query to Walvento. His was a two word response—'in place'.

Vas walked to the pub door as if she was coming in for a drink, then dropped to the floor as blaster fire shot over her head.

From the sounds coming from the back, Walvento was having to fight his way in. Or someone put up a fight and Walvento wasn't in the mood to mess around. She couldn't see Deven or Gon from her spot on the floor, but that didn't mean much. She also couldn't see the shooter.

She felt more than heard her comm click again—'left'.

She rolled to the left as blaster fire hit where she'd been.

"Give up! We have this place surrounded!" Vas yelled as she pulled out both blasters.

"Never! You'll not be taking us alive for your war machine!" The voice was old, cranky, and almost completely drunk. And one Vas recognized immediately.

Vas seriously doubted that Achaius, a two-hundred-year-old Ilerian who'd retired from the merc business ten years ago, was working with their enemies.

It did explain Deven helping the old gunner out though. Most likely Gon was nearby and also keeping an eye on things.

"Achaius, what the hell are you doing? You live hours from here." Not that Achaius being in a pub or drunk was surprising—he'd always lived hard. But he hated the big city. There wasn't really any city on Home that was large enough for that moniker, but Achaius believed that anything where neighbors were closer than an hour's walk was too close—and therefore a big city.

"I came here because they chased us out! First, trying to recruit us old-timers by comm, then showing up on our property! Ain't right! You need to tell Tor Dain she's gone too far this time."

"Achaius, this *is* Vas. I didn't order anyone to chase you out of your homes. As for the comms, Home is under attack. They're checking all the crew and former crew to make sure everyone is okay. Put down your damn weapon and stand up."

Walvento poked open the kitchen door with the nose of his blaster but remained mostly hidden.

"You ain't the captain. You sound too old."

"It's her, and you're lucky she doesn't care about her age." Deven laughed as he stood up. "You also didn't recognize me and I was standing right in front of you. You might want to get your eyes, ears, and memory checked. Since you came into town and all."

Walvento pushed the kitchen door completely open. "He had Phila with him, she chased the staff out the back. I had to hit her to get her to stop attacking me."

Deven hadn't moved, but he held his blaster relaxed in his hand. Yet clearly pointing toward an upended table. Or who was hiding behind it.

"Deven? What the hells man? You were always a good guy." Achaius was sounding a little less drunk, but still confused. And pissed. "And Walvento? What kind of a trick is this? Fake Captain Tor Dain, I've got your men, show yourself."

Vas shook her head and slowly rose. She held both blasters aimed at the tabletop blocking her view of Achaius. "Now do you believe me?"

"You're still old."

"And you won't make it much older if you don't get out from behind that damn table. What the hell were you thinking?"

"I…I don't know, actually." Achaius got up. He was only part Ilerian, mostly that heritage just left him shorter than many beings, and with an extra set of arms. Or in his case, an extra arm. He'd lost one in a fierce battle a year before he retired.

"Put down your caster, please." Deven didn't lower his weapon.

The casters were old-school laser rifles. Not a great weapon in a small, enclosed place like a pub. Which made things more confusing for Vas. "A caster? To overthrow a pub? How was that going to help you fight people trying to recruit you for the war effort? One that doesn't exist, by the way." Vas figured the ongoing issues with the Lethian Assembly and the impending mess with the Clongari, did count as a war effort. But there was no way Achaius would have known that.

"I wasn't going to stay here. Just defend myself. They're following Phila and me. She lives a few miles from my place. We were the only ones who made it out. Never saw any of the others."

Vas put away her blasters and let out a breath. Enough real problems were going on, she was glad this one turned out to just be a bit of a crazy trip. He might not have seen any others because they stayed home and went about their business. "Come back to the hangar, we'll make sure you and Phila are okay, then give you a lift back home. How long ago did you leave?"

Achaius shrugged. "A few hours ago?" He squinted out of the one almost clean window. "Damn, is it daytime? We fled last night." He handed his caster to Deven. He nodded at Gon. "Were you there the entire time?"

Gon nodded and worked his way down to Vas.

There were no other bodies, alive or dead, but the pub was in shambles.

"You get to pay the owners to fix all of this." Vas knew that along with being a loner, Achaius was a money hoarder. This would be nothing for his coffers but could destroy the pub owners.

Achaius hung his head. "Yeah, I will. Phila and I both felt like we were still being followed when we got here. The pub looked like a good place to hide."

"And?" Vas waved her arms around the damaged place. "This isn't hiding."

"I know. It was weird. Something told me to take it over and defend Phila and me. She felt it too." His eyes went round and he looked toward the kitchen. "She's okay, right?"

Walvento nodded. "Yes, she kept fighting so I knocked her out. The blaster shots were only to scare you. And yes, Vas, I'll pay for the damage to the ceiling."

That wasn't normal procedure. But there was a big difference between fighting as mercs and fighting in your home world. Vas appreciated Walvento stepping up.

Deven followed Achaius toward Vas.

"Walvento? Can you and Gon escort Achaius and Phila, once she wakes up, back to the hangar? Tell Terel I'd like her to get specifics on the attack after she checks them out. And give them some rooms to rest in, then take them home once the area around their homes has been secured."

Achaius gave a smile. "Thank you, captain. And I didn't mean you were old."

Vas laughed. "It's been over ten years since we've seen each other—we've both changed since then. And old is better than dead."

Deven handed Achaius' caster to Gon. "Probably safer if he holds it for the trip back."

"Thanks, Deven. Can't believe I didn't recognize you when you offered to help me with the pub. I do need my eyes checked out." Achaius kept shaking his head like a man waking from a nightmare.

Vas mentally made note of that—it could have been something done to him and Phila before they fled. She knew the general area he lived in; all the residents were retired mercs who preferred living far from others. Why would anyone have been trying to get them? Her three who were kidnapped and a bunch of old fighters? There was a connection that she was missing.

Walvento darted back into the kitchen and returned with a groggy and unarmed Phila staggering alongside him. She was a Silante and shorter than Achaius but of a similar age. She'd been a fierce fighter back in the day but retired unexpectedly when Achaius did.

Vas had a clue now as to why. Even if she wasn't sure that Achaius knew.

The two old-timers remained between Gon and Walvento as they headed back to the hangar. After Vas mentioned that she'd felt like she'd been watched on the way here.

Deven started righting the furniture. "The owner and patrons shouldn't have gone far; this all went down minutes before you got here. Good thing you told us to stay here instead of coming back to the hangar." He narrowed his eyes. "How'd you know?"

"Not a clue. But something said there were problems here or on the way here. Even though you hadn't found them yet." Vas pulled up a table and then the chairs. "Probably more Keeper stuff. Whatever Aithnea wants us up on the ship for is important. Did you find out anything about who tried to break into your place?"

"Not a thing. There was a weak psychic trail from where I felt I lost the one tailing me last night, it led us down here, but aside from Achaius nothing was wrong."

"Thanks for saving my place." The owner came in. He was a Welischian breed and scowled around the pub as he spoke and Vas couldn't see his face. He finally looked up. "Captain Tor Dain? Deven? What are you two doing down here? Not that I'm not grateful. Achaius acted like he didn't even know me. Phila too." Salio was another old-timer. He'd been the master gunner who trained Walvento.

"We heard you had some problems." Vas stepped forward and clasped Salio's arm. "Don't worry, the repairs will be paid for. Achaius doesn't seem to know what happened."

Deven greeted Salio as the rest of the staff came back and took over straightening things.

"Well, thank you for coming down in person. It's good to see you two." With a quick smile and a nod, Salio turned back to his crew and started barking orders. He was more social than Walvento but still sounded like a master gunny.

Taking the dismissal, Vas and Deven left.

"I'm going to have a tactical team run out to Achaius' house and the surrounding area after Terel's interviewed both Achaius and Phila. But you and I should get up to Aithnea on the ship. She wasn't happy about whatever she wouldn't talk about over the comm." Vas handed Deven a radio and explained the comm issues with the hotel.

"There is someone up to something here, but I'll be damned if I can guess the endgame. The attack on Terel, Gosta, and Walvento was too easily resolved." Deven held up a hand. "I know, we had help. But still, why go through all of that, then only have them guarded by a small group? And what were they trying to get out of Terel?"

"She said she had no idea. They woke her up, tied her to the chair, and started hitting her not long before we ran in." Vas caught him up on all he'd missed by the time they got to the hangar.

Marwin was coming out as another guard went in.

"Actually, Marwin, I have a job for you and your sister and brother—plus at least four more. Achaius and Phila were attacked in their home area of Northlake. After Terel gives them an all-clear and has found out what she can, I need your group to escort them back and search the surrounding areas."

"Aye, captain!" Marwin gave a salute. "By the way, Ragkor and Therlian are looking for you."

"Thank you," Vas said as Marwin went to gather his team and another guard ran out to replace him. There probably wouldn't be much of a wait for them to leave, Vas wasn't sure what more information Achaius had or if Phila had much more. But Terel would be thorough and if there was anything helpful, she'd find it. She loved medicine, but she also loved sorting out mysteries.

"Where were Ragkor and Therlian?" Deven asked as they walked in.

"They'd been visiting Therlian's daughter. After we got our friends back, I told them to stay put for the night."

"Captain!" Ragkor yelled and saluted. Or started to, then stopped and blushed. Still a Marine. Ragkor was massive. Deven was tall at six and a half feet—Ragkor was over seven feet and had shoulders almost as wide as Xsit was tall. His blond hair was short and sheared so close to his head that it was obvious that he did it daily.

He was mostly human but had some exotic elements and a bit of precog ability of which he wasn't happy about but had come in handy a few times.

Therlian strode alongside him. A former Clionea novice, she was as tall as Deven and almost looked more like a Marine than Ragkor did.

"Good to see you both." Vas clasped their arms. "Any signs of trouble in Outer Highlands?"

Therlian responded first. "No, but I brought Kaena back with us. There's something wrong out there, but I couldn't tell what it was. Has Aithnea said anything?"

"Just that she needs to speak to Deven and me. Let me check something first. Deven can fill you in on what happened." Vas ducked into her office. Therlian never made it past the novice stage of the Clionea nuns. She'd fallen in love and gotten pregnant. And chose family. But she might be helpful with whatever Aithnea was calling them about.

"Are you on your way up?" For a dead woman, Aithnea's voice hadn't lost much of her authority when she wanted to use it. She was worried and pissed.

CHAPTER THIRTY-TWO

"WE JUST GOT BACK. AND will be coming up. But, I wondered if bringing Therlian along might be a good idea."

"I don't…yes, Jasiel is saying yes. Even though she's never met Therlian. But yes, you three need to come up immediately." Aithnea cut the comm.

Vas went back out to the main hangar. "Ragkor, I need you to oversee everything here. Marwin and his siblings will be running some old timers back to Northlake and recon the area. Gosta can fill you in on the rest. Therlian is coming up to the *Destroyer's Curse* with Deven and me to talk to Aithnea. And Jasiel."

Therlian blinked. "Jasiel? As in the founder of the Clionea nuns? I thought she died years ago."

"Her reported death wasn't accurate. Let's go, Aithnea sounded cranky and there's more information you need before we get there." Vas had already been found to be the next Keeper in training when she and the *Traitor's Folly* left here months ago. She'd even asked Therlian for help. But Deven as the Pirate was new. And something it might be best to keep limited knowledge of for now.

Therlian ran to tell her daughter she was leaving, while Vas and Deven went to find a shuttle. Ragkor left to talk to Gosta and Grosslyn. One advantage of a former Marine, he rarely questioned orders.

"You want to fly or me?" Deven was being polite, but Vas motioned for him to take the pilot's seat.

Therlian must have run both ways as Vas was belting into the nav seat when she came up, shut the door, and buckled in. "Ragkor is bursting with questions, by the way." She laughed. "I've gotten to know his tics. It was all he could do to stay quiet."

"Eh, he'll get more answers than he wants from Gosta and Grosslyn." Vas waited until Deven lifted off before turning to Therlian. "By the way, I'm a full Keeper now, and Deven is the current Pirate of Boagada. That's what the nuns want us for. Oh, and we've added another dead nun. Her name is Nitya, she died five-hundred years ago and she's been integrated into the *Destroyer's Curse*."

Therlian let out a whistle. "Anything else?"

Vas gave a short round-up of their trip and that they needed to rebuild the Clionea nuns to save all known space from the Clongari.

"I'm not even sure what to say to that. Any idea why Aithnea wants me up there?"

"Jasiel requested you. No idea, but she knows you're not going to resume the calling."

"Good. I don't mind helping and I'm glad the order is coming back. But that isn't part of my life anymore. It does sound like you have been having all the excitement the past few months, though. We ran patrols, but with that barricade locked, there was little activity anywhere near here."

Jasiel waited for them in the landing bay and was either talking to herself or, more likely, having a serious debate with Aithnea through the ship comm.

Flarik stood partially hidden behind her, looking tense and Flarik-ish. The feathers on the back of her neck were slightly raised.

"Flarik is pregnant?" Therlian picked it up immediately even though there was little to see of Flarik's body. And even if there were, it would be difficult to tell visually. Therlian might have left the order long ago, but she still had some Clionean sensitivities.

"Yup, but I wouldn't ask her about it. She wasn't initially happy about staying with us after she found out." Vas turned to Therlian. "Although, I did use you as an example. Flarik was afraid people wouldn't fear her as much when she was a mother."

Therlian laughed. "If I didn't know her, and saw her right now? I would probably stay in the shuttle. She's still fierce."

"Good. If she asks you about motherhood, remind her of that." Vas unlocked the door and Jasiel came forward. Flarik remained behind the partial shield, glaring.

"Thank you for coming up. It's wonderful to meet you, Therlian. Aithnea told me of you." Jasiel nodded to all three and then hustled them out of the landing bay.

Flarik pulled Vas aside. "I need to speak to you and Deven before you return to the planet."

"Is it urgent?" Vas knew Flarik well enough to know she was seriously upset about something.

"Sort of, but so is what the nuns found. My issue can wait until they are done. I'll be in my room." With a curt nod, she marched down another corridor.

Vas caught up to Jasiel and the rest at the lift. "Where's Aithnea? And are you having comm problems at all up here?" Since the only way that Aithnea and Nitya could communicate outside of the holosuite was through the comms, if whatever was compromising them in the Pilthians' hotel hit the ship, they could be in serious trouble.

Jasiel scowled as Vas filled her in on the Pilthians' comm issues. "No, but I agree that you all might want to be careful with using them on the planet. Aithnea is getting the holosuite ready."

"More training? We're kind of busy planet-side," Vas said.

"That's part of it, and why we need more training."

"You think what's happening on Home is because of what Vas and I are now? How could anyone know?" Deven asked as he walked behind the rest.

"My sister knew about Vas. She might have sensed Deven's part before she died. We have no idea if she told anyone." Nitya's voice came through a nearby comm as they went down the hall. "Very nice to meet you, Therlian. I'm Nitya."

Therlian nodded. "Nice to meet you too. I was never good at most history when I was a novice, but who was your sister?"

"Her name was Kalth, and she was evil. It's a long story." The tone in Nitya's voice was resigned but also conveyed that she wasn't up to talking about it now. "She's finally dead. For good this time."

Judging by the look on her face, the relief in those last words told Therlian all she needed to know.

The holosuite brought a low whistle from Therlian. "This is massive. The strategy holos that could be run is impressive. Any chance we can get some more Hive ships to convert?" It took a lot to bring a smile to Therlian's face, but she was grinning like a drunken Ilerian right now.

"If they don't join us in the next fight, maybe so," Vas said as the door slid shut behind them.

Aithnea appeared in holo form along with a Clionean workout room behind her. "I know, we need to talk first. Some weird things are going on down below. But we need to train as well. Jasiel and I are not in agreement, but I believe these attacks are related to you two and you need to be prepared."

"I didn't say that, I said we don't have enough evidence." Jasiel didn't sound upset although they'd been debating things as the shuttle landed.

"How would they have known when the *Destroyer's Curse* was coming back?" Therlian was still examining the holosuite.

Jasiel nodded. "That's my point. This could be unrelated. But, we did get some odd communication an hour ago, and Nitya is tracking it out of the Commonwealth. Way out. But we haven't locked onto the point of origin yet."

"Because those bastards are bouncing it all over known space." Nitya was pissed.

"This communication is related to the attacks?" Deven asked. "So far we've had the kidnapping of three of our people and whatever happened to Achaius."

"And that's what we know of," Vas added. "Whoever is behind this isn't being stealthy, but I'm not sure of their agenda. Or how they got people on to my planet."

Aithnea sighed and the workout room vanished. "Jasiel and Nitya were right; we need to sort this out first. But I'm not sending you back down without a practice or two. Neither of you should have collapsed like that last night."

Last night she hadn't been sure why Vas and Deven collapsed. Obviously, she'd found something since then.

Vas waved around the empty holosuite. "Can we have some chairs and a screen to see this odd communication? I agree that we need to find out where it's coming from, but knowing what it is would be a start." The command deck would be easier, but this way Aithnea could be seen. Nitya could as well if she wanted.

Chairs, a table, and a widescreen appeared.

"We're not sure. It's heavily encoded and so far unbreakable." Jasiel called up an image on the screen. "It has massive amounts of data in it, and while I think we've blocked it right now, some of it might still be streaming to the planet."

The graphs would probably make more sense to Gosta or Hrrru, but from Deven's scowl, he caught enough to be concerned.

"That's a massive silarian carrier wave. We have to break it." He got to his feet and went closer to the screen. "Terminal." A copy of one of the science terminals from the command deck appeared and he started running different options. "There's a cipher blocking all access." He gave a grim smile. "But there's a lot of power devoted to it. Which means they're fighting to keep things locked."

Therlian also got to her feet, tilted her head, and narrowed her eyes at the screen. "It's in Clionean cant. Or an old form of it."

"What?" Aithnea managed to make that word sound like a swear word. "I would think the three of us would have picked that up…" Aithnea's hologram tilted her head and she squinted at the screen. Then she really started swearing.

Jasiel did the same but with a little less swearing. "Damn. I would say we shouldn't have missed it, but we did. And you're right, Therlian—it's an old form. It was one of the few things already in place when I brought back the nuns nine hundred years ago."

"I wasn't a fan of history," Therlian said. "But I enjoyed learning the cants when I was a novice. Well, that and fighting." She grinned. She still really enjoyed fighting.

"This will take a while to translate as the computers won't be able to. Therlian, would you remain with us?" Aithnea's hologram motioned for the door. "You two are welcome to stay in here, but it might be boring. Just don't leave the ship. We'll get to your training soon."

Deven and Vas left, although Deven did look like he was debating staying.

"Let's go see what Flarik wants." Vas took his arm and led him to the lift. "I'm sure you'll still have plenty of data and information to dig through later."

He sighed. "Good point. I want to know who in the hell sent it as much as what they sent. And from where."

Vas nodded as they went down to Flarik's floor. She'd deliberately picked a level with no one else on it and had spread out over two adjoining rooms.

The swearing and crashing sounds on the other side of the door pointed out they'd found the right room.

"I almost hate to disturb her." Deven paused before knocking.

"Yeah, but she'll get more worked up if we wait."

Deven had barely knocked when the door slid open and a hysterical Flarik grabbed them both and pulled them inside.

Vas had her hand on her blaster. She'd never seen Flarik like this and there had been some weird situations in the past few years. She'd been agitated when they saw her in the landing bay—she was far beyond that now.

Her feathers were standing upright and changing colors wildly. Considering that Wavians had complete control of their feather color from a year old, this was almost as disturbing as the look on Flarik's face. Her eyes were huge.

"Thank the stars you two are here. Someone is trying to steal my baby."

CHAPTER THIRTY-THREE

VAS THEN NOTICED THAT FLARIK'S small bump was gone. She'd laid her egg within the past hour. "When did you lay the egg and who tried to steal it?"

"Right after I left you in the landing bay. I don't know who is trying to steal it, but they are still at it." With a snarl, Flarik ran into the second room with Vas and Deven right behind. "Not this time either!" She screeched at a volume Vas hoped to never hear again.

Vas thought the lights had simply been dim, but after Flarik's yell, they returned to normal. "That darkness was them?"

"Yes." Flarik stomped to the giant nest in the center of the room and sat on her egg. Her feathers settled down color-wise but many of them were still upright.

Deven walked around the nest room slowly, then did the same in the front room before coming back. "How long ago did the attacks start? Right after the egg was laid?"

"Yes. I was recovering when that cloud appeared. They want my baby. I didn't call you as I was hoping they would go away on their own. This wasn't what I needed to speak to you about, but it is of a greater urgency." Her hands were clenching and releasing rapidly. She wanted to strangle whoever was behind this.

"Can you sense anything, Deven?" Vas was creeped out but wasn't sure if it was due to Flarik's odd behavior or a reaction to the weird darkness.

"There's something. But it's fading too fast, I can't pin

point what it is." He swore under his breath. "Damn it, it's completely vanished now."

Vas turned back to Flarik. "Is it similar to anything your people know of?"

"No." Flarik scowled. "Nothing beyond old hen tales anyway." She paused and took a deep breath. "There are ancient stories of the soul takers. That during times of great danger to our people, heroes are born. The soul takers want those babies to build their own power. But it's a bedtime tale. There's nothing real about it. Soul takers don't exist." By the tone in her voice, Flarik didn't completely believe her own words.

Neither did Deven. "That ancient belief, if not the exact term, is found on most worlds with a high level of telepaths. I know this is a sore point for you, but your baby has already shown they are something special."

Modern Wavians tried to suppress any information about telepathic or similar abilities in their people. Vas wasn't sure why, and she sure as hell wasn't going to ask Flarik right now.

Flarik glared at him and adjusted her seat on her egg. A few weeks ago, the nanites and Kantari referred to her unborn child as a queen. One who would be born to save her people in times of terror. And Flarik refused to agree. At least not to anyone else. The flash of doubt on her face indicated she might not be admitting it out loud.

"Flarik, whether you want to believe it or not, there is something unique and special about your baby." Vas kept her voice as calm and soothing as possible. She'd never faced Flarik in a fight, but she knew damn well who would win.

It wouldn't be her.

Deven stayed behind Flarik at Vas' words. Most likely to make sure nothing happened.

Flarik clicked her teeth, glared, and ruffled her feathers.

She finally sighed. "I agree that my child does seem to be something…unique. But right now, we need to protect it."

"I might be able to help with that." Deven came around her. "But I need that thing, whatever it was, to appear again. I wonder…" He hit his comm. "Aithnea, did another odd communication come through about three minutes ago? Or try to?"

Vas swore.

"Yes, not long after you left. But we still haven't translated the cant yet. Is everything okay down there?" The sudden tenseness in her voice said she'd picked up on something.

"Not really. Flarik laid her egg. Something is appearing down here as a darkness and is coming after Flarik's baby."

"That's not good." Nitya's voice came from the wall comm. "Flarik? Do you mind if I run a detailed scan? It won't hurt your baby."

"Thank you, I appreciate anything you can do." Flarik still appeared ready to kill someone, or many someones, but she calmed down enough not to sound like it.

"Everyone stay where you are please, just for a few moments. There will be an odd colored light, but it won't hurt any of you."

"Standing still," Vas said.

The light was strange. Not extremely bright but it seemed to fluctuate colors softly as it moved over the room like a living thing. It remained over Flarik and the nest the longest, then vanished.

"I've found trace elements of something, but can't get a full reading now. I can block anything of that sort from entering your room for a few hours. By then we'll know what we're facing. I will need you to remain in your rooms, however."

Flarik's feathers finally went completely down. "Thank

you. I brought in supplies when I realized it was time for the egg, so we'll be fine here."

"Good. This might also help with sorting out the communications. They are definitely connected. Nitya out."

Vas liked that Nitya usually announced when she was ending a communication. Aithnea simply vanished.

Deven smiled. "I'm not completely sure what she did, but I feel something around this room—something good. What did you originally want to speak to us about?"

Flarik sighed. "I was going to tell you I was expecting the child in a few days. They decided to appear early." She scowled. "I had hoped to have my co-parents here for the arrival of the egg, but the little one thought otherwise." An almost blissful look crossed Flarik's face before she shook it off. "I do wish that I could be planet-side for this newest attack, however. I believe cracking some heads would be therapeutic for me. Since I will have some time to think, I'll see if I can discover anything of use against the attacks occurring on Home." She nodded expectantly.

"We'll see ourselves out." Vas turned for the other room. "If you need us or find out anything, have Nitya run the comm through the ship. We're not sure if the greater comm system has been compromised." Hopefully whatever impacted the comms for the Pilthians in the hotel wouldn't become widespread. Or get to the ships. But it wasn't something she wanted to risk.

"Understood." Flarik snuggled in on her egg and her eyes began to close.

Deven waited until they'd not only left Flarik's room but were on the lift back up to the holosuite. "Her hearing is too acute. But I wonder if the nanites are somehow involved. At least in the communications and whatever was trying to reach the baby."

"They should all still be dormant, right?" The lift stopped but Vas turned Deven toward her before the door opened. "*Right?*" Those damn things were in him as well. If any of them had gone active they had a hell of a lot more to worry about than she thought.

"Mine are dormant, as they promised. We can check the ones in Delimara, but Nitya is tracking her carefully, she'd know if they went live." Deven leaned down closer to her face. "I promise."

Vas narrowed her eyes. When those nanites decided to shut Deven down, he collapsed without warning and couldn't be awakened until they allowed it. She wanted to believe he was right, but she also wasn't going through that again. The nanites had promised to go dormant as long as they were returned to their space on the edge of everything where they were from—the same sector that the Clongari were from. "Fine. But I want Terel to do a full workup when we get back to the planet. If they're not involved, then what else might it be?"

"Damn good question, but there's definitely a connection between the weird communications and that cloud going into Flarik's room." He walked to the holosuite.

"You don't think it was after her egg." It wasn't a question. "But then how did she make it vanish by that scream? Which I never want to hear again by the way."

"I don't believe it was. It felt almost like a living thing. As for her yell, that was a Wavian war cry. You probably didn't feel it but it carries a psychic element to it. That was what made the darkness vanish."

"And you didn't point that out to Flarik." Flarik seemed to be in serious denial about her or her baby having anything to do with telepaths. Never mind that her people had an ancient history of it.

"I thought it was safer not to. If that thing is malevolent, and does come again, I don't want her to not use the yell out of principle. She's going to have to get over her sentiments about Wavian telepaths, but not right now."

The door to the holosuite slid open to show Jasiel,

Therlian, and Aithnea crowded around the one station. Even though they'd added three more to the holo room.

"What have you found?" Vas and Deven joined them but none of them looked up until she spoke.

"Therlian cracked the code." Jasiel beamed as if she'd known all along Therlian would be the one to do it.

Knowing the weird nun powers Jasiel had, she might have.

"What does it say? Any clue as to who sent it, or from where?" Deven got out before Vas could. He was also tall enough to look over the others to see part of the screen.

Jasiel's smile vanished. "It's instructions for a ritual. Not one of ours, even though they're using one of our old cants." She sighed. "Nitya is still trying to track it down. Whoever is sending it is still bouncing the signal all over. The good news is that there's no indication it's hitting the planet, so probably not related to your issues down there."

"I caught the probably." Vas looked at the screen, but even translated it didn't make any sense. Then a painful blazing stabbing shot into her head. She whimpered and dropped to her knees, clutching her head as the symbols and images hit her mind and started rampaging around. "Oh damn. Turn it off."

Deven grabbed her shoulders. "Will you let me block it?"

Vas knew he meant entering her mind to do so. "Just. Make. It. Stop." She barely got the words out through her clenched teeth. It was as if someone was pouring all the information in the universe into her head through a painfully small funnel.

Coolness flowed over her, and as suddenly as it hit, the pain stopped. "What was that?" The words sounded correct in her head but came out of her mouth in a weird language…that she understood, even though it wasn't one she'd heard before. She fell from her knees to her ass as she looked at the others. "That's not good." Same thing as the first sentence, normal in her head—not so much when she spoke.

Same blank looks on everyone's faces around her.

Except Deven. He looked confused. Then his eyes narrowed. "Say something else."

"I don't know what to say, what this is, or why it's happening."

"That's old Asarlaí. The same one Yesenia and those other three Solarian telepaths used." He dropped down next to her and looked at the others. "I can't understand completely what she's saying, but Marli once demonstrated the language. It wasn't one she knew well and was used long before the Asarlaí tried to take over everything a thousand years ago. It was fascinating." He was slipping into entranced academic Deven.

Vas shook his arms and spoke slowly. "How do I stop it?" She needed him to fix her, then he could wander around the mysteries of an extremely dead language.

This time Jasiel gave a small smile. "She asked to stop it. No, I don't speak Asarlaí." A shudder went through her shoulders. "But something about the words is familiar. I think it might be in one of the Keeper books." She frowned. "Or the Pirate of Boagada codes."

Vas nodded. "Stop."

"She said stop." Nitya chimed in from the speaker. "Keep talking and I can create a program to translate it."

Vas dropped her head into her hands. She didn't want it translated; she wanted it out of her head. Even though she understood it, there was no way for her to speak in anything else. "This is the stupidest language I have ever heard of."

Nitya popped in as a hologram and looked far too excited. "She said she hated this language." She paused when Vas shook her head. "No. It's a stupid language. This is fascinating! A connection between the ancient Asarlaí

and the original Clionea nuns? No one ever hypothe-
sized anything like that."

"You like research, don't you?" Vas had nothing against
scholarly folks, the love of her life was one. But she recognized the look on Nitya's face as one she'd seen on
Deven, Terel, Gosta, and Hrrru at various times.

She didn't want to become a project.

Not to mention, how in the hell was she going to take
care of whatever was taking place on the planet without
being able to be understood by her people?

"I do like research! This is so interesting." It took Nitya
a few moments to mentally translate what Vas said, but
she did. Then she turned to Deven. "But it didn't hit you.
Must be either only a Keeper trick, or it will hit later.
Someone sent that code specifically at Vas and maybe
Deven for a reason." Her hologram came closer as if she
was looking for a way to climb into Vas' head.

"Can you fix me?" Vas tried not to whine; it wasn't her
style. But this, on top of everything else, was leading to
whining.

"Ah! She asked if I could fix her." Nitya's hologram
at least had the decency to blush. "Which should have
been my first concern, I do apologize. I believe I can. But
it might take a while. Maybe you two could start your
training workout with Aithnea and Jasiel while I work
on this?"

Vas started to shake her off, but Aithnea clapped. "That
would be perfect. We need to run through some of the
exercises from last night and see what made both of you
leak power and then collapse. It'll be even better if there's
a communication issue to complicate things."

"I hate you sometimes." Vas got to her feet and Deven
followed.

"I caught that one." Aithnea grinned evilly.

The workout was exhausting and moved so quickly

Deven didn't have time to try and translate Vas' Asarlaí speech.

Each time Vas and Deven accessed the mojo they'd used to find their missing people and save them, they crashed immediately after.

"There's something wrong with the thing you're having us tap into." Vas continued to speak weird Asarlaí the entire time even though Nitya was still working on sorting it out. Personally, Vas couldn't find the connection between her picking up the long-dead language, a bizarre, way-out-of-the-Commonwealth communication using one of the nuns' old cants, and the attack on Flarik's still-in-the-shell baby.

Aithnea paused for a moment then nodded as she understood what Vas said. "There's nothing wrong with the system, it's something with the two of you. The tigerian flow of power is a powerful part of the Keeper and Pirate abilities. If you can't use it, we're going to be limited in what you two can do in the final battle."

Both Vas and Deven stopped at her words.

"We're supposed to help bring back the order, but we have to fight the Clongari like this?" Deven grabbed a pair of water tubes and tossed one to Vas. "I haven't had any amazing insights into that, by the way. I don't remember my first time as the Pirate of Boagada, but shouldn't something have changed?"

Jasiel and Aithnea's hologram exchanged looks. Then turned back with smiles.

"They would be subtle changes," Jasiel responded. "As for fighting the Clongari, if we're lucky, we won't have to fight them. Hopefully, no one will have to and they can go back to lurking in their little hellhole of space on their own."

"And if not, then yes, we'll be needing you two to fight as our representatives. Fully trained. Right now, we can't even get you past this level." Aithnea stalked around them both as if their collapsing was deliberate.

"Look, I first need to stop speaking this way. Then we have to sort out who in the hell is attacking Home. *Then* we can move on to the rest." Vas was getting used to the weird language she was speaking, but there was no way that she could command her people while speaking it. It had been an annoying exercise in charades just trying to coordinate the fighting between her and Deven. She wasn't going to do that with her entire crew.

"Nitya is almost there. She's still worki—" An alarm cut Jasiel off before Vas could.

Deven ran to the comm in the holosuite. "Are we under attack?"

"I don't think so. There's a small fighter coming in fast from the Commonwealth border, but they're projected to hit the planet, not any of the ships." Nitya's voice sounded distracted. "I can't reach them. Wait a minute, I think I can now. Patching through."

"Mayday. Mayday. This is the *Crooked Lady* coming in with no power and no control. Get everything out of my way."

Vas and Deven shared a look as the message repeated itself.

"That voice is familiar…Janx?" Vas looked at the comm. It was an auto message, but the wording was also very Janx. Mac's cousin wasn't as much of a smart-ass as he was, but she was close.

She also was a dozer pilot, cleaning up other people's space battles in a massive junk mover named *Betsy*. Vas motioned for Deven to say something. "She won't understand me." Even if she had an auto-responder on, if Janx was alive and conscious, she should be able to communicate.

Deven hit the ship's comm. "*Crooked Lady*, come in. Janx? Is that you? Can we help?"

"Deven? Thank the stars. Not sure how you can help, my ship fell under attack from some pirates right outside of the Commonwealth. It's done for. Just trying to crash in the ocean. Is Vas there?" It was Janx all right, but the amount of machine screams, alarms, and whistles said the *Crooked Lady* wasn't going to be around much longer.

"Yes, but talking is a problem for her at the moment. How much navigation do you have left?"

"Not much. You have a nice big ocean down there. Aiming for that."

Vas hit her comm to Nitya. "Can you connect to the hangar? Maybe we can scramble something to help her." Not only was the comm potentially a problem, but Vas wasn't up to anyone on the planet trying to translate her.

"Aye, captain. I have Gosta, Grosslyn, and Mac. Um, Mac has already taken a shuttle and launched—they picked up Janx's distress call at the same time we did. Gosta thinks the best option is to rescue her after she crashes and is calling for a sailing vessel to head out to sea. Grosslyn asks if you're sure she's a friend or if he can shoot her out of the sky."

Vas rolled her eyes. "Tell him yes. Janx is a friend. And…I can tell it's her." She wasn't sure until that moment, but she knew in her gut that was Mac's cousin, not someone pretending to be her. When and how she traded in her dozer for a flashy high-end fighter was something to deal with once they saved her.

"Deven, I see a shuttle heading my way, but it's too late. Tell them to stay back. I'm entering the atmosphere now." The alarms going off in her ship almost drowned out her words.

"It's Mac."

"Oh shit. I'm going to pick up speed and try to lose him before he does something stupid." Janx and Mac had grown up together and she knew him well.

CHAPTER THIRTY-FOUR

—◆—

DEVEN CALLED THROUGH TO MAC. "Stand down, her ship is out of control. You can follow her to her crash location, but you can't stop it from happening."

"I have to try."

"Damn it, Mac! You'll mess up my eject! Back off!" Janx's voice was still barely heard above the whine of her dying ship—but it was clear enough to know she was pissed.

Vas smiled. Janx hadn't been a pushover during her time with them, not at all. But she'd changed in the past few months. And not only the ship she flew.

"Backing off. I will follow you down." There was more relief than annoyance in Mac's voice, but it was still there.

Vas watched the screen as the sleek and expensive-looking fighter, the *Crooked Lady,* broke through the atmosphere, with Mac's shuttle remaining a safe distance behind.

Within moments, the fighter ditched into the middle of the ocean.

"Is that a parachute?" Vas asked.

"Yep." Deven grinned. "Getting better at understanding you."

"Got her! Her chute is tangled, and she's still outside the shuttle, but she's not dead." Mac yelled into his comm.

"Deven, Gosta wants to know if the ship should still go out there. It's a salvage vessel," Nitya called through the comm.

Deven looked at Vas and she nodded. "Yes, tell him that Mac has the pilot, but we should save the fighter if we can."

"They're on it."

Mac cut back in again. "She's soggy, pissed off, and still tied up in her chute, but I have Janx inside the shuttle and we're returning to the hangar."

"Understood. Make sure Terel checks her out," Deven said before Vas could even open her mouth. Maybe she was predictable.

"I have found it." Nitya's hologram popped up next to Vas.

"Have a cure for this weird language? Found where the transmission is coming from? Who is attacking Home? Any of our ongoing problems?"

Nitya laughed. "This." She slapped the palm of her hand on Vas' forehead.

The force didn't seem strong but it sent Vas flying across the room. She jumped to her feet once she landed. "What in the hell was that for?" Vas stopped yelling as she realized her words weren't coming out in ancient Asarlaí. "I think it worked. Yup, you all hear this, right?"

Everyone nodded.

"Great, but we still don't know who sent the message or why. Deven and I are returning to the planet, but I need you to find out and keep Flarik and her child safe. Therlian? You staying here for now?"

Therlian paused but then nodded. "Yeah. I have people staying with Keara, I can take down one of the remaining shuttles later. I want to help sort this."

"Excellent. Keep us updated." Vas grabbed Deven's arm and swung him out of the holosuite.

"We could still help them." He was always up for research.

"And Aithnea could make us run more training scenarios. You heard her, she has enough recordings of us, including biological data, to figure out any other issues we had. Now move faster." Vas knew that Aithnea wouldn't trap them here—or so she hoped. But, she wasn't up for a fight at this point.

"Agreed." Deven also picked up speed and they were in the shuttle and prepping to leave when Aithnea contacted them.

"Well played. But I'll be running through what we got carefully. You are both far more in touch with the tigerian flow of power than before, but I want to make certain there's nothing else wrong. I'm sure Terel's people can conduct any more tests if needed." Then she was gone.

"Are you going to respond?" Deven cleared the ship's doors and headed the shuttle toward the planet.

"If she wanted one, she wouldn't have cut the comm." Vas closed her eyes, leaned back in the nav chair, and rubbed her temples. "Merc life was so much less stressful."

"I hate to say it, but it was. Damn. What the hell is that?"

Vas opened her eyes but didn't have to ask what. There was a war class vessel within visual range. And it was firing at something much smaller in approach to the planet.

"Mac, you're not in the air, right? Are any of our ships in the air?"

"Only you, captain," Mac said. "Terel is checking out Janx."

"Damn it. Get me Grosslyn." The warship wasn't aiming at her and Deven, but it could be they hadn't been picked up yet. The screen could only go so detailed, but there was definitely something small the larger ship was aiming at.

"Grosslyn here."

Vas quickly told him the coordinates of the incoming ships. "We don't want to contact them directly as that thing could blow us out of the sky." Her shuttles were far better armed than anything on the market, but a single one couldn't hold against something that big. "I can't even tell who it belongs to." Moving closer also wasn't a good idea.

There was a pause, and then Grosslyn was back. "Gosta confirmed that it was a pirate vessel, captain. No officially listed registry and not cleared to be in Commonwealth space. Can I please blow it out of the sky?" That last was a full whine and Vas knew Grosslyn's hand was hovering over the launch buttons for the massive planetary guns.

"Try contacting it first." Vas felt a chill as she watched the large vessel. Either it was her merc skills or weird Keeper mojo, but something was seriously off about that ship. "Actually, have Ragkor contact them. They back off immediately or they get shot down. One warning only. And see what you can find about the ship they're chasing. Judging by what I can see, it's following Janx's trail in. Ask her if she was tailed by whoever shot down her ship."

Vas wasn't happy. There was too much shit happening around and on her formerly extremely secret planet. That it was timed to when she got back made her even more pissed.

"Aye, captain. Do you want Ragkor to contact you?"

"Not yet. Wait and see how this goes down."

Deven was on a direct course to the hangar but detoured to avoid crossing the other ships' flight paths. They needed to get out of the sky quickly, preferably before Grosslyn started firing at anyone. But it was also better to stay unnoticed if possible.

Deven was on approach for the hangar from another angle when the comm crackled.

"Vas here."

"Captain …Vas," Ragkor was getting closer to using her first name without hesitation. "The ship is refusing to respond and they shot out two of Grosslyn's satellites."

"Tell him to fire at will. But, no overkill. Just blow that thing out of the sky. We have no idea if they're reporting to anyone and they don't need to know our full capability. Any information on whatever it is they're chasing?"

"It looks like a modified dozer, captain." Gosta cut in. "Sorry for intruding, we just identified it, but the name is scrambled. The pilot has some serious skills in evasion."

Vas ran her fingers through her hair. The damage was already done, that dozer already knew where Home was. Any chance that Janx showed up at the same time as a dozer being a coincidence was extremely slim.

"Follow the dozer with a gun, but don't fire unless it does something dangerous. But Grosslyn should blow the crap out of that warship. Now."

"Aye." Ragkor clicked off.

The pirate warship was getting better at almost striking the dozer, even with the seemingly random zig-zagging it was doing.

Vas had seen simulations as to how the planetary defense guns would work, but it wasn't the same as really seeing them in action. Two bolts of bright orange light shot up from two different locations on the planet and obliterated the warship.

The explosion was so large that the dozer tumbled for a moment before dropping into the atmosphere.

Deven landed the shuttle in the hangar and Vas watched as the dozer changed direction away from the ocean and followed them down but went to the landing field next to the hangar.

"I want a fully armed crew surrounding that dozer when it lands. Find out who's in it, and what the hell they're doing here." If Mac hadn't pulled Janx from the ocean, she would have said the dozer pilot was her. Janx had sort of been on the run when they parted ways, and if anyone could manage to hide a registered ship's name it would be her.

Grosslyn rushed up to them when Deven and Vas disembarked.

"Did you see it? It worked better than expected. Just two guns. Can you imagine if all of them targeted one ship?" Grosslyn was a fairly sober guy, taciturn was often used to describe him by other crew.

That wasn't the case now. He was like a school kid with too much candy.

"We did. I assume you kept scanning during the entire process? And are scanning now for debris?" Vas folded her arms. In this case, using the guns was warranted. But she couldn't be worried about him being trigger-happy when they had to leave the Commonwealth.

"We have teams on the data and tracking what little debris survived. And there was extremely little. It appears that all of it is burning up in the atmosphere." He was far too happy.

As long as they were taking care of things, Vas wouldn't chastise him. She'd keep an eye on him though.

"I'll check on the dozer pilot," Deven said as they passed the door to the landing field.

"Good call." Vas turned to Gosta. "Where's Janx?"

"Still with Terel, captain. She keeps wanting to leave, and Mac had to threaten to sit on her."

"Cousins." Vas shook her head. "Any updates on the Achaius situation or the Pilthians?"

"The crew you set up escorted Achaius and Phila back home and are keeping in contact with Ragkor, but no signs of trouble yet. However, there is a problem reaching Shien and her people. Grosslyn had the building built on top of an old factory and there's a chance the comms are having trouble with the tunnels underneath. But prior to our invading dozer, I was going to suggest sending a crew to the hotel."

"Damn it." A chill went through Vas and she knew it was from her Keeper training. This was bad. "Get Walvento to set up a stealth crew to cover the entire hotel and any old tunnel entrances. This isn't a comm problem." She gave a flat smile and shook her head. "And no, I can't explain it. But something is horrifically wrong in that hotel."

Gosta gulped and nodded. He was already figuring out when Vas was having one of her Keeper moments.

"I also need you to send out as many drones as you can get ready. Keep them high. But no one goes into that hotel without my order." Vas waited until Gosta left to get things started. She wanted to be involved in this, whatever was wrong was nudging at the edges of her mind. But Janx crashing here, and the two ships after her were a concern also. And she trusted her people to take care of things.

She'd be involved once they figured out how bad things were.

"I'll be in the med bay." Vas started to go to Terel's area but stopped. "And sorry, but for now I need you to remain down here." She'd promised Gosta he could go back to the ship after a day, but all deals were off now.

"I gathered as much. Don't fear, we will take care of this." He gave an awkward smile and scurried off.

Vas shook her head. Gosta wasn't one for platitudes but as long as he was fine with remaining on the planet, she'd take them.

Terel was scowling at a monitor against the wall and punching buttons. Mac was sitting on his cousin's legs, and Janx looked ready to beat him up to make him move.

"Captain! Thank the gods. Can you tell him to let me go?" Janx looked like she had a few months ago—mostly. Her longish blond hair was now in a short spiky bob, or that was what it looked like. Being dunked into the ocean hadn't helped it much.

"Is she glowing?" Vas stopped moving. The glow was faint and fluctuating. Mac didn't seem to notice it.

"Ha! You can see it? Excellent." Terel marched over

with a strange wand. "I'm picking it up on the scans, but can't see it."

"She's glowing?" Mac's voice went up but he didn't move.

"It's nothing. Really. Just a little accident a week or so ago." Janx stopped trying to kick Mac off her legs.

"Who shot up your ship? Where's your dozer? Or was it the one following you in?" Vas pulled up a rolling stool next to Janx's bed but didn't motion for Mac to get off her legs.

Janx helped them out a while ago, along with saving Vas' life. But things and people change. That dead pirate ship drifting in particles around Home, not to mention the group of people slowly invading it, was evidence of that.

Plus, the glowing was odd even if Vas was the only one who could see it. Well, Vas and Janx. Janx hadn't been surprised. It would be interesting to see if Deven could see it. Might be another Keeper and Pirate trick.

Janx grinned. "Always to the point. Fair enough. A friend and I were chased into the Commonwealth by a Racki pirate ship. I think it might have been one of the ones that survived the attack at the pirate enclave a few months ago—it looked familiar and seemed to want to destroy *Betsy* at all costs. Even though I hid her registration, it was insistent. Good thing the barricade came down in time or we would have been caught. Sorry about coming here, but my ship was hit and I had nowhere else to go."

"Where'd you get that ship?" Mac asked before Vas could. "I saw the specs, that was a sweet, and high-end, ride."

Janx laughed. "I won her. I hope she can be salvaged, but she took some serious hits. I disguised my dozer when I won the *Crooked Lady*, and my friend flew *Betsy*. We were aiming for a planet called Solar to regroup before we were attacked." Her eyes went wide. "The dozer came through, right?"

"It went to the landing field and Deven is getting the pilot. It didn't read at all like *Betsy*." *Betsy* was the dozer Janx had when they first met her. Granted, dozers all looked the same to Vas, but the scans should have given some recognition.

"I know." Janx's grin was huge. "I'm not only getting good at disguising people." Her smile dropped. "I'm glad he was able to land her intact, but I know *Betsy* got hit as well."

"Deven will bring whoever is in that dozer in for a check-up first." Terel frowned as she turned away from her monitors. "I'd like to run some more tests on you though. What kind of accident did you say you had a week or so ago?"

Vas knew that although Terel said she'd *like* to run more tests, there was no way Janx was leaving without them. Vas agreed. The glow was gone but there was still something different about Janx. More than her hair.

"It's complicated. Very complicated. Once my friend gets here, we can explain better." She pushed at Mac. "I'm not going anywhere for now. You're cutting off the circulation to my legs."

He jumped off, but grabbed a chair and brought it over. "Who's this mysterious friend of yours? A *boyfriend*?" The two might be cousins, but they interacted far more like siblings. He'd gone from concerned big brother to teasing one in a heartbeat.

Janx blushed and looked away. "We're friends. He helped me in a jam, and we both might be on the run. Sort of. Complete misunderstanding, really."

"Is it related to the accident you had?" Terel had one of her much larger scanners out and was running it over Janx slowly. Whatever it was coming up with wasn't making her happy.

"Sort of? It started with a dead body on Swatlin IV and me having to leave for a job. And him needing to leave." A tic appeared on her cheek and she looked pissed. Then she shook it off. "But the accident was something else. What's the scanner say?"

Terel looked up but moved the screen away from Janx. "I'm still sorting it. Did you get medical help after? And what kind of accident was it?" The emphasis on the word accident indicated that Terel had serious concerns about whatever it was.

She didn't believe whatever happened to Janx was a threat to others, or she would have isolated her immediately. But she wasn't happy.

"It was a little chemical spill. Nothing huge, but knocked me out for a day or so. I didn't go to see a doc, because I felt fine. We did get the *Crooked Lady* out of the deal."

Now it was Vas' turn to frown. "A chemical spill in space? How did it get through your ship?"

"That's the interesting part. We were working—" An alarm cut off Janx's words and she jumped to her feet.

Vas hit her comm as she ran into the main part of the hangar. "What the hell is that?"

The entire hangar was flashing with lights she'd never seen and six of her people were aiming blasters at Deven and another tall man as they walked in.

CHAPTER THIRTY-FIVE

DEVEN RAISED HIS HANDS AND a moment later the dark purple-haired man next to him did as well. The man was well-built but leaner than Deven, and an inch or two taller. His long hair didn't look dyed, and his light teal eyes also appeared unmodified.

He was part human, but like Terel, most likely an exotic of so many mixed species, he didn't fit into one.

"It's okay, I checked him out." Deven sounded relaxed but kept his hands raised. "This is Chasen. Chasen, meet Vas and the rest."

"Don't hurt him!" Janx yelled as she came running out of the med room. The tone was far more than only friends, even if she was in denial about it.

Chasen smiled when he saw her. "Good to know you made it, kid. I saw your ship go down and feared for the worst. Can you tell your friends that I'm harmless? *Betsy* is more or less intact by the way."

"He triggered the sensors. He has something explosive on him." Marwin was closest to both men.

"Damn it, Chasen." Janx glared. "I told you these are friends. Hand it over. *Now*." She might have a crush on her friend, but that didn't mean she completely trusted him. "Seriously."

Chasen reached into his long black coat and pulled free a trisonic detonator. "Sorry, Deven. I've had a rough couple of weeks."

Deven lowered his arms and took the explosive. Small, sneaky, and almost impossible to detect. They were also exceedingly expensive.

And the fact Deven had missed it scared the hell out of Vas. "Lock him up until I sort this out."

"But—" Janx froze the moment Vas turned to face her.

"No. You don't know it, but there is a lot of weird and deadly shit going on here right now. And we've lost communication with an entire hotel. Now you two show up in the middle of it? I trust you, Janx. For now. But your friend is another matter."

"It's okay. It was a stupid move on my part. Sorry, Deven." Chasen looked apologetic, but he'd also tried to bring a sneaky bomb inside her hangar. "I wasn't completely certain that Janx was here of her own will. She's told me some stories about her cousin."

Deven nodded but didn't say anything. Marwin got Chasen's hands behind his back and cuffed him.

Janx looked torn between wanting to defend Chasen and wanting to punch him. She turned away as he and his escorts passed her.

Mac came out with them but remained silent and glaring as Chasen was taken away.

"I'm sorry, Vas. He's rich and doesn't think about consequences. I'm sorry he tricked you, Deven." Janx suddenly looked tired.

Deven joined them but his focus was on the explosive. "It's neutralized now. But it was live when it set off the sensors. And I didn't sense it at all until he revealed it. *What* is your friend?"

Vas watched the device and no switches had been hit. It appeared Chasen turned it off without touching it.

"He's Chasen." Janx shrugged and bit her lip. "He got caught in that chemical spill too. But I know him, he never would have used it."

"Then why did he bring it?"

Janx grimaced as she ran her fingers through her still sea watered hair. "Knowing him? Just to see if he could.

He can be a bit of a jerk. And he might have really been worried about me." She flashed Mac a weak grin.

Deven pocketed the device. "It's good to see you, Janx. Your dozer made it, but will need repairs." He clearly wanted to know more about Chasen, but wasn't going to dig. Yet.

"Thank you all for saving it, and me. Even Chasen. Really, he's not bad." Janx looked around. "Is there somewhere I can get a shower and maybe a nap? I feel okay, really—" Her eyes went wide, she glowed brightly for a moment, then collapsed.

Terel reached her first and started scanning her. "These readings are insane. Everyone, back up. I need a decon suit and chamber immediately. Although might be too late for the suit, I'm already exposed." Bio-security cones sprung up around the two of them and a thin shield appeared. It would keep any deadly particles in with them.

"Let me help." Mac started forward, but Vas grabbed his arm.

"Stay back. Damn it, look at the scan." Even from here, Vas could see the numbers weren't good. Janx hadn't been radioactive a moment ago—but that changed when she collapsed. The full alarms of the hangar hadn't kicked in, so it was isolated to Janx and Terel behind the shield.

Deven threw a decon suit through the shield to Terel and she climbed in and sealed it. Divee and Roha brought out a box decon container on a cart and rolled it toward Terel. They also scrambled into their suits even though Terel motioned for them to stay back. The box was designed for contaminated things rather than people, but Janx would still be able to breathe in it. And they could get her and Terel into one of the decon rooms without risking others.

Janx remained unconscious as Terel lifted her into the box. Divee and Roha wheeled the cart out with Terel swearing at her scanner behind them.

"Don't worry, I'll keep you updated." Terel waved off Vas as she passed. "This is damn weird though."

Deven watched them go. "If Janx was radioactive earlier this entire hangar has been exposed."

"Why are no alarms going off? The auto security only did a localized appearance once Janx collapsed."Vas asked as she hit her comm. "Gosta, run a full diagnostic on the hangar sensors."

Mac watched his cousin as she was wheeled away and turned back to Vas. "She'll be okay, right? It couldn't have been bad if it didn't show up before."

"We don't know. But I want Divee to scan everyone. Starting with you." It said a lot that Mac was more worried about his cousin than himself.

He nodded and followed Divee back into the med area.

"You all heard me, get in line. I don't care if the hangar comes back fine. I've never seen anything like this."Vas joined Mac as Deven and the rest of the people in the hangar followed.

It didn't take long. No one showed any questionable signs and the spot where Janx fell scanned clean. Vas ordered Chasen to be scanned, but he also came back fine.

"I want that dozer checked as well. Any news on the salvage of that fighter ship of Janx's?"

Gosta had come out for something else but nodded. "Already did it, captain. The dozer scanned clean, and they were able to pull up her ship—not sure how repairable it is. I'll have the salvage crew run a level ten scan before bringing it to shore. I've launched the drones and Walvento left with thirty crew to surround the hotel."

"Thank you, keep me updated on the team and the drones. Get Bathie to help you search for anything you both can find about the pirate ship that chased Janx here. There's a chance it was one of the survivors from the pirate enclave a few months ago. I'm certain there's more to Janx's story, but right now let's find our own answers." Vas turned to go to her office with Deven when Xsit came running out of the communications room.

"Captain! People who say they are holding the Pilthians hostage have contacted us! They want to deal."

"Damn it." Even though she'd sent out the drones and her team, part of her had hoped the comm silence was simply an issue with the building. Vas and Deven ran with Xsit to the communications room.

Vas grabbed the headset. "Captain Tor Dain here. Who are you and what do you want?"

"Good to hear your voice, captain. I believe I have some people that you want back. My request is simple—stand down." The speaker's voice was hidden behind a voice modulator and not a great one. The high-end ones sounded like a real person, simply not like the one speaking. This one wavered in between various accents, species, and genders.

"Stand down from what?"

"Stand down from being the Keeper. From bringing back the Clionea nuns. Trying to stop the Clongari. From everything."

"Who is this?"

"An old friend. You're in the way of the people I now work for. Stand down or the hole I blow in this building will take out this place you call a town. You have thirty hours to decide. I'll call back then." Static filled the line.

"Damn it! Someone please tell me they can break the voice modulator and tell me who in the hell that was." The smugness in the voice came through, modulator or not. Whoever they were, it was someone she knew.

"I'm working on it, captain. Even though it sounded like crap, that person was working with high-end equipment." Gosta was running three different searches on neighboring computers.

Most of the people who would be this evil were dead, many by her own hand. A chilling thought hit her. Her brother Borlan had tried to kill her many times, starting when she was a kid. He died, or his clones had, a few times over the last two years.

But how sure was she that they all hadn't simply been his clones dying? Or even that a clone wasn't behind this now? She walked toward her office. "Shit, shit, shit."

"You think it's Borlan." It wasn't a question and Deven kept his voice low as he walked alongside her.

"I don't know. We have no idea how many clones they made, or even for certain who was behind it. The fake Asarlaí black suit fighter clones were unstable. But we have no idea if the others were."

"Marli believed they would all be unstable. Especially after this long." He didn't sound as convinced as she would have liked.

"Since she and her knowledge are long gone, we can't be certain of that. And we need a list of people who might be behind this." Another thought hit her. "I'm going to call Jasiel and the ship. I'm sending them a copy of the recording from the kidnapper. There are connections that we're not seeing. Give me ten to talk to the ship, then grab Gosta and meet me in my office."

Deven gave a salute and walked toward the other offices.

Aithnea answered her call before Nitya or Jasiel did, but she sounded distracted. That changed to pissed when Vas told her what was being demanded for the lives of the Pilthians.

"No one beyond your crew should know anything about the Keeper, the return of the nuns, or the returning Clongari. I know you trust them, but could—"

"No." Vas cut her off. "I trust my crew implicitly. Even more so the ones who were with me the last few months. We're sure Kalth died on that planet, right?" Up until a few minutes ago, Vas would have said that she was sure without a doubt. She'd felt that death in her soul.

Now she doubted everything.

CHAPTER THIRTY-SIX

"KALTH'S DEAD." THE ABSOLUTE CONFIDENCE of Aithnea's words made Vas feel better. Sort of.

"But could any part of her lived on? Someone knows me, knows my planet, and knows about the Keeper." There were too many elements this person knew and they shouldn't be connected.

"Her entire essence was destroyed along with that planet. She wasn't going to be able to move into another body. I felt it. I'll work on the recording, but they didn't say anything about the Pirate? If not, that could indicate their information on you is old."

"They didn't. But damn it, I feel like there's a knife hanging over the entire planet right now. I can't explain it, but I think even if I were to step down, it wouldn't stop them." Vas liked having logical reasons—this vague stuff didn't make her happy.

"You could be right. Jasiel and Nitya are running through the call now. Nitya thinks she can weed out the modulator, but it will take time. I think you need to look at the pattern of the attacks on Home so far. There is something larger going on."

Vas rubbed the side of her face. "I just wanted to come back to Home, rest, then get back out there and save the universe. Is that too much to ask?"

Aithnea laughed. "Now that sounds like the Vas I first met. Always asking, 'why me'."

"I was not." Vas didn't recall that part of being a kid at

all. But her life had been shit at the time, so she might have had justified reasons for feeling that way.

"You were. But that's neither here nor there. You look for things down there, and we'll see what we can find. Nitya was able to pull in some readings from that massive pirate warship that was chasing the dozer. Before you blew it up. Quite extensively, I might add. I take it you might want that data?"

"Yes, please. We didn't have another option. At least Grosslyn only used two guns."

"That Asarlaí woman actually did something good by installing those. I thought they were overkill, but I'm rethinking that opinion. She might have known they would be needed." Aithnea admitting anything positive about Marli was a major change.

"True. I'll see what we can determine, and contact you if we find anything."

"Same." Aithnea ended the call.

Deven and Gosta came in a few moments later. Gosta was carrying at least ten pads and spread them out on the spare desk.

"What are those?"

"Patterns. There have been more events going on here than we knew, and many of them began before we got here." Deven helped spread the pads out. "It works better this way, so I can move them around. Not to mention that Grosslyn hasn't finished his secret surprise of a ship sized monitor here yet."

Vas watched as the entire planet of Home came alive in the collection of pads. Each one showed a section of the planet and was marked with various colors.

"Where did it start?"

Gosta reached over and tapped the uppermost left pad. "As near as I can tell, here. When we were fleeing the Zqui space station. There was a falling meteor reported in the far south. It wasn't near any of the refugee lands, so it was documented and ignored. The only reason it was noted at all was the readings it gave off." He flicked the side of the pad and rows of numbers filled the screen.

"And what are those?" Vas knew that Deven and Gosta probably recognized them immediately, but that wasn't her area of weird expertise.

"It was made to look like a meteor," Deven said. "And it was disguised well. Grosslyn discounted it when it hit because the basic level scans showed nothing except space rock. But this was a pod. Possibly a two, or maybe three person escape pod that was modified to look like a rock."

"Damn it." Vas shook her head. The trajectory was perfect. It hit right in the middle of a large unclaimed desert. "Can we send drones to see if there's anything left to scan?" The people would be long gone, unless they'd spent the time camping out there. But unless they destroyed the pod, there should be something left down there. Even though they had a full flight of drones watching the hotel that the Pilthians were being held in, she knew Gosta and Grosslyn would have more.

Deven grinned. "Already have Grosslyn on it. Waiting for your orders." At her nod, he tapped his comm. "Release the drones, Grosslyn."

"There are a lot of pads here—let's get moving." She noticed the first four were separate from the rest. "This is…?" She motioned to the space between number four and number five. Other people might have been sloppy. Deven wouldn't be.

"Those four happened before we got into the Commonwealth. The rest have occurred since we dropped the barricade." He and Gosta quickly ran through the rest of the initial four. Another disguised pod crashed through the atmosphere in an attempt to appear like a random meteor, this one landed on a tiny unpopulated island to the north a week after the first one. Then a third hit across the continent a week later. The three looked to be at an equal distance from the landing field and town. Not suspicious at all.

"They were clearly checking to make sure they hadn't been spotted but were triangulating something. I assume drones are being sent to those locations also?"

"Yes." Gosta picked up the fourth pad and frowned at it. "This one was the last before we returned to Commonwealth space. It hit about two weeks ago." He clicked something on the pad and an image filled the screen.

"Is that an Asarlaí Fury?" Vas hit the replay a few times. It was fast, and as far as she could tell, hadn't landed, or crashed. But it looked and moved like a Fury.

"That's what we think." Gosta looked like he wanted to go find that Fury himself. "It did at least fifteen passes around the planet before Grosslyn picked it up. I worked back from when that happened and found the loops in the regular survey scans, if they were scanning us, and we have to think they were, there was no indication. Then it appeared to have vanished deeper into Commonwealth space. And the cloaking around our planet was fully operating when all these instances occurred."

"Don't worry, we shuffled the codes, no one should be able to see us now. And I have created an auto reset at random intervals." Deven reached for the next pad.

"Damn it. How did they get our codes? We gave them to Janx, and she probably had them coded in her dozer. Could we be wrong about her?" Vas counted on her gut in battle. This was a different kind of fight, but her gut said Janx wasn't the problem. "I'd say her buddy Chasen, but they were stuck outside of the Commonwealth like we were during those times." She turned to Gosta. "That's been confirmed, right?"

"Aye, captain. But they could be working with someone else. That warship, even." Gosta was usually the type to give people a chance, but he was visibly disturbed right now. Like Vas, he thought of Home as a safe fortress.

The remaining six pads showed smaller incursions, but unless there was a rampaging meteor shower that didn't show anywhere else, they were the same low-level attack as the first three. Nine planet landings in small ships and one stalking Fury.

This wasn't improving Vas' disposition. They needed to figure out what in the hell was going on, what these people were really after, and how to rescue the Pilthians without blowing everything up. She tapped two of the smaller screens. "Two of them landed north of Achaius' homestead. But I still don't know what the point is. They got their people here, they did a piss-poor job of kidnapping three of my senior officers, then attacked a farming community, and are now holding a bunch of Pilthians hostage." Vas walked around the desk and the pads. "I'm not seeing what their point is. Did our prisoner from the cave wake up?"

"He did but is unconscious again. It seems that he had a fake tooth. The poison inside should have killed him, but Terel neutralized it before it could go that far. He's alive, but in a coma." Deven was also glaring at a pad—the one with the recordings of the fly-by-Fury on it. "The only Furies left are ours. Unless someone broke into Marli's compound on her moon."

"Damn it. I hadn't even thought of that. But what was the point of flying around Home? They left when they were spotted—which brings up another question—how did they know they'd been spotted? What in the hell were they scanning and how? A Fury isn't a great ship for that."

Furies were great, albeit extremely unstable, fighters. Using one for recon would be beyond idiotic. Unfortunately, until Home was secure, they couldn't check Marli's moon to see if someone had broken in and taken some of them. The other option, that there were more of the deadly ships loose somewhere, wasn't a good one either.

"We can't tell what they were doing, captain. Or even if the Fury is related to the rest." Gosta pulled up a long-range scan and focused on the nearest system. He was doing a slow and systematic search in the general direction the Fury had gone.

Two weeks ago. It might have flown anywhere and once the barricade dropped it could have left the Commonwealth.

"We have to assume everything is related, at least until something proves otherwise." Vas normally enjoyed solving mysteries, within reason. This one was too much. Even though she knew Deven and Gosta would disagree if the stakes weren't so high. "We don't have time to sort it, sorry boys, but work with the data and the computer on the *Destroyer's Curse*. Find these damn connections."

Gosta appeared torn. He was happy to go back to the ship, but he also clearly wanted to stay here in case of more trouble. He and Deven would still be sorting, but the *Destroyer's Curse* computer would speed things up significantly. It wasn't so much better than the ones here, but it utilized non-Commonwealth data. Also, between them, Gosta and Deven had done some serious modifications to it in the past months.

"Understood." He took the pads and left.

Vas shook her head. "Sorry about that, but we need answers. Now."

"Agreed. See you soon, although we'll probably stay up there overnight." He gave Vas a long enough kiss to remind her what she would be missing. "I'll also check on Flarik and her egg."

Vas watched him walk out. Before she could plan a rescue, she needed to sort out who was behind the call about the Pilthians. The trick with the pads was handy as she could put a different suspect on each and move them about. "Grosslyn? Can you have about fifteen pads brought to my office?"

"Aye, captain. Or a refurbished ship's main screen? I just ran the final check on it."

"You got a ship's screen to work down here?" The screens on most ships were fussy and didn't usually survive to be spare parts, let alone migrate to a planet. Deven had mentioned it, but she knew Grosslyn would have wanted to surprise her.

"Yes. It was a pet project while you were gone. You'd have to come to it though. It has its own office."

Vas laughed and left her office. "I'm on my way, where am I headed?"

CHAPTER THIRTY-SEVEN

CALLING THE LOCATION WITH THE screen a room was generous. It was a glorified closet and the old ship's screen took up the entirety of the longest wall. It had a few chairs and a single table with the controls in it, but there wasn't anyway to fit much more in there.

"Grosslyn, this is impressive." Vas took the chair behind the table and activated the controls as Grosslyn beamed and left.

After two hours, and a dinner made up of bits and pieces brought in from the small hangar commissary, she had a list of over a hundred people who might hate her or her crew enough to do this. And were still alive.

But running that list against those having the ability to pull it off, and having access to knowing about the Clionea nuns, and Vas being the Keeper, left her at zero.

Vas slid back in her chair and rubbed her eyes. This had been another long and frustrating day and they were no closer to resolving anything. Grosslyn popped in briefly to report the drones weren't picking up anything at the hotel, and they'd run a change of shifts for the people circling the building. They hadn't seen anything either. The windows were blocked so well that only a tiny amount of light showed.

Knowing the enemy could make the difference between success and brutal failure—but she might have to go in blind at this point. Spending more time, and risking that the Pilthians' kidnappers weren't going to jump the gun, wasn't going to happen.

Still, Vas wanted to sort out something before she called it a night.

She called up the locations of all the unauthorized landings, then narrowed it to the first three when some instinct said they were the trend she needed to follow. Once she had a theory about those three, she could apply it to the rest. Yes, Deven and Gosta were doing the same thing up on the ship—but different thought processes brought different results. She worked her way down a series of single possible connecting factors, but nothing worked.

Halfway through her list, she started swearing as a correlation beyond them being equal distance from the town appeared. The landings were all near long-dead solbilan mines. She ran the search once more using all nine drops and found that of the other five, three were showing to have been solbilan mines or processing locations.

She hit her comm. "Deven? I found something."

He laughed. "So did we. It took longer than it should have, but Nitya had to upload all the Commonwealth data on this planet since she only had outside of the Commonwealth information. What did you find?"

"There are dead solbilan mines in seven of the nine fake meteor drops." She wouldn't discount the remaining two drops; they weren't randomly chosen. It just might take longer to find the connection.

"That's what we found as well. But according to deep scans by Nitya and Aithnea, those mines aren't dead anymore. Even the mine we rescued Terel and the others from is showing as no longer dormant. Someone or something has reactivated them and they all still have ore. And there's a formerly unknown one deep underground a few clicks from Achaius' home."

"The survey I paid for when I won this place said the minerals were tapped out. How in the hell can someone reactivate empty mines?" Vas probably would have sold this place immediately if she had known there were live, or potentially live, mines on it. Solbilan wasn't a stable element when raw. Or from what she'd heard, as it was before her time—even when processed into spaceships.

"Gosta thinks they weren't depleted, but made to look that way. Someone was hiding them. For a long time."

For over twenty years. Probably longer, as the mines had already been hidden when she had the survey run on the planet. "What? Why? No one even uses solbilan anymore."Vas' sleepiness vanished. What the hell else had been missed in the mineral survey? And why was Home under attack because of some mineral that wasn't even used anymore?

Gosta jumped in on the call. "Actually, captain, there have been studies done on some of the more explosive natures of solbilan. The Commonwealth hid the data seventy years ago, but they were looking into using it as a new class of weapons. They couldn't stabilize it from what I've been able to find and supposedly ended and buried their research thirty years ago."

"And someone brought it back. Has Nitya broken down the voice modulator? I haven't found anyone with the drive, ability, and knowledge needed to be that jackass holding the Pilthians hostage. But we should assume they are connected to the solbilan as well. Their demands to me could be only a part of it."

"It's proving tricky," Deven said. "So far, it's not breaking down to reveal the true voice or any identifying features. Whenever she tries too hard, the entire thing vanishes. She's using copies, but she's not giving up."

"I'm making one more pass at connecting things, then head for bed. I recommend you and Gosta do the same." She knew neither of them would, but figured suggesting it couldn't hurt.

She took down the solbilan information, which was going to be dealt with later. She tossed everything that had happened in the past few months into the funnel of data. Starting when they first left the Commonwealth; the pirate enclave, Ome's ship, the space station, the Enforcers who'd been hunting them, and then everything up to today. Including the solbilan, Janx, and that pirate warship the was now dust circling her planet.

She set up a bunch of queries, looking for patterns both small and large. The system was good, but it still came back with a ten-hour estimated timeline for full results. Not too surprising, it took more than a half hour to enter everything. She yawned, hit the run button, and went to bed.

And spent over an hour tossing. Vas wasn't a fussy sleeper—she was usually so exhausted by the time she finally crashed that she slept like the dead. But something beyond the absence of Deven was gnawing at her.

The bed she was lying on bouncing about became part of her dream until it woke her up enough to realize something was wrong. She hit her comm, "Grosslyn! What the hell is going on?"

"We're under attack, captain." Grosslyn rarely sounded freaked out, but he did now and Vas didn't blame him.

"I gathered that. But by who?" She rolled out of bed, changed, and was out the door before he could respond. Whatever awakened her had stopped now.

Grosslyn was at his command desk and running a dozen screens. "I'm not sure, captain. Some code came through about ten minutes ago and overrode the cloaking program. They're fighting for control of the guns now. No one should be able to do that!" He wasn't as fast as Gosta or Hrrru, but Grosslyn was keeping a good pace as he fought to save access to his guns.

"Ships?"

"They blocked our scanners as well. But…there!" Bathie was at another terminal and swore as she got a new screen up. "Not sure how long I can keep them up, so look fast." From the flickers across the screen, she was grabbing as many stills as she could.

"Vas?" Deven's voice was faint as if crackled through the comm. "There's a pair of ships bombing the planet. Our comms are almost useless and Nitya is trying to get her systems out of repair status to go after them. W—not enough crew on—other ships up here." He broke up mid-sentence, but his meaning was clear. The rest of their ships in orbit didn't have enough crew to fight.

"Bathie got our screens unlocked. But I can't tell what those ships are. And…we lost the screens again."

Bathie waved Mac over and she began expanding on stills of the ships. They were huge but not dark or spikey, so that was a plus. Probably not the Clongari.

"Deven? Do you have enough radios up there?"

"Yes." The comm cut out and Vas grabbed one of the hangar's radios as it crackled to life.

"This helps, but we still are waiting to get enough systems online to go after those ships. What?" The last part was said away from the radio. "Jasiel says those two are Imperium Cruisers from the Doplin Nebula. A little-known group of planets near the far end of Lethian space. They're old, but solid. And not using heavy artillery on their attack. Gosta confirmed both. Their targeting is odd and he's trying to sort the focus."

"It shook up the hangar, but it looks intact. Are these people part of the Lethian Assembly?"

"They didn't used to be, but who knows."

Ragkor came running in. "I can get a skeleton crew together and take up the *Warrior Wench,* unless you want to, captain." He didn't look embarrassed at calling Vas captain this time.

"Hold on, Deven, talk to Grosslyn for a moment. She handed the radio over to Grosslyn and turned to Ragkor. "Grab your crew and take it up. Communicate with the *Destroyer's Curse,* she should be ready to go in a few minutes. Bathie and Mac will send the little info we have up to your ship. Thank you, Ragkor." Vas watched him salute and run off barking orders as he went.

Two ships against two might be a fair fight—or it might not. Vas had never heard of these people, but they had enough bad run-ins with the Lethian Assembly not to trust anything near them.

Xsit stuck her head into the room with wide eyes and waved a headset toward Vas. "That voice is back and demands to speak to you."

"We still have time." She snarled into the speaker of the headset. Another jolt hit and almost knocked her off her feet. "What do you want?"

"Stop bombing this hotel. You're going to get your friends killed before you hurt us." The same voice modulator was in place, but there was audible emotion behind the words this time. Fear.

"We're not bombing anything. The planet is under attack. How do I know those ships aren't whoever *you're* working with?" She mouthed to Xsit to track the caller's location. They might not even be in the hotel themselves.

"My people wouldn't be this sloppy. You're destabilizing the mines—" the voice cut off.

"Damn it. They are after the mines and aren't the ones firing at the planet. At least two groups with their own agendas. Let me speak to Deven." She handed the headset back to Xsit and took the radio back from Grosslyn.

Vas told Deven what the kidnapper said. "Can Aithnea and Jasiel run an analysis on where those explosions are being targeted? We can't keep our sensors up long enough to cover anything."

From Grosslyn's continued swearing, hitting the consoles, and an even faster rate of working—the attacking ships hadn't broken into the planetary guns yet. But they hadn't stopped trying.

"They're both on it. Those vessels shouldn't be anywhere near here. They're extreme isolationists," Deven said. "Hold on, Jasiel wants to speak to you. I'll go find more radios."

"Vas, they seem to be targeting areas near, but not on, the solbilan mines we've found. And a few places we didn't know had solbilan. They're using a pattern, but I can't tell right now what it is and neither can Aithnea."

CHAPTER THIRTY-EIGHT

"THE *WARRIOR WENCH* IS LIFTING; do you want shuttles to run crews up to the other ships?" Mac ran over to her.

Deven overheard him through the radio. "Bad idea, our shuttles couldn't hold their own against those two warships. The only reason they didn't go after us on the station is the heavy shielding and all the ships appear completely unmanned."

"Didn't know about that trick, but good planning on Grosslyn's part." Vas shook her head at Mac. "And good point. They'll see the *Warrior Wench* launch but she's faster than they show as being, and better armed than they."

They got a smaller screen in the hangar, planetary only, to stay on as the *Warrior Wench* made a clear lift-off. The two attacking ships were on the other side of the planet and by the time they turned she was already in orbit.

"Vas? I've been working on a project. It's not extremely large, but it's fast and well-armed." Nitya sounded embarrassed.

"A project? What kind?" The fact that neither Aithnea nor Jasiel weighed in meant they already knew…and were carefully not commenting.

"A stealth fighter. Well, a modified one. Based on five-hundred-year-old plans and current tech that I salvaged. It can take a crew of fifteen but could run with as few as five. I was hoping to finish it and present it to you in a few weeks."

Vas was momentarily stunned. "Does it fly?"

"The specs say so. It's untested, obviously. This ship

has many unused holds, so I didn't think anyone would mind. I don't need sleep, but sometimes have to move away from a project if I've been at it too long. The *Keeper's Tempest* was a break for me."

Her radio was loud enough that Bathie and Mac both looked up with the same shock that was probably on her face. Nitya had built an entire ship, small or not, basically out of scraps. In a ship's hold. In her spare time.

"We can talk later about that name, but thank you. Now, just to get me and a crew up there."

"Ragkor here, we can cover a shuttle to go up if the *Destroyer's Curse* can cover us. Those two ships are still returning this way but are moving slower than before."

"Damn, okay. Deven? Are you, Gosta, Therlian, and Flarik going to be okay up there?" Nitya would do most of the work since she *was* the ship, but better to be sure.

"We're fine, grab your crew, get in the shuttles, and get up here. The *Warrior Wench* is in place and that shiny new ship is waiting for you," Deven said.

"I built it on a lift to the second landing bay, it's tight, but you can fly out from there. I hope you like it, captain." Nitya rarely called Vas that.

"I'm sure it's perfect. We'll contact you when the shuttle takes off." Vas ended the call but kept the radio as she ran. "Mac and Bathie, you're with me." Glazlie, Roha, and Walvento were talking nearby. While all three were often used as muscle, they were also fully trained on multiple ship command deck stations. "You three, come on as well."

No one asked where they were going as they followed Vas to the shuttle. More people were milling around the hangar now, but Vas had enough with her to fly this mystery ship. There were still enough issues going on down here, that she'd rather not deplete her ground forces if she didn't have to.

She waved to the pilot chair. "Mac, please take the honors. The *Warrior Wench* will keep those ships off our back. But you still might need some seriously defensive flying." The screens on the shuttle were working fine and those two slow-moving war birds were still coming at them. Vas explained about Nitya's secret ship. As the current Keeper, Vas wasn't certain how she felt about the name, but she was honored Nitya made it. Not sure how much of an impact it would make, especially since it hadn't been tested before. But three ships were always better than two.

Mac zipped the shuttle under the *Warrior Wench* and toward the space station. Deven and Nitya would keep the *Destroyer's Curse* inside the station's shield until Vas and crew were on the new ship. But there was no way anyone watching would miss when the shuttle entered the station's shield.

The guns from the *Warrior Wench* fired and the shield around the station dropped to let the shuttle in—and let the *Destroyer's Curse* get off their shot at the closest enemy ship.

"Get into your ship fast, I think they were holding back for a reason but that's over." Deven sounded a little rushed, which for him meant a lot rushed.

Mac landed the shuttle in the secondary landing bay and Vas and the rest raced out. There was no way to miss the *Keeper's Tempest*, it was almost the same size as the *Traitor's Folly* had been, but extremely sleek. It also had the name boldly on the side. In gold. Vas shook her head, the *Warrior Wench* was still the fanciest ship in her fleet, but this one would be a strong second.

"I hope she's as fast as she looks." Vas hit the palm lock and the door smoothly opened.

"She's faster than most anything her size, or even smaller," Nitya cut in. "Once you leave the bay, we'll leave the station. Good luck, captain."

"Thank you, you as well." Vas ran to the captain's chair

but let out a low whistle as she looked around. The command deck matched the ship's smaller size, but she was so well outfitted that Vas was going to need to have a long talk with Nitya about how this had been possible.

And if Nitya can make more at some point.

Mac ran for the pilot's sling, and Bathie grinned and went to the nav station.

Roha took a science station, with Glazlie and Walvento hitting communications and weapons respectively.

"Nitya, we're heading out." Vas nodded to Mac and he hit it so hard they almost blasted through the landing bay shield before it was completely raised. "Mac, Nitya won't be happy if you break this on the first time out."

"Aye, captain! But this thing is sweet!" He turned for a moment to grin at her, looking and sounding like a teenager.

"I'm sure it is, but we need to clear those ships." It appeared that the two enemy vessels were slowing even more. More importantly, they had stopped bombing the planet. Vas grabbed her radio to call Grosslyn. "We're in place, no further signs of attacks?"

"No, captain. Even so, we're making sure everyone in the hangar is armed and has radios. The comms keep bouncing." Grosslyn sounded a little less stressed.

"Good call on both. We're going to try reaching those ships, but have Xsit do so as well if you can punch through. Vas out." She was impressed with Grosslyn—marshaling a group of fighters for a potential ground invasion wasn't something he'd ever had to do before.

She hit her ship comm to target both ships. "Unknown ships circling the planet. Identify yourselves and prepare to surrender." Yes, Jasiel had identified them, sort of. But they still hadn't appeared on any database. She'd let them think they were unknown for now.

Not surprisingly, the ships didn't respond. She tried three more times, then called Ragkor and Deven. "They are ignoring me. Both of you fire right over them. Low yield weapons, close, but don't hit them." Granted Walvento was on this ship, but she trusted the people crewing the other two ships to pull it off.

"Should we test our weapons out, captain?" Walvento sounded like a kid desperately wanting to open his naming day gifts.

Vas didn't blame him. "Not yet. Let's see what happens when the other two fire." Deven and Ragkor each took one of the enemy ships and launched low-yield missiles. Vas thought of that class of weapons as nudgers. Even if they hit something they didn't usually cause much damage, but they got attention from non-responding ships.

Usually.

Vas waited a minute, then contacted the enemy ships again. Unlike her comm systems with the planet, the connection was clear and should be going through. They were not responding.

"Walvento, prepare to fire the lowest level of weapons this ship has. Short burst first at the lead ship on my mark, then hit the second. Do not aim for anything crucial." She reminded him of that because there was no idea what these systems could do. A glance at the weapons screen was terrifying and confusing at the same time.

Vas gave one more attempt at reaching the ships. "You are in unauthorized space. We have given you warnings, stand down immediately or we will fire."

She counted the seconds and at the one-minute mark, turned to Walvento. "Fire!"

Both shots were good, and both ships took the hit but still didn't respond. Or retaliate. She hit her comm. So far the communications between the ships was fine and comms were easier than the radios. "Damn it. Gosta? Do we know if there's even anything alive on those ships?" Ghost ships were rare, but they could happen if the crew was killed with systems on automatic. Most times the ships kept going until they ran out of fuel or wandered into unfriendly territory and were blown to bits.

How two ghost ships could have been pre-programmed to break through the planet cloak and bomb specific locations, was something else entirely.

"I am detecting life signs, captain." Gosta sounded calm. "On both ships. But they're oddly masked from my sensors. They're there, and not, almost at the same time."

Vas wished Deven was on this ship, she would have loved to see his face at Gosta being vague. He was the best at being specific.

"That doesn't make sense, Gosta. Are there people who will die if we blast their ships apart or not?"

"Captain…possibly." That word was forced out and his unhappiness at the admission was audible.

"Vas, I agree," Deven said. "With time we could sort out these scans, but I don't think we have time. Ghosts or not, those ships could start bombing the planet again and our only recourse will be to blow them out of the sky."

"Damn it. I need more…hold on my radio is popping." Vas switched to whoever was calling her from the planet. "Vas here."

"Captain, I picked up on communications about those two ships." Xsit was getting in the too-high-pitched-to-hear range. "It's not for us specifically, but it's coming from those three Lethian Assembly ships that are still waiting a few systems outside of the Commonwealth. They are telling anyone who sees those ships to destroy them immediately. I haven't responded."

Vas watched the two ships. They were surrounded and outgunned. And not responding. Why did the Lethians want people to destroy them? "Contact the Lethians. Just mention that you picked up their chatter and want to know why. Do not say who we are, where we are, or that we know where the ships are."

"Aye, captain."

When Xsit clicked off Vas contacted both Deven and Ragkor and told them what Xsit heard. And told Ragkor what Gosta and Deven said about the enemy ships.

Mac spun in his harness when she cleared the calls. "If the Lethian Assembly wants those ships destroyed, they aren't really showing as alive, and they were blowing holes in our world—why don't we see what this ship can do?" The maniacal grin made his eyes wider and more unstable than usual.

"Because we're still not certain if the Lethian Assembly is on our side or not. Or rather, that they aren't on the Clongari's side. There could be prisoners of the Lethian Assembly in some sort of stasis pods on those ships." Doubtful, but Aithnea had always been a fan of 'the enemy of my enemy is my friend' scenarios.

"Fine. But if they are bad? Nitya worked so hard on this ship. It would be a shame if she didn't get to see what it can do." Mac tried to appear logical. Which never worked with him. He was smart, everyone on her crews was, but he didn't like to use it for good often.

Vas stared him down in two seconds. "Nice try. You have no idea what Nitya did, as none of us knew what she was up to." Ignoring the fact that Vas was fairly sure Aithnea and Jasiel knew. "But, you have a point. We should see what this ship can do. *After* we sort out those two ships. They are still from a free nation as far as we know—declaring war on them at the request of the Lethian Assembly isn't the direction we need to be going."

Mac sighed and turned back to his controls. And Walvento surreptitiously lowered his right hand. The hand nearest the weapons controls.

"Orders, captain?" Ragkor asked after a few minutes of no reaction or movement from the ships.

"Gosta? Are you getting any more information?" She didn't mind fighting, and honestly, she wanted to see what this ship could do as well, but starting a war with a sovereign nation that happened to be right where they might need to lead a fleet through to fight the Clongari wasn't a great idea.

Before he could respond, both enemy ships came to life.

"Weapons on both ships are now active and they're engaging the drives." Walvento's hand was back near the weapons pad.

"Captain, they're—" The rest of Ragkor's comment was lost to static.

One of the enemy ships turned back to the planet, the other one was aiming for the station.

CHAPTER THIRTY-NINE

V AS GRABBED HER RADIO AND called Deven and Ragkor. "Stop that ship from getting to the station, blow it out of existence. We'll get the one heading for the planet." The space station had a shield, but it wasn't designed to hold against a crash run. And that's what the ship looked like it was doing.

The *Warrior Wench* and *Destroyer's Curse* got in front of the enemy vessel and began firing. Vas nodded to Mac and he hit the speed to take after the ship heading for Home. When the ships were bombing the planet, they'd kept a standard distance and maintained a stable orbit. This one wasn't planning on either from what Vas could see.

"Roha, confirm the projected path of that ship?" Better to be safe.

"It's coming in too hot, and it's aiming for the hangar and town. And there's an odd chemical coming from it," Roha said. "It's going to burn the atmosphere around the planet as it goes down."

Vas swore. There were hypothetical weapons that could do that—but she'd never seen one in person. "Mac, keep up with that thing. Walvento, fire before it hits the atmosphere and suppress that damn chemical." She hoped this ship had the suppression system the *Destroyer's Curse* did. It was usually used to help with ships on fire.

"Aye, captain." They shouted in unison. The *Keeper's Tempest* picked up more speed than Vas had seen in a ship this size and a massive amount of weapons fired at the enemy vessel. Parts of it would still fall into the planet, but most would burn up and the chemical wouldn't burn Home's atmosphere.

The suppression chemical shot out along with a new set of missiles. These were massive and hit the enemy ship with enough force that it tumbled away from the planet as it exploded.

"Is anything dangerous heading toward Home?" Vas wasn't sure what more they could do, but she wasn't losing her planet or her people.

Roha appeared to be trying to mimic Gosta or Hrrru as she worked on two screens. "No, captain. The chemical was neutralized and the ship was destroyed. The projections show the majority of pieces not going to the planet, they're spinning away from it."

"They were carrying a lot of explosives, captain." Walvento turned from his station. "We hit them hard but that reaction was more than expected."

Vas switched the screen to look back at the station. That ship was the larger of the two enemies and was still on a suicide run. But it wasn't faring any better than its partner as the *Warrior Wench* and the *Destroyer's Curse* demolished it in a series of blasts before it could hit the station's shield.

"Captain?" Vas' radio crackled. "I got ahold of the Lethians." Xsit sounded pissed.

"What did they say?" Not that it mattered really, both ships were space debris now.

"Destroy those ships. They are crewed by Clongari." She paused. "Oh, Grosslyn says you already did. Good job!"

Vas smiled at Xsit's enthusiasm. "Thank you. Tell Grosslyn to keep an eye out for where any parts land and continue monitoring the atmosphere for changes."

"Will do!" Xsit might have been dipping into a few pots of solie again.

"Deven? Ragkor? Everyone okay on your ships?"

"Everything is fine here, captain. But I think we might want to bring a few more crew up for the other ships." Ragkor was calm, but he sounded like he wanted those crew up there now.

Considering how close they got to potentially losing most of their fleet, she agreed. Hopefully, whatever in the hell was happening on the planet wasn't going to become a major ground assault. There'd been no evidence indicating enough people had come to the planet to pull that off. But it was always uncomfortable to split forces during a battle.

"Agreed. Just skeleton crews only at this point. Work on making it happen, Captain Ragkor." Deven could have set things up also, but she needed him to help with everything else.

Deven responded after Ragkor yelled, "Yes, sir!" And cut his end of the call. "We're fine, but Nitya is jumping up and down with excitement to hear feedback on your new ship. Well, she would be if she had a body."

Vas laughed. "Tell her this is an impressive gift. We'll bring it back to the second landing bay once we do a few full planet runs. See you in a while." She looked at Mac. "You heard me, let's see what this baby can do. Roha, keep scanning the planet and the atmosphere. Might as well gather data too."

"Aye, captain!" Both dove into their tasks.

There wasn't much for Glazlie to do on this one, but she had the communications station searching beyond this system just in case. "Not a lot of chatter, but a few ships are coming this way. They don't seem to be together, and they aren't those Lethian Assembly ships. Those are still showing as waiting out past Solar."

Vas walked over to the station. "What's the chatter?" Most likely blowing up the two Clongari-infested Doplin Nebula ships caught the attention of anyone near enough to pick up the explosions. If needed, she and the *Destroyer's Curse* could go meet whoever was coming their way. Too many people had broken through the cloaking on her planet already.

"They are reaching out to the Commonwealth and reporting the explosions." Glazlie shook her head in disgust. "And reporting that the barricade is down. Really? That happened days ago."

"Yeah, but if the Commonwealth didn't make it official, no one noticed. What registries are we looking at and where are they?" A few scanning loops around Home would have been fun in this ship, but Vas was tired of people finding them. She'd take this ship and the *Destroyer's Curse* and speak to them up close.

"One is saying they don't care and are going back to Thail, their home world. The other two are…Garmainian? Well, one is and it sounds like one of Captain Zarith's crew."

Garmain had been a group of three non-Commonwealth worlds of which two, including their capital, had been destroyed by the Asarlaí clones. Zarith had been the captain of one of the few surviving ships and came to help fight against the fake Asarlaí when they'd taken over the Commonwealth.

"Reach out to the Garmainian ship that contacted us. See who they are." Vas radioed to Grosslyn. "Did those ships breach the planetary guns? And is the cloaking back up?"

"No, and yes. Xsit is concerned about the two ships heading our way though."

"Keep the guns ready and the planet cloaked. Ragkor come down to get skeleton crews for all the ships on the station. The *Destroyer's Curse* and this ship will be going to meet our friends where they are." Hopefully, it was Zarith and not someone with ill intent. But better to take the question to them directly.

"Aye, captain." He closed the call.

"Mac, let's see what this ship can really do." She hit her comm. "Stay with us, Deven, we got some people to meet."

Glazlie finally got a response from the Garmainians. "It is Zarith's ship, but Zarith wasn't available to speak. The second in command knows us. They were heading our way to get help after being attacked."

"Tell them to stay where they are, we're on our way. Oh, tell them what ships we're in—they won't know either of these."

Glazlie nodded.

Mac was cruising at a decent pace, with Deven right behind. Nitya made this ship, but she wasn't going to let it beat her.

"Hey, what's this?" The words were barely out of Mac's mouth when he hit a thin panel on the edge of his station and the *Keeper's Tempest* kicked into high gear.

Vas had been in fighters before that couldn't keep up this pace. It reminded her of a Fury but hopefully it was more stable. "Deven? What the hell did Nitya put in this thing? Mac hit a panel and we're taking off." She wasn't too worried, but she was going to speak to Mac after this and point out that asking what something did was better than random testing.

"Nitya says it's a booster. Mac probably doesn't want to run it too long."

"You heard the man, Mac. A few more seconds, then drop it." The ship wasn't shaking, so that was good. But Vas had never heard of anything larger than a two-seater fighter holding this speed.

Mac sighed, waited a few more seconds, then hit the panel. The speed dropped to its normal, still fast, pace.

"Thank you. Not only is this still an untested ship, and we're hoping these Garmainians are our friends, but we really shouldn't risk exposing our secret tech."

"Aye, captain. Good point."

"Glazlie, connect me to that front ship." The systems on her command chair were similar to the ones on the *Destroyer's Curse*—and by default, the *Warrior Wench* as that was what Gosta and his people were trying to replicate when they converted the Hive ship. But still, better to have Glazlie contact them first.

"Coming through to your chair."

Vas hit the comm. "This is Captain Vaslisha Tor Dain, can we be of assistance?"

"Captain Tor Dain? Thank the deities. This is Telian, second in command to Captain Zarith of the Free Garmainian Army. We were attacked outside of the Commonwealth and came here hoping to escape them. Captain Zarith has been injured."

"Who attacked you?" Vas recognized Telian's voice but wanted more information before getting closer. He hadn't been the second when she last saw them.

"Two really old ships that shouldn't have even been flying. Came out of nowhere. They looked like Doplin Nebula, but no one's heard from any of their worlds for almost a year. Not that they were ever social. They hit us hard, didn't say a thing, then vanished."

"Captain?" Roha called out.

"Hold on, Telian." Vas paused the call. "What do you have, Roha?"

"It looks like they were attacked and the weapons were similar to what was used against our planet. No serious damage to either ship though."

Vas drummed her fingers on the arm of her chair. The Garmainians were their allies. At least Zarith's crew was. But she wasn't sure she trusted anyone outside of her people at this point.

"Deven, can you take a shuttle over to the lead ship and assess the situation?" She gave him what information they had so far. Them being attacked by the same ships that had gone after her planet and the station supported their telling the truth. And that those damn Clongari were up to something specific by being in the Commonwealth. Taking over and pillaging the universe was a grand plan, but their more recent interactions were stealthy, and low force.

"You got it. I don't feel anything odd coming from them. But Therlian and I will check. Thinking of bringing them back to Home? If the ships aren't too damaged, having a few more in our fleet when we go back out wouldn't be a bad thing."

"My thinking as well." She started to switch off but changed her mind. "Oh, can Aithnea sense anything? Maybe bring her along? And no, I'm not sure where that thought came from."

"I can't pick up on anything, but I can download into the shuttle and join them," Aithnea responded before Deven could. "A big part of being the Keeper is listening to those hunches."

"Thanks." Vas switched back to the Garmainian ship. "My second and another crew member are coming over to assess the damage." She didn't ask if it was okay. They'd been coming to her for help, this was what they got for now.

"Thank you, Captain Tor Dain. We see them leaving their ship and have our landing bay ready." He clicked off.

"While we wait, evaluations on this ship?" There wasn't a full crew, and even though that wouldn't be many more people for a ship this size, it could make a difference. But she knew these people would notice any ship issues.

"It's great!" Mac almost bounced at his station.

"A little more than that, Mac. Response to changes, stability at those higher speeds, everything."

"Oh. Yeah, it's really responsive. I didn't feel any pull at the fastest speed we got—even with the power booster. I think a fleet of these could improve our chances in any fight."

Walvento turned around. "The weapons are impressive, but far fewer than any of our regular-sized ships. I wouldn't want to go into a fight with only a fleet of these, however. This ship is made for a quick attack and running away." He frowned. "In some ways it reminds me of Ome's Ralith ship."

"That's an interesting point, and I can see that as well. Nitya had our data on that ship, so not surprising that she took some ideas from it. Roha? Glazlie? How'd your stations come through?" There was no way a group of these ships could take on any large fleet. But combined with the larger ships they had, they could be extremely helpful. A class in between Cruisers and Flits.

"It seems fine?" Glazlie shrugged. "Xsit or one of the other communications specialists might want to check it out though."

"Same with the science station," Roha added. "Fast and thorough results to inquiries, but one of the experts should look it over."

Vas made notes and watched Deven's shuttle approach the Garmainian ship. Interestingly, she was beginning to feel calmer about the two Garmainian ships. Hopefully, that was a good sign. With all the texts and scrolls the nuns had about their order and the Keeper, a simple explanation of common reactions, and when to worry about them, would have been damn handy.

"The Garmainian ship feels fine. I'm remaining in the shuttle but am scanning the ship and crew." Aithnea's voice came over the comm.

"Thank you. When we get back, can you search if there are any myths or rumors about the last time the Clongari came to this space? And, aside from hiding, if there's any reason they aren't using their own ships. The first one we saw wasn't trying to hide." Granted, it had been far closer to Clongari space. But for an all-powerful race bent on attacking an entire universe, they weren't giving much away in a show of power.

"Aye, captain." Aithnea cut out.

Vas was never good at waiting, and it didn't look like that was going to change any time soon. "Everyone run a full diagnosis on their sections. Just see what we can find." She knew Nitya would give her a full, and probably extremely over-thorough, data dump on everything in this ship. But, even though she no longer felt like they were flying into a trap, she still hated waiting.

Especially when there was so much weird shit going on her planet.

Chapter Forty

EVERYONE DROPPED INTO RESEARCH AND test mode and Vas did the same. She could access most systems from her command chair, and all seemed to be working fine. There was a metal-covered black button on the inside of the left chair arm. She hit her comm. "Nitya? What's this black button on my chair?" She'd been on enough ships that she knew better than to mess with something that had been made hard to mess with.

"Ah. That's the self-destruct. My research indicated that the normal ones on most ships were overridden by enemies eight percent of the time. That is unacceptable in my opinion. The *Keeper's Tempest* does have the standard countdown self-destruct, but also that button as a last-ditch. It's currently coded to only you, so even if someone pried the casing off, they'd need you and your alive fingers to set it."

Vas gave a sad smile. "Like a Clionea nun's last rite." She'd been witness when Aithnea called her before she sent herself and all the nuns to the great beyond. That it didn't stick didn't make their deaths any less tragic. "Any delay?"

"Thirty seconds. Enough for a final prayer." The sadness in Nitya's voice was uncommon for her. She'd been dead for hundreds of years before Aithnea and the rest of the nuns died, but she was aware of what they sacrificed.

Aithnea and her nuns gave their lives to protect Vas and her crew for something important they were supposed to do. Vas believed it was saving the Commonwealth from the Asarlaí clones.

Until Aithnea and her nuns failed to move on after that. Now it looked like it was a much larger task. Like reinstating the Clionea nuns and saving all of known space from the Clongari.

"Vas, we've checked everything out. Captain Zarith is unconscious in the med bay and there's damage to their deck. But everything seems legit," Deven's voice was calm.

Aithnea popped in right after him. "I agree. I've reached out to this ship and the other one. They're who they say they are. Neither ship is mortally wounded, but they need our help. They'd both lose a fight against an escape pod at this point."

"And helping them might give us at least two more ships for the fight against the Clongari."

"Yes." That was echoed by both.

"Lead them back to Home. The *Destroyer's Curse* will go first so Grosslyn doesn't blast them out of the sky." With the recent incursions, Vas knew Grosslyn would be keeping one hand on the firing control for the planetary guns. She told Gosta and Nitya to follow the *Keeper's Tempest* back to the station. At their acknowledgments, she turned to Mac. "Take us to Home, Mac. At normal speed. And no, you don't get to keep fussing with this ship when we get back."

His heavy sigh confirmed what she'd suspected. He was going to ask to stay on the *Destroyer's Curse* and investigate the *Keeper's Tempest*.

The trip back to the station and into the *Destroyer's Curse* landing bay was uneventful. While the *Keeper's Tempest* could easily land on a planet, Vas wanted Nitya to run full studies on their engagement and this first test of the new ship.

"Anything to be apprised of, Gosta?" Vas asked as she left the *Keeper's Tempest* in the landing bay. Mac was the last out of the ship and she finally grabbed his arm to pull him away when his steps slowed.

"The recent activity in the solbilan mines is slowing down," Gosta said. "At least the ones bombed by the Clongari ships. The ship debris is heading away from the planet. And Grosslyn says they've had no more contact from the kidnappers."

"The mines are going dormant?" Vas didn't know enough about mines to know how in the hell they were made active again in the first place. But either they had always been active and had been hidden for over twenty years, or they'd actually been dead and were made active again.

She didn't like either option. Or more importantly, why it was happening.

"Sort of?" Gosta sounded like he trusted what was appearing to occur even less than she did.

"Do you need any of us to stay up here with you?" She would have liked to talk ships with Nitya, but she needed to get Shien and her people safely freed, get whoever the assholes were who'd invaded her planet locked up, and find out what in the hell the Clongari and the Lethian Assembly were doing.

Besides, Nitya would probably be in a deep dive looking at the results of the *Keeper's Tempest*'s maiden run.

"Not really, captain. Do you need me to return to the planet?" Gosta asked.

Vas smiled as the last part was barely said above a whisper. He had everything he needed here.

"No, please remain here and keep an eye on things. There will be skeleton crews going to all the ships on the station, so coordinate with them. And see if you can find anything at all on the Clongari's behavior. They aren't currently acting like universe destroyers."

"Aye, captain. Oh, Nitya asked about Starchaser ships. Are those parts still on the *Warrior Wench*?"

When Vas obtained the *Warrior Wench,* someone had been storing a lot of highly illegal Starchaser ship parts inside it. They'd used a few for repairing the broken Furies that Deven picked up from Marli, but she'd hidden the rest inside the ship.

"I'd have to check with Ragkor, but honestly he might not have even known they were there. Why does she want them?"

"I'd guess that she is planning on using them to create more ships. Apparently, this ship has a lot of spare parts stored in it, even a destroyed Fury. She utilized some of the Fury's more stable parts in the *Keeper's Tempest* and found enough research to determine the two ship types were similar. Just as we did."

Although they'd never gotten to the bottom of it, they'd speculated that whoever had the Starchaser parts wanted them for something other than simply building Starchasers. Unless they were planning on using the illegal ships outside of the Commonwealth.

Vas thought of Marli's moon. Aside from making sure it was secure after the Pilthians fled—and were destroyed—they hadn't done anything about it.

But Deven was sure that Marli had more Furies stored there.

"Would some more Fury parts help as well?" While a fleet of the *Keeper's* class of ships couldn't win a fight, they could be damn helpful. Sometimes having more than just massive fighters in a battle turned the tide.

"She says yes. And apologizes for not contacting you directly—she's digging into some systems of the *Keeper's Tempest* already."

Vas looked back as she, Mac, and the rest walked toward the shuttle. The ship looked normal, but Nitya's work wouldn't be visible. "Tell her to wait, but we'll send someone over to Marli's moon once we sort out the hostage situation. And the invaders. And the mines. But we'll get on it."

"Aye, captain," from the tone of his voice, Gosta was already distracted.

Vas hit her comm to Deven. "You on the way?"

"Yes. I'll have the two Garmainians dock at the far end of the station, then bring the shuttle down to Home with Zarith and the other injured. I had to use the radio, but Terel is prepping for medical assistance."

"Good. We're heading down now." Vas signed off and looped her arm around Mac's shoulders as he tried to slip out of her grasp. "Sorry, bucko. I need you on the planet right now. You'll get a chance to play with the new toy soon enough." If Nitya could make more, she'd see about giving Mac his own ship. At least for this fight.

His sigh was loud enough that Vas was surprised Gosta didn't hear it up on the command deck. But he followed Roha, Glazlie, and Walvento into the shuttle.

The trip back to Home was uneventful, but they passed five shuttles heading back to the station with the crews. Vas still hated splitting her crews with Home under attack, but their ships were in danger as well, and many of them couldn't land on a planet.

"Captain!" Grosslyn yelled louder than necessary as he came out of his office and saw them coming into the hangar. "The hostage takers have called twice now but will only speak to you. I told them you were indisposed at the moment. I didn't know that they needed to know you were off-planet."

Vas nodded. "Good idea. Is Ragkor back down here?" She knew there would be a minimal crew on the *Warrior Wench*, but he might be more helpful down here right now.

"He's running a check on the rest of the new shuttles." Grosslyn's wince as the words came out was audible and he raised his hands as if to ward off blows. "Seriously, captain, I didn't tap into the fund to pay for them either."

Vas sighed. It seemed like such a low-level issue right now but she would eventually need to find out where Grosslyn got all the money for the space station, the hotel, and now, the new shuttles. Not that she didn't appreciate the timing on them. "We'll deal with all of that later. Tell Ragkor to come to my office once he gets back."

Grosslyn saluted as he went back to whatever he was doing. That was rare and almost disturbing and indicated how unsettled he was about where those funds came from.

Terel followed Vas to her office. "I know I have incoming injured; I take it the Garmainians are still on our side?" They hadn't started there and the way allegiances seemed to be flopping around, Vas didn't blame her question. She also knew that enemy or not, Terel would take care of any patient—it was whether they needed to be restrained first.

"Yes, they are. How is Janx?"

Terel sighed and shook her head. "Still unconscious. Not showing any radioactivity. Me either obviously, thanks for asking. But she's asleep. It's not even a coma—just an extreme case of exhaustion. And all of her readings are like a normal twenty-five-year-old human."

Vas laughed. "I figured when you came out of the med bay that you were clear. Let me know once she wakes. Anything new from her friend, Chasen?" He was also lower on her list of worries, but she felt that like Janx, he might be important. Call it a Keeper's hunch, but something told her they needed Janx for the upcoming battle. And Chasen.

Whether it was something inherent about Mac's cousin, or whatever weird thing that happened to her during the accident, as she called it, Vas couldn't tell.

"Aside from the fact that Delilah wants to adopt him

and he can eat more food than Walvento and Gon combined? Not much. He says he won't talk about what happened to them until Janx wakes up."

"It looks like your new patients are here." Vas nodded toward the guarded hangar door as Deven escorted five med beds toward the med bay.

"On it." Terel waved as she ran over and started barking orders.

Vas shut the door to her office after waving to Deven. She wanted to see any new data on the hotel and the area around it before she called the hostage takers back. And she wanted Deven to be listening in on the call.

Reviewing the cameras from the past few hours revealed no activity around the hotel, until a short time ago. Marwin and Castel, garbed in black and staying low, went out and set up two new pieces of tech aimed at the hotel. Then slunk away. She hit her comm then remembered the issue with them on the planet and called Grosslyn on her radio. "What did Marwin and Castel set up about twenty minutes ago?"

"Ah, sorry. We cobbled together a heat scanner that would go through the hotel walls. It should be live on channel five."

"Thank you. Anything else?" She was already switching to the surveillance channel on her monitor.

"I can't think of anything. I'm sorry, it's been hectic."

"I understand." Vas cut the call as the hotel appeared. They couldn't scan earlier because Grosslyn had specially made the walls to be scan-resistant for privacy for high-level visitors. Who only existed in his head. But this worked. She let out a sigh of relief at the heat signatures popping up on the screen. Either there were a hell of a lot of kidnappers, or the Pilthians were all still alive.

The rest of the vids since she'd gone up to the station weren't informative, but at least they had something to work with now.

"Anything useful? Terel's already working on Zarith and the rest, by the way." Deven came in, handed Vas a huge cup of solie, and pulled up a chair next to her desk. "And how was your new ship?"

Vas took the cup gratefully. "They got heat sensors to go through those damn walls Grosslyn put in." She drank while he looked at the results. "And the kidnappers have contacted the hangar twice. I'm going to see if anything's changed, but wanted to get you in here first. Janx is still unconscious, Chasen is eating everything, and Nitya wants Starchaser and Fury parts. The *Keeper's Tempest* is impressive. I still can't believe she created it with what was on the *Destroyer's Curse* and without any of us knowing."

Deven laughed. "Good to know about the ship. We can work on getting parts to Nitya once we get the Pilthians freed."

"My idea exactly. Shall we see what our friendly kidnappers want now? I didn't ask, but I take it no one has broken through that voice modulator yet?" Vas hoped the people behind this would have realized by now they weren't getting their ridiculous demands of her giving up being the Keeper and not fighting the Clongari.

They'd seemed upset about the attacks on the solbilan mines though. She wondered if they realized that the Clongari had been behind it.

Deven's scowl answered her question—as of yet no one knew who was behind the invasion of Home or the kidnapping of the Pilthians.

"Let's contact them, then." Grosslyn gave Vas a contact code for the radio, but it still took almost five minutes for it to be picked up. Most likely making sure the voice modulator was in place.

Chapter Forty-One

———◆———

"You called?" Vas had the volume turned up so Deven could hear the responses.

"Where were you? We granted you time and that time has passed. The Pilthians will begin to die now."

"I was stopping your friends, the Clongari, from bombing the mines and trying to destroy this planet. Had they succeeded, that voice modulator wouldn't have saved you. Why are you working for them if they tried to kill you?"

There was a pause and Deven leaned closer. "They wouldn't do that. They work for us, not the other way." But there was fear in the voice that the modulator couldn't hide.

"They don't believe that's the case. Along with being in the ships that were bombing the mines, which are all going inactive by the way, they were going to destroy the atmosphere on this planet. We have vids, do you want to see them? Now who in the hell are you?"

Vas was about to ask if they were still there after another long pause when the radio crackled and the voice came back. It was still modulated but less so than before.

"This turn of events is being confirmed by my people. Send us the data. We will hold off our demands for now." The line went dead.

"Damn, I almost feel like I can tell who they are. There's something familiar, even with that modulator." Vas finished her solie and turned to Deven. "Can you have Gosta send the data of those ships and the mines to the kidnappers? Plus that last run to blow up the atmosphere." Her ships had better security than the hangar—just in case the people in that hotel had their own version of Gosta and were planning on trying to hack in from the sent vids and data.

"On it. Oh, and Jasiel is continuing to work on the weird transmission that invaded your head up in the ship. She still believes that it and the attacking force against Flarik's child are connected. She did ask if you'd started speaking old languages again."

"Not that I know of. There are too many things going on in a place that no one should be aware of. And I'm getting annoyed at not being able to sort them out."

Xsit called through the radio. "Captain? Terel's in surgery with the Garmainian captain, but the guards are calling from the lockup, Mac's cousin is awake. I thought you might want to speak to her?"

"Thank you, yes we do. Please don't tell Mac yet." She nodded to Deven and they went for the door.

"Not a peep."

Vas and Deven went to the hangar's lockup. Janx wasn't a prisoner, but Terel had figured she didn't want her waking up and wandering about. Which was an excellent thought. There were too many elements out and about already, and Janx was known to attract trouble.

The guards nodded and stepped back as she and Deven went in. The first cell had medical equipment as the only surviving attacker from the mines was still unconscious and hooked up to a bunch of machines.

The Hivian prisoner from Solar was awake and leaning back as he read a holo novel on his bunk. He smiled and waved as they passed. Probably still extremely happy to be alive given what happened to the rest of the people he'd been with.

Janx was a few empty cells down, her cell was also filled with medical equipment. But unlike the others, she was awake, sitting up, and rubbing the back of her head.

"What did I do?" She blinked blearily at Vas, Deven, and the bars of the cell.

"You went radioactive, collapsed, and weren't responding. Terel said there was no sign of any radioactivity remaining, but you wouldn't wake up. You don't seem surprised at being in a cell." Vas grinned and unlocked the door.

"It's happened a few times. Not the radioactive part, but that's probably from the accident." Her eyes went wide. "I didn't hurt anyone, did I?"

"No. Terel was with you but she came out unscathed. Do you feel up to talking about what's going on now?"

She nodded. "Where's Chasen?"

Deven gave a short laugh. "He *is* locked up. That trisonic detonator that he casually brought in could have blown up this entire side of town. And we found ten more of those things in your dozer."

"There were twenty, you missed some." Chasen couldn't be seen but his voice came from the far end of the row of cells. "I can give you an entire list of the ordinance we liberated before those bastards came after us."

Janx first smiled at hearing his voice, then scowled at what he was saying. Or maybe at his cocky tone.

"It's not what it sounds like. The people we took those things from were up to no good. We had to stop them."

"Who did you take them from?" Vas looked down toward Chasen's cell. "We can talk in my office if you'd like. Maybe get you some food?"

Deven grinned as Janx leaped to her feet and almost ran out of the cell.

"Thank you. I'm starving." She glared down toward Chasen's cell. "And I don't need someone who is being a jerk to cut in with comments."

"I'm stating facts. Can you have that lovely Delilah bring me more food?"

Janx shook her head and stalked out of the cell area.

Deven started to answer Chasen but Vas shook her head. "Let's not encourage him."

Vas did swing by where Delilah was setting up for another full hangar lunch. "We are paying you, right? Not that I don't appreciate what you're doing, but you are running a business." She almost grabbed a plate but Delilah shook her off.

"I am, although Grosslyn and I are still in disagreement about the amount. I don't need the money, Vas. I run the diner to stay active and see people. As for lunch, I'll bring a full spread for the three of you. Just go get comfy in your office." She grinned at Janx. "I'm Delilah by the way. Chasen has told me all about you." The way she winked; Vas was pretty sure that Chasen hadn't intended to tell her much—not that that ever stopped Delilah.

Janx grinned. "Never believe everything he says. Like my cousin, he's a con man. But thank you in advance for the food."

"You're most welcome. Now go settle and we'll bring it in." Delilah patted Janx like she was six and sent them off.

"That's Delilah? Nice lady." Janx waited until they were inside Vas' office before speaking.

"You thought Chasen was flirting." Vas nodded toward a table and they sat around it.

Janx blushed. "He is a flirt. To get extra food he'd flirt with an Elline."

"Has he always been like that? The eating, the suspicion, the rest?" Deven was keeping his voice light, but Vas knew he was picking up on something.

"Sort of." Janx shrugged. "His behaviors became stronger after the accident. But he was always a troublemaker and often hungry. It's stronger now." She frowned slightly, there was something else she wasn't ready to tell them. Then her smile returned.

The door opened and Delilah and two of her crew

brought in enough food for at least fifteen people. "Not my call." She responded to Vas' question before she even spoke. "Your nun friend, Aithnea, called down and said you two needed extra food. Especially Vas. 'Even if Vas says no' were her exact words." She folded her arms and almost looked like she was channeling Aithnea. "I'm not messing with a dead Clionea nun Mother Superior."

Delilah waited until all three had full plates and started eating, before nodding and leaving.

"We don't need to know everything that's happened since you left us at the station, but who was trying to blow the crap out of you and your friend?"

"A pirate companion of the Racki ship we accidentally destroyed during the accident. They'd both been following my dozer and Chasen started getting twitchy. He'd had an issue back on Swatlin IV and was accused of something he swears he didn't do." She frowned. "Or so he recalls. There's a chunk of missing time that he's not sure of. Mostly revolving around a massive party he'd had. But I recognized the ship that accidentally blew up later on—I'm almost positive it was one of the ones that held back during that slaughter at the pirate enclave. The one that chased us here looked sort of familiar, but there was something off."

"Captain? We have a secure call coming in on the radio from the hotel." Xsit sounded excited. It wasn't the voice-modulated person.

"Transfer it." Vas grabbed the radio. "Vas here."

"Vas?" The voice was low and scratchy. "It's me, Shien. A few of us have been free since they took my people, but we can't get out or free anyone else. I sabotaged the comm system to make it harder for them to track us, but they're closing in. Or they were. The guards seem to be pulling back and fighting among themselves."

"Damn good to hear your voice. How recently did the

change happen? I spoke to the one calling the shots and gave them some unhappy information."

"Yes. Maybe a half hour ago? That's why we risked contacting you. What was the news?"

Vas summed up the attacks and that the Clongari were behind it.

"Damn, that's not good, none of it. What do you want us to do?"

Vas looked to Deven. What she wanted to do was for them to hang tight until they could sort this out. But they might not be able to communicate with Shien again. Not to mention if the hostage takers were worried about the Clongari working against them, they could become desperate.

Deven spoke up. "How many have you seen?"

"Twenty. Maybe less now, there's been some blaster fire but not in any areas where my people are being held. Maybe they'll all kill themselves and save us the trouble."

"Right now, sabotage what you can. We're going to get inside and get you out."

His smile made it seem far simpler than it would be. But Vas knew he'd caught something that changed things.

"You still all have your comms, right?"

"Yes, but like I said, I sabotaged them. I found a radio in the closet of my room before they attacked us."

Vas grinned. It was making their own communication awkward, but it should be seriously messing up the kidnappers' plans. "Yup, it's hitting everywhere on the planet. I'd like to see how you did it when you're out."

"That's a deal, captain."

Janx remained silently eating, but her eyes were huge as she listened.

"Take the comms and smash them. There will be dust inside, use it to mark your path." Deven turned on the monitor that showed the hotel under heat scan. "Test one now."

There was some faint muttering and then a brighter dot appeared down in the lower part of the building on the scan.

"We see you. There are tunnels from the structure that go under the hotel." Vas pulled out the hotel printout. "Smash all of your comms, and keep the radio on Code 223 frequency. It's more secure. Then take the people you have and go to the southwest corner of the basement. Look for a small cabinet." She shrugged. There wasn't information attached to it, just an odd short door. One that led to the tunnels. "Get the people with you out, and make sure the door is secured. Keep leaving your trail, and heading southwest until you hit a way out." Like the doorway, it wasn't well marked.

"How are you getting out my people? These cretins do have explosives inside the hotel."

Janx was still eating but switching between the monitor and the map. She grinned. "Hi, Shien, it's Janx. My friend Chasen and I can get inside and neutralize the explosives. Vas and Deven can work on getting everyone out."

Vas raised an eyebrow, but Janx appeared extremely confident.

"Keep the radio on that code and smash those comms. We'll see you soon." Vas hadn't wanted to end the call, but splitting Shien's attention could be fatal.

Shien signed off and the increased lumination from the connector dust inside the comms grew on the monitor as the people with her smashed theirs and started moving.

Vas kept the heat scan up on the monitor but turned to Janx. "And how are you and Chasen going to neutralize those explosives?" She adjusted the view on the heat scan and both the people and the explosives were now visible.

"It's hard to explain. He and I have a trick that came from the accident. Well, after the accident during a job, that wasn't what they said it was. It was how we got the *Crooked Lady*. They had her under guard and explosives.

She's an amazing ship and I couldn't stand to see her destroyed." She waved her hands. "Sorry, longer story. Anyway, whatever weird thing that happened to us, together we can neutralize explosives. Chasen might be able to do it alone, but I helped get us in." She nodded to Deven. "That trisonic detonator was off when he handed it to you, right? If you run a full check on it, it's not an explosive anymore. Maybe Gosta can do something with the spare parts." She took a deep breath. "I can phase through things. And bring something or someone with me. Sorry, didn't mention it before, it's been a weird day."

"Phase through? As in…?" Deven motioned to the wall behind him.

Janx shrugged, shoved the last bit of sandwich into her mouth, walked to the wall, and very slowly went through it.

Vas and Deven ran to the wall just as Janx returned equally slowly.

"It doesn't hurt, just feels kinda weird. Chasen hates it."

"I….don't even know what to say." Vas walked around Janx, but she seemed the same. She poked her shoulder to make sure. "Can you go faster?"

"No, we didn't do much testing. But as of now, I'm limited to what you saw. We'll need to be hidden while we go through. I thought back here where there are fewer guards." She tapped the map in the back and looked at the monitor as many of the images moved toward the center. "Even fewer now. They didn't like your news."

Vas watched the shifts. "We have to move. Deven, get our people together, heavy armor and weapons. No more than forty or we'll be too hard to hide. Janx, let's go talk to your friend and get moving."

CHAPTER FORTY-TWO

DEVEN JOGGED OFF TO SPEAK to Grosslyn and wave down Ragkor who'd just returned to the hangar.

Vas and Janx went to the row of cells. "How difficult is Chasen going to be? If he can't neutralize those explosives, this plan won't work." They didn't have options, if the kidnappers were taking out each other, it wouldn't be long before they went after their hostages.

But Chasen was a risk.

Janx's wince indicated Vas wasn't the only one having concerns. "Chasen doesn't trust big government. I know you're not that, but you do have a fleet and your own planet. You're probably larger than many small nations outside of the Commonwealth. He might need some convincing."

Vas paused outside of the cell row doorway. "I'm going to let you go first, we don't have time to play games and we need both of you to pull this off. The lives of all of those Pilthians, and possibly many people in the town, are riding on you two." Evacuating the town would be a solid idea. But they didn't have time and she knew the level of stubbornness in her people.

They wouldn't leave.

Janx nodded, fluffed up her spikey hair, clenched her fists, and narrowed her eyes. "I'll soften him up, then you come in and finish him off."

Vas laughed. "I thought you liked him?"

"He's my friend. But we have to make this work." With

a look that reminded Vas of Mac when he was scheming, Janx marched down the corridor.

The cell row was long enough that while Vas could tell that Janx hadn't gone inside his cell, she was having an extremely tense low-level discussion with him.

So much for her softening him up. Vas couldn't make out the words, but the tone on Janx's end was not friendly.

After a few moments, she waved for Vas to come down.

Chasen was a striking man, but his face was locked into a frown right now. "What do you need with us?"

Vas figured that whatever Janx told him pissed him off. He'd been trying to be annoyingly charming before. There was no sign of that now.

"I like this version better. More sincere." She nodded to Janx and stepped closer to the bars. "I have no idea who you are, and honestly, I don't care. But my friend Janx says that you two might be able to save a few hundred people, and that I do care about. You invaded my private world, possess a stolen ship, and a dozer wanted on suspicious activity. You also brought a trisonic detonator into my hangar. I could lock you up and throw away the key. In my *real* prison." She waved around at the cells. "Not these nice ones." She didn't have anything beyond these on the planet—they didn't need them—but he didn't need to know that.

Chasen shrugged and folded his arms. But Vas caught a concerned glance toward Janx.

"I'd have to lock up Janx as well. She's guilty by associ-ation. In everything." There was something that both of them were hiding.

Chasen's face changed and Vas knew she'd found the key. She had no idea what was going on with these two and she didn't want to know, as long as they could do what Janx claimed.

"I'll have my people help repair both of your ships after

we free the Pilthians." It wasn't much, but considering that Janx and Chasen couldn't get off her world without help at this point, it might nudge him over.

"Pilthians? They're dead." Chasen went back into lockdown mode.

"Not at all." Vas turned to Janx. "Tell the man. You met Shien and Khirson when you stayed with us at the station."

Janx seemed surprised by Chasen's reaction but nodded. "Vas is right. That's who we would be saving. Vas and her people rescued a colony of them and they've been traveling together." She started to ask more—probably like asking why Chasen was freaked out about it—but didn't.

He watched them both carefully. "I believe Janx. I used to know a group of Pilthians, long ago. I'm glad there are still some alive. You have a deal, captain. Fix the ships and let us go once we save the Pilthians. Janx and I will neutralize those explosives."

Janx gave a sigh of relief. Chasen might be her friend, and she might have more than simply friend feelings for him, but she didn't fully know what he was going to do.

Vas unlocked the cell, although she was almost tempted to have Janx pull him out since Janx said he didn't like it. "Let's get you both set up. Does armor hinder your phasing?"

"Not sure." Janx shrugged. "This is still new and I never tried it with armor."

"Get a full set on for both of you. Then Janx, take yourself and Chasen through a wall."

They'd started walking down the cell corridor, but Chasen stopped at Vas' words.

Vas folded her arms and stepped back to Chasen. He was taller than her, but that didn't matter at all. "Janx told me it's not fun for you to go through things, but do you want to find out when you're trying to sneak in? Keeping you both hidden long enough to phase in will be problematic enough."

He was silent for a few moments, then resumed walking. "Understood. Where's the armor?"

Vas pointed them both toward Grosslyn. Janx and Chasen would be doing the heavy lifting. Vas, Deven, Ragkor, and the rest would be coverage and work on getting the hostages taken out.

She gave a brief overview of their plan to the crew that was going, sketching over how Janx and Chasen could do what they were going to do. It said a lot about her crew that no one asked a thing. They were also all fully armed and in armor. If this wasn't Home, heading out like this might cause issues. One advantage of a planet of mercs. Even if there hadn't been odd things going on, no one would question forty heavily armed people roaming the streets.

As long as it was their own people.

Just to be sure, she'd had Gosta contact anyone living within two blocks of the hotel and told them Vas needed them to bug out for a few hours.

Vas got her armor on after prepping the teams and went where Janx and Chasen finished getting geared up.

"Ready to test?"

Janx nodded. Chasen paused but eventually nodded as well. She took his hand and without any warning, walked into the wall.

Even seeing it before didn't prepare Vas for the oddness of watching two people slowly vanish. Grosslyn looked like he was going to be ill as they slid through and he quickly turned away.

He glanced back when they were gone. "How long until…" He shut up as Janx began coming back. She looked fine, but Chasen appeared to be joining Grosslyn in the sick department. He also rubbed his arms and shook himself once they made it through.

"It worked like normal." Janx smiled as if she'd just walked through a garden. "I didn't feel anything different." She turned to Chasen. His pale skin made his teal eyes seem creepy. "Was it different for you?"

"If you mean did it not try and tear my insides out? No, it still did. Let's get this thing done." He gave himself another shake and dropped Janx's hand. "Don't forget that you're fixing our ships, captain."

"I stick by my deals." She held out her arm to point where Deven waited to lead them. Ragkor and Marwin would be taking two of the teams to surround the front and sides of the building and distract the kidnappers. Vas would take a slightly smaller team through the back and work with Deven on getting the rescued hostages out.

After Janx and Chasen did their job, Vas hoped that they could delay the repairs of their ships long enough to get Jasiel and Aithnea to see what they could tell about those two. Vas hadn't been able to tell at first, but she was now picking up an odd Keeper sense issue with both of them. Their weird new talents could be a temporary reaction to an odd chemical spill.

Or something deeper.

Evening started to fall as they hit the streets. Current and retired mercs alike nodded to the groups, then stepped out of their way.

Deven, Janx, and Chasen moved quickly and Vas lost sight of them after a few moments. She'd have to check with Deven afterward but he might be using telepathy—or some funky Pirate trick—to hide them. He had a masker with him but those only worked on stationary targets. He'd use it to keep Janx and Chasen hidden while they disappeared into the wall. This was something else.

The other two groups spread out at their assigned locations and Vas and her group followed the path Deven would have taken. Vas would have liked to have warned

Shien about the plan, but she couldn't take the chance she'd been discovered.

Hopefully, they wouldn't have to kill the one behind this during the attack. Vas wanted to take care of the person behind the voice herself.

Deven was standing near a wall but was so still Vas almost missed him. He acknowledged her with a nod that the other two had gone inside and the people with Vas spread out. This group would be focused on saving the Pilthians and getting them out safely once the defenses were breached and the explosives neutralized.

The sound of blaster fire from the front of the building worked to draw the kidnappers' attention—at least if the responding fire was any indication.

"Any trouble getting in?" Vas kept her voice to a whisper as she scanned the area. The guards they'd seen were inside the building, not outside it. But that didn't mean they hadn't left someone outside here.

"No, but that is weird to watch. I can't say I envy Chasen. I hope it doesn't slow down his abilities." There was a slight tinge of envy in his voice. Knowing Deven, once things settled down he'd be working on how to replicate the trick.

"Me too. We need someone to check them both out after we free the Pilthians—never heard of a chemical spill doing this."

Deven nodded, then held up his hand as a light crunch came from the strand of trees behind the hotel. Half of their team spun around and aimed their sights.

CHAPTER FORTY-THREE

V AS HELD UP HER NEW toy, a stunner that Gosta had improved. Better than a blaster on the low level, it supposedly would stun and freeze the person at the same instant.

Of course, it hadn't been fully tested yet.

But it would be silent. Or so he claimed. Blasters made sounds and reducing them could only go so far. A fully silent one would be handy in extreme stealth operations.

An armed guard, looking confused, stumbled out of the trees. He didn't even raise his weapon as Vas shot him with Gosta's toy.

She thought it failed as the man blinked and raised his blaster. Then he slowly froze in place. Along with the look of surprise on his face.

Not as disturbing as Janx's trick, but close.

"I hope Gosta can undo that." Along with the lack of noise, Vas wanted prisoners to question. Which wouldn't work if Gosta couldn't fix him.

There was an increased volley of weapons coming from the front, but no additional guards came out of the trees. Vas sent two of her people and they quickly verified that no one was there.

A hand came through the wall and Vas motioned for her people to move closer with weapons raised. Janx and Chasen had moved much faster than she'd expected, or they'd missed some explosives.

Janx appeared, pulling a stunned Shien behind her. Shien blinked and rubbed her arms, but didn't appear to be nearly as upset about the trip through the walls as Chasen had been.

"That was different." Shien gave an involuntary shiver but then regained control. "I asked Janx to bring me out. Once her friend is done taking care of the explosives, I believe we can get almost everyone out—through the door." She nodded to the locked door behind them as Janx went back into the wall next to it. "Janx agreed but we didn't have time to break the lock now. Khirson and five of my closest advisors were moved into a secure room in the center of the building as soon as the weapons fire started." Her brows lowered and she clenched her fists. "I saw them but couldn't do anything." Shien was a fighter as well as a queen. Vas understood how she felt. Not only was Khirson Shien's consort, but those were her people. The kidnappers weren't keeping them without a serious fight.

Deven had his right hand on the wall and was listening to something inside. "Janx is coming back again." The explosives were scattered throughout the hotel and designed to do as much damage as possible to the building, the people inside, and the surrounding few blocks. Chasen and Janx were going room to room, through the walls if necessary, and taking them out. Chasen wasn't happy about multiple wall phasing but it was better than getting caught.

Janx was alone this time. "We have another problem. Someone grabbed Chasen when I was bringing Shien out and there are still at least three active explosives."

"Damn it." Vas hated when plans went sideways. "Hold on." She used her radio to pass the updates to Ragkor and Marwin. "Stay in place for now, but be ready if we have to take another route." Having her people break in with those explosives still live was dangerous for everyone—including the people behind this that Vas had a personal interest in questioning.

"I'm going in," Vas said as Deven took a step forward to join Janx. "I might not have another chance if we have to blow these bastards up." She turned to Shien. "We will get your people out, including Khirson and the ones with him. And we'll find Chasen." She clasped Janx's shoulder. The new Janx was more confident than the one she'd originally met—but Chasen being taken had freaked her out.

Janx stayed silent but gave a sharp nod and blinked rapidly. Then she held out her hand.

Vas grabbed her hand and took a deep breath as they started through. She didn't think she really needed to, but it was automatic. The feeling of the wall as her hand and arm followed Janx was cool and smoother than she'd expected. As the rest of her went through Vas was overwhelmed by the feeling of massive space. Not only the space between the molecules of the wall, which seemed to go on forever, but the space of the entire universe.

It was beautiful and she found that she never wanted to leave. She was everything and everything was her.

A sharp jerk brought her out of the new reality and into an empty room.

"Are you okay?" Janx kept her voice low but leaned forward to stare into Vas' eyes. "Your eyes…. changed. But now they're normal again. Is your vision okay?"

"Yeah. Sorry, that was odd. But I'm fine." Vas added the entire outcome to her list of things to ask Aithnea and Jasiel. "Where did you leave Chasen?" She kept Gosta's new stunner handy, but she also had two blasters set on kill—she didn't want to use them but she would if needed.

She was getting tired of the people she wanted to question either dying or going into comas.

Janx gave her one more worried look, then nodded and went to the door of the room. Vas expected that she'd pass through it but instead, she cracked open the door, nodded, and snuck through the door.

Vas had no idea what doing the phasing thing did to Janx, but it was always better to not use a trick too many times.

The building was dim, emergency lights were on, but not much else. Then Vas saw an armed guard. She froze, but Janx continued walking until Vas grabbed her arm and shook her head.

She thought maybe the phasing was affecting Janx's eyesight as she obviously didn't see the guard waiting to ambush them.

Then Vas blinked and he came into better focus. She could see his heart rate, his breaths, the sweat running down his back. He hadn't asked for this, but a job was a job and he'd always liked killing people when it was needed. She shoved the rest of his thoughts away.

"Shit." Vas kept her voice low but he reacted like he heard her. He was on the other side of a wall, waiting for them to get through the door two feet from him. And yet, she'd seen him. "Stay," she whispered and motioned to Janx to hold her place. It would take too long for Janx to phase through the wall before the guard saw them.

Vas busted through the door and dove with her stunner firing at the startled guard. The weapon worked quickly this time; the guard froze a moment after being hit.

Janx came running through as well and looked around frantically. Vas rolled to her feet and nodded to Janx. She could explain what happened later—if she could figure it out.

They continued to a larger room, probably designed to be a meeting room. Grosslyn had some strange ideas about this place.

There was no reality where Vas was having conferences on her planet. No matter what he thought.

"I left him here," Janx whispered and pointed to a section of wall.

Vas felt an odd urge and stared at the wall. Unlike seeing their now frozen friend, there was nothing on the other side. She walked over and put her hand on the wall.

And almost dropped to her knees as sights, sounds, and emotions hit her. Yup, faint feelings and images—like ghosts—of Chasen and ten guards. He fought back, they were trying to subdue him, not kill him. While he was a strong fighter, eventually one of the guards got close enough to get a hypo into him, and he collapsed.

They dragged him off.

Vas moved to the doorway and grinned as she couldn't completely see Chasen or his attackers anymore, but she felt the direction they went. "This way," she whispered and then started after the trail. This had to be some weird-ass, never brought up before, Keeper trick. She really wished Aithnea and Jasiel had given her a list.

Or maybe her Keeper abilities got jostled by Janx's wall passing trick.

She felt Janx's emotions as she jogged behind her. A running bundle of questions, fears, and doubt that Vas hadn't gone crazy. Vas kept running. This new whatever-it-was could be extremely handy, but not if everyone's emotions came along with it.

Vas slowed as she heard the unfortunate sounds of someone being beaten on the other side of the next door. Unfortunately, Janx heard them as well and tried to keep going. Vas grabbed her arm and shook her head.

Then she focused on the space behind the wall. Yup, two guards right inside the door and four more beating up Chasen. They weren't even asking anything that she could tell. Or maybe they'd already tried and this was the result.

Chasen was a nuisance, but right now he was part of her crew. Vas leaned closer to whisper to Janx and told her what she saw—and felt. "You take the two guards at the door; I'll get the rest." She switched to her regular blasters. They didn't need all the guards.

Janx looked ready to argue but Vas shook her off. "Or stay here."

At Janx's nod, Vas whipped open the door and shot the four beating up Chasen.

There were the sounds of bones crunching as Janx dispatched the two at the door.

Chasen wasn't as pretty as he'd been, but he didn't appear too injured. He got to his feet without assistance when Vas cut the bindings holding him to the chair.

Janx ran forward and grabbed him the moment he got to his feet. Chasen let her hug him and returned it, before he stepped back.

"What did they want?" Vas remained glancing between him and the walls around them. Either her new trick wasn't working now, or there was nothing to see—or feel—in the nearest rooms.

A flash of fury crossed Chasen's face, then it simmered down to anger. "Nothing. They drugged me, took my weapons, and beat the crap out of me. They never said a damn thing."

Vas glared at the six dead guards around them. Maybe the stunner might have been a better option. "Where did the others go?"

"The drugs immobilized me until we got to this room, but it looked like they went through that door in the back. Or they have the same abilities that Janx has. I could see both of the nearest doors and no one went through them."

Vas patted down the closest dead guards, taking their weapons and handing two to Chasen. They were a different class than the rest and probably belonged to him anyway.

"Thanks. Take the rest as well?" Chasen nodded to the weapons near the guards.

"All yours." During a merc job, Vas wasn't averse to claiming weapons as spoils. But she was still having trouble getting her mind around this job being on her home planet. "But, you might need to lend them to others as we free them. How's your head by the way? Up to neutralizing more explosives? Janx said there are still three more." She'd like to have the two of them with her when she went to free Khirson and the five with him, but time was running out. The distraction of the attacks out front would only work for a little longer.

"Four. Before they grabbed me, I…sensed…another explosive." He gave an awkward shrug.

"Wait, not only can you neutralize explosives, you can feel them? Damn, boyo, merc groups would pay millions of credits to get you two on their teams." If once all of this was over, Vas decided to remain as a merc captain, she'd definitely track them both down to join. They also needed to figure out how these two became the way they now were. And see about replicating it.

"Sort of. I didn't notice it in the dozer, or the hangar, and you had plenty of ordinance there. But here…yeah. I can feel where they are. As for joining a merc group?" His laugh had little mirth in it. "I don't play well with large groups of others. But maybe Janx would?"

"She turned me down once already." Vas beat Janx's response with a grin. You two find and neutralize the explosives. Don't separate or get caught. Once you're done, tap three two three on your radio to me. I'll hit two for leave and one to stay put. If I don't respond immediately, get the hell out of this building and find Deven. Don't forget to unlock that door and start getting out any Pilthians you find." She hadn't planned on taking on all the kidnappers left alive in here on her own, but there wasn't time to get Deven or the others in. And there was the risk that if the people behind this realized they were screwed, they could start killing hostages.

Janx opened her mouth to argue but Vas shook her head. "Nope. My op, my rules. Let me leave first." She had oriented herself and now knew where Shien said Khirson and the other five were in relation to where she was.

Vas ran through the far door, the one Chasen said the other four attackers left through. Her weird seeing through walls trick seemed to be working, but she didn't pick up on any guards waiting to ambush her.

Down two more halls filled with hotel rooms, and then a sharp left. She heard the voices before she sensed them. The room ahead of her was a suite, far too fancy for something on Home judging by the elaborate double doors.

The voices were low and angry. But not low enough. Vas slowly moved toward the doors, the stunner in one hand and the blaster in the other. Which one she used was going to depend on the situation.

She swore under her breath as the sounds of another beating were heard. The voices were clearer now and seemed to be unrelated to the beatings. Why beat up prisoners if you weren't trying to get information out of them?

"—can't get out. But she's demanding we destroy those bastards out front. Before we can leave this planet."

"She's an idiot. Not sure why she was put in charge except that she knew the captain. We should kill these people and get out of here. The escape ships aren't far from here and they won't catch us before we're out of range. This job is a bust."

"How'd you figure? Did you see the specs on those damn planetary guns? We'd be space dust as soon as we cleared the atmosphere. And we *will* be noticed."

Vas narrowed her eyes. Two guards, one male human,

and one female Hivian, both giving off massive amounts of stress. They talked tough, and there was no doubt they'd kill Khirson and the others without an issue. But they were scared. Not of Vas and the guns but whoever was behind the woman in charge.

That probably ruled out a Borlan clone as the one behind the voice modulator but the options were still open.

Their conversation became less helpful as the guards moved away from the door and joined the five people beating up the Pilthians. Much easier to do when your victims are tied up.

Vas shook out her shoulders and slowed her breathing. The Keeper ways were handy even for everyday fighting. Hopefully when this was over she could keep the aspects that she liked.

Calmed and centered and with a clear view in her head of the location of everyone in the room, Vas kicked the door on the right open, dodged low to the side, and came up shooting with her blaster. She got one guard when another one hit a button on top of a tower with his hand and her blaster's power died.

Damn it. A remote blocker and since it hadn't been on originally, she didn't sense it. She grabbed the knife she wore on her belt and ran forward.

The entire room slowed down. Or that's how it appeared to her. With a yell, she launched herself off an overturned stool and tackled the two Hivians near Khirson. She knifed one and kicked the second so hard that he flew out of one of the room's windows.

Hopefully, he didn't land on any of her people.

Vas felt like she was moving at normal speed, but no one, even the Pilthians, were reacting like she was. They were all slowing down.

Sometimes it was good to be the Keeper. Vas lifted Khirson out of his chair, breaking the rope that held him.

Then gave him her knife. "Free the others." She went after the rest of the guards with her bare hands before they could get out of the room. There was no doubt that the person behind this mess knew they'd been breached, but the fewer reinforcements for their side, the better.

Khirson had a bloody lip and a chipped tooth, but he grinned as he slowly cut free the other Pilthians. Or at least it looked slowly to her.

Vas pummeled the remaining guards, leaving two unconscious but killing the rest. Including the two she'd heard talking. These weren't mercs fighting a sanctioned battle. These were killers hired to do that.

She looked down the hall when she reached the door, then shut it the best she could. And almost collapsed. She wasn't surprised, this was too much like when she and Deven went after rescuing Terel and the others in the mine. Lots of power, then nothing afterward. But this time she controlled the reaction and recovered quickly.

She might not complain about Aithnea's obsession with training as much anymore. Maybe.

Khirson had the other five Pilthians up and free. He handed Vas two of the longer pieces of rope and her knife and the other five patted down the guards for weapons.

"And someone turn off that blaster blocker please." Vas restrained the two unconscious guards, a Lethian and a Hivian, and shoved them up against the wall.

The sounds of blaster fire from out front of the building stopped but then picked up even louder. Her people weren't supposed to breach the building until they had confirmation that the explosives were all neutralized.

Janx hadn't sent anything yet.

"Do you know where the rest of your people are?" She asked Khirson once he'd added two snub blasters and a long knife to his ensemble.

"Unless they moved them. But we need to find Shien."

A soft knock at the door hit at the same time Vas' radio gave a series of clicks—three-two-three.

Vas clicked for go, then motioned for Khirson to go to the other side of the door. Unlike before, Vas couldn't tell who was out there. At first.

Then she grinned and swung open the door. "Shien, I found them." She stepped back as Shien and six of Vas' people who'd been covering the back came in.

Shien and Khirson smiled at each other but didn't give any further demonstration of affection. Pilthians were warriors at heart, their reunion would be private.

"Deven took another group along with Janx and is heading toward the main holding for the prisoners," Shien said. "More of your people, led by someone named Grosslyn, came to cover the back."

Vas was still feeling a little winded, but that stopped her in her tracks. Grosslyn having left the hangar to help them in the mine had been startling enough. That he brought out fighters and was standing guard himself was shocking.

"I'm not even sure what to say to that. Is everyone fine to fight?" Vas knew Pilthians were stubborn, but hopefully, there were no false heroics. Khirson appeared to have taken the worst, but she didn't want anyone to fight when they shouldn't.

Shien gave a grim smile. "And if any of you aren't okay and claim otherwise, I won't be happy."

The Pilthians all nodded.

"Let's go free the rest of your people. If anyone comes across any leaders of the kidnappers, try to take them alive. Particularly any female ones. But if it's them or you, no worries." Vas checked her weapons, sometimes a blocker could have lasting effects. But they all seemed fine.

The cluster of prisoners was still showing in the basement, but they continued to register as warm, so that was good.

Vas felt Deven, Janx, and Chasen as they came up a side hall heading to the stairs to the basement, then the other twenty people with them. Between the two groups, they had about thirty-five fighters.

"Good to see you all, they've already used a blocker once, where they had Khirson and his people. Be ready to fight hand-to-hand or with blades when we go to get them out." She gave them the same info on trying to keep the leaders alive and that they were especially looking for a woman.

Deven nodded as everyone finished checking their weapons. "You heard her."

The noise out front seemed to be dying down, but Vas knew her people would only slow down if there wasn't a response. She grabbed her radio and reached Grosslyn. That he only sounded slightly freaked out was a hopeful sign. She told him about the stashed escape ships nearby and asked him to warn whoever was watching the hangar and Gosta to keep watch for them.

"Maybe I should go back to the hangar." His tone was less freaked out and more concerned that he might miss out on blowing something up.

"Stay where you are. This is good for you. We should be out soon and need to get the Pilthians to the hangar and our prisoners locked up." Granted, she might not remember exactly where she left them, but she knew the floor. The one she wanted was the woman running this op on the ground. She was disappointed that the bigger fish weren't here, but she wanted to capture one who knew her.

"Understood. Grosslyn out."

Deven chuckled as he ran alongside her. "He was extremely determined when he came running up. He's also wearing heavy riot armor including helmet and shield."

"Hey, he came out."Vas almost tumbled as an explosion rocked the stairwell. She looked around but everyone seemed to be okay. They all picked up their speed.

A second one came as the last of her people and the Pilthians left the stairs. Cracks shot up the stairwell.

"Grosslyn? What's going on?" According to the scanner, the prisoners were in the basement toward the back.

That was where the explosions were coming from.

"We're under attack! Ragkor and his people came around to this side, they're trying to get us out—"There was another explosion and Grosslyn's radio cut off.

Vas nodded to Deven and they led their people toward the room where the Pilthians had been taken.

She started swearing when she saw the wide doors blasted open from the outside. Holding up her fist for the others to wait, Vas and Deven silently ran to the shattered doors and looked inside.

It was a madhouse. Guards were fighting the Pilthians, but it looked like their intention was to get to something in the back. Not that they appeared to be holding back. But no one was using blasters.

"Holster your weapons, and charge!"Vas yelled as she ran forward. No super speed this time, at least not at first. But the guards were extremely outnumbered.

And none of them looked like anyone important.

Damn it. Vas had to find who was behind the voice modulator. She had plenty of enemies, but this one knew too much to be allowed to escape.

The fighting was getting ugly as the guards became desperate. There were a few of them piled against the walls. Judging by the way the current ones had to blow the doors open, Vas would guess the Pilthians had taken advantage of the attacks and taken out the people holding them.

The question was, what was in the back of the room?

A few more deep rumbles indicated the attacks from

outside were still happening. Grosslyn's hotel might not last too much longer.

Deven was watching the back as well and Vas felt a change come over her. The people around them slowed down. Not at the same level they had the prior time, but they were much easier to move around.

She and Deven nodded to each other as they ran to the back. There was an odd collection of mechanical structures there. So odd that it took Vas' sped up mind a few moments to sort it out.

It was a reconstructed bomb. A deep space exploration one used for clearing planetary debris.

Janx caught up to them and started swearing. "That's not one of mine, but dozers carry those. We have to get out before it blows."

CHAPTER FORTY-FOUR

"IS THERE ANY WAY TO disarm it?" Vas doubted it. The monster was unlike anything she'd seen before and appeared to be massively intricate. And huge.

"If there is, I've never heard of it. They're designed to destroy everything within a few hundred miles. On a planet, it would destroy at least half of this world. It's illegal to have them on a planet for that reason. They're even created on distant space stations." Janx sounded calm but her facial reactions said otherwise. She was terrified.

Chasen didn't move forward but watched the wall of explosives carefully. "I don't know that I can completely neutralize it, but I can try. It's far more complicated than the ones they had around the hotel."

"If you can get everyone out, Chasen and I can work on that bomb." Deven nodded as the last kidnappers in the room were killed.

"I can help. I'm the only one here with any experience with those things." Janx might be terrified but she wasn't going to let Chasen do it without her.

Plus, she had a good point.

Shien and Khirson were gathering their people and making sure the injured had support.

Vas wanted to stay with Deven, Chasen, and Janx, but she needed to make sure the Pilthians got out. There were far more injured than she thought.

"I'll help them get out." She grabbed Deven for a tight kiss. "You do not get to die this time." Then looked at the other two. "None of you."

She signaled to Shien and Khirson and they led the Pilthians out the door.

The locked outer door wasn't defended. Vas wasn't sure how many kidnappers were left, and she still hadn't found the woman behind it. A few shots with her blasters and the doors shattered. Shien and Khirson gestured for their people to run out.

Grosslyn waved and Ragkor ran forward to help the injured Pilthians.

Vas grabbed Shien's arm. "I'm going to help the other three. Get everyone back to the hangar. Not that it matters, if we fail."

Shien nodded. "Thank you." Then she ran with the last of the Pilthians outside.

Vas didn't hear any weapons fire, so hopefully any remaining fighting was taking place only out front. She wasn't sure what she could do to deal with that bomb, but something Keeperish told her she needed to be back there with it.

The steady stream of swearing as she jogged closer to the blown-up doors told her they hadn't resolved it yet. On the plus side, they also hadn't blown up half the planet.

The three were clustered around the massive explosive and seemed to be working on different aspects.

Vas dropped to one knee as images caught her. This bomb was of the same type that Aithnea secured around the nun's last compound and how she blew them, and the forces attacking them, up. Unfortunately, she also knew they didn't have time to reach Aithnea. There was no countdown device visible, but Vas felt it internally now. That thing was going to blow in five minutes and thirty-two seconds.

Her vision changed. Similar to the weird thing that happened when she walked through the wall with Janx—but also different. She was seeing the explosive on a different level. A lot of levels. It was as if there was a full schematic in front of her.

They could do this. Janx, Chasen, Deven, and herself were the parts needed to stop it.

Vas jogged forward. "I know what to do. But we're almost out of time. Do exactly what I say."

Janx gasped as she turned around. "Your eyes…"

"Probably weird again, yeah. We'll sort that out later." If there was a later.

Deven and Chasen both turned but didn't say anything about her eyes. If they survived this, she'd ask them what her eyes looked like.

"Deven, stay near me, we're taking apart this section." Vas took Deven's hand and grinned as the images now in her head went to his mind. That Keeper and Pirate connection was handy.

"Chasen, you do this." This transfer of information was different from the one with Deven, but Chasen's eyes widened. His ability to neutralize the explosive would work once the interference was dealt with.

"Understood." He stepped over a few feet to where Vas sent him.

"Janx, this is your job." Vas tried not to freak her out too much, but Janx had to go inside the bomb. Vas took her hand to show her what she needed to do.

Janx slowly nodded and joined Chasen. She was pale, but not shaking. She would stay linked to Chasen, but not be dragging him inside with her.

"As the Keeper has spoken," Deven said it, but the other two nodded as well.

Vas was creeped out, but first things first. No one was destroying her planet.

The pattern in her head solidified as she took her place. Every person was a piece and they all had to move at the same time. She took a deep calming breath, nodded to the other three, and put her hands on a series of wires.

She could see them clearly even though only the smallest part of them showed.

"Green, yellow, purple," she said out loud.

Janx slowly slipped into the bomb with Chasen holding her hand.

Deven closed his eyes and moved small parts of the explosive to get to the inner workings for him and Vas.

Then the entire procedure was repeated as they worked through to the heart of the bomb.

It felt like days and sweat was flowing down Vas' back as the clicks echoed in her head that it had been defused.

She stepped back. It was now past the five-minute countdown and the bomb remained in place as the clock ticked to six minutes.

Vas leaned over to the side and threw up. Luckily, there wasn't a lot of food, but it felt like that, plus what they'd just done, took everything from her.

"How are you all feeling?" She hadn't noticed dropping to the floor until she looked over and saw the other three were unconscious. Fortunately, Janx made it free of the bomb before passing out.

Vas hit her comm and also her radio. "Terel? Anyone? We need a med evac—STAT!" Then the world spun and everything went black.

Moments later, Vas heard sounds, loud voices all speaking to her at once. But it wasn't her crew. And they were damn annoying. If she could punch them, or even open her eyes, she would.

Then she heard one voice speaking in that weird old fashioned Asarlaí that the communications on the *Destroyer's Curse* had shoved into her head. It was gibberish at first, but then she understood it. They wanted her to save them. Whoever 'they' were. Only she and her Xali could save them. That word didn't translate, but felt like it meant a group of some kind.

"Shut up. Please."

"I'm trying to save your life, damn you." Terel's voice cut through all the others, even the pushy Asarlaí one.

"Good." Vas still couldn't move, but in some cultures dying people heard their ancestors as they faded away. She didn't believe that but was glad the voices left.

"Whatever in the hell you four were doing almost killed all of you. Don't move."

Vas would have laughed, but she didn't have the capacity for that. Breathing was hard enough—even with the mask Terel had on her. She felt her body rise, then settle on a mobile med bed. The movement was jarring, but she was glad to still feel anything.

Her mind went to Deven, Janx, and Chasen, but she somehow knew they were okay. Knowing that about Deven, and being sure of it, was comforting. Knowing that about the other two was weird, but not something to sort out at this point.

She still couldn't open her eyes but felt the sun on her face as they ran out of the building. They'd been there all night. "How…"

"Whatever you're trying to say, don't. Don't speak, don't open your eyes, don't even twitch. If you die before I can get you back to my lab, so help me, I'll bring you back and kill you myself."

Vas smiled but had a feeling it didn't show. Terel was scared, but anger was a good sign. When she became extremely kind to a patient it meant things were fatal. She had no doubt that Terel would do what she threatened though, so Vas focused on remaining still.

None of the voices from her head came back until she was in the med bay of the hangar. Then they were so faint, she wasn't certain she wasn't imagining them.

"She's in code!" That was loud and so were the machines placed on her. Then the machine beeping slowed down and the voices in her head vanished.

"You're going to be fine, but I need you to sleep." Terel's words came right before a cold spot hit Vas' neck and the world went black again.

———◆———

The sounds of a calm medical lab were wonderful to hear and Vas took a chance on opening her eyes. No one was hovering over her, so that was a good sign. She knew without looking that Deven was on one side of her with Janx and Chasen on the other. Weird. As long as she couldn't see inside anyone's head, she was fine.

"The captain is awake!" Mac yelled as he ran to her.

"This is a medical ward, Mac. The others might still be asleep," Vas' voice felt rough and seemed barely loud enough to reach her own ears.

"Not anymore," Deven's voice was also scratchy and faint, but Vas thought it was the best thing she'd ever heard. Thinking he was okay on some weird mental level was one thing—hearing it was completely another.

"Thank you, Mac." Terel appeared within Vas' line of sight. "Go watch your cousin."

Mac grinned at Vas, then took off.

"We all made it?" Vas not only meant the four of them but the rest of her crew and the Pilthians. But forming words was difficult.

Terel hovered over her. "There were three fatalities among the Pilthians and many injuries. But everyone should survive. You four almost died though. Gosta came down from the ship to see for himself the giant explosive where we found you all. He says it's completely inert and can't figure out how you did it."

Vas took an offered water tube and drank all of it. "That might be a better question for Aithnea and Jasiel. I think it was something to do with the Keeper and the Pirate."

Terel looked where Janx and Chasen were still unconscious. "And those two?"

"No idea. They linked with me, or I linked with them. It's fading now." Vas hoped. She could still sense them, but she thought it felt weaker.

"Hmmm." Terel gave her the 'I don't believe you look,' and continued checking Vas' vitals.

"Check her eyes." Deven was being examined by Larrisa but managed to get that out.

"Your eyes? What's wrong with them?" Terel's look was predatory.

Vas would have glared at Deven if she could count on being able to sit up without falling over. "They're fine. They apparently changed at one point. I could see through things. Pretty sure that's another Jasiel and Aithnea issue. That they never warned me about. I will be so happy when this is over and they have their new Keeper and Pirate to kick around."

"They went black with tiny flecks of light." Janx wasn't sitting up that Vas could see, but she sounded okay. "It happened twice that I saw. Sorry, Vas. Never lie to your doctor."

Terel grinned. "I knew I liked her. Can we trade her for her cousin?"

"Funny." Mac stayed near Janx's bed.

"How do my eyes look now?" Vas continued trying to sit up until Divee raised the head of her med bed to support her.

"Fine. Not that it means much. The four of you are depleted of some essential chemicals and nutrients. That's not what almost killed you though, I'm still sorting that. But we need to fix that imbalance quickly so new problems don't come along." Terel pulled up a weird-looking glove with lots of tubes coming out of it. "You woke up first, you get the first dose."

Vas opened her mouth to complain, but the glove was secured on her hand before she got a word out. It was clammy and not coming off.

"There ya go. Now, Deven, you're next."

Chasen regained consciousness and had enough energy to struggle before he realized where he was and why, as Terel got a glove on Janx after Deven.

Ragkor came in while they all waited for the gloves to do whatever they were doing.

"Everyone's going to be okay?" He gave his pleasant, 'I'm going to keep smiling no matter what the answer is' smile.

"Things were that bad?" Vas knew that look.

"No, captain…Vas. Everything was under control." He nodded and assumed a military-at-rest stance.

Mac looked up from Janx's bed. "You all died for a short time, nothing big really." He ignored the glare Ragkor shot him.

Vas noticed Terel head toward Ragkor probably to chase him out. "Did any ships escape? The enemy had pods of some sort not far from the hotel." Reviewing everything that happened should wait until she could sit up unassisted, but that was crucial.

"Nothing that we saw. Gosta was monitoring from the *Destroyer's Curse* while we were at the fight zone. Then Nitya took over when he came down here."

"Ships? There were escape ships? On my planet?" Grosslyn was still wearing some of his battle armor as he stuck his head into the med bay.

"Our enemies claimed to have some. And I still never found the woman supposedly behind the ground crew. The one who knew too much about me." Vas would go over the bodies and the prisoners to see if she recognized anyone. But she had a bad feeling whoever it was had escaped. Even if she couldn't get off the planet. Yet.

"Xsit took over monitoring, I'll confirm with her." Grosslyn started to march off, then spun back. "Glad to see you all survived." With a terse nod, he left.

"How long before we're finished fueling up?" Vas tried

to move her hand with the glove, but it was frozen in place.

"Another few minutes. While we're here though, I want to take some images of your eyes." Terel wheeled over a massive machine. "They look fine now, but something was wrong."

Vas agreed only after Terel promised to let her call Aithnea and Jasiel afterward. If she could, she'd order them both to come to the planet. But, while Jasiel could do so easily, Aithnea's mobility was more complicated.

Not to mention that she doubted either would listen to her orders.

Terel finished taking more views of Vas' eyes than Vas could guess at about the same time that the glove released its grip on Vas' hand.

"You can call them now. I'll get back to you when I sort out your eyes." The tone of Terel's voice—annoyed—meant that no great insight had been seen in the images as they came through. Not that it would stop her from searching.

Vas slowly sat on the edge of the bed, then got to her feet. She could contact the ship here, but she didn't want to disturb the others. There were rows of injured, mostly Pilthians, behind them. Not to mention, the call might not be pretty. Normally she wouldn't mind, but there was a mystique about the Clionea nuns and she might as well maintain it when she could.

She nodded to the greetings from her crew but kept going as she slowly walked to her office. Showing weakness when it was warranted wasn't a problem, but she wanted to hash this out with Jasiel and Aithnea while she was still pissed. This bit of her and Deven almost dying because of some mystical crap was getting old.

"Vas, we were going to check on you." Jasiel sounded too chipper as she picked up the call.

"Bullshit. You knew something went wrong. Again.

This time not only Deven and I almost died—but two more people got pulled in. What the hell caused me to see through shit? And know how to disarm an extremely complicated and deadly bomb? And die. Not almost." Terel had made a point of saying almost, but in this case, she believed Mac. They'd died.

"Oh. Let me get Aithnea. I think we need to go down there."

"You can't tell me?"

"It's better in person, and I need to see these other two. This shouldn't have happened this soon."

Vas leaned back in her chair and took a few deep breaths. "What?"

"It's complicated. Let me tell Flarik, Therlian, and Nitya that we're leaving. And get Aithnea into a chip. Could a few more crew come back up here?"

"I can have Ragkor take some people up. Get down here." Vas cut the comm and folded over her desk.

Deven knocked as he walked in. "Drink more water, it'll help." He wasn't moving stiffly at all, but he recovered from everything faster than she did. Including death. He handed her a pair of water tubes as he pulled up a chair. "I take it the nuns had no answers?"

"They're coming down. But apparently, something happened before it was supposed to." She finished a water tube. "Did you hear any voices when we collapsed?"

His eyes narrowed. "No, but obviously you did. What did they say?"

"I couldn't understand them. Or at least most of them. One was in that weird Asarlaí language. They said myself and my 'Xali' had to rescue them. Everything translated in my head but that term."

His eyes narrowed. "Xali. That's not Asarlaí. Not even the old version. That's an older form of my people's language. It means sworn pod group. People who are linked until death."

CHAPTER FORTY-FIVE

VAS SWORE. "I THOUGHT THE Kilesh didn't deal with the Asarlaí? Why would some beings using an Asarlaí language use that word?"

"I have no idea." Deven ran his hand through his hair. "It's such an old term that I only recognize it from stories as a kid. All the mythical heroes of our fables were part of a Xali. Bonded to death and beyond. I never heard of it being real though."

"Why can't anything about any of this be straight-forward? Find out who to fight, kick their collective asses, and move on. I feel like by the time we figure it out, it'll be too late."

The door opened. "Because you are the Keeper." Jasiel's face was grim and she carried a large tablet. Aithnea's equally annoyed face peered out of it.

"This is all more Keeper crap that you forgot to mention? I appreciate the training, to a point. But more information about what to expect would be even better. Deven, myself, and two others died out there. Not nearly died, but dead died."

"Where are the other two?" Aithnea's voice coming out of the tablet was louder than Vas would have expected, but still disturbing as she tried to look around.

Vas thought about moving this to the small holodeck in the hangar, but she was annoyed enough not to want to make things easier for Aithnea.

"How'd you get a shuttle down here this quickly?" Deven also had the same tinge of annoyance in his voice.

He was far harder to upset than Vas was but he was clearly coming to the end of his tolerance.

Vas' annoyance went up that she hadn't even caught that. She folded her arms and glared. Speed was often an issue. Yet they did nun mojo and got down here in twenty minutes?

"We have ways to speed things along." Jasiel raised her hand. "But they take a lot out of us and shouldn't be used except in emergencies. This trip was warranted. But we need to see these other two people. And we have to hear everything that's happened recently. Even the smallest detail could be vital."

As much as Vas wanted to stall to annoy the two nuns, she agreed that things needed to be resolved. Not to mention she still felt the connection to Janx and Chasen. It was fainter than before, but there. She knew they were both still in the med bay and Terel wanted to lock up Chasen. Again.

"Fine. We should go get them before Terel locks them *both* up."

Deven gave her an odd look but didn't say anything as he got to his feet.

Jasiel opened her mouth to say something but shut it when Vas turned her glare in her direction.

The hangar was an odd combination of busy and empty. There were fewer people in it than previously, but they were all busy and quiet.

The med bay wasn't quiet.

Mac and Terel had moved to the outer area and shut the doors leading to the sick beds. They were facing off against Janx and Chasen.

"Whatever is going on, stop it." Vas walked into the middle of them and held her hands out facing each pair. "Janx and Chasen, meet Sister Jasiel and Sister Aithnea of the Clionea order. Yes, Aithnea is in that tablet because she's dead. No time to cover all of that. For ease of this mess, we're going to the holosuite to sort things out." Vas turned to Terel. "Unless there is a medical reason that these two can't leave or you wanted to lock them up in the brig?"

Terel's eyes went wide, but she shook her head. "Not if you're taking them elsewhere. I won't intrude on your talk, there are still patients to help. But I'll need the important points afterward." Her look toward Janx was neutral but hostile toward Chasen.

"Agreed. Come on, folks." Vas held up her hand as Mac tried to follow them. "I'm pretty sure there are some things you should be doing. Or I can have Grosslyn find something for you."

Mac froze. "I'm fine. Bye, Janx, we'll chat later." He left so fast that there was nothing to see but a red-haired blur.

"You can't force us to do anything." Chasen hadn't been this difficult when he first arrived and was locked up. But there was a tightness around his eyes and he kept rubbing the side of his head.

"He's fine, right?" Janx moved closer to him.

"He was." Terel turned to Chasen. "Damn it, get back on the table."

"I'm fine. Just suddenly got a headache." He sighed. "Fine, Janx, I'll go with them."

Janx hadn't said a thing and looked at Vas in surprise.

Jasiel started pushing them toward the door. "We need to be in the holosuite, now."

Terel shrugged and went back to her other patients.

Janx remained next to Chasen and Vas stayed ahead of them. The holosuite was small but they all fit and once she called up a holo room with trees and chairs it felt less confined. Jasiel took her pad to the computer screen and soon Aithnea's hologram appeared.

"These are the two." Aithnea was using her best mother-superior tone as she put her hands behind her back and marched around them. "I'd say this is highly unusual, but this entire situation has been that way." She paused and watched them both with narrowed eyes. "Let me fix this first." Without warning, she tapped both Chasen and Janx in the middle of their foreheads. Both shook their heads and blinked, but the stress lines on Chasen's face vanished.

"Thank you." He dropped into a chair. "What caused that?"

"The connection between you four. An odd one for certain. It's not gone, by the way, I lessened the impact. When did the two of you gain these new powers?"

Janx sat but looked at Vas in surprise.

Vas shrugged. "The nuns know things. And if I'm right, we're all stuck together for the duration." Providing Chasen could dial back his attitude before she killed him.

Chasen sat up. "We can't stay. There are too many people after us."

"Easy, boyo. You're safer with this lot." Aithnea almost sounded like she was channeling Marli, but she winked when Vas looked at her.

The short version of their accident didn't completely resolve the questions from Aithnea and Jasiel, but it gave them enough to work with. Mostly they were interested in the date it happened. It meant nothing to Vas, but Jasiel and Aithnea shared a concerned look about it.

"Now, what happened in that hotel?" Jasiel had taken a seat and held a pen and pad in her hands. "The more details, the fewer times we have to repeat this. Aside from keeping this planet from blowing up, something significant happened out there."

Vas began and ran through everything from her side to the end. Aithnea remained pacing around them but stopped when Vas got to the explosive and what it was.

"There is no way that could have been by chance. After we sort this, I need to see this thing." Aithnea spoke more to herself than the rest of them.

Deven watched her, appearing to wait to see if Aithnea was going to add to that. He went on with the events from his point of view when she didn't.

Then Jasiel nodded toward Janx to say what she saw and did. Here both Aithnea and Jasiel asked questions. Mostly about Janx's abilities. That neither had said anything about Vas seeing through walls or bombs indicated her abilities hadn't been completely unexpected.

Chasen was difficult at first, then surrendered and shared his side of what had taken place in the hotel. Aithnea had a lot of questions for him—most of which revolved around his new bomb-neutralizing trick. She'd continued to walk around the table, but Vas watched her face carefully. Something about Chasen was making her extremely concerned.

The silence that followed was almost as disturbing as the look on Aithnea's face. Jasiel was schooling her expression better but she also didn't appear happy.

"What do you now think is going on that has surprised both of you and you're now trying to sort out without freaking us out?" Vas aimed her scowl at both of the nuns.

"That you four are a Xali, as the strange voice said you were. Something not seen since long before my time." Jasiel spoke when Aithnea simply nodded and stopped pacing. "Historically, Xali are linked in many ways in order to complete a major life-or-death task. You are picking up on each other's abilities in subtle ways right now. But it will get worse and you'll need to be able to deal with it."

Janx looked at both nuns. "But we did the life-or-death thing. Stopped that bomb, saved the Pilthians, and this planet. It's done now."

"That was the crux, the unifying event to tie you all together." Jasiel started pacing. "I have a feeling that your intended destiny right now might have contributed to how you were both changed by your accident. These things are often foretold, even if not in clear easy to understand ways."

"Agreed. And there's more," Aithnea said. "I believe that you two are the future Keeper and Pirate. Once the Clionea nuns are returned to their standing level, you will both be vital to their success."

Chasen sighed and rubbed his temples. "We have weird powers, that weren't completely caused by the accident, and we're now tied to Vas and Deven for some unknown reason. And if we survive that, Janx and I are working for the Clionea nuns? Who aren't even around anymore?" He tipped his head to Jasiel. "Present company excluded."

"Yes." Aithnea smiled.

"None of any of that makes sense." Janx held up her hand. "There is a lot of crap going on, Chasen and I have pissed off some extremely powerful people. We can't sit around waiting for them to find us."

"Again, the four of you are far stronger together than you are if separated. Whoever is looking for you, can't be nearly as bad as what the real danger is. And at this point, I think only death could disconnect you four, so it's not a valid concern. As for an unknown reason, Chasen?" Aithnea's laugh was flat. "It's known. Bring back the Clionea nuns, gather a force as never seen before, and destroy the Clongari before they destroy everything in the known, and probably unknown, universe. Failure isn't an option for any of you."

The room went silent and even Chasen appeared subdued.

"How does this work? Knowing where these two are all the time might be handy in a fight, but day-to-day, it's going to get old. Fast." Vas wasn't happy about any of this, aside from naming Janx and Chasen as the next Keeper and Pirate once the nuns were reformed. Seeing an end to the entire Keeper bit did make her happy.

"I can subdue that effect for now." Deven got to his feet and turned to the nuns. "Unless you two have some ideas?"

"This aspect is most likely related to your specific telepathic ability, so please, go ahead." Aithnea snapped her fingers and a computer console appeared in between the trees. "I'm listing all the abilities you each currently have; you'll need to understand them all to make this work." She paused and looked at the four. Then smiled. "I believe that this doubling up, as it were, will help call the new nuns to us much faster. And get them ready to fight."

Vas narrowed her eyes. "Not here though, right? I don't need more strangers on my planet."

Aithnea's look became distant. "Too late for that. They're already coming this way. Do you sense them, Jasiel?"

Jasiel closed her eyes, then grinned as she opened them. "They are, and I didn't even have to get drunk this time. Sorry, Vas, your nuns are coming. Here. Soon. Like now."

Xsit's call on the comm a moment later wasn't too surprising. "Captain? Several small ships are coming this way. Grosslyn has the cloaks up, but they seem to be aiming right for us. He wants to shoot them down."

Vas swore at both nuns before she responded to Xsit. "Tell him no. Reach out to them and send them to…" She looked toward Deven for a location. The last thing she wanted was more strangers in this town.

He nodded. "Send them to the Maoli islands. The main island has a landing strip and a research station is there, but not much else. Instruct them all to remain in their ships."

"Aye." Xsit ended the comm call.

"Damn it, you couldn't wait until we got off world, could you?" Vas glared at Aithnea and Jasiel. "We still haven't found the woman behind the attack here, and now we're going to have random ships dropping in." She got up as a thought hit her. "How many nuns are we expecting? And how in the hell did they know where we are?"

"Easy." Jasiel also rose and held up her hands. "First off, we didn't make it happen—you four did, unintentionally. It was most likely expedited by what you did against that explosive. Very Clionea nun thing to do. Secondly, every time the nuns have been recreated, it's different. Even if I hadn't been completely drunk at the time, I couldn't have told you how I gathered them eight hundred years ago."

Aithnea pursed her lips in thought. "Probably a few hundred, I'd think. This is an accelerated situation. But they won't all come at once. Gather these, then prepare to put your forces together for the battle that's coming. The rest will find you as you travel. As for how they knew this world was here? It's a strong calling. It would take more than simple cloaking tech to stop them."

Chasen opened his mouth to argue, then shook his head and dropped it. "You're right, Janx."

Again, Janx's eyes went wide. "I didn't say anything."

"Yes, you did. You said we didn't have a choice." He looked around at everyone's faces. "She didn't say it out loud, did she? Great. Are we telepaths now?"

"No, but I am." Deven turned to Aithnea. "You said we'd be sharing abilities in this Xali. It's happening now?"

"Like I said, this was way before any of our time. But there is a strong connection with you four. And the way you described taking apart that modified dozer explosive?" Aithnea shook her head. "I used those things for decades to protect the monastery and I know you four shouldn't have been able to do what you did." She appeared to want to take apart all of them to find out what they'd done. But finally shook it off.

"Let me guess, there's training for this?" Vas got up. "I don't have time for training right now. Whoever was behind this attack on my planet is still out there."

"I wish we had training." Aithnea looked shockingly lost. "This is all unprecedented. Jasiel and I have been trying to stay on top of this, but everything before this was unprecedented as well. There is nothing to train, as we have never heard of whatever in the hell this is."

Jasiel watched her friend have a rare meltdown, then finally stepped in. "I agree. But I do believe there can be training." She held up her hands before Vas could respond. "Not a lot, and yes, finding the person behind the attacks here is important. We can't move on until that's resolved. But if you four can't work together all the time, we might as well give up now." Her glare silenced everyone, even Aithnea.

Vas finally nodded. "Agreed. A weapon is useless if you can't use it. But, it's not only up to us four. We have to get everyone together on this. Any Commonwealth worlds who will help, and as many people and ships as we can get outside. After I find the bitch behind this mess."

Aithnea and Jasiel stayed in the holosuite to work out their details and the other four left.

"We're going to just hang out here and try and figure out what we're supposed to do?" Janx lowered her voice as they walked. "Chasen wasn't kidding about us having powerful enemies looking for us. The Darmon enclave owned the moon that ended up exploding during the accident. It was where their main storehouse was."

"I haven't heard of them. Outside of the Common-wealth, I take it?" Even though Vas and her crew had spent months trapped outside of the Commonwealth, they hadn't had much engagement with the people there—or rather, with the mob people. Which, based on Janx and Chasen's faces, and elevated heart rates, was what they were.

The sensing them on that heart rate level bit was also going to have to stop. Soon.

"Yes. Extremely dangerous, and they make a point of

avoiding anything even remotely related to the Commonwealth." Chasen sounded a little less freaked out than Janx, but not a lot. "I'd heard of them before our run-in. But I didn't realize that Janx's job was for clean up for them. Things went wrong, maybe in part because of what those nuns set up intentionally or not, but the moon blew up. It was a gralian plat-dium mine. One of the few left and larger than anything ever recorded. Now they won't stop chasing us. That pirate ship your people destroyed was one of theirs. The fact that it was willing to cross into the Commonwealth to kill us is a bad sign." Now that Chasen wasn't being aggressively annoying, he seemed reasonable.

They were walking past the communications office and Xsit came running out. Her bright yellow feathers were extended, and her pupils were huge.

Too much solie again.

"Captain! The Garmainian second-in-command wants to know if he should blow up the vessels coming in. And he needs to speak only to you." She shoved a headset into Vas' hands.

"Fine." Using the headset would be faster than comms. "Hi Telian, this is Vas. Please, do not blow up any ships coming our way. Thank you for your concern." Honestly, she'd forgotten about the Garmainians. And the fact that their captain and other injured were in the med bay. However, even with everything else going on, she knew Terel would have said something if Captain Zarith hadn't made it.

"Are you sure? There are some questionable ships coming your way. There are four Hivians." His accent was different, but his tone echoed Grosslyn's suspicious nature.

"Yes, we're sure. Again, thank you. How are the repairs going?"

"We should have both ships completely done in a few

days, about the time that your doctor said our captain and the rest of the injured should be ready to leave."

Vas looked to Deven. This Garmainian was a combination of Mac and Grosslyn—and had nothing to chase or blow up. Frustrated and excitable people could make serious mistakes.

Deven held out his hand for the headset.

"Hold on, Telian." She smiled at Deven as he put the headset on. "Thanks. I'm going to go have Grosslyn find our new pod mates a place to stay for a while, then see if any of the prisoners seem familiar."

Deven nodded and started making up things that he needed Telian to look for out there. A slow and low planetary patrol by a shuttle would be helpful as well.

Vas motioned for Chasen and Janx to follow her. "Don't look so worried, Grosslyn isn't going to lock either of you up. Nor put you in that hotel. You will probably need a place where you can do a lot of training with the nuns. They're big on training."

"I still don't understand what we're going to do." Janx waved around the hangar. "You have a lot of people here, couldn't two of them be these whatever these people are?"

"Sorry. Neither Deven nor I had a choice, it just happens. Most likely Jasiel and Aithnea will give you far more backstory and history as to why you two were chosen than anyone would ever need. If they do, remind them that I said they need to do a speed training. The Clongari being bold enough to come into the Commonwealth— even disguised—is a bad sign. We don't have time for mysticism."

Chasen and Janx looked at each other and nodded.

"Excellent." Vas stopped in front of Grosslyn's office and popped her head in. He was chatting with Delilah. "Hate to break this up, but I need to officially introduce our two newest members: Chasen and Janx. They'll be training with Jasiel and Aithnea, but need a place to stay until we leave. Preferably not in the hangar." She intended for her and Deven to move out of the hangar this evening, it would be rude not to offer that for them.

"Good to see you again." Delilah jumped to her feet and vigorously shook both of their hands. There's an open apartment next door to my diner." She turned to Grosslyn.

"Ah, yes, that's open. If it's okay with the captain?" Grosslyn was an excellent planetary manager, but not so much on picking up on quick changes. From the way he kept narrowing his eyes at both of them, he still saw Janx and Chasen as criminals and threats.

"Sounds perfect. And don't worry about paying for your meals at her diner, I'll cover what Delilah doesn't." Vas knew Delilah would keep an eye on the two of them for her.

Delilah didn't wait for either to respond, just slipped her arms into theirs and led them out. "I'll show you around, get you fed, then send you back here for more training, I'm sure. Grosslyn can send your things, right?"

Grosslyn looked caught between smiling, frowning, and scowling. But he shrugged and nodded.

CHAPTER FORTY-SIX

VAS WENT TO THE CELLS and slowly walked through the prisoners. There were fewer than she'd expected and she would need to make sure this was due to them dying, not escaping.

Not a single one even looked remotely familiar.

The person behind this attack was still on the planet.

Vas knew Grosslyn was beating himself up for not catching the attackers when they'd landed over the past few weeks. She didn't blame him, and she also knew his mood meant that not even a rock was coming on or off this planet without his being aware of it.

Deven joined her walking through the hangar after having set Telian on some helpful, but not completely necessary tasks. Between Telian and Grosslyn, no one was going anywhere without being tracked. Xsit reported that so far all the future nuns were following orders and landing at the coordinates sent to them. Almost all of them were fighters from a wide variety of peoples both inside and outside of the Commonwealth. Vas hadn't thought of it before but it made sense. The Clionea nuns weren't under any jurisdiction, even though they'd been in the Commonwealth.

"You know that eventually, they'll bring us in for training with Janx and Chasen." Deven nodded as Jasiel met the other two when they came back from Delilah's and dragged them back to the holosuite.

"I agree we need training to work together, but right now, I need to find the one behind this." Vas stopped her march to Grosslyn's office when she saw Shien and Khirson leaving the med bay. "And they might have some clues."

"Shien, can we speak to you? Both of you?" Vas asked as she went to them.

The two had been in conversation but Shien gave a regal head tilt. "How may we assist? Thank you again for rescuing my people. And from what I understand, not blowing us all up."

"You're welcome. I'm sorry your people went through that, and that we couldn't save everyone. Let's go to my office if you don't mind." Vas looked around the still mostly empty hangar. She trusted these people. But someone had too much information on her and the Clionea nuns. The odds that it was one of her own were slim, but not zero.

Vas explained about the modulated voice and what they'd been demanding to save the Pilthians. Shien grew more annoyed as the information came out, no one held her people prisoner and lived to tell about it. It would be a race to see who killed the woman behind this first.

As long as Vas could find out who it was and how they knew way more than they should, Shien and her people could do what they wanted to her.

"Did either of you notice anything that might help us find her?" Vas knew even the smallest bit could change a war.

"Nothing. I mostly hid from them." Shien turned to Khirson. "But you were locked up. Were there any clues?"

"I might have heard something. Moments before the guards grabbed me and the other five, I heard a woman giving orders. She was furious at something and said someone had betrayed her. Not sure if the victim was the one who'd done it, but I heard a blaster shot and the thud of a falling body right after. She wasn't with the ones who came in and separated us though." His eyes narrowed. "Could I hear the voice-modulated threats? I have a sensitive ear."

Deven went to another desk and pulled up the recordings. "Right here. We've tried everything to break down the voice behind it."

"I'm not sure I can identify it, but I can tell you if the voice I heard was the same one. It might help a little."

"Here you go. If you sit here you can play it as often as needed." Deven got up from the desk and Khirson took his place.

Khirson replayed the calls a few times while Shien tried to think of any information her people might have told her about the kidnappers. Mostly she'd been with the injured since they'd been rescued.

"It's her," Khirson finally said. "There's an odd cadence to her speech that the modulator only partially gets rid of."

"You found it that quickly?" Vas wasn't going to argue, but none of her people had been able to do anything with it.

He looked up with a grin. "Like I said, I have extremely good hearing. And a good memory. I'm adjusting the modulator aspect out of this section to match the voice that I heard." He played the snippet again.

Vas and Deven listened closely, but the modulator was still doing too good of a job.

Khirson nodded. "I'll keep working on it. Don't worry, I'll crack it."

He might have started as trying to see if it was the woman he'd heard, but Vas had worked with him long enough to be able to tell when he was on a mission.

"Thank you, Khirson."

Shien favored her consort with a fond smile—once he'd looked away. The Pilthians had a far less publicly demonstrative way of dealing with affection than many species.

"I am certain that your people can find another temporary location for us, but I believe after our adventures we would prefer to return to our section on the *Destroyer's Curse* for this final battle. It truly has become home to us." Shien laughed. "At least a nice temporary one. Never fear, Vas, we're not going to move in there permanently."

"I was thinking of moving more of the crews to the ships now anyway," Vas explained about the new nuns who were arriving. Mostly she hadn't discussed the Keeper or nun situations with Shien, she had enough to deal with. But since it appeared that the Pilthians were going to join them in this battle—she needed to know.

"That will work out well for us and you then. I'd heard you might be captaining a different ship than the *Destroyer's Curse?*"

"News travels fast. I thought about it, but having Nitya and her new ship take the lead in this battle seems right. I'm not going to lie; I've missed the *Warrior Wench* and will go back to it when we're finished saving the universe. But I think I'll finish this on *Destroyer's Curse.*" Vas looked over at Deven and Khirson working on breaking down the tiniest parts of sound from the recording. "What are your plans after?"

Shien looked over at the two men and smiled. "Seriously thinking of taking up the offer from Solar. A new world all our own at some point would be nice, and perhaps we could gather more of our people. But I want something small and out of the way for now. And, no offense, not in the Commonwealth."

"I completely understand."

Deven and Khirson were chatting softly as they worked, and their sudden stop caught Vas' attention.

Deven's look of concern when he turned to her solidified that. "You should hear this. But keep an open mind."

Vas was already on her feet and she and Shien joined them.

"What?"

"It's not a single voice," Deven said with a nod to Khirson. "It wasn't that noticeable when Khirson heard her, but once you remove the voice modulator and start picking it apart there are two voices, blended."

Vas waited for the rest. "And? Damn it, Deven, who are the two voices?"

Khirson played the recording loudly. "Easier if you hear them."

Vas found herself clenching the edge of the desk at the first unmodulated word. "The empress. Pretty sure she was dead." Then a lower timber cut in under the words. Honestly, if Khirson and Deven hadn't been futzing with it, she probably wouldn't have caught the second voice. Saying the same words, at the same moment. Just separated in pitch.

"Borlan." There wasn't a question and judging by the look in Deven's eyes, she was right.

"That's who it sounded like to me, but he was your brother."

"They're both dead—or so we thought. I know the bastard on the *Defiant Ruin* was Borlan. And there was no way he survived that explosion. This person is a clone? Of the two of them? Damn it, who's behind this?" Vas' goal of finding the person behind this attack was so she could sort this out and find out how much they knew. But if they were a clone, there wouldn't be many answers even if they found her-them.

"That would be my guess." Deven played the cleaned-up recording again. Confirming both voices. "The only advantage is that Gosta will most likely be able to narrow their rather unique genetic makeup down and find them. As for who? Not a clue."

CHAPTER FORTY-SEVEN

K HIRSON CONTINUED TO WORK ON the recordings for another hour, then finally gave up as there was nothing else he could draw out of them.

He and Shien left to speak to Terel about moving their injured and the rest of their people up to the *Destroyer's Curse.*

Gosta was settling down to do a full analysis of the neutralized dozer explosive when Vas caught him and told him who, or what, they were looking for.

"I'm on it, captain." He gave a glance at his other project but was already setting up scans when she left.

"You know, you can rest. It's late, and nothing is going to resolve itself immediately." Jasiel was leaving the holosuite and had Aithnea in her pad. Neither appeared ready to sleep but had obviously finished working with Janx and Chasen as the holosuite was blank and empty.

"I know, and Deven already took our stuff over to his place. Hopefully, we'll get to spend at least one night there. I keep thinking about who in the hell is bringing back these clones? They were already falling apart a year ago. The place that was making them is destroyed. What the hell have we missed?"

"I wasn't around for that adventure, but Aithnea filled me in. You said you had an Asarlaí friend who had a secret moon?"

"Yes, although she said the Asarlaí didn't go for clones—even they thought they were blasphemous."

"True, they didn't. It was one of the things I liked about them—and her." Aithnea's voice was muffled as

Jasiel was holding the pad against her body. Which she quickly resolved. "But Marli had a lot of inventions and other tech around her. Those ships she had. Could someone have moved onto her moon and used her resources and their knowledge to create a new clone lab?"

"They couldn't get in. Deven secured everything after those murdering Pilthians left." She stopped and swore. "But there was a fly-by around the Home from a Fury while we were gone. No one aside from us or Marli's moon should have those."

Gosta looked up as Vas and Jasiel came running into his office. "I haven't established the parameters for the search for the clone. And it will take a while once they're up to search the entire planet. Just because they couldn't blast out of here doesn't mean they are still in town."

"I know, and that's important, very much so. This shouldn't be as difficult. Can you use the systems on the *Destroyer's Curse* and the satellites to determine if there's been activity on or around Marli's moon?"

Gosta wasn't surprised often but his eyes went wide and his throat bob dipped a few times. "Do we think someone broke through Deven and Marli's defenses?" He might have been surprised, but he was quickly working on another computer.

"They might have. While your friend despised clones, any tech area of hers would have the required machines to make them." Jasiel stepped forward and held up the pad so Aithnea could view Gosta's screen.

"I hadn't thought of that, but I assure you, Deven's protection of that moon after the Pilthians were removed… oh." Gosta tapped a few more buttons, then started swearing. An exceedingly uncommon thing for him. "There is activity on the moon now. Not a lot and to be honest, the moon is still cloaked and shielded."

Vas, Jasiel, and Aithnea moved behind him.

"Damn it. How in the hell did someone break in? How

far back can you go to see when this began?" The events with Khirson's original crew occurred right before Vas and the *Traitor's Folly* left the Commonwealth on their mission. But she knew Deven had secured that damn moon extremely well afterward.

"That will take longer," Gosta paused. "And I might need to go back to the *Destroyer's Curse* for a deeper look." He didn't look at Vas, a sure indication he believed that she'd say no.

"Why does everyone think I don't want people up there?" She waved Gosta off before he could answer. "Never mind. Things have changed, everyone has had downtime and can start moving back up to the ship. Yes, I will be taking the *Destroyer's Curse* out when we go back into space. And the Pilthians will be joining us." She clasped his shoulder. "You gather your things and head up, notify me if you see anything else. We might be doing a fly-by on that moon before we leave the Commonwealth." She turned to Jasiel. "You two ladies should probably work on getting the new nuns set up. I'll speak to them tomorrow. *After* I have had a relaxing night with my second-in-command. Get rest, all of you. We're going to be moving soon." With a smile she didn't feel, Vas left.

The hangar was completely empty now that it was late, but Vas knew Terel would still be working. Even if she called it 'just finishing up a few little things'.

They were rarely little and often took hours.

It took a few minutes to track her down, there were fewer filled beds than earlier, so that was good.

Divee was fighting yawns as Terel was going over some charts with him.

"Divee, get some sleep. Terel, you too, or at least go to your room."

Terel spun and waved a chart at Vas. "Just have a few more things…" She stopped when Vas barked out a laugh.

"Nope. I came by to say we're moving more of the

crew back up to the *Destroyer's Curse* and the rest of the ships tonight and tomorrow. I'd like you to be ready to move, but come with me when I address our new nuns. Which means you need to get some sleep."

Divee began to slowly move toward the door but froze when Terel coughed.

"Never mind," Terel said. "Get some rest, our captain will most likely work us to the bone tomorrow."

Vas smiled at Divee and he scurried out.

"Now, what else did you need to tell me?" Terel put down her charts, folded her arms, and glared at Vas.

"The person behind the attack, who we do think is still on the planet, is a clone. As far as we can tell they're a combination of the late empress and my equally late, and unlamented, brother. Gosta is working on tracking them down since as a clone of two dead people they'll stand out on a tight scan."

"Damn it, I thought the clones were dead."

"We all did. Someone brought them back, or at least this one. And they might be using Marli's moon, or rather, using the resources there, to do so. Gosta's also looking into when that started but there is activity there that shouldn't be."

"I can help. Not with the moon information, but I can modify my equipment to help find the clone. Or clones."

"I'd thought of that too. Where there's one, there's often more. In the morning, have Divee and Larrisa scan the dead and the prisoners for any evidence of cloning."

"But I—"

Vas cut her off. "Can listen to your captain who needs to rely on you a lot, and get some damn sleep." She took Terel's arm. "Seriously. There are way too many balls in the air right now for me to have any chance of sorting out. I need you at your best." Then Vas yawned.

Terel fought it, but she echoed the yawn. "Funny. That doesn't mean that I'm tired."

"Then get that way. I'll be at Deven's if you need us. Otherwise, I'll see you here at 8 hours or Delilah's before." Vas waited until Terel began shutting down the screens. The night shift docs were already in place and flashed grateful smiles at Vas as Terel left.

"I'm staying in one of the rooms here, but I will go to sleep. Stay out of trouble until tomorrow, please." Now that she'd been pulled away, Terel was starting to slump. She was always the last to admit to being tired. Considering how stubborn everyone in Vas' crew was, that said a lot.

Vas told the night crew in communications where she and Deven would be then headed over there.

With all the ambushes and attacks lately, she didn't think it was odd to approach Deven's house with her stun blaster out.

But he answered the door before she hit the final step and bowed for her to come inside. She hugged him as an amazing smell hit her. "Capsina fish? Where did you get it?" Vas loved seafood of all kinds despite growing up on a world with no real seafood to speak of. But capsina fish was her absolute favorite.

"It was supposed to be a surprise, and they still don't have many that aren't little. But Grosslyn and Ragkor created a lake not far from here and had it stocked with capsina while we were gone. They would have told you, but things have been hectic. I got them to give me three full-sized ones." He stepped into the kitchen and Vas almost swooned. Three golden-fried, deep orange fish were finishing up on the stove along with a massive pile of vegetables.

"So, you're eating the veggies?" Three fish would be too much for even her. They were fat and longer than her forearm.

"If you can eat them all without being sick, you are

welcome to them. Now go wash up and take a seat. I'm serving."

Vas ended up only eating a fish and a half, along with a good helping of vegetables.

Deven had a fire going in the living room, even though it wasn't cold, and settling into his arms with it crackling along and being extremely full almost caused her to fall asleep.

Then she jerked awake and reached for her blaster— that she'd taken off.

"Easy there, you're safe." Deven rubbed her shoulders and kissed the top of her head. "I figured you were asleep."

"I almost was, which wasn't my intention." She shook her head. "I feel like something is going to go wrong."

Deven turned her so he could see her face better. "You do seem worried, which isn't normal for you. But, this is Home and it's been invaded. And two people who should be dead, and technically are dead, are roaming around on it. You might not spend much time here, but this planet was your safe place. Until this visit."

Vas pulled his face closer and kissed him with enough passion to remind him that she wasn't sleepy. "Okay, doctor, I was going to make sure Nariel was along on this trip, but if you're going to be the psychologist, maybe we don't need her." She kissed him again before he could respond. "I will always listen to your advice, by the way."

He grinned. "Just not always take it."

"Of course not. What would that say about our relationship? But you hit extremely valid points, and I agree with them. I also believe you're wearing too many clothes." She pulled his shirt over his head.

"Agreed. And I suggest that you are as well." He pulled off her shirt and ran his fingers to untangle her braided hair. "After we save the universe, I would also suggest that we find our own island here and simply get rid of clothes altogether."

Vas ran her hands over his chest and grinned. "Now that advice I agree with."

———◆———

Vas woke as the light was cracking its way through the front blinds. She and Deven spent the night in the front room on the sofa in a pile of blankets and limbs. She put her head back on his chest. This was what life should be. After spending her entire existence trying to fight for other people's dreams—she had found the one she wanted.

She'd almost fallen back asleep when the front door crashed in and the unwelcome sound of a blaster powering up came into the room.

CHAPTER FORTY-EIGHT

VAS AND DEVEN BOTH DOVE over the sofa as a blaster fired into it. That it was damaged, but was not in shreds, meant whoever was firing had the weapon on the lowest setting. Possibly even stun.

They wanted Vas and Deven alive.

Deven reached under the table behind them and brought out two blasters and handed one to Vas. He might not act like he was ever worried, but he was prepared for anything.

"Surrender and I won't kill you." That was an unsurprising but still annoying voice. The empress might be dead, but her voice carried on.

"You're a screwed up, failed clone of the late Empress Wilthuny and my dumb ass brother, Borlan. Why should we believe you?" Vas listened carefully, but she only heard one pair of feet walking through the front room on the right. Very slowly.

Deven frowned and pointed to the left. He had better hearing than Vas and she belatedly heard the softer tread echoing the first steps along the wall.

"We work for people who want to make a deal with the Keeper and the Pirate. We can make it so that your powers never have to be passed along. You can rule the Commonwealth."

"Oh gods, you don't know either of us at all. That sounds awful. By the way, tell your buddy to freeze or my second will blast them."

Deven was lying off to the side and had his blaster tracking the non-speaker.

"There are far more of us than of you. And if we continue attacking your world you either have to stop going after the Clongari, or let this world fall. Your choice, *sister.*" The last line was delivered by only Borlan's voice.

Even knowing it wasn't him didn't stop Vas from responding. She'd wanted to capture the clone and get information from them—even if it was limited. But at his words, she went into full Keeper rage, threw aside her borrowed blaster, and darted over the sofa. Her speed caught even her by surprise and she got to see the same shock on the mutated face before her. Wilthuny and Borlan didn't make a good combination and Vas knew what would be haunting her nightmares for the next few years.

She moved so fast that she knocked the blaster out of their hands as she slammed them to the ground. A tiny voice said she needed the clone alive. A louder voice said it needed to die.

The brief firing of a blaster followed by a scream told her Deven had taken care of the other one.

Vas was moving so fast that her fists were only a blur even to herself. She briefly realized she was fighting while naked, but that wasn't enough to stop her.

The strong arm that grabbed her around her waist and lifted her in the air did that.

Twisting around confirmed it was Deven.

"Let me kill them. You can't stop me." She kicked her legs in the air in an attempt to break free and get back to the fight.

Deven released her and handed her a blanket then wrapped one around his waist. "Wasn't going to try, but even clones don't live long with a broken neck. Which you did when you first hit them, by the way. I was letting you go until you felt better, but we've attracted attention." He tipped his blaster toward the shattered door.

Vas wrapped the blanket around herself after she grabbed her borrowed blaster.

"Easy, captain! Just us." Mac came in first then raised his blaster and his eyes when he saw she and Deven were fine. And in blankets.

"Hey, I had to deal with your naked ass running around my ship. At least we're covered." Vas powered down the blaster and looked to the other attacker. Whether it was also a clone or not, she wasn't the only one who needed to work out frustration on an enemy. They were little more than a smear on the carpet.

Deven also powered down his blaster. "I wanted one of them alive, but it didn't happen. How'd you know to come out here?"

"Janx called us. She and Chasen were attacked and said more attackers were coming here." Mac looked at the two beaten bodies. "They shot theirs, though."

"Thank you. Can you call a crew to come pick up the bodies from here and Janx's place? Terel needs to run full scans on what's left." Vas looked down at her blanket. "And leave someone to stand guard while we get more presentable." None of her people were what anyone would call prudes, but seeing their captain like this was making Mac and the three crew with him uncomfortable.

"Aye, captain!" The four echoed it as they ran outside. Mac called for backup on his comm, then remained with his back to the shattered front door. The other three remained closer to the road with weapons drawn.

"Shall we?" Deven held out his hand to escort her to the shower. "I was planning on a gourmet breakfast before we headed in, but I think we might want to pick something up at Delilah's instead."

Vas gave him a solid kiss. "Good idea. The last one there loses." She raced toward the bathroom. Shared showers were many wonderful things—quick wasn't one of them.

Mac stood at the busted door, tunelessly humming to himself, as they came out. He jumped when Vas touched his shoulder. "Captain! Deven! Good, you're ready." If his face flushed any brighter it could be seen from space.

"We're dressed, you mean." Vas nodded as Divee and a med team came jogging up. They had covered med beds. Not so much a worry of contamination, but to keep all the parts inside.

Mac must have mentioned the condition of the bodies.

"Any news from Gosta on the scans of Marli's moon?" Vas stood back as Divee and crew loaded the bodies up. There was always the chance this hadn't been the only clone.

"Not yet. He said he's close, but the reactivated solbilan in some of the mines is causing issues, even from up in the *Destroyer's Curse*. Things are bouncing around—his words."

Deven had finished repacking and handed Vas her bag. "The mines were shutting."

"They were. Then something brought some of them back to registering as active." Mac shook his head. "The scientists are having a field day. Massive excitement for that lot."

No one on any of Vas' crews was dumb, but some liked learning more than others. Mac was more of a learn what he had to in order to do the fun stuff kind of guy.

"We're picking up food at Delilah's to bring back. Anyone else who wants to can do so as well, but I will need a clean-up crew out here." Deven waited until Divee and the covered med beds left, then hit a button on the wall. The entire building developed a shield. He looked around when Vas whistled. "Exterior shield. Put it in last time we were here. I hope it's never needed again. It doesn't work great for people who want to keep breathing inside it."

Mac and the other three crew joined them heading to Delilah's but all four seemed more interested in playing security as they went than food.

"We're fine, Mac." Vas was touched by his paranoia but didn't feel it was warranted.

"I know." He shrugged but continued to skulk around everything they passed.

Although disappointed that Vas and Deven wouldn't be eating in, Delilah still set the group up with enough food to fill the hangar. "The two young ones did the same—but I gave them almost as much as I'm giving you. Whatever they're going through, it's burning a lot of calories." She narrowed her eyes. "Will they be on your ship when you leave?"

"Yes, they're going to be training with the nuns." Vas ate a pastry as the rest was distributed among Mac and the crew to carry back.

"Speaking of which, which ship will they be on?" Delilah was always inquisitive, but there seemed more to it this time.

"Probably the *Destroyer's Curse*, possibly the *Aoenyth* once we pick it up from Solar. They're the two largest and I'm not sure what the nuns need. Why?" Vas waved for Mac and crew to start back with the food—Deven remained with her. From the quizzical look on his face, he picked up something odd as well.

"What would you say if some of us old-timers joined in on this fight? Not sure why, but there have been a few of us feeling the urge to go to space again. I have my little ship, but tagging along uninvited doesn't feel right."

Vas was shocked. Delilah had been one hell of a fighter back in the day, but she'd retired long ago. "All of you are welcome, but why ask about the nuns?"

Delilah looked around her diner with a sigh. "It might be time for me to find some religion. As long as they don't mind an old telepath joining."

"They would love to have you join," Deven said. "You felt the call?"

"I did. And a few other older fighters too, they're heading to the hangar, but we can go to the Maoli islands if you'd rather. Only the women, but many of the old-timer men want to get into the fight too. We love it here. But this is something we need to do." Delilah reached behind the counter and lifted a pack almost as large as herself. "I'm ready to head out, captain. Even sent a few crates of kitchen supplies ahead." She grinned. "Just in case."

Vas laughed. She knew regardless of what Delilah said, she'd get her ship and follow them if Vas said no. "I'm sure the nuns will be happy to have you all, and if they don't, I will be."

"Great." Delilah slipped her massive pack on and turned to her staff. "You know the drill. Keep serving, smiling, and only kill if we're invaded." Then she walked out the door.

Vas and Deven followed her.

"That was an abrupt goodbye." Vas was impressed that the bag didn't pull the tiny woman over. But she'd seen her in combat carrying men twice her size.

"Oh, we had our weeping farewells after I sent Janx and Chasen off with food. I knew then I needed to go on this fight. I shouldn't go off to the Maoli islands first? I want to do things right."

Deven pointed up as shuttles and smaller fighters passed over, heading toward the landing field. "I believe the new nuns have been screened and are already coming in."

Vas hit her comm to Jasiel. "Are we taking all of them? We're going to have some more." The *Destroyer's Curse* was second in size only to the *Aoenyth,* but the Pilthians occupied a third of it. Depending on how many new nuns they had, they might have to consider separating the group before they rejoined the *Aoenyth.*

"Everyone scanned true—and they're all experienced fighters. There will be more younger ones coming along eventually, but for this battle, we need people who can fight."

Vas shared a grin with Delilah. "Good that you said that, we've got some more for you to meet. Very experienced ones. I'll tell you more when we get to the hangar."

"There's only twenty-three of us nun-called. The men are about thirty and Achaius is leading them. He's still pissed that those invaders chased him from his home and he wants payback."

"He realizes the ones who attacked him are dead, right?" Deven asked as they walked into the hangar.

"Yes. But that's never stopped him from wanting revenge. He'll find the people who hired them. And keep working his way up. Phila is coming as well, but she's not joining the nuns." Delilah winked.

Achaius might or might not have figured it out, but everyone else had. He better catch on soon, Phila was a better fighter than he was.

The hangar was far busier than it had been last night and a steady stream of the new nun recruits was coming in from the landing field. They all had professional-looking gear and kits.

Ragkor jogged over as soon as he saw Vas. "I've heard you're staying with the *Destroyer's Curse*?"

"I am. Deven and I are connected to the Clionea nuns for this. You don't mind hanging on to the *Warrior Wench* for this fight?" She glanced over and noticed that Jasiel was in deep conversation with Therlian. "They might be stealing Therlian as well. If so, pick who you feel is strongest to captain the *Victorious Dead*."

He glanced over. "Aye, captain. Sorry…Vas. By the way, those three Lethian Assembly ships that halted outside of Commonwealth space turned, and fled."

"Fled? From what? Are they being tracked?" Deven grabbed a box of food for him and Vas before the masses descended.

"Gosta and Flarik are tracking them from orbit, but I don't think they've sorted out what spooked them. The

Commonwealth is still going on its daily way. I'll go see about adjusting the rosters." Ragkor raised his hand but caught it before he saluted.

"Thank you. Can you also make sure all the ships are ready? Fully crewed and have as many fighters on them as they can hold. And check with the *Aoenyth* if they need anything. We'll pick them up on the way out." Vas was used to being the one in charge of jobs. While no one was paying them to push back the Clongari, this was the biggest job they'd ever faced.

But all that Keeper training changed her thinking. Her focus couldn't be on the movement of ships and crew. Not to mention that Ragkor and the crews themselves knew what to do.

She, Deven, Janx, Chasen, and all the nuns had their own agenda.

That she wasn't completely certain what it was yet, didn't stop it from being true. Like the women fighters streaming into the hangar—both older ones from Home, and the new arrivals—they just knew they were needed.

Ragkor watched the people around them and nodded. "Aye…Vas. We'll be ready."

CHAPTER FORTY-NINE

GROSSLYN CAME OVER AFTER RAGKOR went to sort the troops. "No signs of any new ships. It seems they all arrived at once. I heard you were attacked at Deven's home?"

Vas let Deven fill him in.

"Probably a good call on killing them, captain." Grosslyn nodded sagely. "Do we have a launch time for the campaign?" Although Vas and crew hadn't run a merc job in a few years, Grosslyn snapped right back into his admin position. He might not be a fighter, but he made damn sure everything was ready.

"Not yet. I'm turning over control of most of the fleet to Ragkor for this, though I'll get us started, we'll work together. The Clionea nuns will be with Deven and me on the *Destroyer's Curse.*"

"Aye, captain. I'm sending some more Flits up to that one. Even if you take all the fighters who came in with the nuns, that ship can hold a lot of cargo."

Vas wasn't sure, but it almost looked like Grosslyn drooled as he said that. It always seemed in the past there was never enough room for everything he wanted to put on the ship during a job.

"Yes, it can. Load what is reasonable, but just because it's got space, doesn't mean you have to fill it all. And confirm everything with Nitya." She wasn't sure how much space Nitya had taken over for the *Keeper's Tempest* or any other side projects she might have started.

Grosslyn nodded and went to yell at someone for not moving a pallet the way he wanted.

Vas and Deven finished eating and went to check on Terel in the med bay.

"Glad you could finally join us. I sent Captain Zarith and the other injured Garmainians back to their ship. By the way, those two bodies you sent me were pretty destroyed. A few anger issues?" Terel kept her face neutral, which always meant she wasn't feeling that way. "Only one was a clone, and yes, it did have make-up that tracked to your brother as well as the empress." She scowled. "And five other unknown genetic codes. It's as if the clones continued to degrade, as we saw, but someone created new ones from more and more others. If you hadn't killed it, it wouldn't have survived much longer."

Vas' comm chirped before they could resolve anything. "Vas here."

"Captain," Xsit sounded stressed, but not exceedingly so. Yet. Her voice wasn't in the too-high-to-hear range. "We've got three incoming ships but they aren't identifying themselves. They're not little fighters."

"Shit. Hold on, we'll be right there." Vas turned to Terel. "Do what you have to do. Get that chip and bring it to the *Destroyer's Curse*. Ask the nanites for help but explain they have to go dormant immediately after or we can't get them home."

Terel nodded and switched to another screen and contacted the *Destroyer's Curse* med bay when Vas and Deven ran out of the lab.

"What do we have?" Vas ran into Grosslyn's office. Xsit was at the communication desk while Grosslyn was swearing and pulling up screens.

"They aren't responding to anyone. The ships docked at the space station, including the Garmainians, have been sending hails as well. They're not a danger at this distance, but they will be soon." He switched the largest screen to a space shot. "They're big enough they will cause serious trouble if we don't shoot them down first."

Vas knew Grosslyn's wanting to shoot things down was a deal with him, but there was a tinge of fear in his voice.

"Can you get a closer shot of that lead ship?" Deven had excellent eyesight, but even squinting didn't give him enough details.

"I can boost it a little more," Grosslyn swore under his breath, but a few moments later the image was clear.

"A Welischian ship? I didn't know they had ships." Grosslyn stepped back. "They're still friendly, right? Why aren't they answering?"

"They have ships, they are friendly, and damned if I know." Vas called up to Gosta. "Gosta, at least one of those approaching ships is Welischian, can you scan them for problems?" There was a chance that the ships weren't coming to attack at all.

"Aye, captain. Flarik is checking also. They're disabled. Life support is still on and engines, obviously. But everything else is dead."

"On all three?" Deven was moving the image of the ships around, all looked to be identical in class.

"Yes. Let me try something to get through to them." Gosta didn't wait for approval before he cut the call.

"Is Hrrru on one of them?" Xsit continued to attempt contact but she was worried for her friend.

"I would think so if they are Welischians and not more ships taken over by the Clongari." Vas watched, but the ships seemed to be slowing. "Xsit, call Abiel from Solar. See if they sent these ships. Also, get a hold of the *Aoenyth*. I need to know what's going on in that system."

At both of their nods, Vas and Deven went to gather the last of their things from Vas' office.

"I'd envisioned coming back here when we were stuck on that station. This wasn't what I thought a reunion would be like." Vas laughed as she shut down the systems.

Grosslyn stuck his head in. "People and things are heading up to the ships now. We got reports that indicate all the solbilan mines are active. Koli wants to send full geo crews out to check, but he feels they've been active for a long time and were masked somehow."

"The Clongari ships that were bombarding the planet were shutting them down though, right?" Deven already had everything of his packed.

"Yeah, he's still sorting that out too," Grosslyn said.

Vas finished packing. "When we're gone, keep a full crew working on those things. If they were masked before, mask them again. Or better yet, shut them down." Solbilan wasn't as valuable as it once had been but still had many uses—not all of them were benign.

"They could be valuable down the line."

"And they will attract attention to our hidden planet. Might I remind you that as long as we are an active merc crew—fighting for paying jobs or not—we need to keep this place secret."

"Aye, captain." He started to turn to go out then stopped. "Sorry, too many things. The *Aoenyth* says that three Welischian cruisers briefly came by Solar from the Welischian home world. Seems they've been busy this past year. Hrrru, Qaan, and a group from Solar went with them, but all three ships were fine when they crossed into Commonwealth space two days ago. He wants to know if they should come to us?"

Vas didn't like that timeline. Those cruisers wouldn't have taken that long to get here. "No, we'll still come to them. But thank you. Any contact with Abiel on the planet?"

He shook his head. "Xsit is still trying to reach him."

"Thank you." Vas and Deven followed him to the hangar.

Delilah and a cluster of older women fighters were talking with Jasiel and, judging by the way she was holding up the pad, Aithnea. Jasiel saw them and waved them over.

"I see you already knew of our new recruits?" Jasiel's smile was good to see. "All of them scanned clear—and were legitimately called for this. We've got a chance to pull this off."

Vas wasn't as optimistic about bringing the nuns back actually reversing the Clongari invasion. But more fighters were always good.

The hangar was organized chaos as the med teams, troops, and supplies went to the shuttles. The *Warrior Wench* was still on the ground, receiving personal care in the loading from Grosslyn.

Vas grinned as she went out. She might not be taking this ship for this battle, but it was damn good to see her.

Ragkor was also supervising the load-in and waved. "You sure you don't want her back for this?"

"Tempting. But no. It feels right to be in *Destroyer's Curse*. I assume the nuns stole Therlian?"

"Yeah, I sent Xieliap to replace her as captain on the *Victorious Dead*. She's excited and ready." Xieliap was a Jeliasian, one who'd joined Vas' crew after the battle with the Asarlaí clones. Excited wasn't really their thing. But the tall, thin fighters were deadly and Vas was glad she and a few others had joined.

"Excellent choice. We'll see you up there." Vas nodded to the shuttle Mac had already claimed. "Where are Janx and Chasen?" She hadn't been worried not seeing them in the hangar, but they should have been around.

"Jasiel said they went up in an earlier shuttle." Deven nodded to Mac to keep the pilot seat as they came on board.

"Wait for us new nuns!" Delilah and four more retirees, all looking extremely excited, came running to the shuttle.

"Come on in, lots of room." Vas waved to the storage space for their packs. This shuttle could take a few more, but if no one else came soon, they'd head up. There was plenty of room on the *Destroyer's Curse* for all the extra fighters, according to Nitya who'd briefly contacted her, but they wanted to sort things, and getting the shuttles in first would be helpful.

The Pilthians and their vessels were already up there.

"I take it you're all excited to be coming over to the religious side of things?" Vas smiled at the other four.

"I am with the amount of fighting," Clara said. "No offense to back in the merc days, I did love those. But these nuns are serious ass-kickers." Her grin was one step short of maniacal.

"Ready to launch, captain?" Mac was bouncing in his seat. "No one else who is coming out right now is aiming for this shuttle."

There were still three other shuttles for the *Destroyer's Curse* ready to go, plus ones from the other ships waiting along with the nuns' fighters. "Lift off as you want."

Vas called Grosslyn. "Still waiting to hear from you about Abiel."

"Just about to call you. They're fine on Solar, just a communication hiccup. But he said he thought the Welischian ships were going somewhere else before coming here. The coordinates look like Marli's moon."

Vas shared a look with Deven. They wanted to check things out there before leaving the Commonwealth. She hadn't forgotten the image of the Fury circling Home. "Thank you. Any idea why?"

"No. But he said Yesenia and a group of people like her went with the lead ship. He didn't say what they were doing." Whether Grosslyn was being cautious about saying telepaths, or Abiel had been—it was clear who he was talking about.

Telepaths. They sent a bunch of high-powered telepaths to Marli's moon. Even without knowing what motivated them, there was no ignoring that place now.

"Thank you, Grosslyn. We're heading to the ship. Send Xsit and the remaining crew up now. Keep us updated."

"Aye." There was a twinge of disappointment in his voice—he was curious enough to know who Yesenia and the others were. It wasn't a huge secret, but he didn't need to know at this point.

"I'll set a course to Marli's moon when we get up there, captain." Mac didn't look back but he was too excited about the idea. He really liked the Furies and was certain he could find some on her moon.

"Settle down. We still need to find out how to get through to Hrrru and gain control of those three cruisers." Vas smiled as she watched the shuttles and smaller craft heading up to the station and the various ships. She hadn't found out where Grosslyn got the funds for it, or his hotel, but at this point, she didn't care.

"I thought you didn't want to have a fleet." Deven leaned into her as he watched.

"I don't. Didn't. Still not sure. But they are damn impressive, aren't they?"

"That they are." Deven smiled.

"It's good to be back out here." Delilah was in the seat behind Vas and had her face pressed against the window. "Forgot how emotional space can be."

The other four old campaigners murmured in agreement.

"Shuttle, please enter the second landing bay," Nitya said as Mac made his approach.

They were greeted by Therlian in the soft gray robes of a Clionea nun novitiate. "Good to see you all. I've been put in charge of keeping all of our novices together. After me, ladies. Your accommodations await."

If Delilah or any of the others were taken aback by someone a third of their age calling them novices, none of them showed it and they all quietly followed Therlian.

"Should I go back down?" Mac hadn't left his seat yet.

"No, go to the deck and help Gosta with whatever he's doing to reach Hrrru. I think there are enough ships down there to get everyone back up." She noticed the activity around the bay. "Whoever is still down there, anyway." It seemed that she wasn't the only one ready to get back into space.

Mac grabbed his pack and followed Vas and Deven out. "Aye, captain." He ran toward the lift.

"Ready to go to Marli's moon once we sort out the Welischians?" Vas asked Deven as they caught the next lift. The *Warrior Wench* was still her ship, but this one felt good to come home to as well.

"I wanted to spend some time there after we took care of this. But between that fly-by Fury and whatever happened to the Welischians, we need to go now. Do you think Nitya would be able to make room for some Furies?"

Vas paused the lift and folded her arms. "That sounds extremely confident that there are some there."

He nodded slowly. "I started thinking about it when I saw the vid of that one. Marli was a tricky person, Asarlaí or not. She would have had back-ups for back-ups." He rubbed the back of his head and shrugged. "And I have a hunch. One that grew stronger as we got away from the planet. I don't know what the connection is between those Welischian ships' current situation and Marli's moon, but there's something."

"Agreed. And I'm sure Nitya would be more than happy to welcome some Furies." She hit the speaker in the lift. "Right, Nitya?"

"Yes. Sorry, I wasn't trying to listen in. Kind of difficult when everyone's talking inside you."

"Don't worry." Vas released the hold on the lift and the doors opened to the command deck.

And Gosta shouting.

CHAPTER FIFTY

VAS RAN TO GOSTA, BUT it was a happy shout, even with fist pumps that she'd rarely seen him do.

His grin was disturbing. "I found a way in. I've reached Hrrru on the front ship and he was able to use the same trick to contact the other two cruisers. They've had no control over anything since they got to Marli's moon. Entire system blocked out. Even knocked out the telepaths until right before I reached him. Something hit them from the moon to take everything out and send them to Home." He scowled.

"Marli had a trap." Deven slid into his chair and shook his head. "I would have thought having a bunch of telepaths would help against such a thing, but they must have tripped something and her trap took them out as well. The lead ship is the key to breaking the system. Her trap sent them to us to deal with."

Vas took over the captain's chair from Bathie. "Wouldn't that have been good to share with us? I know she made plans before we went off to that final battle."

"Knowing her, she did. There's probably a lot of information out there on her moon." He shook his head. "I should have gone over there after we recovered from destroying the Asarlaí clones, but it was still hard to believe she was gone. And with the Pilthians, I only checked to make sure her private places were secure—didn't go inside."

Vas watched the slow progress of the Welischian vessels. She'd rather not meet up with them this close to Home in case they weren't who they were pretending to be. "Are all nuns, crew, and items for this ship on board?"

"Aye, captain," Bathie responded from her science station. "The nuns' fighters are all on board as well as the shuttles. Jasiel, Aithnea, and Therlian have claimed the largest holosuite for their nun training, and all of them, even Janx and Chasen are there. There are two smaller holosuites that Nitya uncovered. She wanted you to know where they were." A section of the ship appeared. Two holosuites were near the large storage areas.

Vas nodded. Never knew when they'd be handy and disturbing the training of a group of women called to save a universe wasn't a good idea. She hit her comm. "Flarik? How are you and your baby?" The egg shouldn't have hatched yet, but from the information she'd been able to find, this birth had been anything but normal.

"We are fine. I am glad to have you back on the ship. Nitya has a safety program protecting my egg, so I will be taking a station on the command deck now."

"Good to hear, we'll see you soon." It was nice to hear Flarik sounding more like herself.

"Med bay checking in," Terel called up. "We're ready to go. I'll be working on that chip from the clone and the nanites. Delimara is still in a coma and I believe I can separate some without waking her."

Vas was glad to hear the last part. Delimara was a Kantari, a vicious xenophobic species. After her people came on the Zqui space station to kill her, Vas would have dumped her. But they still felt she had information they needed. And then the nanites made their presence known.

If Delimara and the nanites in her died, the nanites in Deven would kill him.

"Keep me updated. We'll be heading out soon to meet the Welischian ships. After they're sorted, we'll be swinging by Marli's moon."

"Aye, captain!" Terel ended the call.

Gosta frowned. "Do you think going to that moon with all the fleet is a good idea? Not that they're not trustworthy, but Marli's defense system might not be."

"Good point. I'd already gotten out of the habit of thinking about a fleet. I think you might be right, though. We have no idea what the Welischians did to trigger the defenses, but it could be bad if we had everyone with us."

"Agreed." Deven looked up from his station. "Even though I was able to get us through her security when we brought the Pilthians there before, that doesn't mean she didn't set up the system to modify itself. I'd say us and the ship Hrrru is on, once we clear all three Welischian ships."

Vas nodded. Even though having Yesenia and the other telepaths hadn't helped them before, Deven obviously believed it would now. "We can have Ragkor take the fleet to Solar and wait for us there once we're ready to head to the moon. Gosta? Can you create a drone with an emergency responder that will launch if our systems are breached? Have it head to Ragkor if launched." If Deven couldn't get past whatever Marli had left behind, at least Ragkor and the rest could come back to rescue them.

Hopefully.

Gosta gave a head bob. "Aye, captain. And I've been pulling in what information I can from the ship Hrrru is on—hopefully we can prepare some defenses against what was done to the Welischians."

"All ships reporting ready, captain." Xsit grinned from her station, like most of the crew, she was glad to be back on the ship.

"Then let's go fix those ships," Vas called the *Warrior Wench*. "Ragkor, have the flee follow us." They weren't that far away from the Welischians, and while she could send Ragkor and the rest of the fleet off to Solar now, it might be best to begin this as a unit.

Gosta continued communicating with Hrrru, an old system of taps that came through the life support system. He tried to explain it to Vas earlier, but after a few sentences, she waved him off with a smile. He understood it and could make it work, that was enough for her.

Deven pulled up the fleet on the main screen. "Pretty impressive. But we are going to need more if we're going into Clongari space."

"I know. I hoped we could just push them back, but I think we're past that point now. I wish we knew if the Nhali or the Lethian Assembly were on their side or not." Vas didn't like enemies she didn't know and there wasn't much information on the Clongari in the Commonwealth database. But something about them was hitting her hard. She noticed it as they left the space station. Most likely another one of those weird Keeper things, but the thin lines around Deven's eyes said he felt it as well.

Like she was being tracked by a sniper she couldn't see.

Which meant it was a Keeper and Pirate thing. She was extremely happy when Jasiel and Aithnea stated that while Janx and Chasen would be helping on this job, they would take over as the Keeper and Pirate afterward. She also noticed that having the Pirate forget what happened during their time wasn't mentioned.

The Clongari hadn't made a massive show yet, but they were deadly killers who cared nothing for any other forms of life. Deep in her gut, Vas knew they had to do more than simply push them back into their space. They had to destroy them.

"Hrrru says that they still can't stop. They're slowing, possibly because they are getting closer to Home, but none of the three ships can stop." Gosta tilted his head as he listened to his communication with Hrrru. "And Yesenia wanted to warn all our telepaths about the satellites around Marli's moon that target them *before* the moon disables the ships."

Deven frowned. "There weren't any satellites like that before."

"Maybe her program added them after the Pilthians. We don't know what they attempted before they fled," Flarik spoke as she went to a science station. Neat and calm as normal. But the look in her eyes still indicated she'd like to kill people. Most likely the ones who'd attacked her child, but any bad person would do. Or even a reasonably bad person.

"I could see her designing it to do that. And again, I wish we'd gone back sooner." Deven shrugged. "Tell Yesenia thank you and we'll warn our telepaths."

"I can get their landing bay open, but not sure how long it will stay that way if we can't gain control of their system." Gosta went back to his coding after Vas nodded that she understood. There wasn't much to be done about that, and no time to figure a better solution. She didn't want those ships getting closer to Home.

"How close are we getting to that lead ship, captain? I assume that's what we're going after first?" Mac was slowing down the *Destroyer's Curse* but would need to come alongside the other vessel to match it.

"Hold back, I think a shuttle would be the best idea… or the *Keeper's Tempest*. It has more control than any of the shuttles and more weapons if needed." Vas hoped they didn't have to blow up any of the Welischian ships. Even though Gosta was sure he was communicating with Hrrru, ships had been taken over before.

"Aye, captain. Request to be allowed to join?" Mac looked ready to launch himself out of the pilot seat. Vas didn't blame him; the *Keeper's Tempest* was a fun ride.

"Yes, but hold on running down there just yet. Gosta, you, Deven, myself—"

"And me." Flarik had her eyes closed as she spoke, but when they opened they were even more predatory than before. "I can't explain it, but my child believes I will be needed." She spoke as calmly as if an egg telepathically speaking to her was the most normal thing in the world. Considering how she had denied all telepathic abilities for her people until recently, that was fairly amazing.

And not something Vas was going to question. She nodded to Flarik.

"Is medical needed? I'm still working on the nanite situation but Pela can go." Terel had resumed listening to deck communication—which was handy.

Vas looked to Gosta but he shrugged. "Hrrru indicated everyone was fine, once the telepaths recovered. But?"

She agreed. They didn't know what they were really going into. "Yes, please have Pela meet us in the third landing bay. Full field kit." Then she called Roha and Marwin to join them in battle armor and heavy weapons. The rest of them would pick up their armor and weapons en route. She could apologize to the Welischian captain if it wasn't needed.

"Bathie, you have the deck. Hold position to pace the...what's the ship called?"

"The *Ffrwyth ein llafur.*" Deven's tongue twisted on that one. "It means fruits of our labor, roughly. Fitting for an agricultural culture. "

"Hrrru's ship. Sorry, I'm not even going to attempt that one. Just stay with them and have Ragkor keep the fleet back. Out of explosives' way." Hopefully, it wouldn't come to that, but between her Keeper sensitivity and the way life had turned on her in the past year—she wasn't taking chances.

Bathie took the command chair and had Xsit contact Ragkor as the rest of them left the deck. Mac beat them all to the *Keeper's Tempest,* but at first, Vas thought he'd done so without weapons or gear.

Her thoughts must have been clear on her face, as he reached over and held up his full gear and two blasters. "I'm ready, captain. Can I fly it?"

Vas watched him squirm for a moment, then finally nodded. "Fine, but we're only going over to that Welischian vessel, nothing fancy." She paused as a thought hit her. "Gosta, get that bay open on the Welischian ship when we get closer. Mac, the moment we're off on the *Keeper's Tempest,* you take off. I don't want this ship trapped inside."

Mac patted the side of the ship with a dreamy look. "Agreed. I mean, yes, captain."

Since most of them hadn't been on the *Keeper's Tempest* before, there was a lot of ogling and touching as everyone boarded.

Deven let loose a low whistle. "This is damned impressive. But the shape does remind me of Ome's ship."

"I did utilize what I found from images of the Ralith ship." Nitya's voice came through the ship's comm. "Even though it was created and controlled by a madman, it is quite extraordinary."

"I like it," Pela said with too much glee. Unlike some of Vas' crew, Pela wasn't one of the ship enthusiasts. Or so Vas thought. She'd have to warn Terel that might be changing.

"I have the bay on the other ship ready to open." Gosta was hunched over his pad. "But will wait until we get closer. Should I notify Hrrru that we're coming? I doubt they even know we're this close to them."

Deven pulled himself away from checking out the ship and shook his head. "No. Hopefully, it is him on there. However, it's better to play things safe."

A flash of concern crossed Gosta's face, but he nodded.

"Approaching the ship now," Mac unnecessarily called out. Vas was surprised at how reasonably he was flying.

Most likely he wanted to make sure that he was allowed to pilot the *Keeper's Tempest* again.

"Hit it, Gosta," Deven said.

They were close enough to see the landing bay doors open, if stiffly. Whatever had shut down the systems was fighting back. Another good reason to get the *Keeper's Tempest* out of their landing bay as soon as possible.

The advantage of having a well-trained crew; they moved quickly. Vas and Deven were the last ones out once the bay was cleared. As soon as the hatch shut and they were clear, Mac fled.

The bay doors slid shut behind him.

"Coincidence?" Roha had her massive blaster with her and slowly turned to cover all angles as she spoke.

"Or not." Vas froze as armored fighters, not Welischians that she could tell based on the height, ran into the bay with weapons raised.

"Surrender or we'll blast you out to join your ship."

CHAPTER FIFTY-ONE

V AS RAISED HER HANDS AND motioned for her crew to do the same. No one dropped their weapons, but they did raise their hands. Gosta didn't raise his hands but scowled at the enemies as he glanced between them and his pad.

That gave Vas pause. Gosta was many things, a fierce fighter wasn't one. Yet he wasn't obeying the people facing them. Vas lowered her arms, and at a nod from Gosta, took a step forward. Then a second.

"Stop or we'll blast you." The being was too tall to be a Welischian, and the voice was oddly moderated.

"Auto defense?" Deven also lowered his arms and moved forward.

"That's what they scan as. But the weapons aren't active. At all. They could club us with them, I suppose." Gosta hadn't moved forward but wasn't concerned.

Having an auto defense was considered high-end by some shipmakers. Vas refused to let them be on any of her ships. But having them without active weapons was absurd.

The doors slid open and Hrrru came racing in with four other Welischians armed with blasters. Including an extremely annoyed-looking Qaan. The tall half-Welischian tried to grab Hrrru as he ran past her, but he dodged around her.

"Gosta! Vas! Deven!" Hrrru ran and hugged everyone so fast there was no way to stop him. "You came!"

"I told you they could be a trap. You should have let the autos check them out." Qaan lowered her blaster but didn't put it away. The three others stayed behind her but did the same with their blasters.

"The autos would be more effective if they had live weapons." Deven stepped forward and nodded to the frozen automatons as he passed.

"We barely got them functioning," Hrrru said after he finished hugging Roha. "The systems are slowly coming back, but we're defenseless against anyone coming on board. There was no way for us to tell who was boarding us, or even if there were other ships around nearby. Why didn't you tell me you were coming?"

Qaan gave a flat smile. "Because they weren't completely certain that we hadn't been compromised. I would have done the same. Your friend's moon hit us hard."

Vas stepped around the automatons as well. "Can we go to your deck and see what can be done to fix things? Then I'd like to know why you went to Marli's moon." She aimed the last at Hrrru. It was extremely doubtful that anyone on this ship aside from him would have even heard of Marli or her secret home.

Qaan stepped back and motioned for the other three Welischians to lead. Vas and Deven followed. Flarik and Pela were directly behind them, and then Marwin and Roha, neither one smiling, brought up the rear. After a minor standoff where they wanted Qaan to go ahead of them and she refused to budge.

Vas motioned for them to come along ahead of Qaan and she flashed her a real smile.

The ship was dimly lit, but Vas wasn't sure if that was because of the bugs in their system or that no one was down here. The lights flickered to half-power as they went down the corridor.

Vas caught up to Gosta and Hrrru. "Now, why did you take these three ships, that we didn't know about, to a super-secret moon?"

Welischians didn't blush, or if they did, their furry faces would have hidden it. But his wince was visible. "I had a dream, captain. I know, dreams aren't real. But this one was. There was a secret weapon on that moon, one we had to find. It could turn the fight against the Clongari."

Qaan was at the end of the line, but she was listening. "It wasn't only him. The human telepaths, especially Yesenia and Abiel, had similar dreams."

"Welischians are numb to telepathy," Deven said.

"Most of us are." Qaan didn't expand on that and didn't sound like she was going to.

"Why was this dream directed at Solar?" Vas admired the corridor they were going down. Functional but also elegant. This ship might have been made by a formerly non-space-faring people, but that wasn't true now—they belonged in the stars.

"We were hoping that once we found you, you could tell us. Abiel remained on Solar, but we have Yesenia and fifteen other telepaths on board this ship." Hrrru split his focus between Gosta and Deven.

Vas knew Terel had found trace Asarlaí elements in the blood of Yesenia and a few other Solar telepaths. But she didn't think this should be common knowledge. Deven's frown indicated he was thinking the same. Somehow Marli's base was reaching out to Asarlaí blood, no matter how weak. How Hrrru picked up on it was another matter.

The command deck was impressive. Not as large as the *Destroyer's Curse*, but bigger than the *Warrior Wench*. And more than a little similar.

Vas noticed Hrrru appearing more concerned as she, Gosta, and Deven looked around the deck.

He finally nodded. "Yes, I might have borrowed some ideas for this. They were mostly done building the ships when I came along, but they weren't ready to join the fight against the Lethian Assembly. I gave them suggestions for the command deck layout." He first appeared embarrassed but then raised his chin.

Vas laughed. "Borrow away. The *Warrior Wench* is a well-designed ship. And *Destroyer's Curse's* design would be too large."

Gosta looked around, nodded, and then scurried over to a science station. "Might I run a diagnostic from here?" He was armed with a few pads and even a small console.

"Please do." Qaan waved to all the empty stations. The command deck was only half full. "We're still decreasing speed, but we can't stop. We didn't get the automaton defenses to work until a few minutes before you opened the bay doors. They're for emergencies, but their weapons were active before the shutdown."

Flarik walked to another empty station. "Were you able to record anything when the attack happened?" She still appeared like she wanted to fight something, but that wasn't unexpected.

Vas did notice that aside from Qaan and Hrrru, the Welischians stayed clear of her.

Also not unexpected.

"We got some. We honestly weren't certain what to expect as we arrived in orbit around the moon, so I had them record as much as possible." Qaan hadn't said it, but it was clear that she was the captain.

Qaan pulled the system up for Flarik. "Would you two like to speak to Yesenia and the others? I have them restricted to the medical bay." Qaan shrugged. "They aren't amused. But they agreed to our terms when they came on board my ship."

Yup, she was the captain.

"Yes. Pela, Devin, and I will go. Roha and Marwin will remain here." They put away their weapons, but with full body armor, or even without in Roha's case, they were impressive. They took a relaxed military stance and nodded in agreement.

Pela followed on Qaan's heels as they left. "Your people did all of this in secret? That's impressive."

"Thank you. When we began, we believed the Commonwealth had taken over Solar. We didn't want our ships falling to them." She smiled at Vas and Deven. "Thank you again for showing us that wasn't the case."

"I doubt the Lethians could have held that ruse for long once the Commonwealth barricade fell. But glad we cleared it up." Vas continued to admire the spaces they were passing through. She'd always said she would have loved to have gotten more of Hrrru's people on her crew. It was good to know that thought was valid. They belonged in space; it had only taken a while for them to realize that.

The med bay was different from the *Warrior Wench*, but that made sense, as the medical areas needed to reflect the needs of the people flying the ship.

Yesenia had been speaking to a Welischian doctor at the side of her bed, rather forcefully, although she remained in her bed when they came in.

"Vas! Deven! Thank goodness you found us." She started to swing out of the bed but the short doctor had no trouble pushing her back in.

"I can scan them, if you don't mind?" Pela held up her equipment toward the doctor. "I assume your medical bay was hit with the same issue the rest of the ship was?"

Qaan gave her doctor a nod. "It was, thank you. And perhaps Deven can check them on a different level?"

"By all means." Deven and Pela went to Yesenia first, but all the telepaths wanted to tell their story at once.

Vas waved them all down. "Don't worry, we'll get to that. I assume all of you had the call to come here? A place you didn't know even existed?"

Aside from Yesenia, who was paying attention to Pela and Deven, the telepaths all nodded. "Do you mind if we take blood tests to bring back to our principal doc?

She's testing a hypothesis." Vas had a feeling they were all going to show the same Asarlaí markers as Yesenia. Why in the hell some Asarlaís had settled on an obscure planet, one they'd abandoned supposedly, was something to be worked out later.

They looked at each other and then nodded in agreement.

"I'll do the tests as I check all of you." Pela drew blood from Yesenia even though she knew Terel already had her on file.

Probably not a bad idea, they could see if whatever hit them from the moon changed Yesenia's blood in any way.

As Pela worked through the telepaths, with the ship's doctor answering what she could about when they'd been unconscious, Vas and Deven started in the back row and did their own interviews.

Even if all of them had trace elements of Asarlaí blood, Vas wanted to know what prompted the dreams—and why now. Not to mention if the dreams were created by some system on Marli's moon, why did that same system attack the telepaths when they arrived?

Marli had been ornery, tricky, and often difficult, but she usually had a reason for her actions. She had to have known about Asarlaí descendants existing on Solar, even if extremely removed. So why call them and then attack them?

Vas stepped back and let Deven do the asking, but after the first five, they realized the responses were shockingly similar to what Hrrru had reported.

"Are we sure Hrrru doesn't have any telepathic abilities?" Vas muttered to Deven as they went toward the next bank of beds.

"He's been tested like everyone on the crew," Deven said. "Unless something changed? But they are all repeating similar stories and there'd be no reason to have created a lie."

The next five were the same and they passed Pela and the Welischian doctor as they did their exams and blood draws.

The next was different though. He was a Jeliasian, the only one in the group. Vas' interaction with them for the most part was limited to the battle against the Asarlaí clones. They were a tall, thin species with small upright ears that were almost always moving. This one was no exception. They were also fierce fighters and extremely paranoid.

"I had a dream, but it was of a battle far larger than anything ever known. Worse than when the Asarlaí hundreds of years ago and the fake Asarlaí attacked the Commonwealth." He gave a slight smile. "Before moving to Solar, I was with Kamin's ship—we joined you in that final fight." He shook the smile off. "My dream stole all the air in my lungs. Darkness blocked out all the stars. Sharp, terrible ships attacked by the thousands, all of them three times the size of this one. The coldness. Dread." His face paled and sweat beaded on his face.

Deven grabbed him and forced the man to look up. "Stay with me. What's your name?"

"Lios, of the third house of Kamin." His voice was weaker and his eyes were rolling back.

"Lios, listen to me carefully. Something is calling you, don't follow it. Only hear my voice." Deven spoke low and softly but there was a power behind his words.

Vas felt a twinge as Deven went into the man's mind. She felt it was more than a little weird, but it was probably another Keeper and Pirate thing. She couldn't tell what was going on, but Deven's jaw was getting tighter. "Fight against it." The words were barely audible, but Vas caught them.

Lios spasmed and the readings on the screen above his bed spiked sharply then crashed. He passed out and Deven collapsed over him.

CHAPTER FIFTY-TWO

VAS YELLED FOR PELA AND the Welischian doctor and pulled Deven off of Lios.

"They both collapsed." She grabbed Deven's head, closed her eyes, and mentally reached out to him. Regardless of what Deven continued to imply, Vas didn't have telepathic abilities. But right now, her Keeper instincts were telling her that she had to pull him back and anchor him.

Pela tried to help her but Vas shook her head but didn't step back or open her eyes. "Help Lios."

Deven's mind was darkness and chaos. He was there, she could feel him, but whatever had been in Lios' mind was trying to overwhelm him.

"*Oh, like hell you will. I won't let that happen.*" Vas snarled at the darkness in Deven's mind.

"*Vas? Is that you? Oh, this is unexpected. I finally managed to die? Thank the elements!*"

Vas almost released Deven when she heard the voice in her head—it was clearly computer generated and was fighting through the darkness, but wasn't the cause of it.

It was Marli.

"*How are you in my damn head? Or Deven's head? Yes, you are dead. Or so we thought.*"

"*Oh, if you're hearing this, I've gone to the great beyond. Whatever it is, I should have gone there a few hundred years ago. This is a response of the security system from my moon. Someone triggered it. Someone near you at this moment.*"

"*Deven?*"

"*No. I don't recognize whoever they are.*"

Vas opened her eyes and looked at Lios. Pela and the Welischians were hooking him up to every machine they had, but he was growing paler.

"Him, yes. Not his fault. He had a hitchhiker. Not cool. Trying to get into my secret moon by pretending to be Asarlaí."

Vas almost dropped to her knees as Deven convulsed and a massive surge of energy jumped from him into Lios.

Lios jerked as well, hard enough to throw Pela and the Welischians back. The equipment over his head went blank, then came back to a soothing beeping sound.

"There. Wakey, wakey Deven." The voice was awfully flip for a computer generated one. But if anyone could imbue personality into a computer, it would be Marli.

"Marli?" Deven's eyes opened and he looked around.

"Stay still, weird shit is going on." Vas kept her hands on his temples, but the darkness that had been inside his mind was gone.

"Are you what called the telepaths and Welischians from Solar? Why did you attack them when they got there?" Vas was still working through Deven's head, so she felt him catch up on the situation.

"I am. That world was called something else long ago, but Solar works. They might be the last hope for this universe. And while I'm sure that I already miss you both in the afterlife, I don't need all of you to be joining me this soon." There was a pause. *"The system attacked when it sensed the one over there. He was compromised."* The last word was spat out with enough venom that Vas rocked back. *"We will not let them destroy this reality. Even if we are no longer here. There are enough children to defend the universe."* Another pause. *"Power is restored to all the ships. Come back to my moon. There is much you will need."* The voice vanished so quickly Vas stumbled into Deven.

"Are you okay?" He grabbed her arms as he sat up.

"Are you?" Vas rubbed the side of her head. "I really

do think either Marli or Savan were the Pirate at some point—even if Jasiel and Aithnea can't confirm it. I have a Keeperish urge to go to Marli's moon."

"I'm fine, but I have the same feeling. That projection in our heads was unique. And disturbing." He turned to Lios and the medical team. "How is he?"

"He's unconscious, but all of his numbers are getting into the normal range. He was moments away from dying. Whatever you two did, it worked." The Welischian doctor gave a quick nod.

"There was something killing him, then it stopped." Pela was making enough notes to keep even Terel happy.

Vas hoped Lios was the only one with this issue. Although the Marli-voice didn't say it, there was no doubt in Vas' mind that this had been a Clongari attack. Had they gotten to Marli's moon, any advantage Vas and her people might gain from it would be lost.

She wanted to know why a species that was reportedly so powerful was being this sneaky in their attacks, but there was no doubt they were still working on their goal.

"Captain?" Flarik called through the comm. "The ship is recovering system control. Communications, helm control, everything. Same with the other two Welischian vessels. The three ships are coming to a halt, and Ragkor has the fleet doing the same."

Vas looked at Deven. "That's the fastest response from Marli ever recorded. Too bad it was after she was dead." She hit her comm. "Thank you, Flarik. We think we've found what caused the attack on the Welischians, but we need to check some more before we head to the moon. Once we're clear, Ragkor and the fleet can head for Solar." She wasn't certain why they still needed to go there since they had the ships and telepaths, but something was nagging at her that they still needed something. Another Keeper thing.

"Aye, captain." Flarik clicked off.

"What happened?" Lios' voice was weak and he kept blinking, but his color was back.

"What do you recall?" Pela was closer than the Welischian doctors.

"Some weird dreams." He looked around. "I'm not on Solar, am I? That's the last thing I recall."

"We need to do more tests." The primary Welischian doctor smiled, but it didn't reach her eyes. "Right now, I believe you need privacy and rest." She nodded and two orderlies came and rolled Lios away from the others.

He shrugged. "That's fine. I'm really tired." He passed out as they went into a distant room.

"You think whatever got him is still there? Is he a telepath also?" Deven waited until the door to the inner room was shut.

The Welischian doctor nodded. "He is a telepath, not a strong one, but he came along with the others when we were getting ready to go into the Commonwealth. Until they all collapsed, he seemed normal. That's what worries me. We don't know if his confusion is genuine and he's back to himself or not."

"Good point," Deven said. "I can examine him more carefully later, but we probably want to move him to one of your other ships for now. We need to go back to the moon and I'm not sure he won't trigger an attack."

Vas nodded in agreement. She still wanted to bring the telepaths and the Welischians to Marli's moon, but there was too much at stake concerning Lios.

"I can keep him sedated and stay with him on our second ship, the *Cartref.* They have an excellent medical bay and many secure rooms. I take it this ship is going with you?"

"Yes, unless Qaan doesn't want to. We're sending everyone else back to Solar to wait for us." Vas nodded to the rest. "I think Pela had a few more folks to get blood from? We did get Lios' before the incident, right?"

Pela nodded. "Just three more, and yup, I already have Lios's blood." She patted the kit at her side. "I'd like to stay with the patient though. If Qaan doesn't mind, and of course you and the captain of that ship." She nodded to the Welischian doctor.

"I'm fine with it, and I'm sure Qaan will be fine."

"I'm fine with it. You probably want to send what you have to Terel before you go over there," Vas said as she and Deven started out of the med bay. "You know how touchy she gets."

"Aye, captain. Never mess with Terel's samples." Pela grinned.

Vas and Deven returned to the command deck. The ship had been impressive with most of its systems offline, it was even more so when it was fully functioning.

Qaan was busy talking to the other two Welischian captains, but Gosta and Flarik were comparing screens as they worked.

"Everything checks out, captain. The ships are fine. What happened?" Gosta finally stopped pulling up data.

Vas gave a summary, not putting a lot of emphasis on the Marli computer system. It wasn't that she didn't trust Qaan and crew, but until they were certain what was done to Lios, keeping the information limited was probably for the best.

In fact, bringing this ship might not be necessary.

"Yes, they should come here. All are clear except the one getting ready to leave that ship." Marli's computer voice needed to learn boundaries as having that voice in her head, answering something Vas was just thinking of, almost made Vas scream.

"You can't just pop in my head all the time. Or anyone else's head. Is Lios a danger to anyone right now? Or even himself?" Although random mental visits would be a very Marli thing to do, she didn't like them and she didn't want Deven or anyone else of their crew being hit with them.

"He isn't a danger to anyone now. Had I not stopped them, he would have been. The beings you know as Clongari got to him on the planet you call Solar—the people of that planet will need to be warned."

"Thank you."

Deven was watching her, but she knew that he probably had an idea of what she was doing. Gosta, Flarik, and the rest were giving her odd looks.

When she figured the Marli-bot had left her head, Vas turned to the others. ""We have some interaction with an auto system Marli left on her moon. It says that we won't be attacked this time. I'd like your ship to join the *Destroyer's Curse*, and the other two to join our fleet back at Solar." Vas watched Qaan for a reaction, but she just shrugged.

"That's fine. We planned to join your fleet anyway—once we found whatever was calling the telepaths to that moon. The rest are clear, correct?"

"According to the Marli-bot, yes. And even Lios should be fine, eventually. There could be others who were infected like he was still on Solar however." Hopefully, more information on that would be discussed once they got inside Marli's secret compound.

Once Deven, Flarik, and Gosta ran a full scan of all the ship's functions, Vas called for Mac to come get them in the *Keeper's Tempest*.

She updated Ragkor on their flight back to the *Destroyer's Curse*. As usual, he took it in stride and said he would keep the fleet at a distance from Solar until they knew more information about how Lios was infected.

Vas and the rest returned to the command deck and prepared to go to Marli's moon. Once Lios and Pela were on the *Cartref,* Ragkor led the rest of the fleet toward the Commonwealth border and Solar.

"The captain from the Welischian ship is calling for you, captain." They needed to find a shorter name for that vessel. Although it could be a deliberate choice of the Welischians.

"Vas here, are there any problems?"

Qaan laughed. "Not this time. We're ready when you are and intend to stay behind that ship of yours. My crew is shy about that moon now—especially the telepaths."

"I don't blame them. Tell me if any others have problems or your ship starts acting oddly." Vas nodded to Mac and Gosta and the *Destroyer's Curse* headed for Marli's moon.

Chapter Fifty-Three

———

THEY WERE ALMOST WITHIN SIGHT of the moon when Gosta turned to her and put something small and distant up on the main screen. "We have a tail, captain. I didn't pick them up until Ragkor and the rest left. They're hanging back, but are definitely following either us or the Welischians."

"How long until we can see them?" Vas squinted at the massive magnification but there was no way to make out the ship. Except that it was a large fighter, about the same size as the *Keeper's Tempest*.

"Working on it," Deven swore. "They're good, whoever they are. They have too good of an idea of how far we can see. They don't care that we know they're there because they know we can't identify them."

"Want me to take the *Keeper's Tempest* and see who they are, captain?" Mac didn't jump out of his seat but looked ready to.

"No. Continue watching them, but slow down and warn Qaan."

"Captain, my child is reacting to whatever is following us. We believe it is the Ralith ship." Flarik had returned to her room after they came back from the Welischian ship but was obviously listening in to the command deck.

"Damn it, what's Ome up to?" Vas wasn't going to question what Flarik and her unhatched child sensed— there was something mystical about that baby whether Flarik wanted to admit it or not.

"He's slowing down at the same pace we are, captain." Gosta didn't doubt Flarik either.

It would be their luck that Ome would invade the Commonwealth right now.

Vas had no idea how he knew about Marli or her moon, but he knew far too many things that he shouldn't.

"Captain?" Xsit's chirp was already in the higher registers. "Ome is calling us. You. He specifically wants to speak to you on a secure channel. In your ready room. His words, captain." The yellow feathers on the back of her head were poking straight up.

"Fine. Deven, you have the com, warn Qaan that we'll be stopping for a bit." Knowing it was Ome behind them did change a few things. She didn't have to worry about leading some stranger to Marli's moon—with his resources, she was certain he already knew where it was.

Vas shut the door to her ready room and told Xsit to transfer the call.

"What do you want, Ome?" Vas couldn't be as rude as she'd like—the man could destroy both of these ships without a moment's thought.

"Thank you for taking my call, Vas. It's lovely hearing your voice. Had some adventures back on your planet, I take it?"

Vas took a deep breath and dropped into her chair. "Yes. We're fine now. What can we do for you?"

"I know you're going to that Asarlaí moon. Would you like to hear that I can't get past their security? I can't. Rich, isn't it? Something *I* can't break? But we found one of their Furies a while ago. Broken down, not even able to fly, derelict in space. We fixed it. I need more."

Vas had no idea how many people Ome had working with him, or who was in that ship. He could have left everyone who'd helped him create it on desolate planets and be doing this on his own. But she did know that while he'd been unable to gain access to Marli's moon, he wouldn't stop until he got what he wanted.

"You are not allowed here." This time the Marli-bot's voice came through the comms for both Vas and Ome to hear. "I will destroy you. The Clongari must be stopped. What I left behind is to be used for only that."

"Ah, the Asarlaí speaks. Only you're not alive anymore, are you? I'm glad to meet you, though. Would it make a difference if I said that myself and my people want the same thing? My home has already been taken over by the Clongari," Ome spat the word out, a sharp difference from his almost jovial way of speaking before. "We must destroy them."

Vas felt a chill. There wasn't a doubt about him wanting to destroy the Clongari—especially if his home system had fallen. But she had a foreboding of what would happen to the rest of the universe after the Clongari were dead, if he had that type of power.

The Marli-bot felt it as well or it wouldn't have been so aggressive. Even though as far as Vas knew, Marli had never run into Ome before or after his transformation.

However, being a member of the largest group of world-dominating beings, probably gave her an insight into spotting them.

"You would not stop there. I can feel it." There was a flatness in the bot's voice.

Vas figured the Marli-bot was picking it up from inside of Vas' head, but she was grateful she hadn't said anything.

Not a lot of things scared Vas, but Ome did.

"If I promise to be good? I only need three more of your Furies. Not even in working order. I solemnly swear that after the Clongari have been destroyed, no one in this Universe will see me again."

"*He's hiding something,*" the Marli-bot spoke inside Vas' head.

"*He's almost like an Asarlaí in his wants and drives. He might say no one will see him again because he'll destroy every-one else along with the Clongari.*" Vas wasn't sure how she ended up in the position of being between these two, but it didn't make her happy.

"That is good to know. I will make a deal. He won't be allowed near the moon, but along with what was left for you, I will send out three broken Furies for him. Nothing more. Let me do the talking."

"I'm fine with that."

"Ome, you are too duplicitous for us to simply agree with your promise. Destroying everyone would also make them unable to see you. If you swear by the power of your Ralith ship to only use the Furies, all of them, in order to combat the Clongari, and swear to leave all known space and never return after they have been defeated, we shall consider it. But you must swear *on your ship.*" There was an odd seriousness in the Marli-bot's voice on the last line.

Vas was missing something. She could swear on any and all of her ships, but it didn't mean she would follow through because of it. Obviously, there was yet another odd nuance to the Ralith ship creation.

"I can promise—"

"No. Swear on your ship, or I will blast you apart where you sit." Marli-bot was fully pissed off Asarlaí now.

Something Vas had been lucky not to hear too often. She wasn't certain if the Ralith ship could be destroyed by anything, but the Marli-bot sounded confident of it.

Ome muttered something that was too low for the comm to pick up. Finally, he raised his voice. "I, Ome Thilianopolous, swear by my Ralith ship and all it commands that my people and I will leave all known space as determined by Vaslisha Tor Dain after the Clongari have been destroyed. To never return."

Vas thought that was bold of him, as she had an extremely broad definition of known space.

"Agreed. So it shall be." Then the Marli-bot said a few words in that ancient Asarlaí language.

And an odd wave flowed through the ship.

"You will wait where you are, and Vas will bring you the Furies. Moving from that place before then would be considered a breach of contract and will result in the destruction of your vessel."

"Agreed. Contact me when you've brought out my ships. Ome out."

Ome was a lot of things, but petulant wasn't usually one of them.

"That will make him not try to take over everything once the Clongari are defeated?" Vas wasn't certain she had the same belief in those words that the Marli-bot did.

"Yes. There is a…different type of component tied into creating a Ralith ship. My people couldn't successfully create them because of that. His completion of that task indicates he is vulnerable. What happens to him, happens to the ship, and vice versa. He cannot follow through on his original plan. Fortunately, his hatred of the Clongari is stronger than his drive for universe domination."

"Or at least this universe." Vas got up. If she felt that wave, the rest of the ship did as well.

"Extremely true. However, there's always the chance that he won't survive the battle." That was a reassuring thought.

"Is there anything we need to know before coming to the moon?" Vas asked as she reached her door.

"No, just be prepared to be awed." The bot sounded extremely Marli-ish with that and then clicked off.

"Captain, there was a wave of some sort. We all felt it, as well as the Welischian ship but the systems aren't showing anything." Gosta was working on three computers at this point. He wasn't a fan of unexplained phenomena.

Deven got up from the command chair as she approached. "It was something telepathic, at least what myself and all the telepaths felt. The ones on the Welischian ship were extremely concerned."

"Was anyone hurt?" Vas never trusted Marli when she was alive, she trusted this version of her even less.

"No, only startled. Did Ome do something?"

Vas laughed. "He found someone smarter than him. The Marli-bot knows about Ralith ships and knew how to control Ome with his." She quickly explained the deal between the two.

Mac's eyes were wide as he turned toward her. "And that will work? Just his say so?"

"I know, those were my thoughts as well. But there's something even odder about that ship than we thought. Ome was seriously pissed and worried when he swore on it."

"And we don't have much in the way of options," Deven added. "The best thing we can hope for is that he will fight to the death against the Clongari. His and theirs, if we're lucky."

"The Marli-bot said the same." Vas nodded to Xsit. "Notify Qaan that we're moving again. Mac, take us out."

No one on the command deck appeared happy, and Vas didn't blame them. But Deven was right, there were few options and none of them were good.

The rest of the trip to the moon was short and calm. Vas, however, was running too many various scenarios in her head to relax. She was grateful about Ome stepping down—but part of her kept focusing on the fact that it was done so via an odd bot of a dead Asarlaí. She couldn't shake the feeling that something was about to bite them in the ass.

Hard.

CHAPTER FIFTY-FOUR

THE MOON APPEARED TO BE as Vas remembered it. Dull, lifeless, and unassuming. All the sensors reflected the same data until they got into orbit. Rather, in orbit right outside of the linked hidden satellites that Gosta picked up as they approached.

"You can pass them. I've told them to stand down." The Marli-bot's voice in Vas' ear wasn't as surprising at this point, but Vas hoped it didn't tag along for the battle. Or the trip there.

"Thank you." Vas turned to Mac and Gosta. "Take us past the satellites and maintain a standard orbit."

An odd pressure hit her head. Judging by the twitches around her, the heads of everyone else as they drew closer to the moon. But the feeling was quick and immediately vanished.

Even Mac didn't have time to complain.

"Captain, Captain Qaan says her telepaths are all complaining about headaches…or they were. They're fine now." Xsit shrugged.

"Captain, what just happened?" Shien called in on the comm but she sounded tense.

"Just crossing a barrier. Are your people okay?" As far as Vas knew telepathy wasn't common in Pilthians, but it was hard to tell anything when they didn't disclose a lot.

"We are now. Just some headaches. I've sent my medics to Terel for more supplies. The ship is okay though?"

"Yes, we're fine. But I should tell everyone that. Thank you for calling up." Vas ended the call and opened the ship-wide comm to let everyone else know before Terel and the med bay became overwhelmed.

On a hunch, she called down to the holosuite. If there had been something wrong with the new nuns, Vas figured that Nitya would tell her if Jasiel and Aithnea couldn't.

"Aithnea here, class is in session, do you want to join?" She sounded too chipper and slightly out of breath for anything to be seriously wrong.

"Just making sure everything's okay down there. We're at Marli's moon and she had some defenses."

"Ah, the Marli-bot. She spoke to us as well. Carry on!" Then she cut the call. Aithnea might be dead, but rapidly training a hundred or so new nuns was giving her a lot of joy.

"Where do we…" Vas cut herself off as a map took over the main screen with a huge, 'go here' red arrow.

Gosta punched buttons but the map remained in place. "That's not me, captain."

"Very Marli-like." Deven hid his laugh but not as well as he could have.

"*Thank you for the map. But you could have simply told us.*" Vas thought in her head.

"*This was faster. I recommend coming down in your shuttles, not the fighters. And…. I believe that the entity running your ship should come as well. I can transfer her to the first shuttle in your bay.*"

"Nitya? Are you okay with being moved?" Vas figured that the Marli-bot probably hadn't checked with Nitya first. Not to mention, while they had been able to do the serious repairs to the *Destroyer's Curse* while n the space station at Home, Nitya was still the heart of the ship.

"She reached out to me; I am okay to leave the ship for a few hours and would like to review the Furies and parts directly." Nitya rarely showed excitement but she sounded energized now.

"Let's do this," Vas called out a few teams to go down. She would go in the first shuttle along with Nitya and Mac. She wanted enough pilots along that if there were actual usable Furies there, they could bring them back without towing them. She had a feeling the ones being sent to Ome would have to be towed.

Deven piloted the second shuttle, and Khirson came up to pilot the third along with three other Pilthian pilots. The Pilthians were part of this thing, and Vas wanted to include more of them.

Qaan reported that Hrrru would be piloting down Yesenia and five other telepaths. Qaan would be flying down the rest in a second shuttle from their ship.

The telepaths still had no idea what drew them there, and Deven said he hadn't noticed anything aside from the pressure caused by the barrier they crossed.

Vas had a feeling that it was the trace of Asarlaí blood that Terel confirmed was found in all the blood work from the telepaths on Qaan's ship that was calling them. Interestingly, it was so extremely faint in Lios' blood that it had taken five screenings to find it. Terel wasn't sure what that meant, or at least she wasn't hazarding a guess.

There was no turbulence, not even standard minor buffeting, as they approached the moon. Mac pouted that while he'd been included, he wasn't flying.

Vas told him to suck it up after his third heavy sigh.

The landing was smooth even though the terrain looked rocky and desolate. Marli was good at hiding things.

This wasn't the same area they'd brought the Pilthians to. That was far further south and none of the satellites, shields, or defenses had been in place.

Most likely the betrayal of the majority of the Pilthians on that ship lead to the change in the moon's defenses. And the activation of the Marli-bot. If it had been active back then, Vas was sure it would have reached out to her or Deven when they approached with the refugee Pilthians.

The five shuttles easily fit on the landing strip—which was huge when it wasn't being hidden.

"I'm bringing Nitya inside the building. She should be a part of this," Marli-bot spoke in Vas' head as everyone got out of the shuttles.

Yesenia waved when she saw Vas, but the Solar telepaths stuck together. Vas had heard of genetics doing strange things, but Terel explained that the Asarlaí blood wasn't strong in any of them. At least not strong enough to have any impact on them.

Or so it seemed. Vas was questioning it severely at this point.

"Do you notice anything different?" Vas asked Deven as he and the rest of her landing crew joined her.

"Not really. Let's see what she left for us. And what called them here." He nodded to the other telepaths as they all walked toward the disguised building. Vas hadn't seen Marli's home before but Deven had spoken of it.

As they got closer, it still appeared to be a massive pile of rocks.

Deven waited until their crew, the Solar telepaths, the Pilthians, Hrrru, Qaan, and her people joined them. "We probably want to stick together when we go in. And I recommend not touching anything inside unless the bot says you can. Marli was an extremely private woman and there are probably traps everywhere."

"This is true." A simplistic robot, vaguely Marli-shaped—in her human form—appeared to be walking out of the rocks. "Welcome to Marli's home. I feel like I know many of you." She gave a tip of her head to them, then turned and walked back toward the rocks. "Come this way please."

Vas and Deven shared a look then followed her in.

The front room was spacious, far more than a single

person, even an Asarlaí, would need. It was also filled with a lot of chairs.

Vas had a feeling they were the exact number of chairs as everyone who'd come down.

"Hello, captain," Nitya's voice came from a speaker in the wall. "It looks like we can get help here." Nitya's normally emotionless voice sounded extremely overwhelmed, although she was trying to hide it. Most likely she was going to get the Furies and parts she wanted. Grosslyn was able to give Nitya some Fury and Starchaser parts before they left Home, but while she'd been grateful, she felt they wouldn't be enough. She had visions of a mini fleet of ships like the *Keeper's Tempest* and was certain she could build it in time if she got enough parts.

"It's nice having beings here." Marli-bot nodded toward the speaker. "There's not much time, and you will need to take much back with you, but Marli knew there would come a day when the Clongari would return. Unfortunately, she felt it would be in a few thousand years, but she hadn't calculated on the Clionea nuns dying. And she believed the telepaths with Asarlaí blood would be enough along with the nuns to keep the Clongari at bay."

Deven narrowed his eyes. "Marli knew about them? How?" He looked over to the confused telepaths and shrugged. "I'm sorry you had to find out this way."

Yesenia already knew and from the look on her face, she'd guessed about the others.

"Yes, she did. It wasn't one of her projects. By the time it came about, she'd already separated from the rest of the Asarlaí, but she knew of the genetic attempts. Ten thousand beings on an Asarlaí controlled planet were exposed to Asarlaí genetics, and only a small amount of the ancestors of these survived. They didn't do it to hold back the Clongari however, the Asarlaí felt they would never fall. They were trying to make different genetic beings with Asarlaí abilities, for reasons that Marli never did find out." The Marli-bot moved closer to the telepaths and had a gentle smile. "I can't leave this moon—not beyond speaking to others at any rate. But if you let me, I can activate more of your Asarlaíness."

Judging by looks on all their faces, and the faces of most of the people in the room, that wasn't a welcome idea.

"You want to change us into Asarlaí? Most people don't recall they existed. My family's original home world was destroyed by them in the final battle. We've never forgotten." The man was solid and looked like a heavy-worlder. As he got to his feet, he also appeared to be judging whether he could destroy the Marli-bot or not.

Deven also got to his feet and stood in front of the Marli-bot. "Even if you have some of their blood, and keep in mind that your ancestors have carried it with no problems for over eight hundred years, you could never become an Asarlaí." He glanced back at the Marli-bot. "What she wants to do is change your blood enough to confuse the Clongari. You won't change. And even active, I'd guess it's too late to stop the invasion." He'd turned back to the telepaths but the Marli-bot nodded sharply behind him.

"Then why?" This telepath was a tall, thin, human woman. She wasn't as upset as the heavy-worlder, but she was pissed. "Why call us here if it won't do any good?"

"It was Marli's system that called you here, not I. However, the Asarlaí need to be present for this battle, even if they can't stop it from happening. And all of you have varying Asarlaí telepathic abilities. Didn't you wonder why the only ones called were telepaths? You can't stop the Clongari from invading. Their attempts so far have been limited, but that will change. They will come. But if you accept the gifts that I can give you, all of you," she looked around and met everyone's eyes, "we can make sure they do not win."

CHAPTER FIFTY-FIVE

THERE WAS MORE DISCUSSION, BUT it slowly died down. Especially when the Marli-bot and Nitya gave a graphic representation of what would happen to all the worlds, Commonwealth or not, if the Clongari succeeded in their full assault.

Massive destruction and brutal enslavement of the few survivors. The entire structure of the universe would change, making it unlivable for most current species. But perfect for the Clongari, who required encounter suits to function outside of their space.

The heavy-worlder, Don, shook his head at the information. "How can anyone know that's what would actually happen? The Clongari are only myths, this is all theory and conjecture." He didn't get to his feet this time but did tighten his arms across his chest.

"The Asarlaí originally rose to power against the Clongari invaders thousands of years ago when they and the Clionea nuns—the first ones of that order—pushed through the Clongari defenses and sent them back to their own section of space. Billions of beings died in the Clongari attacks before they were defeated and darkness almost overtook this Universe. It was before Marli was born, but she knew the stories. The Clongari almost did it before and they have the ability to complete what they attempted thousands of years ago. If they succeed, there will be nothing left." Marli-bot kept her voice neutral, but her right fist clenched as she spoke.

Qaan remained silent, but now rose and turned to the telepaths. "You are technically part of our crew, but while

I know some of you would have joined us in this fight regardless, some only came because you were called. That being said, no one here will force you to join us on this. We will be going back to Solar briefly after this, and we can leave you there. No one will think badly of you."

The Marli-bot started to open her mouth but shut it quickly and took a step back.

One by one almost all the telepaths got to their feet, led by Yesenia.

"I want to fight. Do what you need to do, but I'm not sitting out." She looked like she wanted to take them all on by herself.

Vas was grateful that being around Yesenia no longer gave her a pressure headache. Her theory was something to do with Yesenia's Asarlaí blood. She was grateful that didn't appear to be the case, as being around this many of them might have driven her mad.

The rest joined in after Yesenia's statement, stating they needed to defend their world and all the others.

Aside from Don, who remained sitting. He wasn't speaking out loud but he did appear to be having a conversation in his head. Or with the Marli-bot.

The discussion must have become heated, as his face grew darker. Vas was about to tell the Marli-bot to back down when she saw Yesenia's face. She was furious and she must have been the one mentally arguing with Don.

Don finally shook his head. "Fine, I agree. But if I become one of those soulless Asarlaí," he turned to the Marli-bot, "no offense, I'm hunting everyone down. After we destroy the Clongari." He got to his feet. "Let's do this."

The Marli-bot moved the telepaths to another room. After giving the rest instructions where to find what they needed.

Nitya led the way, hopping from speaker to speaker down a long underground hallway.

"This will make such a difference. The telepaths too, but I can get a few more ships like the *Keeper's Tempest* done and ready to fight by the time we get to the Lethian Assembly borders…" Her voice dropped as a massive amount of lights flicked on and a warehouse larger than the entirety of Vas' main town on Home came into view. "Oh, my."

Vas echoed Nitya's muttered response. There was a large group of Furies, most in excellent shape from what Vas could tell. Also, a pile of parts. The parts alone were the size of the *Destroyer's Curse's* landing bay.

"These are all functioning Furies? And we can take them?" Vas spoke out loud, but the Marli-bot responded in her head.

"*Yes. The worst of the broken ones can go to the Ralith. The rest and the bulk of the parts are yours. Nitya already has plans for them.*"

"*Thank you.*" Vas turned to the others. It would have been damn handy to have had these while they were facing the Asarlaí clones in the fight to free the Commonwealth, but this was better than not at all. "These are ours. Mac, do not get inside that one. They need to be checked out first."

He took a tiny step away from the Fury he had his hand on. "But I do get to fly one, right? I've been trained." Mac was right about that. Aside from Vas and Deven, he was the only one with prior training on the Furies.

"Yes, but I'm not sure how we're going to get them all out of here."

Again, the Marli-bot did her mental fly-by. "*I can give the basics to all of your pilots. And they can be linked together. You can have three Furies flying under the command of a single pilot. I'll show you that too. The ones not with you can receive the same training in your holosuite once you rejoin them.*"

"Why didn't Marli bring these out before?" Deven walked up to the closest row of Furies.

Vas shook her head as she followed him. "I was about to ask you that. She just had these things sitting around? And begrudgingly gave you those three broken ones?"

"Marli didn't have all these originally. Or she did, but access to them could only be given after she died." The Marli-bot's voice came over the speakers and paused. "It's complicated. But she believed they should only be used if there was no other option to save the Universe. They were only recently brought to my attention."

Deven continued looking over the collection of deadly ships. "You remotely commanded the Fury that flew by Home a short while ago."

"Yes. I was testing things out. Her instructions were to only release them to you and Vas. Continue looking them over, don't worry, none of them can fly until I release them. I must get back to work with the others."

Vas turned to Khirson and the other pilots who were holding back. "You heard the bot, check them out. But, and I can't overstate this, the mythical power of these things is matched by their unpredictability. Maybe our bot has a way to mitigate that, but don't count on it."

The group of pilots quickly dispersed to prowl through the assembled Furies. Vas stayed back after looking through a few. She'd had two destroyed under her. She watched Deven closely as he looked at one from a distance. While the ones she piloted broke down, she made it back to their ship.

Deven and Jakiin had pushed theirs to explode. Deven might have come back, but she noticed he wasn't standing that close to the ships.

"How are you feeling?" Vas knew Deven was only slightly more likely to talk about his feelings than she was. But this had to be hard.

"Not sure, to be honest. I remember Jakiin's Fury blowing up a split second before mine did. Then nothing until you found me on that plane." He wrapped one arm around her shoulders and hugged her. "I'm not sure I ever told you, but I think that you almost dying and finding me in limbo, or whatever that was, helped bring me back."

Vas slipped her arm around his waist and held him. "Normal people don't come back from being blown apart. Marli said there were changes to you when she gave you those three Furies, maybe the bot can access what they were." Marli was essential in combining the three people that Deven came back as into himself. But she never really explained much about any of it.

However, even she seemed surprised at Deven's return—before she covered it up with Asarlaí bravado.

"True. It depends on what was told to the bot. Part of me is afraid to find out. My people are extremely difficult to kill, but what I did was bizarre even for us." His hand clenched her shoulder as he watched the pilots climb into Furies. "I'm almost glad that many of these will become Nitya's fighters. She assured me that the explosive aspects of the Fury firing system were not added to the *Keeper's Tempest*."

"Then they also won't be as deadly against our enemies. But it's a worthy trade. Anyone who flies one of the surviving Furies needs to fully understand what they can do, and the repercussions." Vas watched the excited faces as the pilots went through the ships.

Yeah, they were going to need to have a very long talk.

Furies were one of the most dangerous ships ever built. They were fast and heavily armed. And could take out ships ten times their size.

They also had a bad reputation for blowing up in mid-fight. She and her crew had taken advantage of that when they had to try and save a group of ten refugee ships from the invading Asarlaí clones. Deven and Jakiin had gone out intending to blow up and take enough of the enemy with them that the rest could escape.

Vas tried to ignore it most days, but there was still a dark pit in her soul that remained from when Deven had blown up his Fury.

Marli-bot and the Solar telepaths, all appearing far more subdued than when they left, came down the hall.

"I believe they are ready. Their presence, and that of their Asarlaí ancestors, will be felt by the Clongari. Could all the pilots come forward please?"

Mac was the last, but even he came out of the Fury he was looking at before Vas had to drag him out. "Janx is going to be sad that she missed this." The tone in his voice wasn't of sadness for his cousin, but glee at rubbing it in.

"You need all of us? Three of us have flown them before." Deven nodded to Vas and Mac.

"Yes, there are elements you wouldn't have learned—such as linking ships. Please have everyone stand in a circle around me, a tight one." Marli-bot moved back toward the wall so the circle was completed by the curved wall itself.

"Now what?" Yesenia kept looking back at the Furies. She might not be a serious fighter ship fan, but it seemed that was changing.

"Now you become Fury pilots." The Marli-bot's grin looked alarmingly like the real Marli as she raised her hands. The entire room went dark until a current of light appeared on the left side of the wall and shot out before Vas could warn anyone.

The arc of electricity shot through everyone in a moment.

Vas dropped to the floor as the lights came on and aside from Deven and the Marli-bot everyone else was in the same position.

There was too much stuff in her head to remember how to get to her feet.

Deven turned to the Marli-bot as he rubbed his forehead and frowned. "That was too high of a level, help them."

The bot shrugged but didn't apologize. "It happens." This time the lights didn't vanish and a lighter current flowed through everyone sitting on the ground.

Vas felt the tingle this time, unlike the first time when she just dropped to the ground and was flooded with information. Deven helped her up and the rest of the group all got to their feet.

"This is amazing." Yesenia grinned. "I feel like I've flown these ships for years. Thank you." She nodded to the Marli-bot.

"You are welcome, but I was simply following what the original Marli programmed. You can connect the ships in groups of three and take them out." She pressed an indent in the wall and the roof retracted.

Vas turned to Qaan. "Could you sort them out? And we'll need at least three more pilots to take our shuttles and the broken Fury parts out as well. We need to speak to our host."

Qaan nodded and joined the others to organize them. Hrrru was on the edge of everything but had received the same mental zap of instructions everyone else did. He'd been making some life changes recently, but Vas knew he never liked the Furies.

"Hrrru? I know you're on leave from my crew, but would you mind flying one of the shuttles with Fury parts back to the *Destroyer's Curse*? If you don't mind not flying one of the Furies this time."

The relief on his furry face showed that she'd picked correctly. "I can do that, captain. I'll stay with Captain Qaan until we reach Solar, but I notified her I'll be returning to your ship for the final battle." A face with so much fur shouldn't be able to show that much emotion; he'd clearly enjoyed being with more of his people, but wanted to be with his crew when the time came.

Vas hugged him and then stepped back. "I will be honored to have you back. Thank you."

Hrrru grinned and ran to look into securing a load of Fury parts to be towed in by a shuttle.

"We should make sure to keep the ones for Ome separate, it would be better if we do that first and send him on his way before the rest of the Furies come up." Deven nodded to the pile at the far end. Marli-bot kept her part of the deal, there were probably enough pieces there to create three full Furies. There were just *a lot* of pieces.

Vas and Deven moved over to the Marli-bot.

"Thank you for this. I know you're just following commands; however, I also know Marli would have given you a way out." Deven smiled. "We had a few questions about a few things Marli might have left or said."

The Marli-bot nodded and motioned for them to follow. "I will do what I can. I believe your people have things well at hand and Nitya can reach me if something goes wrong."

She led them to a smaller room off of the big front room. "I understand that biologicals enjoy resting and food and drink. I can order both if you would like."

"We're fine, but thank you," Vas said. "We're wondering if you could access answers to a few things that Marli might have in her database."

The Marli-bot sat with them and tilted her head. "What is it you need?" She'd been extremely Marli-like for most of their interactions, but she seemed like a robot now, or an extremely advanced computer on legs.

Deven quickly told her what Marli had told him a few years ago—that he'd changed in the twenty years before. He also told her about dying and coming back as three people.

The Marli-bot leaned forward. "You are a biologic. How did that happen?"

"That's something we're not certain even Marli knew, but there's a good chance they were connected." He paused. "And it might have been something that occurred when I was the Pirate of Boagada, the first time."

Vas hadn't connected that to the rest, but it seemed there were a lot of connections going on in the weirdness of their lives.

"My data indicates that the Pirates of Boagada do not recall what they did during their tenure. Although, Marli found a way for Savan to bypass that."

Vas turned to Deven. "Yup, Savan was one. Is there any way to find out when he was it and any information about what he did?"

"Not at this time. The information might be coded in the deep files, but it feels like it was a long time ago for mortal biologics." The Marli-bot paused and tilted her head. "I might be able to access how Marli was able to pull in what Savan did. But it will take time. Along with determining what could have changed to allow Deven to return as three unique forms. Even though I can't travel with you in this battle, I can communicate with you. I will research these items."

"Thank you." Deven got to his feet.

"Yes, thank you. Do you think you could communicate with us via the comms instead of in my head? That's extremely startling." Vas didn't want to think what could happen if the Marli-bot contacted her in the middle of a fight. She also stood up.

"I can do that. I will also remain in contact with Nitya." The Marli-bot rose and turned toward a wall, then came to Vas and Deven with two crates. "These were items that Marli left to you. Along with this moon and myself, obviously. If you do not wish for me to maintain the protection over your moon, I can shut myself down at any time."

Deven responded first. "No, please stay and continue

protecting this place. Ome might not be the most determined invader if we fall."

Vas nodded. "And you are given autonomous standing. Now, and if we don't come back. Hold out as long as you can."

The Marli-bot nodded. "Thank you. If everything collapses, this moon will self-destruct once enough enemies are close enough to feel it." She gave a grim smile. "I have spent time studying the Clionea nuns and their last rites. I will go with honor."

Vas clasped her arm. "They would be proud. Thank you again."

They left the building to the activity of getting the shuttles loaded and attached to their hauls and a bunch of impatient Fury pilots.

Hrrru was waving from the shuttle Vas had flown down. "I attached the parts for Ome to a tow on this shuttle, I thought one of you would like to be there to drop it off."

Vas and Deven nodded.

"You could both do it if you want. Qaan said she would take one of the shuttles if you both went."

"She's a smart lady. I'd say that even though he swore on his ship, and we don't have to actually see him, I'd like both of us to be there." Vas smiled at Deven. "Especially since I know you won't back down on taking them up."

"You're also a wise woman." He grinned and motioned to the open shuttle door. "Shall we?"

"By all means." Vas looked around at the waiting Furies. "We might have an uprising if we don't let them get in the air soon."

CHAPTER FIFTY-SIX

———◆———

THE TRIP TO OME'S RALITH ship was mostly silent. Vas was thinking about what might be in those crates she and Deven were given, and just what information about Deven the Marli-bot would uncover.

She was a little concerned about what might be revealed if Deven gained access to what happened to him as the Pirate the first time. Not all secrets should come to light.

"If you give me that side-eye, worried look one more time, I'm taking it personally." Deven was piloting and didn't take his eyes off the front window as he spoke.

"Sorry. Just having second thoughts about all the things the Marli-bot might find."

"It's better that we know. But I know what you mean. Do you want to contact him?"

Vas sighed. Ome's ship was waiting right where it was supposed to be. "He better not screw this up."

"But if he does, he and his ship vanish. I got a little bit out of the Marli-bot about the Ralith ship, including that tidbit. That's a plus."

"True." Vas hit the comm. "Ome, we've got your parts as agreed."

"Great, do you have time to come inside?" The Ralith ship wasn't much larger than the *Keeper's Tempest*, the shuttle couldn't fit in it. Not that Vas would have considered it.

"No. Thanks, though. We're going to release the tow. It has a limited power source, but you should have time to get it loaded. We have a universe to save." She tried to keep her voice light; Ome was too good at reading things and he didn't need to know how stressed she was about this drop.

"Come on, you want to see this ship, I know you do." He sounded oddly distracted and a chill went down Vas' spine. She cut the mic to Ome.

"Deven, drop the tow and pull back. Now." She couldn't explain it but something was horribly wrong.

Deven didn't question her and released the parts and their tow, and then moved the shuttle in the opposite direction. Ome would have to go after the tow and away from their shuttle.

Vas felt better, but still off.

"What are you doing? Come on, we're friends now." Ome's voice had a tenseness it hadn't had a moment ago.

Deven started swearing and punched the shuttle to race away just as two missiles shot out of the Ralith ship.

"Damn it! He was going to blow us up?" Vas looked at the screen as the missiles looped around to follow them. Until a Fury came racing up and blew the missiles apart.

Mac's voice came over the shuttle comm but it was directed at Ome. "Take your parts and go. The next shot blows the tow apart."

Vas smiled. The Ralith ship might be indestructible, but the parts on that tow weren't.

Ome didn't respond, but his ship grabbed the tow and left so quickly it was as if he vanished.

"What the hell was he up to?" Deven was reading output from the weapons fired and growing pissed as he did. "Those missiles weren't going to blow us up, they were going to immobilize this shuttle. He was planning on taking us before the *Destroyer's Curse* could send help."

"Are you both okay?" Mac called over. "Marli, well, the bot, freaked out a few minutes ago and said I had to get up here. I think she might have been putting a tracker on Ome's ship at the time."

"Yes, thanks to you and the bot. Damn him." Vas' hands

were shaking. She'd faced far worse encounters but something about this one chilled her soul. She didn't doubt that Ome hated the Clongari; there was real venom in his voice when he spoke of them. But he also had another agenda that involved capturing her and Deven.

Vas hit her comm to the moon. "Thank you, Marli, for the assist. Did you tag that bastard's ship? And you can send the rest of our people up now."

"I did, but it will take a while to catch up to him. I'm glad you're both okay. The rest of your people are coming up now." The Marli-bot clicked off.

The Marli-bot was fairly close to human, but Vas didn't know if bots could sound worried. This one did.

Deven got them back into the *Destroyer's Curse* and the other two shuttles followed. The Furies would be flying into the second and third bays under Nitya's guidance.

"How did we know?" Vas asked as she slowly got out of the shuttle.

"I'm not sure. You felt it first, but then I did."

"Vas?! Are you both okay?" Aithnea's panicked voice came through Vas' comm.

"Yes, did you warn us? Ome was planning on kidnapping Deven and me."

"We all did. It's a long story. Once everyone is on board and we're heading to Solar, come down to the holosuite." Aithnea's voice vanished.

"This entire thing is adding more weirdness to our weird situation." Vas shook out her arms to relieve some of the tingling. "I'm going to the deck; can you make sure everyone gets back? I know Nitya wants to start making her ships immediately, but I think we need to get to Solar as soon as possible."

Deven gave her a quick kiss. "On it." He jogged to the corridor for the other landing bays.

Vas almost felt normal by the time she got to the

command deck. Bathie had already left the command chair and Gosta was pulling up images.

"As soon as all of our people and ships are on board, and Qaan's people are settled on her ship, we need to head to Solar. Gosta, did you track Ome's ship at all?"

He turned to her. "I saw what happened and scanned the residue for the missiles. I couldn't have moved us there in time once we realized he'd betrayed us. Aithnea and Jasiel almost shook this ship apart trying to reach you. Ome cut our comms to you." Gosta was mostly an easy-going guy—it made him not the best merc. But right now, he looked like he wanted to change that.

"He didn't even break his deal with the Marli-bot." Vas shook her head. They should have been tighter on what he could and couldn't do. Not that there had been a lot of time.

Mac came running on the deck. "Deven told me to get up here and head out. All of our Furies and shuttles are in and Qaan is ready to leave as well. The Marli-bot sent Nitya up directly." He grinned. "I did some good shooting with that Fury! Deven even said so." He slid into his pilot sling.

Vas nodded to him and wondered what Deven was thinking. Praise where it was due was good—most times. There wasn't a doubt in her mind that if Mac hadn't come when he did, she and Deven wouldn't be on this ship right now.

But encouraging Mac was a dangerous thing.

"We're locked and ready," Deven's voice came from her comm, judging by the background noise he was still in the landing bays.

"Mac just told me. We're heading out." She nodded to Gosta, and the *Destroyer's Curse* headed out of the Commonwealth.

Vas waited until Deven came back on deck before

calling to the holosuite. "I assume now is okay? I'm bringing Deven as well."

Jasiel answered. "That will work fine. The nuns are on a project in the primary suite, Aithnea and I will meet you in the smaller one."

"I'll be there as well. Ome's behavior surprised Marli." Nitya sounded furious.

"On our way." Vas grabbed Deven before he could sit. "We're going to find out how the nuns knew what was going on and how they let us know."

"This should be interesting." They walked to the lift. "We have twenty-five Furies that Nitya isn't taking apart, not yet anyway. From what was reported, linking the ships together worked perfectly on the flight up here. They obviously didn't test the linked firing, but we can run a few tests after Solar. Do you still think there is some Falian thring there? And that it's worth the risk to haul them with us?"

Vas shrugged as they approached the smaller holosuite door. She had that odd thought when they were originally planning on going back to Solar, and briefly told Deven about it. A dream, nothing more. But the urgency hadn't left. "We might ask our friends in the holosuite. That dream did pop up out of nowhere. But yeah, once I got over the weirdness of it—I do think having those seeds to throw at Clongari planets, or transfer into their ships, would help our cause." At the very least, they should mess them up enough in order to launch an attack.

Deven was about to slide open the holosuite door but paused. "Transfer them into their ships?"

"Yup. Just came to me. If we can partially activate them before we have Gosta fling them in their engines? We could do serious damage even before the seeds fully germinated." She'd almost feel bad about such an idea, but the Clongari would do the same if they could. "We'd have to do as many as we can in one shot, you know they'll block us after the first round." That Gosta would be able to do it was a given. She just might need to get him to start figuring it out soon.

"Come on, we all have things to do." Aithnea's voice came out of the room as soon as the door opened.

Vas and Deven entered to find Jasiel, Aithnea, and Nitya—the last two in hologram form, sitting behind a table with two chairs in front of them.

The stern setup wasn't lost on Vas and she narrowed her eyes as she and Deven took their seats.

"And why are you three looking cranky? We appreciate what you all did, by the way." Vas met and held their gazes.

"We're not cranky." Aithnea stopped at Jasiel's snort. "Okay, maybe I am. You two shouldn't have needed our help to sort out what that Ralith runner was going to do. He wanted the Keeper and the Pirate of Boagada for his own nefarious reasons. You should have felt it." She leaned forward, pure pissed off Mother Superior.

"We didn't. There have been a few things going on." Vas frowned. "And that's what this is about. If we had more training we wouldn't have needed help from the nuns."

"No. Although, I'm not sure that would have been the case even if you had the training needed." Jasiel ignored Aithnea's glare. "Ome is unique. I'd say he was before becoming what he is now and the connection to the Ralith is augmenting that extremely. His shielding of his mind with that ship is something we can't underestimate."

The discussion boiled down to Aithnea still demanding more training until Vas and Deven told the three of them about the Marli-bot's conversation that Savan had once been the Pirate of Boagada, the original Marli managing to override the nuns' block on what Savan had done during that time, and that the same might be possible for Deven's past. And why it could be important.

Even Aithnea looked stunned at that information.

"We believed no one could break the block on the Pirate, although it doesn't seem to be in place with Deven this time." Jasiel finally spoke up. "However, we also never thought an Asarlaí was still alive and puttering around messing with our people."

Aithnea nodded. "I wasn't a huge fan of Marli, although she did sacrifice herself at the end, which was an extremely Clionea thing to do. And she was strong enough to break through the locked memories of the Pirate." She sighed.

"Do you think that it could be important for us to know what Deven did during his first stint?" Vas still wasn't sure how she felt—it might help Deven, or make things worse. She didn't know how that information could help with their current crisis.

"Yes."

"No."

Jasiel and Aithnea glared at each other as their opposing answers came out at the same time. Nitya just shrugged. While she'd been a nun when she was alive, she hadn't been a high-ranking one like the other two.

"Breaking the cover for the Pirate shouldn't be done. Ever." Aithnea's glare intensified.

"We're facing an opponent that hasn't been outside of their section of space for an exceedingly long time. I doubt that the first Clionea nuns would care about keeping Deven's events secret at this point." Jasiel was far calmer than her friend as she returned her look.

"Is it true that the Clionea nuns and the Asarlaí worked together to send back the Clongari that first time?" Nitya ignored the tension coming from Aithnea.

Jasiel nodded. "Yes. As much as the order wanted to ignore that part. We did work with the Asarlaí to defeat the Clongari. Which I understand we will sort of be doing again."

Vas had already given a brief rundown of the Asarlaí activation process for Yesenia and her group earlier, so she just nodded to confirm.

"Captain, we have a problem. Solar is under attack." Gosta's call through the holosuite brought everyone to their feet. Even if Aithnea and Nitya couldn't take their holobodies out of the room.

CHAPTER FIFTY-SEVEN

———◆———

"IT'S THE LETHIAN ASSEMBLY AGAIN. They have ten ships and hit the planet and fleet about twenty minutes ago."

"We're on our way. Damn it, why didn't Ragkor contact us earlier?" Vas and Deven raced for the lift with Jasiel right behind them.

"He and the rest of our fleet were blocked until just a few moments ago. The Ralith ship tore through here right after the Lethians arrived. He didn't attack any ships but completely decimated all communications. At least it appears he did it for the Lethian Assembly ships as well. Ragkor said they stopped their actions at the same time he and the rest of the fleet lost communications." Gosta sounded like he really wanted to be the one to destroy Ome.

He was going to have to fight Vas for that honor.

"We have to find a way to stop his communication blocks from happening. He might want to destroy the Clongari like we do, but he doesn't care how he does it. Or who else he takes down." Jasiel raced into the lift as the doors shut. "I'm definitely in better shape now than I was before I found you all." She grinned but was breathing heavily. "If you don't mind, I'd like to claim one of the extra science stations for the duration."

"It's yours and glad to have you up here." Vas waved at the open science stations as they got on deck. Khirson had resumed one, and Flarik had taken one as well. "You're in good company." Vas ran for the command chair. "Good to see you, Flarik and Khirson. Looks like we're in for a fight."

Deven took his station. "We're fifteen minutes away from Solar. Why in the hell did Ome hit their communications? Aside from him being an asshole. He couldn't have thought any of those ships, ours or the Lothians, could catch him. Or hit him for that matter."

"He didn't want anyone to know where he went." Flarik's grin wasn't nice. "He changed direction sharply once out of here, but why go through it in the first place?" Flarik was a professional at finding tiny weaknesses in her opponents and developing ways to exploit them. She was one of the top lawyers in the Commonwealth for a reason.

"He didn't think our fleet was there and he wanted something from the planet?" Gosta started pulling up data. "I can piece together his trajectory from the information from the fleet. He swung into Solar's space too deep to have been expecting our ships. The best detail came from Captain Zarith's flagship." He flipped it to the large screen to show the Garmainians' data on a star chart.

"It was as if he didn't see our rather large fleet, or the Lethians, until he was upon them. He didn't fire on anyone, but that communications block was massive." Vas watched as Ome's ship raced off. "I wonder if the Marli-bot was able to do more than just try to track him."

"Captain, Abiel from Solar is trying to reach you," Xsit said.

"Send it through." Vas hit her comm. "Abiel, what can we do for you? I see the Lethians returned."

"Yes, unfortunately. It was a good thing that your fleet was already on its way here. We were getting ready to launch our ships when all planet and ship-wide communications went out. Are you almost here?"

"On our way. We want to speak with you in person when we get there." She could ask about the Falian thring seeds now, but she thought she'd be more convincing in person. Not to mention, while she knew they were there, the urge was even stronger now, explaining that to him over the comm could be difficult.

"Aye, captain. We'll see you soon." He ended the call.

"The Lethians are pulling back, but not to the gate," Gosta called out.

"Xsit, get me Ragkor." Vas watched the slow retreat of the Lethians. Why leave now when their communications were restored? The *Destroyer's Curse* and the Welischian ship wouldn't have made that much of a difference. Unless their communications hadn't come back. "Belay that. Reach out to the lead Lethian ship. Standard hail."

Xsit attempted the call five times with no response before Vas finally told her to resume contacting Ragkor.

"Vas, good to see you. We were just about to go after the Lethians." Ragkor was definitely in his element—he might not be a Marine anymore, but a good space battle was still a favorite for him.

"Have you tried contacting the Lethians since your communications came back?" It appeared to her that the enemy ships were increasing speed as they went for the gate. "Hold a moment." Vas turned to Gosta. "Are we close enough to tag any of those damn ships?"

He frowned. "Probably not...but my new drones could." His grin was scarier than his frown.

"New drones? When did you have time?"

"Here and there. Stealth drones. Made from ones we've captured, but impossible to see or pick up on most screens. They carry weapons and trackers, and are extremely fast." He was excessively smug, but it was warranted if they could do what he claimed.

"Yes, please. Thank you, by the way."

Vas watched as ten small blips left her ship and vanished from the screen.

"Nicely done." Deven adjusted the screens a few times, but they were gone.

"You need a special tracker to see them." Gosta put up another screen. "I wanted to make sure they worked before I added the system to the ship. Or the rest of the fleet."

The new screen was basic but showed the dots joining the Lethian fleet. The image continued as the Lethians left through the gate.

"They're jumping through distant gates." Gosta was doing fifteen things again.

"Why?" Mac didn't turn to look. "We know where they're going, back home. Right?"

"Unless that's the entire point—they weren't going back to Lethian space. Damn it. We should have scanned them before they took off." Vas looked at the data they were pulling in, but it was basic—where they were going, and that they continued to move.

"You think those might have been Clongari." Deven didn't ask a question.

"Yup, and so do you. This makes no sense. We've seen a Clongari ship, they're big and nasty-looking. I get that perhaps Clongari can't cope in our Universe, but they've shown they can inside their ships. Probably better than they could in a bunch of stolen Lethian ships."

Flarik was quietly glaring at the main screen, then ran her analysis. "The only reason to hide is when you don't have the power for a full attack. Which doesn't coincide with the information the Marli-bot sent up." She looked up as everyone turned to her. "I apologize. She sent me data concerning the original Clongari invasion, from the Asarlaí side. She felt my child needed to be informed. Or rather, warned. I'm still processing it, but the Clongari in that first attack were a serious threat. Their ships filled the sky of every world they went after."

"Until they reached the Asarlaí." Deven continued to watch the screen as the Lethian ships seemingly took random hops through gates.

"And the Clionea nuns. The two groups together defeated them. Then a blood oath, one that no longer exists now, made the survivors flee to the far end of known space. The blood of the nuns and the Asarlaí held that for over a thousand years."

"But if they can sense the Asarlaí and nuns were gone, couldn't they realize they're back now as well?" Mac did glance around this time, but then swung back to his pilot station.

"It's believed it's too late to stop their invasion. The new nuns are being rushed through training, but they are new and the telepaths with Asarlaí blood are also new." Jasiel looked around. "Obviously, whatever that Marli-bot did activated them. Otherwise, it would have been clear there were still Asarlaí around even when Marli died. Although there was Asarlaí blood on Solar for generations, it didn't appear during that time."

"How do we proceed?" Vas knew one of the first items, once they sorted out Solar and found the seeds, would be getting Flarik to share the rest of her intel. They also needed to figure out why the Marli-bot felt Flarik's still unhatched child needed that information.

"I'll continue monitoring them, and find out if any of our fleet gathered more information," Gosta said.

"Excellent. I want everyone on alert. The obvious aggressors might have left, but we can't be certain there aren't more." Vas got up. "Right now, I need Deven and Gosta with me on a visit to Solar. We'll need full ground scanners as well. Bathie, you have the chair. Roha, please take over tracking at Gosta's station." She knew he wouldn't be happy about leaving, but she had a feeling he should be there concerning the Falian thring seeds. Which she hadn't shared with anyone other than Deven.

Gosta appeared ready to argue, then simply nodded and followed Vas and Deven to the lift.

"Might I ask why, captain?"

"I need you to track down some Falian thring seeds on Solar for us. But they're hidden too well to scan from space."

"How do you…" he paused when she shrugged and tapped the side of her head. "Ah. A Keeper thing?"

Vas wasn't sure, but at this point, anything weird was going into that category. She just nodded. "I believe we can use the power of those seeds to take out a few Clongari ships. If we ever see any of them."

"If they work the way we think they will, then even the Lethian Assembly ships would be slowed down if not destroyed by your plan." Deven smiled. "Providing they are on the Clongari side or are being run by the Clongari."

Gosta watched them as they got down to the landing bay. "Might I inquire what the plan is?" Not knowing things didn't sit well with him.

"Once we get the seeds, and get to the edge of Clongari space, we want you to hack into as many enemy ships as you can and transfer the seeds into their engines. Well, once the seed activation process has been increased." Vas didn't get a chance to surprise Gosta often—but she did this time.

"I…into their engines. Activated." He nodded furiously.

"Think it will slow them down?" Vas grabbed some heavy scanner equipment, along with an extra blaster as they passed a locker. Deven did the same, but Gosta stood there blinking and nodding.

"I believe it might blow them up." He grabbed three

scanners. "When this is over, this secret power of yours is gone, right?"

"I hope so."

"Too bad," but he said it so softly as he walked to the shuttle that Vas wasn't completely sure what she heard.

CHAPTER FIFTY-EIGHT

THE TRIP DOWN TO THE planet was uneventful. Abiel and Lucan met them at the small landing strip.

"Qaan is also coming down. That group of telepaths joined her last minute, but they wanted to get more supplies and personal items before the fight." Abiel motioned for them to follow, but Lucan remained at the strip. If Qaan didn't take Lucan with her crew this time, she was going to have a stowaway on her ship.

Vas made quick introductions for Gosta as they walked.

The house looked completely repaired, albeit more obviously defended than before. "How are the politics going? Looks like you're not worried about being known anymore?" Deven waved to the reinforced door and metal shutters for the windows. Abiel had been far stealthier about his activities before.

"Still a work in progress. I might become the new leader of our planet—but after the threat is gone." He frowned and waved for them to take seats in the front room. "It took a few hard days, but I convinced the other region leaders that the threat of the Clongari is real. Now, as lovely as it is to see you, and to meet you, Gosta, I don't believe you came for a social call."

"No." Vas leaned forward and brought up the destructive power of the Falian thring seeds. Particularly in the engine of a ship.

Abiel rocked back in his seat. "Impressive, but you two destroyed those seeds." He watched Vas and Deven then scowled. "Didn't you? You said they could destroy this planet, given what the Asarlaí did to it."

"We thought we did." Deven was soothing as he explained that a new source on the planet was found. Not only could it help the war effort, but if they removed it, there would be less threat to the planet. Telepathy might or might not work since Abiel was also a telepath, but Vas was pretty sure Deven was more powerful—and the Pirate of Boagada.

Abiel was relaxing quickly. "But how are you going to find them? They could be anywhere. We might not be a huge planet, but we are still a planet."

"I found it!" Gosta had been scanning as Deven worked on Abiel but he jumped up as he shouted. "Oh, sorry. Do go on." But he didn't sit.

"We're fine, Gosta, where is it?" Vas felt Deven release the hold he had over Abiel. They just didn't have time to convince him.

"Here. We'll need to take the shuttle." Gosta tapped on his pad with a frown. "Might need to have someone bring down a second shuttle. There's a lot of seeds there. It's deep in what looks like an old mine."

Vas' stomach lurched. They'd never found out what the deal was with the solbilan mines on Home. "What kind of mine?"

Gosta nodded to himself as he pulled in more data. He ran the results two more times before looking up. "It appears it's an old solbilan mine."

Abiel watched the three of them. "Solar was a mining planet a long time ago. But the solbilan has been gone for hundreds of years. Why are you all upset?"

"We're finding some odd connections with those mines. And I doubt the placement of the seeds was accidental. Let me get the second shuttle to come down. Maybe a third?" Vas stood up to call her ship but watched Gosta.

He gave a short nod. "It's difficult to get a clear reading, but it probably wouldn't hurt."

Vas left the front room and called Bathie. Mac would bring down one shuttle and Glazlie the second. Plus a few extra crew members to help load, although she overheard Abiel offering to have his people help also as she came back into the room.

Gosta sent Mac and Glazlie the coordinates and the discussion went to ships joining the fleet.

"I know Yesenia and the other telepaths have another job to fill, but I'd like her and Lucan to co-captain the ship *Solar,* and join your fleet. The Welischians have three more warships to send that are coming from their home world and should be here in a few hours. The ones here will protect Solar as long as they can." He didn't add, 'if you fail' but it was clear.

Deven smiled. "We'd be honored to have them and your ship join us."

"I'd go along, I was intending to." Abiel gave a small grimace. "But, I'm getting older now. Reflexes aren't what they used to be. And someone has to keep an eye on this planet."

"We're on our way, captain," Mac called down. "We'll meet you at the coordinates."

"Thank you, Mac. Don't leave your shuttles when you land. Any of you." Vas had no idea where that thought came from, but she wasn't arguing with it.

"Aye, captain. Mac out."

"Let's head over. Do your folks want to ride with us or take their own transport?" Vas asked as everyone got to their feet.

"I've got a shuttle I can bring them down in. If Gosta will send me the exact coordinates, we'll meet you there." Abiel didn't appear happy about his admission of not being up to command his ship, but he was recovering. It took a strong leader to realize when his desires weren't the best option for his people.

Gosta transferred the information to Abiel while Vas,

Deven, and Gosta took their shuttle to the mines. It was only a few minutes jaunt in the shuttle, but there was enough rough terrain that a ground vehicle would have had serious issues. There had probably been roads leading to the mines when they had been active, but they were long gone now.

The other two shuttles were waiting, and for once it looked like Mac had followed orders and everyone remained inside.

Which was good. She still couldn't nail down where the feeling was coming from, but the skin on the back of her neck was itching more the closer they got to the site.

Deven set them down, but didn't pop the hatch. "You're seriously worried about something. Do we move ahead? The seeds would probably help us, but if this is a trap, it's not worth it."

"That's the problem, I'm not sure what it is. It could just be more remnants of my whole issue of dealing with mines as a kid. Even though the ones on my home world were dead by then, the people Borlan was working with specifically took me there."

"Or it could be something from the Keeper. I didn't sense anything earlier, but I have concerns now." Deven watched her carefully.

Vas took a deep calming breath and ran through some of the Keeper protocols that Jasiel and Aithnea had been beating into her head. Not only was she stronger and faster as the Keeper, but her mind worked differently.

The view outside the shuttle faded and she saw shapes instead of hills and rocks. There had been a darkness there, but it was fading now. She opened her eyes. "Let's do this, but I want Marwin and Glazlie to stay on guard above with the shuttles and not help move the seeds.

Deven and Gosta nodded as Vas called to Mac and Glazlie to bring everyone out and the new orders for Glazlie and her brother.

Abiel and his crew landed their shuttle just as she got Glazlie and Marwin in place as snipers. Close enough to cover the shuttles and the entrance to the mine, but still remain hidden.

He nodded to them as he and his crew left his shuttle, but didn't seem surprised. "Probably a good idea. I didn't recognize it at first, but this is sort of the badlands of this region. Or it was fifty years ago. No one comes out here much."

"Yeah, it looks rough." Vas motioned to the rest of her crew. "Follow us down, no idea how the seeds are being stored." The ones in the barn were in containers. But there was no idea how long these had been here.

Everyone had headlamps as well as wristlamps and they trooped into the cavernous entrance. Signs of the old mine were fading but here or there a track or the shattered remains of an ore cart appeared. The feeling of foreboding lessened as they went in further, so that was good. Hopefully.

"Sealed crates ahead, captain." Mac had slowly taken the lead as they went down. Most likely in case there were any hidden riches down here.

"Scan them please, Mac." Vas stood back. This room was massive and had more crates than she could take up in a single round—even with three shuttles. If they were all the seeds, she needed another plan. Abiel started twitching when they saw the massive amount of crates. Most likely imagining what these could have done to the planet.

"This entire section appears to be the seeds," Mac yelled from the side he'd gone down. Still, a lot, and more than enough to help the cause. Plus, the smaller amount would be more reasonable to bring up in a single run. "The rest.... weapons? High-end explosives? Umm, does Gosta want to check what I'm seeing? This is a high-end stash."

Gosta went to the far side of the room and began muttering loudly. Then the mutters turned to swearing and he and Mac came back.

"Captain, that half of the cavern appears to be as Mac said, weapons. Various ones from Commonwealth worlds, non-Commonwealth worlds, some that aren't even identifiable aside from they are designed to kill people." He checked his scanner again, then shook his head. "And they were only left here a few years ago. The Falian thring seed cases are at least a hundred years old."

Abiel's eyes were round. "This can't be good. But, I have to admit, we'd love to take some of the weapons off your hands for planetary defense—and for the *Solar*. We have weapons on the ship, but we'll be increasing the crew size."

"That's more than fair. I need teams to sweep for traps around all the cases; seeds and weapons alike. Then we start hauling them out." From what she could see, even the hundred-plus years old seed containers were solid enough to move.

"At least we know now where the seeds in that barn came from," Deven said as the teams swept through their scans.

"True, but how in the hell did anyone know they were here? Granted, they would have scanned, but what did they do, a manual, ground-level scan of the entire planet?" Vas shook her head. "Based on what?"

"And why leave all these weapons if they were planning on exploding this planet? There's more than one group involved." Abiel had his people stand back while Mac, Gosta, and the rest of Vas' crew ran their scans.

"We might never know," Deven said.

Vas' comm clicked. "Captain? This is Glazlie, we have visitors. Two ground vehicles designed for this terrain. They haven't spotted us or the shuttles but the shuttles will be visible to them in about five minutes at their current speed."

Abiel shook his head. "Ask what direction they're coming from. We would have seen ground transports on our way down here."

Vas relayed the message.

"They're coming from the south. There's a clump of pretty nasty mountains not far from here and that's where they appear to be coming from."

Abiel's people pulled out their weapons. Considering he'd had traitors in his midst before, Vas dropped her hand to her blaster and noticed Deven did the same.

Abiel nodded to his crew and they started back out of the cave. "Local marauders. Damn it. I told the council they were still down here. Vas, these are rebels who have tried to take over Solar before. Their numbers keep shrinking but they're still around. And they probably know what we've found."

"Are you certain they aren't working with someone off-world? Those weapons are from all over." Deven stepped closer to the mouth of the cavern, both blasters in his hands.

Abiel shrugged. "They've been around for years, but that's not to say they started here. Or that they brought these weapons. How good are your two snipers?"

"Exceedingly good. Is there a shot they should take?"

"Yes, the transports being used are for extreme terrain, but not good in a firefight. Avoid the tires, they're well-protected, but the engines aren't. A shot directly into the grill of each will stop them. But that's a crazy shot."

"They're brother and sister and work hard to be the best. I trust them to make it." Vas nodded to Deven. "I'll stay here to make sure nothing blows up, you go tell Glazlie and Marwin what their jobs are." She'd rather not use comms for the snipers just in case those marauders were more than they appeared.

Deven and Abiel ran out, although Abiel appeared to be going to see these great shots. Vas knew even tracking speeding vehicles over rough terrain, Glazlie and Marwin would hit the targets.

Vas hit her comm to Deven. "Standard op procedure." At his affirmation, he ended the call. She didn't believe a group of rampaging locals could have another group circling around, but they also shouldn't have had access to the contents of this mine. 'Standard op' told Deven to run a full scan outside and prepare for a regular merc incursion.

Gosta came back from the weapons side of the cavern. "No explosive trip wires linked to any cases or the ground underneath. We should be able to get them all out." The rest of her crew came back with the same results from the seed side.

"I need half of you to go outside and station yourselves for hostiles. Current ones are coming from the south, but don't trust that. The other half stay with me and protect this cavern. Local rebels or not, they aren't getting the seeds or the weapons." Vas didn't feel like these marauders were what was making her feel on edge about this. But they still shouldn't be discounted.

"Got them, captain!" Marwin called on Vas' comm. "Glazlie did too. Too bad Walvento and Huglin aren't here, we'll have to make sure they know. Damn it. The transports stopped but didn't blow up. Rather their hoods did, but the crews are out and running this way. Pick them off?"

"Yes, and good shooting you two." The triplets and Walvento were the most competitive people Vas knew. Once they moved past their goal of dying in a blaze of glory during a battle at any rate. Vas told them she'd find a way to bring them back from the dead if they did that. They'd moved past it.

Walvento was just plain competitive with weapons.

Vas and the crew remaining inside the mine moved closer to the entrance and took defensive positions. It was unlikely whoever was attacking would get past her snipers, Deven, and the crew, not to mention Abiel's people. But she didn't get to be one of the best mercs in the Commonwealth by not being paranoid. If there was the slightest chance it could happen, prepare for it.

The sound of blasters came from outside, although because of the formation of rocks, she couldn't see anyone.

A horrific feeling hit her and she ducked just in time as a shot went into the rock where her head had been.

"Come on, Captain. Ome won't pick us up without those weapons." The voice answered why Ome swung by the system. He might have planned to come to the planet, scoop up the weapons for himself, and leave without being noticed.

That was blown to hell when Vas' fleet and the Lethians were having a pissing match in orbit over Solar—so he dropped off his brothers.

"Which one are you?" Vas projected as much annoyed boredom as she could into her voice.

"Pol. Look, we won't hurt your people. We can even take care of the second wave of locals racing this way. Just step back, let us grab a few boxes of the weapons, and we'll be gone."

Vas switched her comm to warn Deven what was going on. Chances were it was just the two brothers—they and Ome would be cocky enough to think they wouldn't run into problems.

"Understood," Deven's voice was low, then he cut off. He might already have spotted them.

Vas still didn't respond to Pol but turned to Gosta. "They came down to this planet somehow. Can you scan for their shuttle? I'm done with them and their damn brother." An idea hit her. "First, can you make it seem like there are active explosives in this entire cavern? They don't need to show for long."

Gosta nodded and started furiously hitting the pads.

She wondered if Ome was watching this from a nearby system.

"Pol, my friend. I feel like we are dear friends now. The only way you're getting these is if you find a way to get them in the afterlife. This entire cavern is wired with explosives. And I'm holding the deadman switch. If you make any move towards us—or those marauders do—I'm dropping it." The ruse wouldn't last long, but hopefully, it would be enough to keep them off balance.

"I have them in sight. Take the kill shot?" Deven's voice was still low.

Vas knew that even though he wasn't as competitive as the triplets or Walvento, Deven was an excellent shot. She gave a deep sigh. "As much as I'd like to, we don't need Ome hunting us. Legs only." Killing the brothers would make her life easier in the short run, but Ome was a vengeful son of a bitch and would quickly destroy her and probably the rest of her fleet. But she wanted the brothers out of the picture for a while.

Blaster fire and yells indicated Pol and Relin were far too close to the mine for her liking.

"Got them with the stun blasters. Figured we wanted them out more than hurting. Although I was tempted." Deven sounded like he was scrambling down. "Mac and I are securing them and dragging them to one of the shuttles. Might be more marauders coming in."

Vas turned back to Gosta. "Can you track more incoming ground transports as well as look for whatever the brothers came down in?" At his nod, she sighed and looked back at the pile of crates on the weapons' side. She'd hoped to quickly sort some out for Abiel, then take the rest up to her ship. But she'd caught how specific Pol had been about certain crates. Which meant she had to figure out what the hell was in there.

"Captain, the leader of the marauders wants to speak to you," Mac called over the comm. "Oh, and our guests are locked up."

"That was quick. Are the marauders surrendering?"

"Not really. He has a blaster at my head." Mac was calm, but her people were trained for this.

"Shit. Give him the comm."

"Stop punching me!" Mac sounded more annoyed than hurt. "He says in person. All weapons down."

As soon as Vas heard Mac was being held, she'd opened her comm to all of her people on the planet. There wasn't time to go through and tell them all.

"Tell him that I am coming out. Unarmed." She handed Gosta her obvious blasters but kept her snub-nosed one tucked into her boot top, hidden by her pants. Along with a throwing knife in the other boot. Then she hit the comm to Glazlie. "Do you have Mac and the enemy in your sights?"

"Aye, captain, we both do."

"Hold off getting a shot, even if it opens. I'm going to leave my comm open when I speak to him but if I say 'dive' take the shot. I don't want to fight these people to get what we came for, but we will if we have to." There were much larger enemies out there and spending ammo on low-level punks was a waste of resources.

Glazlie agreed and Vas left the mine. The fighting stopped, so there was no way to know how many hostiles were still out there. But it was easy to see Mac and his cloaked friend. She couldn't even tell what species the leader was, just that he was tall and bipedal.

Vas raised her arms as she walked forward.

"Stop and turn around slowly." The voice was low but they could be using a voice modulator. "And keep your arms up."

"This isn't my first time doing this, bucko." Vas had no intention of lowering her arms. Not yet at any rate. "What do you want?" Her circle completed, she continued walking toward them.

"We want a ship and passage off this damn rock."

Vas paused. That wasn't what she expected. "Why were you on this damn rock to begin with?"

"It's complicated. But we're done now. We just received notice that our home world was destroyed. We need to fight."

CHAPTER FIFTY-NINE

———

"WHAT WORLD WOULD THAT BE?" Vas kept her arms up, but relaxed her shoulders. There was a weird familiarity to the cloaked person.

"None of your business. I know who you are, you're a Commonwealth merc that this useless planet hired to come get rid of us."

"Partially correct. I am currently a former Commonwealth merc. Not hired by this world to do anything and with enough firepower to blow you and your people off this planet. We had no idea you were here, nor do I really care. I'm right in the middle of a large event right now, and am seriously leaning toward letting the locals just lock you all up. Well, the rest of your people, anyway. Holding my man hostage is a bad idea."

Part of her wanted to shout 'dive' and let the idiot die. But her Keeper senses were picking up on something. These Keeper things would be a hell of a lot more useful if they were clearer. Another time she actually missed not having Aithnea kicking around in her head.

"There's no way you can shoot me before I kill him." The voice laughed but it wasn't pleasant. "But fine. My home world was Jalian. My crew and I came here to see if the rumors were true about some seeds to help our world. Not that it matters, but we were the last world of Pilthians."

Vas watched him carefully. Most likely his people, or what was left of them, were descendants of the third Pilthian sleeper ship that left the Commonwealth fifty years ago. Or perhaps some of the people who'd mysteriously fled their Commonwealth home not long after the sleepers left.

"First off, asking for help would have gone a long way. Secondly, your people aren't the last Pilthians—there's a large group with their queen up in one of my ships. Thirdly—Mac, duck!"

Mac slipped but didn't get too far, before the gunman and he were both stunned. Vas grinned. Deven had been listening in and switched to his stun blaster.

The Pilthian was unconscious and Mac stumbled about. But he still kicked the man twice. "That's for trying to break my jaw. Damn it, I got swiped by that stun shot." He blinked rapidly and dropped to a seated position.

"They've rounded up the other marauders and yup, all are Pilthian," Glazlie called in.

Abiel walked over to the gunman and nudged his blaster out of reach before pulling back the man's hood. "Pilthians were hiding in our badlands? I've heard of Jalian, a small world on the edge of the Nhali system. Didn't hear they were Pilthians though."

Her crew brought the rest of the unconscious marauders to the shuttles. Prisoners or not, Vas knew Shien would want to speak to them. She sighed. About forty or so. Plus, Pol and Relin. "The three shuttles will take up the prisoners—after they're secured. Then we'll start moving cargo." She nodded to Deven to organize it then stepped off to the side to call Shien.

Shien was equal parts excited at finding more of her people, saddened at the loss of their world, and annoyed at the aggressive behavior of the survivors. And yes, she and Khirson would be waiting for them in the brig.

Gosta and the remaining crew in the mine were given a new task, to identify the weapons as quickly as they could just by scans. Mac recovered from his partial stun, so Vas sent him to help. She kept Glazlie and Marwin on sniper duty just in case, although nothing was moving in the land around the mine.

"More Pilthians. I assume Shien was happy about that?" Deven came down to the mine. "Hopefully whatever destroyed their planet gave them time to get some people off first."

"Hopefully. She's happy and pissed and will be having nice long talks with our new friends. Are Pol and Relin still out?"

"Yes, there might have been double stun hits on both. Glazlie and Marwin weren't happy about those two being here."

Vas looked up into the clear sky. "And most likely their brother is coming back. I have Gosta and some others trying to speed-identify the weapons. Whatever ones Ome wanted, we can't leave here."

"Agreed." Deven went down to help, but Vas waited as Abiel jogged up.

"Your prisoners are loaded up and my folks are ready to start bringing the crates out."

"Just the seeds first, we need to sort the weapons. If whatever Ome was looking for remains here, your entire world won't be safe. And trust me, you don't want to meet him."

Abiel gave a terse nod, then motioned for his people to head back into the mine.

Getting the mostly unconscious and secured prisoners off the shuttles and returning to Solar took less time than expected. They quickly stuffed all the Falian thring seeds into the three shuttles and sent them off again.

Her comm pinged as they were finishing sorting the weapons. She still had no clue what Ome wanted but Abiel agreed that his people would keep the simplest of them. Hopefully, they'd figure out what Ome was after before they left Solar.

"Captain, Hrrru here. I'm back on the *Destroyer's Curse*.

There's no sign of Ome or any more Lethians coming through the gate. But something big is passing through a few systems over. Single vessel, but if these scans are right, it's as large as half of our fleet."

"Damn it. Glad to have you back Hrrru, keep scanning. One more run after this one and we can leave. Track any system that ship has been through."

"Aye, Captain. Hrrru out."

Vas smiled. It was good to have him back. They'd been using high-end scanners to look at the weapons, so at least most of the crates weren't opened.

The three scattered around Deven's feet were, though. And he looked ready to kill a few dozen people. The way that his hands kept clenching, he'd prefer to do it without weapons.

"Easy there, you're scaring the crew." Vas kept her voice light. She'd never seen him this furious before.

"These are Kilesh destructors. A design my people threw away decades ago because they're too dangerous and unstable. This has to be what that maniac wants."

The weapons did look deadly. "They're hand weapons though. I can see where keeping them away from Ome, or anyone else for that matter, is a good thing, but he doesn't usually go for hand-to-hand combat."

"They can be modified. These haven't been. But put them together, pair them with something like a mutated Fury? They'd match that Ralith ship in destructive power. Before they blew up and took anything in the same system out with them." Deven took a few deep breaths. "And these are new. The rest of the weapons might have been here a little longer, but these things have been here only a month."

"Are they going to be safe to transport, or should we destroy them here?" Vas figured they'd have to blow them up from space and even then she didn't trust that Ome wouldn't find a way to save them. Having him more or less on their side against the Clongari was becoming problematic.

"I've no idea what would happen if we tried to destroy them. I've got Mac piloting one of the shuttles up with the seeds. He's got a list of items to have Jasiel find to help make those weapons safe until we can find a secure way to get rid of them." Deven sighed. "The Pirates of Boagada recognized them before I did. And, more importantly, they knew that the nuns could neutralize them for now. I don't think we can spend any more time down here."

Vas told him about Hrrru's finding a large mysterious ship in a distant system as the rest of the weapons were sorted. Abiel's shuttle was packed and would go up to the *Solar* to transfer most of the weapons.

"I'd like to see you two when things aren't going to hell." Abiel hugged them both. "Good luck and I hope we can all look back at this over drinks." Then he and his people left.

Deven made a temporary restraint for the Kilesh destructors after Jasiel called down with the specs and sent supplies down with Mac.

They put the rest of the weapons and crew in two of the shuttles. Vas and Deven would fly the Kilesh destructors up.

"Your people are up to something. Or some of them are. How close is Kilesh to Jalian?" She'd mentally felt a twinge from him when the Pilthian mentioned his home world.

"Too close for the destruction of Jalian to be good. I don't go back there often, but it is still my home." He dropped into his thoughts for the rest of the flight.

The *Solar* was close to the rest of her fleet, along with three more extremely impressive Welischian warships. It might have taken the Welischians a while to decide to go to space, but they made a damn good show when they did. The six up there now could be their own fleet.

Vas tried to rally the Commonwealth when they were still at Home, but the best she'd been able to do was leave a bunch of messages. No help would be coming from them and they didn't have time to hunt down any Commonwealth worlds who might be interested in fighting on their own.

Therefore, she was surprised to see a group of ships coming toward them from the Commonwealth.

CHAPTER SIXTY

V AS HIT HER COMM. "XSIT? Who are those ships and have they hailed you?" The scanner on the shuttle was more limited than the ones on the ships, but it did look like those ships had just come into range.

"They just appeared and the lead one is hailing us. Do you want to speak to them?"

"Yes." Vas was mostly curious as to what they were doing. "Vas here."

"Damn woman! You are hard to find when you want to be!" Carrix's voice was even more gravelly than before, but good to hear. "We heard through the useless Commonwealth government, that you are gathering a crew to fight the real threat. And not whatever caused them to create that barricade. Also, glad to know you're still alive. You could have called."

Vas laughed. "Things have been busy since we crashed the barricade, but damn good to hear you. You've got a lot of ships that don't seem to be Silantian."

"Nope, my people weren't the only ones picking up on chatter outside the Commonwealth—even before they put up that barricade. Once I saw your fleet move, we gathered and followed. A bit surprised to find you here, though. Solar isn't a hotspot."

"It's complicated, but we're getting ready to head out. Are those ships with you following your command?" Carrix was a damn good leader and it would make life easier to have two fleets instead of a fleet and twenty or so independent ships.

And she didn't want to annex more ships into her

fleet, even though Ragkor was technically in charge. She would do what she could with the fleet before the Keeper's actions kicked in.

"Yes, it was tricky, but once they understood the full threat of the Clongari, they agreed. What do we need to know?"

"Let me get to my ready room and I'll fill you in."

"Deal. Carrix out."

"I'll take the Kilesh destructors to their holding area. Nitya has managed to find a remote, unused, and easily cut-off section of the ship for them—next to our dead Clongari body. Although she's not happy." Deven opened the shuttle doors.

"You wouldn't be either. Those things are menaces. But I can keep them safe." Nitya didn't sound happy but was also distracted.

"Are you already building more ships like the *Keeper*?"

"Just setting things up. But I think we'll be happy to have them. I've also run full diagnostics on the intact Furies, they're as solid as they can be."

"Thank you. I'll be in my ready room if you need me."

"Understood. Nitya, out."

Vas waved down Bathie as she started to get up from the command chair when Vas came out of the lift. "Not just yet, need to talk with our second fleet leader. Have we identified all the ships with Carrix?"

Gosta nodded. "Hrrru and I have almost finished and will be sending the list to your ready room." His grin pointed out how happy he was that Hrrru was back— even if they were still looking at a fight they might not win.

"Excellent. And good to see you back, Hrrru." Vas flashed him a smile, then went to her ready room.

She went through her messages, but aside from one from Carrix from a few hours ago, and Grosslyn saying they'd mustered a militia from the former refugees in the southern continent, there was nothing. The Commonwealth government would probably get a hold of her if her fleets defeated the Clongari.

Full retirement after this sounded even better.

Updating Carrix was quick and easy—just what she needed right now. They signed off after an agreement to meet for serious drinking after they kicked Clongari ass.

Vas laughed as he signed off. But she was extremely glad that he and his Commonwealth fleet joined them. The Clongari were doing mostly stealth strikes, and using other non-Clongari ships so far. She knew the closer they got to Clongari space, that was going to end.

The Clongari were trying to take out the threats they could deal with first, before their full attack.

"Gosta, are we ready and plotted?" Vas asked as she took the command chair.

"Aye, captain."

"Mac? Ready to go?"

"Aye, captain."

"Xsit, are we in communication with all of our fleet and Carrix's flagship? Is Ragkor ready?"

"All ready, captain." Xsit didn't sound as confident as the other two, but there were a lot of ships to keep track of, even though Ragkor was sharing the load. Another reason that while Vas was grateful as hell for Carrix bringing these ships, she was even more glad that he was commanding them.

Deven turned from his station. "Everyone has checked in as ready to go, captain. Shien said her people are hoping for a serious fight. Oh, and the Pilthians from Solar are still unconscious Terel gave them an extra sedative, along with Ome's brothers, but Khirson recognized some of the facial markings. The older ones among them are from that third sleeper ship that left his world fifty years ago."

"Thank you. Warn the fleet that we'll be moving soon. Gosta and Hrrru, did you send them a flight pattern?"

She'd found out during the Asarlaí wars that it helped
if ships knew where their place was. She wanted them
together, but not too close.

No reason to make it easier to take out the fleet in a
single massive shot.

"Aye, captain! Ragkor first, then the rest. Carrix has a
copy as well." Hrrru grinned from his station.

Vas hit her comm. "Ragkor? Do you want to get us
going or should I?"

"You should have the honors, Vas." He paused, "Unless
there are Keeper tasks right now?"

She laughed. "Not yet, but don't give them ideas."
Vas nodded to Xsit and opened the full all ships comm.
"We're about to head out for a fight not just for our people, but for everyone in known space. Probably unknown
space as well. The Clongari will be brutal in their fighting once we get closer to their domain. I want all of you
to know that whatever happens, I'm proud to serve with
you. You all have your gate and travel routes, let's get this
started." She nodded to Xsit who cut the all ship comm
and to Gosta and Mac to head out.

Solar only had one functioning gate, so in this case
all of the ships would have to go through the same one.
With her own twelve, two Garmainians, six Welischians,
the *Solar*, and Carrix's twenty-one, they would be going
through rapidly.

Destroyer's Curse led the way with *Warrior Wench* guarding the flank.

They were passing through the gate when a blood-cur-
dling scream came from the lift.

Flarik had gone to her room, but was back in the lift
and yelling at a level that most likely shook the walls of
homes back on Solar.

"They stole my baby!"

CHAPTER SIXTY-ONE

V AS AND DEVEN RACED TO Flarik, but she kept screaming and collapsed.

They grabbed her and held her before she could do any damage to herself as she flailed her fists.

"They…they…" Flarik's feathers changed to deep red with black and gray running through them.

"They broke through my shields; I couldn't see them," Nitya's voice was heartbroken as it came through a wall comm.

"It was not your fault. I will destroy them." Flarik had stopped yelling but her feathers still held their colors. "Their children will never be born. I call upon my co-parents to aid me."

Vas held her tighter, then looked to Deven and he nodded. She knew what she needed to say. "We honor our pledge. The three of us will command this ship and find the child. The ones who stole the child will be ripped apart."

Flarik pulled back and watched them carefully. "Thank you."

They finished clearing the gate and Mac moved them out of the way for the rest of the ships coming through.

"I know we will…" Flarik froze and tilted her head sharply. Then she smiled. "It will be okay. I felt her. She is still inside her egg, but she knows where she is and will eat the hearts of her captors when born." She blinked and laughed. "That is *my* daughter. Together, we will find her."

Flarik kept her feathers their dramatic and scary color as she let them help her to her feet.

"Do you know who took her? Where they went?" Deven guided Flarik to the science station she often took.

"They were Lethian Assembly curs, betrayers of all people, including their own. They go to meet their masters, the Clongari." Flarik smoothed her feathers and nodded. "I will be all right." She looked around the command deck as if she'd had an outburst in a high court. "I apologize for my outburst. Do carry on." Her imperious nod was good to see.

Vas wanted to send Flarik back to her room, to have time to recover, but from the predatory look on Flarik's face, that wouldn't work. Instead, Vas patted her shoulder and returned to her command chair. "You heard her, get ready for our gate jump."

Deven took his seat and the deck crew studiously ignored Flarik.

The two fleets of ships cleared the gate in good time, especially for the first time working together. By the time the *Warrior Wench* came through, they were sorted for the next jump. Vas and Ragkor had planned out a few jumps to get the groups working together. Even the Welischians and the *Solar* only had a small learning curve. In wartime, it was important to come out and be in position the moment a gate was cleared. By the fourth jump, everyone was doing that.

"Captain? There's a large fleet of ships that just entered this system from that far gate, close to fifty…or more." Hrrru cleared his throat as his voice almost went into Xsit's range. "They are coming this way at exceptional speed."

"We're being hailed, captain," Xsit said. "Rather, *Regent Flarik* is being hailed. They need to speak to her and only her, immediately."

Flarik scowled at the screen but the ships were still too distant to be identified. "Might I use the ready room, Vas?" She got to her feet and again smoothed her red and black feathers—the gray had vanished.

"By all means." Vas watched as Flarik stalked off. She wasn't hysterical anymore, but she was going to need to kill a lot of bad people very soon.

"Captain? Those ships are Wavian. Their call is sending out a code for the Imperial Wavian Fleet." Xsit's feathers went up as she spoke. That many Wavians would concern anyone, especially a member of an avian prey species. "They are not returning my hails, however."

"Hold off until Flarik speaks to them. But how did they know to come here? And why?"

The lift opened and a frazzled Jasiel came out. "Flarik called them. Using all of the nuns, by the way. She simply took us over with her screams. I believe the Wavian armada will be joining us whether we want it or not."

Vas looked at Deven, but he shrugged. "There are a lot of layers going on right now."

"That's an understatement."

"Captain? Ragkor, Carrix, Zalith, and Qaan are calling," Xsit said.

"Tie them together and send them to my chair." Vas quickly explained these ships were here to help and that Ragkor would now take full control of the fleet—excluding *Destroyer's Curse* and the Imperial Wavian Fleet. There wasn't much grumbling, mostly a little awe at the impressive Wavian ships. Vas kept Ragkor on the comm as the rest went to tell their ships to stand down.

She wasn't going to tell everyone what happened, but he needed to know. She quickly explained the attack on Flarik's child.

He was silent for a few moments. "I am so sorry her child was taken. What can we do?" There was a lot of controlled anger behind his words.

"Right now, whatever Flarik says. She, Deven, and I will be working with the nuns and the Wavians on this."

"Aye, captain. Ragkor out." He was angrier than she'd ever heard him and at this point might be fighting to not chase after the kidnappers himself.

Flarik came out appearing calmer. "They answered the call of the queen and the queen's regents. They will join in our battle and will follow the lead of this ship and her captains. My child will be saved and the aggressors will die." She calmly took her seat at her science station.

Deven nodded. "Regents? Captains?"

"As my co-parents, you both are now co-regents in the Wavian empire. And we are all seen as the captains of this ship." She glanced between the two of them but it didn't look like a point that could be debated.

Vas shrugged. "I'm fine with the co-captains—I trust you both. Not sure what you need us to do as co-regents." Hopefully, that would only stay in place until this fight was over. The idea of spending her life on a Wavian world until Flarik's child came of age was terrifying.

"I will tell you when you are needed." Flarik nodded. "I suggested that my people take the end of our grouping as they are the most powerful. Although, they are your people now as well." Her smile while still wearing her scary feathers was disturbing.

"Sounds good to me. Mac, take us out."

Flarik was communicating with someone, most likely her people as she was speaking Wavian. She laughed as she ended the short call. "They agree to endeavor to remain in the rear and not take all of the spoils from the rest."

Vas lifted an eyebrow, there was probably a lot more.

Flarik's laugh this time was more genuine. "That's a close translation. I and the lead of the Imperial Wavian Fleet will work on incorporating them into our attack plans when we reach the edge of Lethian space. Unless you two would like to be included?" That she even asked spoke a lot about the importance of Vas and Deven as co-regents.

Vas and Deven shook their heads.

"We will leave that task to you." Deven did an elaborate bow from his seat and Flarik grinned before turning back to her station.

Jasiel came to Vas' command chair but watched Flarik carefully. "I have to say we were all surprised at Flarik's power when she called upon us. But it did open us up to seeing the aggressors directly for a brief moment. They are Lethian but have killed as many of their people who didn't agree with them as others. They want to offer the baby to the Clongari as tribute. If the queen is who they believe she is, she could destroy the Clongari."

Vas shook her head and dropped her voice. Flarik had excellent hearing but she was busy chatting with one of her people again. "Then wouldn't bringing the baby to them be a mistake?" She meant alive but distracted or not, she wasn't saying that anywhere near Flarik.

"That's where it's interesting. The information we had, from that Kantari woman in your med bay, was there was a destroyer. Aithnea and I agree that after going over the evidence, it is the child. But there is a second translation, that having the baby will *create* a destroyer to work on the Clongari's side. If the Clongari aren't as strong as we feared, having something to help them would be handy for them."

"Then it could go either way?" Leave Flarik's baby with the kidnappers and hope she turns out to be on her people's side? This entire fight was a gamble, but that was pushing it too far.

"I'd say the odds are far better in our favor. Don't forget, the connection between Flarik and her child is extremely strong," Jasiel said.

"Jasiel? If you're done puttering around, we have more training," Aithnea's annoyed voice popping out of Jasiel's comm was nice to hear. A bit of normalcy.

Jasiel laughed and hit her comm. "I'm on my way." With a nod to Vas, she left the deck.

They were nearing Nhali space when Terel called up from the med bay. The sound of electronic alarms almost drowned out her words. "I need security down here now!"

Vas and Deven both jumped to their feet. "What's wrong?" Vas asked as she motioned for Marwin and Roha to join them.

"Delimara died, the nanites woke up, and they are now demanding to be let out of the bio bed. They're about to crack through the shield!"

CHAPTER SIXTY-TWO

———◆———

VAS TURNED TO DEVEN AS they hit the lift with Marwin and Roha behind them. "How do you feel?" There were nanites in him as well, but they all agreed to remain dormant until they were returned to their normal space.

Which was still a distance away. That they'd killed Delimara wasn't a good sign.

"I feel fine. As far as I can tell the nanites are still dormant. What the hell happened?" His question went unanswered as the lift opened and he, Vas, Roha, and Marwin all ran for the med bay with weapons out.

The room was chaotic, but the med alarms had been turned off. Delimara, or her body being used by the nanites, was still trying to break open the bio bed. Her eyes were dead and the nanites didn't seem to have the same level of strength they had when they took her over.

"When did she die?" Vas approached and held her blaster against the bio bed shield.

"About ten minutes ago. I was about to conduct the autopsy when the nanites took over. How are you feeling, Deven?"

He shrugged. "Fine. Did the nanites kill her?"

"I have no idea. I thought so?"

"No. She let self die. Would kill us. Need out." The weird disembodied nanite voice came out of Delimara's open but unmoving mouth. "Dying."

Deven started twitching. "Damn it. They're telling the truth. Stop it!" At his yell, the nanites stopped making him move. "She woke enough to kill herself. A bomb inside her was triggered to go off when we hit this section of Nhali space—which we missed the last time we were here. Damn it. She was working for a secret group of her people when we found her. They want the Clongari to win." He released the shield from the bio bed before Terel could stop him.

Delimara sat up and appeared to calm down, but didn't try to get out of bed. "Thank you. The body tried to kill us as well. We stopped it from exploding."

"Thank you." Vas wasn't sure what to say but blowing up before the war would have sucked.

"Her people not trusted." The voice was pulling itself together more. "We will go to war. Die fighting. This one will not last long, but we will use it to save all worlds from the killers." It was still disturbing seeing Delimara's slack face as words came from her. But the nanites were gaining more control.

Vas turned to Terel. "How did we miss this? And she went through all that just to blow us up if we got to the Nhali? That's a long stretch to assume it would help her cause."

"I have no idea." Terel pointed to the machines behind her. "It was extremely well hidden. The nanites were living in her and until the bomb started to activate, they didn't know it was there."

"Is Deven safe?" Vas spun on the nanites. Deven supposedly had fewer in him than Delimara had, but that was taking their word.

"Yes. We still want to go home, if we live, but need to make sure there is still a place to go."

"Could you shut down for a bit? Let Terel do a check-up on you?" Vas had been more attuned to everything around her since Flarik's scream. And she instinctively knew Deven was safe even as she'd asked the question.

Also, they could trust these nanites. Originally, they'd

only cared about returning to their people, now they wanted to help save their people.

"Of course. Thank you for not spacing us." Delimara's eyes closed and the body fell back into the bio bed.

Terel scowled at the dead Kantari. "Fine. Let me see how things are going. I've never examined a newly dead Kantari now being animated by nanites. You all go about your business. I'll tell you what I find." She pointedly turned her back on Vas and the rest.

Vas and Deven nodded for Roha and Marwin to stand down then they all returned to the command deck.

"Think that will help? The nanites running Delimara around as some sort of weapon?" Vas had no idea what the nanites could do. And evil or not, Delimara was still only one person.

"It's more of it probably won't hurt. And that's my best guess." He was almost to his station and turned. "It wasn't from my esper skills, or at least not them alone, but I realized I believe those nanites." He shrugged.

Vas sighed. "Same."

"Captain, Ragkor wants to know if we're picking up some Kantari as well. There's a fleet of them coming to this system."

Vas motioned for the call to be sent to her chair. "Ragkor, we have information that the Kantari are not on our side. Are there any Nhali or Lethian Assembly ships with them?" The Clongari were determined to keep this fleet away from their borders, so they'd probably pull in any allies that they controlled to throw them in front of the fleet.

"No. Yes," Ragkor swore under his breath and Gosta started muttering loudly and pulled up a screen.

The Kantari ships were smaller than most other warships. But that worked better with their culture. There were about thirty, but a strange field was blocking what was behind them.

Gosta and Ragkor busted through it. Another twenty ships—larger than the Kantari. Nhali, Lethian, and Racki were lagging behind the static field.

"Captain, I think our best option would be to spread out wide here and here." Ragkor was all polite Marine, as a chart flipped to one of their screens.

With the addition of the Wavians, they had far more ships than the aggressors.

"They have no intention of winning this fight." Deven remained at his station but stared at the chart. "They were sent here to delay us, even if they all died."

Vas drummed her fingers on the arm of her chair. Her people wanted a fight. But this might be a trap. "If they want to slow us down then we can't fight them. Not here, anyway."

The deck went silent and Vas turned to Flarik. The red and black feathers were still disturbing, but she wasn't upset. "I agree. This is a trap to delay us. My child is not on any of those ships. I recommend we leave this sector immediately. The Imperial Wavian Fleet Admiral agrees." She tilted her head and watched the screen. "Then blow up the gate. I believe Gosta has drones that will do that successfully with the right calculations."

"Did you hear that, Ragkor?" Vas left her comm on. Flarik was a co-captain now.

"I did. And while I know we'd all love to destroy them, we have to think about the larger battle. Not to mention with odds this much against them, any real threat would have fled by now."

"Agreed."

Ragkor signed off to notify the rest of the fleet of their decision and that they would continue as planned. Vas figured there would be some pushback, but they weren't her concern.

Deven glanced back and narrowed his eyes. "What's that grin for?"

"Nothing. It's just nice that we have a massive fleet behind us and between Ragkor and Flarik, I'm not in charge of anything beyond this ship." She'd made it work when they were fighting the Asarlaí clones back in the Commonwealth, but it had been a much smaller fleet. Not to mention it still wasn't how she liked to fight.

"Captain? The original Kantari led group is still coming our way and another group is heading for the gate," Gosta called out as the screen shifted.

"And I've been tracking that big ship we picked up back at Solar." Hrrru's eyes were wide when he turned around. "It's coming here. Through the gate we're heading for. And it's a Clongari ship. One of those big, spiky ones."

CHAPTER SIXTY-THREE

"VAS? THERE'S SOMETHING VERY WRONG with whatever's coming through the gate. Recommend we get fighters out." Nitya rarely gave battle advice, but she was freaked out now. "I have ten Keeper class ships ready, plus yours, twenty-five Furies, thirty Flits, and the Pilthian fighters are ready. Just need pilots. Soon."

Vas hit her comm to Ragkor and shared what Nitya said as Deven called out pilots. Ragkor at first didn't understand, but Nitya jumped into the comm.

"Small fighters only. The larger ships need to hold back. No time to explain." Nitya was still incredibly stressed and distracted.

"Understood. I'll tell the fleet." He signed off.

"We have a group of nuns ready to fight," Aithnea called up. "Not all of them brought their ships but they have twenty to add. Or they can help pilot others."

Vas nodded to Deven. "Deven's coordinating the pilots, but have them go down to the landing bays."

Mac got to his feet and Vas remembered the telepaths were on the *Solar*. There were twelve of her people, including her and Deven, who could fly the Furies.

"Yesenia, we need all of your people who were trained on the Furies to get over here immediately."

"Captain, we are on our way over now."

"Thank you." Vas switched over to Nitya. "You heard that? Bring their shuttle into the Fury bay. We're coming down."

There was a chance they had enough Fury pilots without her and Deven, but something in her head said they needed to be out there.

Deven had gone to the landing bay as he rallied pilots, so Vas grabbed Mac and ran for the lift.

"Flarik, you have the deck," Vas yelled as the doors shut.

The landing bay was busy but surprisingly silent. Images of the approaching two fleets and the massive Clongari battlecruiser were on all of the screens overhead.

Deven waved her over. "I wasn't sure if you wanted a Fury or the *Keeper's Tempest.*"

"I'll take a Fury this time. More pilots can fly something like the *Tempest.*"

Yesenia and her crew got out of their shuttle and went into the bay.

"Thank you for coming. Your people remember how deadly these are, right? Hesitation and fear are not good in a fight."

Yesenia had her wild red hair back in a tight braid, not unlike Vas'. She gave a grim smile. "Life is dangerous. And if using these helps us shove that Clongari battlecruiser into the hell it came from, we're ready."

The pilots with her cheered and ran for their Furies. Mac gave Vas a nod and ran after them.

Deven joined her. "The Wavians have zip fighters, almost as deadly as the Furies but not as dangerous to fly. They're ready and will launch when the regents give the order." He took the second to the last Fury.

Vas called Ragkor, "Give us a minute then have all of your fighters launch. The Wavians are sending a group as well." All launching at once could be impressive, but in this case, it was more to make sure they had the element of surprise.

Their larger ships would hold back the Kantari, Lethians, Racki, and Nhali. The fighters would swarm the Clongari. Nitya could explain later why she said only small ships—but right now they just needed to survive.

The fighters launched in waves; having three landing bays was damn handy.

The Fury handled extremely well as Vas led the rest out. Soon the space between them and the gate was filled with hundreds of fighters.

Ragkor gave out orders for all of them, even the Wavians followed when Flarik sent them a separate message. Vas was a merc and a damn good one, but in this case, having a military strategy was better. Everyone knew the goal here was to strike the Clongari hard and fast and pull back. The larger ships were already adjusting to meet the Kantari.

The Clongari battlecruiser barely fit through the gate and was even more spiky than the others they'd seen.

"Wave one! Now!" Ragkor yelled and the Furies, KT class ships, and the Pilthians flew forward.

Vas hadn't flown a Fury in battle in almost two years but it felt right. As long as none of them blew up.

The Clongari ship was slow and still clearing the gate when her wave attacked. Vas fired enough to do damage, but not use everything in the weapons bank.

The Clongari didn't show that they even noticed at first. Then impacts were seen across the surface. They were designed to fight larger ships; this was like a bunch of poisonous flies taking down a hydra beast. Lots of tiny hits.

The second wave flew in on the tail of Vas' wave and more explosions along the surface were seen. After the third wave, made up mostly of the Wavian zip fighters, Vas noticed the Clongari ship had stopped moving forward and the tips of the spikes all over were starting to glow blue.

Vas hit her comm. "Ragkor, we might have a problem. They're charging something."

"Damn it, I see it. All waves, be aware that the enemy is charging weapons."

The third wave completed their run, but Ragkor must have told the fourth wave to hold back. Unfortunately, ten Garmainian fighters either ignored him or didn't get the message. They raced forward just as the spikes of the enemy ship flared brightly.

An arc of a beam weapon focused from about a quarter of the points on the Clongari ship hit the center of the ten, spinning them off into space. The weapon appeared to be designed for larger ships, but it still destroyed at least three of the Garmainians and sent the rest into out-of-control spins.

Ragkor called out to all of the fighters, "Everyone pull back!"

The Clongari didn't fire again but resumed moving forward. Whether it was from the Keeper or the weird connection with Flarik, Vas had a flash of what they needed to do. She called Deven and Ragkor and told them.

"Captain, risking all of the Furies—"

"Is a calculated risk. We'll never make it to the Clongari border if we can't destroy this ship. The Furies are the only things that have a chance." The trick would be to get them linked to hit the same target at the same time. And not explode.

"I can connect us all," Deven responded. "It's apparently a Pirate thing. I'd say the Pirates of Boagada were all telepaths."

"Even our non-telepaths? Mac and a few others from our ship are out here too." She'd send them back on this run but knew that Mac at least would refuse. They didn't have time to debate it.

The Clongari ship still wasn't moving fast, but it was picking up speed.

"Normally, no. The effort would distract me and them. But whatever those nuns did to the Pirate...I can do this." He told Vas and Ragkor where they'd hit.

Ragkor wasn't happy, but he agreed. "This is all you. What should we do?"

"Stand back…damn it." Vas' swearing increased as Clongari fighters came out of the huge ship. "You'll be keeping those away from us."

"Aye, captain. Ragkor out."

"This is Deven. Yes, I'm in your head. We have one shot to stop that weapon on the Clongari ship, we have to work together. No wild stunts. No risk taking. Follow my directions." Deven's voice and his plan hit Vas. He'd always been a powerful telepath, but Vas had never heard of something like this.

"Vas, Deven, the nuns are with you. Let us support your flight." Jasiel's voice didn't come from the comm, but it felt like a comforting touch. "We can't fight for you, but we can protect you."

"Anything you can do—do it," Vas yelled as Deven's plan went active and all of the Furies moved as one for the Clongari ship.

A shimmering shield enveloped the twenty-five Furies as they focused on a specific location on the Clongari ship.

The Clongari fighters were intercepted by Ragkor's fleet of fighters and pulled away.

"Now!" Deven's yell was felt as well as heard and Vas found herself firing at the target in her head.

Every single Fury did the same.

The Clongari fighters tried to return to their ship, but the rest of the fighter crews kept them busy and unable to return.

The Furies flew low over the Clongari battlecruiser, then up and around for a second run at the same spot. The skin of the Clongari ship cracked and small explosions ran along it.

The weapons on the spiky ends went out after the first run. But as they were going for their third run, a grouping from the other side of the ship fired and two Furies spun off into space.

They didn't explode, but the nuns' shielding around them grew stronger as they spun away.

"One more," Deven yelled, and the remaining Furies dove. This time they hit the Clongari ship with everything they had.

Vas' ship rattled hard as she pulled up from the crackling Clongari warship. The rest of the Furies seemed to be having trouble as well, but they all cleared the area.

"Captain! Deven! All of you need to get further away!" Gosta yelled into her comm. "The Clongari ship is going to explode!"

CHAPTER SIXTY-FOUR

VAS FELT DEVEN INFORM THE rest as they fled. Her cameras were still aimed at the surface of the Clongari ship behind them, they'd hit it hard but it had been twenty-five fighters against a monster-sized ship that could hold six *Destroyer's Curses* in it.

The best they could hope for was to disable it or make it leave.

Or Gosta could be right.

The Clongari ship halted and the menacing blue lights died. The cracks on its surface spread over the entire vessel and the Clongari fighters tried to return to it.

The Wavians blocked them at every attempt.

"You need to move faster!" Aithnea's voice came from the comm this time and Vas felt her ship call up more speed.

"We're trying, damn it!"

"You're going to lose your shields, but this is better." Aithnea cut off and the glow around the twenty-three active Furies vanished.

Then it reappeared around the Clongari ship.

A group of Flits and KTs came forward and held between the Clongari warship and the rest of the fleets. Vas figured it was the nuns as the rest of their crews held back.

The Clongari battlecruiser exploded, and the sharp points circling it became missiles. If the shield wasn't in place, a lot of ships would have been run through by the barbs. The pieces were forced back by the shield and the line of nun-flown fighters.

Three Flits took hits as smaller pieces got through the initial shield. The Flits wouldn't fly again without serious repairs, but hopefully, the pilots survived.

The rest of the nuns' ships moved closer. Vas felt a wave coming from their ships. It was powerful, but she only caught the edge of it—as if someone was shouting but she was too far away to hear the words.

The Clongari fighters pulled back and zipped past the remains of their dead ship and toward the gate.

"Gosta! Can we track them?" Vas yelled into her comm. She knew even he couldn't get a drone on them, but maybe something.

"I can't. But they would have picked up unique particles from the exploding ship. Hrrru believes he can find where they jumped. At least if we move quickly."

"Ragkor? How goes the fighting with the Kantari and friends?"

"The few survivors are running. I assume we can't chase them?"

Vas laughed as her Fury rattled its way toward the *Destroyer's Curse*. "Good assumption. Have all ships stand down and reclaim all of the fighters. We need to leave as soon as possible."

"Aye, captain. Ragkor out."

Vas roughly landed the Fury but it continued to rattle. "Nitya? The Furies are in bad shape, is it safe to have them here?"

Even behind the landing bay shield, she heard the same noises coming from the rest as they came in.

"I'm scanning them and neutralizing their firing mechanisms as they come in. You've drained all the weapons, so they should be safe, but this will make certain."

"Thank you." Vas hit her comm as she headed up to the command deck. "Terel? How many injured?"

"At this point, thirty," Terel's voice was tight and clipped. "Three fatalities from our ship that we know of, and two Flits aren't responding. Of the injured, only four are going to be confined to their med bed for the duration. You could have all died."

"It's part of war, Terel. You know that."

"I know. But this wasn't even the war. It was a ruse, a test. And the Furies were almost destroyed." She paused. "Never mind. I'll keep you updated."

Vas knew better than to push when she heard that tone. And Terel wasn't wrong. But when that battlecruiser appeared all bets were off.

She just hoped wasting all of the Furies in the fight had been worth it.

Flarik looked comfortable in the command seat, so Vas waved her off and went to her ready room. She was pulling up recordings of the fight when Aithnea spoke through the comm.

"Yes, the loss of the Furies is hard, but you did what you needed to do. That Clongari ship could have destroyed this fleet."

"Are you in my head again? You were in the ship."

"No, that was different. Your thoughts are rather pushy right now. As for the Furies, they served their purpose. Marli would have been proud." That she said that without any sarcasm said a lot.

"Those nuns were pretty damn impressive. All of them."

"I know, we were, weren't we?"

Vas knew Aithnea popped out again so went back to looking at the fight. The vids didn't offer much more information, but this was just a brief viewing of an unfiltered feed. Vas knew Hrrru and Gosta would find anything of value.

"Vas?" Terel didn't sound upset as she called through the comm. "Could you and Deven come down to sick bay? The nanites have a proposition."

Vas headed for the ready room door. "Am I going to like it?"

"Probably not."

"On my way." Vas ran toward the lift and caught Deven coming up. "Our nanite friends are up to something again. Terel needs us."

"Got it. Nitya has not only shut down but has shielded all of the Furies."

"Good. I would have liked to have that firepower longer, but they did what we couldn't. Deven, how in the hell are we going to fight more of those? We won't even have the Furies anymore." Vas was tough, but right now terror was catching up with her.

Deven paused the lift, turned her to him, and tilted her face up. "We will go down swinging. Isn't that what you say in impossible merc battles?"

"This isn't just a fight gone wrong—" Vas' comment was cut off by Deven's passionate kiss.

"But how are we going to—" She got out as they broke apart.

This time the kiss was so intense she had to remind herself they were in a stopped lift.

Finally, she pulled back. "As always, you know the perfect thing to say. Or do. Thank you. We go down swinging."

Deven laughed and released the lift.

The med bay was busy with injured, but calmer than before. Nanite Delimara was sitting at a bank of monitors running scenarios. Terel kept glancing over at them with a frown. Then she saw Vas and Deven.

"Thank you. I think the nanites have lost their mind or minds. Seriously." She continued to watch the Nanite Delimara but didn't bring them closer.

"Terel, we're all busy, you especially. Can't we just ask them?"

"Yes. They told me, but it'll be better coming from them." Terel marched over to the bank of monitors. "You work it out. I have injured to treat." She stalked off.

The nanite Kantari turned to them and gave a close approximation of a smile. "We are pleased you survived. We have a proposal. We require your furious ships."

"The Furies? They're all out of firepower and not holding together very well. I don't know what you could do with them."

"Weapons. Flying. We can create with them." The nanites had sounded better than before but were breaking up now. "Too much for slowing down for you. Sorry. We will take the wreckages, create a new vessel, and attack those you call Clongari. The queen has told us."

Vas and Deven shared a look. "The Wavian queen?" Maybe the nanites had royalty.

"Yes. She is the best chance to accomplish our goals. We have studied how your ships fly, and now can do this." Delimara turned to Deven. "We don't expect to survive, in fact, we intend not to. But not all of us will be needed. Before we fly, may some of us come to join in your body?"

Deven looked surprised. This was a wildly unexpected turn of events even for this trip.

"Yes, of course. Can you tell us what you're going to do?"

"Do you both say yes? The ship has agreed if you both do."

Vas hit her comm. "Nitya? You're okay with this? They'd be working in your bay."

"Yes. What they are planning is far above my ability, but it holds promise."

"I'm grabbing at anything now. We should ask our co-captain Flarik, though," Vas said as Deven nodded.

They didn't even have to explain what it was. Flarik was already involved. "My child told me, it has power."

Vas shrugged. "Okay, Del— what should we call you?"

"Delimara works. We do not have names in our culture. Thank you, captains."

Delimara got to her feet and they went to the lifts. Delimara went down to the landing bay; Vas and Deven went back to the command deck.

Ragkor's face filled one of the smaller screens. "Good, you're all here. I was telling Captain Flarik of our updates. We're ready to travel whenever you are."

Vas and Deven both turned to Flarik, who flashed a toothy grin. "Follow those bastards, Mac."

CHAPTER SIXTY-FIVE

———

THEY FACED A FEW MORE distraction-style attacks. Again, not enough enemy ships to have a chance against this group—even without fifty Wavian warships. But after a full week, no more Clongari ships even appeared on the long-range scanners.

Vas was in her ready room going over the fight strategy. They would be at the edge of Lethian space by the end of day. At that point, there would be nothing beyond that except for the nanites' space and the Clongari worlds.

Nitya voiced a few concerns about what monstrosity the nanites were making in her hold, but they weren't letting anyone see their 'furious ship' as they continued to call it.

"Captain? The Marli-bot is calling." Xsit sounded a bit concerned, most likely because the bot did sound like Marli.

"Send it through." Vas sat back and stretched. There were still too many unknowns against the Clongari.

"Vas. I have created new vessels for your telepaths. Are they on your ship?"

Vas narrowed her eyes even though she knew the bot couldn't see her. "There are a few here, but most of them are on the *Solar*. What kind of ships? You said you gave us what you had. And how can you get them to us?"

"They are my creation. Marli gave me autonomy in my education. These are called Marli ships. They are single-seat fighters that are smaller than but similar to the Ralith ship but without the complicated heritage. They are also telepathically controlled. I talked to Nitya when she was here, and I utilized some of what she does. They are fast, deadly, and can slice through a Clongari ship. I have ten of them heading your way by the same type of drones I used to test-fly that Fury around your planet." She paused. "I hope they help you. Marli would want you to survive. So do I." The last was soft.

"Thank you. When should they be here?"

"Captain! Fighters speeding this way! Ten Ralith ships!" Hrrru was close to hysterical and Vas didn't blame him.

"Those are them. I will have seven go to the *Solar* and three to your ship. Stay alive, Admiral Vas." Then the call ended.

Vas smiled. Marli always wanted to call her Admiral. "It's okay, Hrrru, those aren't Raliths. Nitya, let the three ships coming our way into the landing bay." She ran out to the command deck. "Deven, I need you to pick the three strongest telepaths from our crew—aside from you—and head down to the landing bay." Vas ran for the lift. She contacted Yesenia and quickly filled her in on the ships coming their way, and who they were for. Yesenia said thank you and cut the call.

The three ships were a deep silvery blue; something unique but eye-catching.

"Captain, these ships are impressive. The Marli-bot briefly mentioned wanting to build them, but I didn't expect this. They are completely telepathically con-trolled," Nitya said.

Vas laughed at the awe in Nitya's voice as she went to the first ship. The door slid open silently and she looked around for any hidden telepaths.

"The power you have as a Keeper will let you control these." The words were a recording.

"Thanks." There was no way she was trusting her Keeper's powers to fly one of these, but at least she could go inside.

It was small inside, and most of its size was taken up by

engines and weapons. But Mac would weep if he saw it. Or try to find a way to become a telepath.

Deven and three others came into the landing bay. The Marli-bot had mentally contacted them briefly—most likely all telepaths on the two ships—so they weren't shocked. But there was a lot of ship admiration going on as they familiarized themselves with the vessels.

"I assume I'm not taking one." Deven came up next to her.

"No. I think we have a different job, one that needs Janx and Chasen." She held up her hand. "No clue where that idea came from, the nuns aren't as forthcoming as the Marli-bot."

"I heard that," Aithnea's voice came through a nearby speaker. "But you're right. The four of you need to be on the *Keeper's Tempest* during the final battle. You'll lead a group of nuns flying their own ships and the rest of the KT class ships."

"You don't happen to have information on when that fight will be, or what we'll face before then, do you?"

"Nope. Oh, have Nitya send that Clongari corpse out with those seeds you found. It'll help."

Vas started to ask how, then shrugged. Aithnea might know, but she wouldn't be able to tell her. "Thanks."

The three telepaths were silent as they went over their ships, so Vas and Deven left.

"We're sending a dead body with the seeds, I heard?"

"Yeah, at least it's good for something." She had no idea what, but it would be off her ship.

Flarik was almost dancing when they returned to the command deck. "Joyous news! Our baby has hatched! Her name is Ysolte. It's much longer in native Wavian. She selected it herself."

Vas never thought she'd see Flarik beaming about anything, let alone a child—but that's what happened.

Then Flarik ran forward and hugged both of them

hard enough to pop joints. Her feathers were still red with black, but her grin lit up her entire face.

It was more disturbing than when she was angry.

"Is there anything we need to do?"

"How can we rescue her?"

"She is where she needs to be. The *fartolks* who took her are treating her extremely well so she will be in excellent shape when they give her to the Clongari."

Vas knew *fartolks* was a Wavian swear word, but not what it meant beyond that.

If Flarik wasn't worried, then she wouldn't be either.

"Captain, the Ralith ship just entered the sector." Gosta was calm. Having the Wavian empire at their backs made one cocky—Vas would never tell him who she thought would win against Ome.

Vas watched as the distinctive ship came toward them but at a reduced speed. It stopped a respectable distance away before Xsit called out that there was a call from Ome.

"You can't have your brothers back."

"That's not why I'm calling, Captain Tor Dain—"

"You can't have the Kilesh Destroyers either."

"Now see here, captain. I'm trying to be reasonable. We do have a war to win, you know. Just my brothers.... and what happened to the weapons. Information, nothing more."

Vas narrowed her eyes. "You're not a ground forces type of guy, why would you want those?"

"None of your business, keep the weapons. Do I have to take my brothers by force?"

She knew he easily saw the massive fleet of ships behind her. "Even for you? Against that?"

"It would hurt, but yeah. I'm sending over a shuttle for them."

Vas was about to tell him to find a new hell when something poked at her. In her head from three sources:

Keeper mojo, nanites, and….Flarik's baby, Ysolte? All three were telling her to free Pol and Relin. "Yes." Vas wasn't happy about agreeing but the three in her head were showing her why it was.

That they were all showing different things and were about to explode her mind made their attempt pointless.

But deep inside, she agreed.

"Nitya, allow Ome's shuttle to land. We're bringing down his brothers." She nodded to Deven, Glazlie, and Marwin to join her as she finished her call to Ome.

"Wise choice, captain," Ome said quickly then cut the comm.

Vas joined Deven in the landing bay watching Ome's shuttle as Glazlie and Marwin brought Pol and Relin down. Both were tightly bound and had been roughed up.

Vas didn't condone brutality against prisoners unless they fought—she knew these two had fought.

"I'm tired of seeing you two on my ship. Stay with your brother this time." Vas nodded for them to be taken to Ome's shuttle, but called out to them when they were halfway there. "By the way, Ome swore on the Ralith ship that he would leave this universe after the fight. If he fails to do so, he and the ship and all on it will be destroyed by the Ralith." She assumed that was what would happen, the Marli-bot hadn't been as clear as possible about that.

The brothers stopped and Marwin and Glazlie turned back to Vas. But then the brothers started walking again. Slower this time, but they didn't look back at her. They knew the odds of their brother adhering to anything.

She sent Marwin to guard the brig and Glazlie to the command deck as the Ralith shuttle left. Then she turned to Deven. "You still think we have a chance?" She reached up to give him a solid kiss. "And did you get anything of use from the brothers?" That had hit her almost the moment after the initial push that they had to let the brothers go—there was something important in one or both of their heads.

"I did." He kissed her back. "At first it looked like there wasn't anything—but thanks to your nudge, Pol gave up that his brother would kill them anyway without the weapons. And what Ome was going to do with them." His smile dropped. "I'll speak to the nanites, they'll want the Kilesh destroyers on their ship."

"Increased explosive power?"

He nodded. "We don't want to be within two systems of that thing when it explodes if those weapons get added."

CHAPTER SIXTY-SIX

VAS RETURNED TO THE COMMAND deck and watched the Ralith ship take off moments after the shuttle returned. Most ships that size couldn't hold a shuttle, but Vas knew Ome's ship was anything but normal.

Gosta and Hrrru were preparing the seeds and Clongari body parts for dispatch and would launch the moment Vas commanded it. Gosta estimated they could hit three ships' engines before the codes changed and they were locked out. As long as they all went at once.

Hrrru being Hrrru, he'd saved a smaller amount of the combination, just in case they could get a fourth.

Fighters from all the ships ran test runs to make sure they could work together. The telepaths did a few test runs with their new ships. They were incredible ships and moved in formations that usually only extremely experienced pilots could pull off.

Vas had to practically tie Mac into his pilot sling as he watched the Marli ships test runs. Non-telepath or not, if they all survived, he was finding a way to get one.

At least he wasn't pining away for the *Keeper's Tempest* now.

"Ragkor? How are the troops?" They'd continued through a few systems without using gates to make themselves harder to find.

"Restless. My fighters are happy, but that's just a test run."

"Agreed. But within ten hours we'll be in Clongari space." She paused. "How many planets are dark so far?"

She had plenty of brains on the *Destroyer's Curse*, but so did he. She'd asked him to set a dedicated deep space tracking of all worlds that were presumed destroyed.

"Twenty-four. The Kilesh worlds appear changed—past fighting most likely, but you can tell Deven they're still there."

Vas relaxed a bit. "No currently active attacks?"

"Not since we started going through here. It's those Wavians, they're scaring everyone off. When we go back to merc work we need to see if they'll lend us one of those warships."

"We can ask, but doubtful." Even as a co-regent to the baby queen, she doubted the Wavians would lend her ships. "Keep on track, get some rest, and prepare for battle."

Ragkor signed off and Deven walked up to her chair. "Speaking of which, *we* need rest. Just a few hours."

"I feel like I'm missing something." Vas sighed as she got to her feet. "I spoke to Janx and she feels the same. This is too easy. They didn't want us out here or they would have moved faster destroying the other worlds—and not sent those sneak attacks after us. Why aren't they throwing more ships at us? Aside from the one Clongari battlecruiser, we haven't faced much defense."

Deven frowned. "I ran into Chasen coming up from the landing bay. He's bringing stuff on to the *Keeper's Tempest*; he feels the same."

Vas shivered and slid into his arms as the lift doors shut. Before she could say anything, the lift jerked to a stop, knocking them off their feet. Alarms rang out from multiple levels outside the lift and an annoying one inside of it.

At least until Deven got to his feet and ripped the alarm out.

"Gosta? Terel? Anyone?" Vas hit her comm. Only static came back.

She continued to call while Deven took apart the lift.

"We're going to have to force the doors and crawl out. Whatever happened, it was big." Deven had wires hanging out all along the door and nodded. He moved a few around and the lift doors opened half-way. "Now!"

Vas squished out and Deven managed to as well. They were a few feet below the next level but made it up. This door opened easier.

They were on the med bay level and while the alarms were fewer now, the emergency lights were flashing and people were running around. Most heading for the smaller second lift which appeared to be functioning.

Vas and Deven ran to the med bay. Terel was busy but they ran to her monitor and tried to call the command deck. It took a while and the image was bad, but Bathie appeared.

"What in the hell hit us?"

"We're not sure, captain. An unknown weapon hit ten of our ships, and us. We only got a glancing blow. Two Wavians were destroyed on impact. The other eight damaged ships are still intact and have life support, but they're out of the fight. The Wavians and Flarik are having a loud discussion in your ready room." Considering the distance between the command chair and the ready room—that was loud.

"Damn. Deven and I were stuck in the main lift—it's dead right below the med level. Have Gosta and Hrrru check the other lifts. Are the badge comms working at all?"

"Not that we've seen. Ragkor has ordered fighters out of all ships who are able. But whoever hit us is gone. Will report once we have more data." Bathie cut off sharper than normal. She was an extremely calm merc, but the attack had rattled her badly.

Deven managed to get a view of outside their ship on the monitor and Vas didn't blame Bathie at all. The Wavians had moved away from their two fallen ships. The other seriously damaged vessels were too far away to tell for sure who they were, but they were listing.

"How in the hell did something destroy two of those Wavian ships? And then simply vanish?"

Deven fussed with the monitor but shook his head. "Hopefully I can see more once we get back to the deck—but maybe they're still here."

Vas didn't like the idea of that but was willing to wait until they took one of the smaller lifts up. She jogged to Terel who was directing triage. "What do you need?"

"Right now, just to get our systems back. Then find the assholes behind this." War was one thing; sneak attacks didn't sit well with Terel.

Nor with Vas. "Agreed. Call if you need anything specific." Then she and Deven made their way through a few smaller lifts to the command deck.

Flarik was back at her station, but kept clacking her teeth and snarling at the screens she was watching.

Vas took a deep breath and swung over to her. "I'm sorry two of your ships were lost."

"Thank you. I don't believe we can control my people. They will not sit back after such an insult." She took a few deep breaths and visibly calmed.

"Did they find out who attacked us?"

"No. And that is why they remain here. They honor the baby queen, and us as co-regents, but that only goes so far in the face of such an attack."

"If we lose them before we face the Clongari we will most likely lose the battle."

"I know." Flarik turned sharply back to her screen.

"Captain! We have eighty percent shields back; engines and weapons are online and holding. Walvento demands the first shot by the way," Hrrru called out as he sharply saluted.

Odd, but Vas would take it.

"Communications is still scrambled, captain." The feathers on the back of Xsit's head were standing up and she appeared ready to start taking apart her station, probably with a sledgehammer.

Deven looked up from his station. "Let's see if part of the attack was directed at communications."

"You think Ome was involved? Could he have done this without being seen at all?"

"We're still not sure what all that damn ship can do. And he's been messing up communications everywhere he goes."

"Yes, Deven and Captain, there's a marker designed to hit all ship's comms." Gosta flipped screens with the big one in the front. "And then there's this." It was a grainy but usable vid of a beam of light as it passed through two Wavian ships in slow motion. "That's as slow as I can get it. Nothing appears at any faster speed. They moved faster than we could catch on any system. The eight other ships were damaged by explosives but no light hit them."

"It went through them and blew them up from inside. Cowards. Spineless cowards." Flarik snarled as she watched the slow-motion destruction. "The Wavians need to see this."

There wasn't a question about it and Vas wasn't going to fight. Most likely they'd lost the Wavians' support after this attack, might as well keep them on their side. Vas nodded to Gosta to send it to Flarik's station.

Vas used the comm at her chair to call Ragkor and tell him.

"I thought Ome couldn't do anything to us, or his ship would kill him?" Ragkor came in clearer now.

"Unfortunately, it was that he had to leave if we won. He'd been marginally on our side, we thought. I think—" Vas cut herself off as Gosta waved both hands over his head. "Hold on. Yes, Gosta?"

"There's a trail, it only shows up a few moments before

the beam of light—which is the ship—but it's trackable. We should all be able to configure our sensors to pick it up."

"Excellent work. Send it to Ragkor and the rest of the entire group—Wavians as well." The Wavians hadn't moved to leave yet, so she'd treat them as if they were staying.

Gosta and Hrrru started sending the data when Mac yelled out. "Clongari warships, five of them coming in through the gate!"

"Captain Vas. We have readied our furious ship. Can the other return down here so we may leave more of us behind?"

Deven was already running for the smaller lift.

"Can you take out those five ships?" Vas asked the nanites.

"Yes. You will have to pull back. We will not launch until the queen tells us."

Vas turned to Flarik but she just shrugged. The nanites didn't care much for the rest of the biological forms, but Ysolte had won them over. Somehow.

"Captain, a group of Lethian Assembly, Nhali, Racki, and Kantari ships just came through the far gate." Gosta was moving fast as he scanned everything he could.

"No indications of the Ralith ship, captain." Hrrru was also multitasking.

"Damn it," Deven called up from the landing bay. "The telepaths and the *Keeper's Tempest* need to get out there. Ome, or something else too much like a Ralith ship, is out there, and the fighters won't be as affected as the ships are."

CHAPTER SIXTY-SEVEN

———◆———

VAS CALLED TO JANX BUT she and Chasen were already on their way to the landing bays. The three telepath pilots were also on their way, and Yesenia had her pilots leaving the *Solar*. A group of nuns came down as well with Jasiel leading them.

"They'll follow you and the Marli ships. They're taking the KTs or their own ships." Jasiel looked envious as the nuns, including Delilah, ran for their ships.

"You could join them, you know," Vas said.

"I know, but I'm called to remain here. If we get through this, and Aithnea and the rest finish their final task and move on, I have to be the one to lead the nuns." She scowled. "And sort out a new mother superior. I tried to convince Therlian, but she said no."

"But I said it kindly." Therlian raced past them into one of the KTs.

"I could have told you." Vas watched as Deven, Janx, and Chasen made final checks of the *Keeper's Tempest*. "You'll find someone."

"Easy for you to say." Jasiel became serious. "Be careful out there, all of you, but especially you four. There has never been a group like you and I feel you could slip through the cracks. If so, this fight is over."

"That's a cheery pep talk. Keep an eye on my crew." Vas nodded and ran into the *Keeper's Tempest*.

There was an odd tingle as she entered the ship. It had to do with the three with her, and all the people fighting along with them. Including the nanites, Flarik's baby queen, and the essences of the Keepers before her.

Weird was an understatement.

"We're ready when you are, Vas. Although I'm not completely sure how our abilities are going to work in a ship." Janx was in black body armor, more suited for hand-to-hand fighting than a space fight. But an opalescent sheen indicated it could also adapt into a space suit. Chasen was dressed the same. Those were high-end suits and most likely were lifted from whoever they'd been running from.

"This is unique for all of us, so just roll with what you feel. There will be a lot of elements going on, trust the telepaths and the nuns to protect you and get you through." Aithnea dropped off the comm before anyone could respond.

"What did that mean?" Chasen finally asked.

"Who knows? Welcome to the inscrutable nuns." Vas checked the pilot console as Deven finished the nav check. "Let's do this," Vas said as they left the landing bay with three telepath Marli ships, twenty KTs, and another fifteen random small fighters following behind them.

"Captain?" Bathie called from the command deck. "Gosta says he's been told to launch the attack on the enemy engines."

"On which?"

"Two Clongari and two Racki, captain." Gosta cut in. "Xsit is fixing the communications by the way. But the baby queen believes we can damage or destroy two Clongari ships."

Vas wanted to know if that was the case, why not go after all of them. But there were too many weird things going on, and this wasn't the time to question her people.

"Ysolte is on the lead Lethian ship. It's a small cruiser and will meet the largest Clongari ship in moments. Once her transfer is completed, we go. *Everything.*" Flarik hadn't taken the command chair from Bathie, by the time Vas left, although as co-captain she could. But she was still in charge.

"The non-Clongari ships are launching fighters, captain." Hrrru wasn't yelling, yet, but even at this distance, she could see why he might start. Hundreds of fighters filled the space in front of them.

"Bathie, release the rest of the fighters when Ragkor and Carrix send theirs. Flarik? Are your people staying with us?"

"They are until they find who attacked them. There is conflict within the fleet. I will apprise you if they decide to change." Flarik cut off more abruptly than Aithnea usually did.

"Everyone in my wave ready?" Vas called to the three telepaths and the nuns. Confirmations all around so she left the landing bay.

Yesenia and the rest of the Marli ships waited and followed as Vas' group flew past. Smaller waves of dots behind them indicated Ragkor was releasing more fighters. The largest ships, including the Wavians, for now, repositioned themselves.

"The Lethian cruiser has docked with the Clongari. Ysolte is probably on there now." Janx called out from her station.

"Damn it, I was hoping we'd find those invisible ships before this went down." Vas paused. "Gosta, do you recall what those Racki did to hide themselves during the pirate conclave?" There were four massive Racki ships in sight, but it didn't mean that was all they had.

"Yes, adjust your red filter by .0856. Good thinking, captain. I'll tell Ragkor as well."

Deven switched the red filter over the moment Gosta called it. Three additional shapes now came into view lurking behind the bulky Clongari. Unlike the normal round Racki ships, these looked like Ome's ship but triple-sized.

"How are they doing that?" Janx refreshed her screen a few times, toggling back and forth where the ships were. "And they're using solbilan? Damn. Probably no chance of capturing one is there?"

Deven laughed. "You sound like Mac. But no. Now that we can get a read on them, those ships are too unstable. And we need to make sure none of our ships are near them when they explode."

"Captain, I've been ordered to launch the seeds and parts now," Gosta said.

"Fire away." Vas waited as the seeds were fired. There was no immediate response, but Gosta and Hrrru calculated it would take a while to process.

The two Racki targets exploded first.

The rest of the ships with them, including the Clongari, rapidly moved away as their fighters engaged Ragkor, Carrix, and the Wavian fighters.

Then two of the Clongari exploded. Not as dramatically as the Racki, but they were larger and honestly, she didn't think they'd be able to get through them at all.

Both Clongari ships shot out random arcs of the blue electricity that had come from the spiky parts of the ship. But only their ships were close enough to be impacted.

Then the two Clongari warships were finished off by their own people.

"Nice loyalty." Janx shook her head. "Although to be fair, those two Clongari were done for, just going slower than the Racki did."

"The invisible fighters are coming for us. I'm going to lead them away from the rest of the fighting." Vas prepared to leave and Deven put in a course. "Oh, Yesenia, stay back and keep tracking the Clongari ship that the baby is in. If there's a chance that something is going wrong before we get back, rescue the baby without us."

"Aye, Captain Vas." Yesenia sounded like she was having too much fun with this. But she was still young.

Vas took off with Janx and Chasen tracking the three modified Racki ships. "Do you think they know we see them?" Now that their sensors were adjusted the three were impossible to miss.

"I'd say no. Their flight pattern doesn't seem aggressive. More curious." Janx waved at the screen but it simply looked normal to Vas.

She didn't want to get too far away, but taking these ships out would help a lot. The fighters seemed matched, but if the Wavians did decide to abandon them, they wouldn't be able to hold against even three Clongari fighters.

"Suggestions as to how to take them out?"

The weird linking to the other three that she'd noticed on Home hit Vas hard. But it wasn't just the three, but everything around them. She knew exactly where those three ships were, where they were heading…and the plan to charge into her forces and take out all the ships.

"Nope," Vas said out loud as the other three worked on readying weapons and calculating the distance and speed needed.

They were going to hit all three with weapons fire and push them into each other. Thoughts were going so fast, talking would only slow them down.

The three Racki ships opened their weapons bank, just as Vas—or rather Vas-Deven-Janx-Chasen punched their engines. The other three were spread out, but the *Keeper's Tempest* was a lot faster than it looked.

Not to mention those ships believed they couldn't be seen.

All three took hits in their weapons ports—perfectly.

Vas spun away from the three exploding ships and she, Deven, Janx, and Chasen linked hands. Through thought and whatever weird mojo Janx had, they reached out to the three ships and pushed them into each other. Chasen added a kick by activating any remaining explosives and weapons on all three ships.

The three ships exploded in a massive fireball and Vas almost wept with exhaustion. She felt like she'd just faced a four-day siege.

But neither she nor Deven looked like they were going to collapse, so that was a plus.

"Captain, the time is now." Flarik was calm, but there was a lot of tension in her voice. "And you will be the one to explain to our people that you destroyed their enemies."

"Not a problem. Hey, if Deven and I are co-regents, then part of the Wavian Empire did destroy them." Vas turned the *Keeper's Tempest* back to the Clongari.

"That is a valid point. Thank you. By the way, five more Clongari ships are coming through the gate and the nanites are going to launch whether we agree or not."

"Damn. We're on our way. But don't try to stop the nanites. Just remind them we need to rescue the baby first." Vas switched to Yesenia. "We're heading toward you. Follow our lead." The telepaths and nuns were far enough away from the main fighting that no one was engaging them yet.

Which was good, as from what Vas understood, it was going to take the Asarlaí telepaths, the nuns, and the Xali of the four in this ship, to free Ysolte and destroy the Clongari.

Yesenia's group fell in behind them and Vas felt an odd tickle in the back of her mind. "Is that the telepaths?"

"And the nuns," Deven rubbed the side of his head. "The nuns aren't telepathic, at least most of them aren't. But the Keepers and the Pirates are holding them together as one."

They were heading toward the Clongari ship that Ysolte was on when the new group of five Clongari came through the gate.

CHAPTER SIXTY-EIGHT

"**D**AMN IT! WE CAN'T DESTROY that many!" Vas' swearing sputtered out as the Wavian warships moved on the new Clongari group.

"Yes, we can, let's do this!" Vas ignored the fact that cognitively she wouldn't be able to say what they needed to do—but instinctively she did. More Keeper stuff floating in her head. She was grateful for the times it had helped, but she was going to be very glad when she was no longer the Keeper.

The Clongari vessel Ysolte was on was in front of two other Clongari ships—and five of the others were coming their way.

"We can't stop that many…oh." Janx stopped when the same thought hit all of them. Ysolte was calling the other Clongari to her.

"That is one powerful hatchling," Chasen sounded in awe.

Vas and Deven spun the *Keeper's Tempest* to face the Clongari ship Ysolte was on. The Asarlaí telepaths and nuns spaced their ships out alongside them.

A warm and foreign thought hit Vas. "*Thank you for coming. I am ready to go now.*" Ysolte.

Vas punched the engines and they darted forward as the rest of their fighters swarmed the Clongari ship. Which was currently experiencing violent shudders from some unknown source.

Vas found herself, along with the other three, directing Ysolte to an escape pod. Once it launched, Vas raced for ward to grab it in their hold. She felt a warm feeling of thanks come from the pod.

"Captain? We're holding it back as best as we can, but we're still too close to that ship and it's going to explode." Chasen was no longer calm as he squinted in pain.

"We will help. Get away but the queen will still gather enemy ships." The nanites called in as their furious ship raced by.

In answer, two more of the remaining Clongari ships were moving closer to the exploding one.

There was fighting all around, but dealing with Lethians and their like was easier. Even so, three of the nuns' ships zipped off to chase something.

The explosion of the colliding Clongari ships, along with the furious ship of the nanites near the gate lit up everything and alarms went off in the *Keeper's Tempest* as they were hit with an explosive wave.

"Damn, that's impressive. I think they'll see that back on Home. Is it close enough to destroy that gate?"

"It looks like it already has," Janx said. "It's just collapsing slowly. There's one more Clongari ship left, and it's claiming surrender."

"It's doing what?" Then Vas heard the call in her head too. They were citing ancient law and that their time in this realm was over.

"They destroyed at least twenty-four worlds, killed millions of people, and they want us to let them go?" Vas knew the overwhelming feeling of vengeance came from the Keepers—all of them.

And Vas didn't mind it at all.

She slapped her palm down and fired.

And found her shot blocked by a shield around the Ralith ship that appeared in front of the Clongari.

So much for Ome being on their side.

"What in the hell are you doing?" Vas yelled into her comm at Ome.

"What is best for me, obviously. The Clongari have asked me to join them. As they're paying me an insane amount of money to find a way out of this debacle, I can't let you destroy this ship. Move along now."

"We had a deal."

"That I never intended to honor, even if we did win. Didn't you notice I wasn't here for the lovely fighting?"

Vas grinned as the ten telepath Marli ships all turned toward Ome.

"And as you were told when you accepted the gift, betrayal will destroy you. The Ralith will always win." Marli-bot's voice flooded their ship and probably all the others. Ome had said he wasn't going to honor his promise.

Vas figured the Marli ships would destroy the Ralith ship but they just maintained a perimeter.

Ome yelled as alarms rang out inside his ship. "No! You can't do this!"

Before Vas could respond, the Ralith ship exploded. The Marli ships fired on the remains, turning the once deadly ship into space dust.

Ragkor and the Wavians were holding in front of the remaining Clongari ship. The distant gate appeared inactive.

"Captain, we're discussing whether this ship can leave, be destroyed, or be held for court judgment in the Wavian Tribunal System."

Vas muted her comm. "Ideas? Anyone?" She still felt the tight connection to these three, but nothing from anyone else. She wanted to blow them out of the sky.

Although eons in the Wavian judicial system might be more painful.

Deven shook his head and winced. "The nanites inside me are all awake now, not just the ones I gathered from Delimara. They say to transfer them to the Clongari ship and let it go."

"They wanted to go home."

"They will but I think our nuns were talking to them. They feel they can convince the rest of the Clongari government to leave them and all of us alone."

Vas wanted to protest, but this might be for the best—if it worked. "Fine, how do we get them there?"

"*Take the pod I am in, co-parent.*" Vas felt a chill as Ysolte spoke in her mind.

"Janx and Chasen, rescue our queen from the pod, Deven transfer your nanites into it, and let's finish this."

The fighting wound down as many of the Kantari, Racki, Nhali, and even Lethian Assembly ships fled when most of the Clongari ship exploded.

Deven came back, rubbing his arms as if suddenly cold. "That was odd. The nanites have definitely changed." He reclaimed his seat as Janx and Chasen also returned.

"The queen is resting in a bunk." Janx smiled. "She is lovely, by the way."

"Captain?" Gosta cut into Vas' comm. "There are ten more Clongari warships in transit to that far gate. They'll be in this sector in a few minutes."

"Damn it, thank you Gosta." She turned to Deven. "Send the escape pod. And what in the hell is that?" A piece of what she assumed was wreckage joined and pushed the escape pod to the Clongari.

"We all thank you." The nanites responded. The debris was from their furious ship exploding.

"You're welcome. I hope this works for you."

"It will." The nanites cut off communications as the pod and ship wreckage raced into the Clongari landing bay. How they did it without being shot down, Vas would love to know.

The nanites acted fast, as the Clongari ship turned to leave, but not toward the distant gate.

"Captain? Orders?" Ragkor was all Marine right now.

"Stand down. Let that ship leave. But we need to stop

the incoming ones." Vas ran her fingers through her hair. She was exhausted and she had to think that everyone in their fleets were as well. Not to mention weapon levels had to be close to non-existent by now for everyone.

"Understood, Ragkor, out."

A moment later, Gosta was on the comm. "Captain, it's a long-distance image, but it appears the freed Clongari is joining the others on the other side of the gate."

"I'd say the nanites failed. We prepare to fight."

Jasiel cut in. "Vas? Let the ship go. Some of our friends from *beyond* have joined us to boost the nun signal, as it were. There is a plan."

"The nuns who died with Aithnea?" Vas knew it was weird that Aithnea had come back, but the rest were in limbo.

"Yes. The end is near. One way or another, they will be freed."

"Ragkor, the released ship is joining the incoming ones. Everyone stand down."

"Captain?" Confusion and concern filled his voice.

"Yup. Orders." She cut the call and contacted Flarik when some of the Wavians started to act on the Clongari change in direction.

"Ysolte and I will convince them." Flarik sounded far too serene.

The nanite Clongari ship made it to the incoming ten ships without incident. In a quick movement, tentacles lashed out from the nanite ship to strike all of the others. They froze but then turned to return through the gate.

"Thank you. They will negotiate now." The nanites still sounded like Delimara even though the body was gone.

"You're welcome." The last Clongari ship vanished through the gate.

The silence in her head was startling. "I can't feel any of you anymore." Vas grinned.

"No offense, but thank goodness," Janx said.

They turned back to the *Destroyer's Curse* as the fighters returned to their ships and medical support went to the heavily damaged ships.

Vas patted the sides of the landing bay wall as they worked their way to the command deck.

"After we get the ships and crew repaired and healed, what's our next job?" Deven walked alongside her

Vas smiled and slid her arms around Deven's waist. "Have I told you of a lovely island I found on Home?"

He bent down to kiss her. "How long will that last?"

"As long as we want. Retirement sounds damn good right now."

———◆———

THAT'S A WRAP!

ENDING A SERIES IS ALWAYS hard, these people have moved into my head, and they're like old friends.

Thank you so much for following Vas, Deven, Flarik, Mac, and the entire crew on six adventures! They're off for a well-deserved rest.

Other adventures in and out of this world can be found on my website *https://marieandreas.com/*

You can also sign up on Amazon to follow me and they will keep you updated on new releases *https://www. amazon.com/Marie-Andreas/e/B00SX81KIM/*

ACKNOWLEDGMENTS

WRITING IS EASY—TAKE A BUNCH of weird ideas and mush them together. And then lie about how easy it is. Writing is hard, I love it, but it's hard. It would be impossible without a lot of other folks.

I'd like to thank everyone who has ever supported me, read chapters, edited, let me cry on their shoulder, read my books, given nice reviews, and/or bought me soothing beverages. I could never have done this without ALL of you. I can't list you all here, but you mean the world to me.

My awesome round of editors/beta/proofreaders: Lisa Andreas, Lynne Mayfield, and Ilana Schoonover. Any errors or mistakes that remain are completely mine.

Thank you to Aleta Rafton for the amazing cover!!

Thank you to The Killion Group for the print interior

To all my readers—thank you for coming along for the ride!

About the Author

Marie is a multi-award-winning fantasy and science fiction author with a serious reading addiction. If she wasn't writing about all the people in her head, she'd be lurking about coffee shops annoying total strangers with her stories. So really, writing is a way of saving the masses. She lives in the fantasyland known as Southern California and dreams of castles and forests.

She is a proud member of SFWA (Science Fiction and Fantasy Writers Association) and NINC (Novelists, Inc.).

When not saving the masses from coffee shop shenanigans, Marie likes to visit the UK and keeps hoping someone will give her a nice summer home in the Forest of Dean or Conwy, Wales.